SPIN

BCC PRESS

BY COMMON CONSENT PRESS is a non-profit publisher dedicated to producing affordable, high-quality books that help define and shape the Latter-day Saint experience. BCC Press publishes books that address all aspects of Mormon life. Our mission includes finding manuscripts that will contribute to the lives of thoughtful Latter-day Saints, mentoring authors and nurturing projects to completion, and distributing important books to the Mormon audience at the lowest possible cost.

SPIN

JOHN BENNION

ART BY

AMY BENNION

Spin
Copyright © 2022 by John Bennion

All rights reserved. Printed in the United States of America. No part of this book may be used or reproduced in any manner whatsoever without written permission except in the case of brief quotations embodied in critical articles or reviews.

For information contact
By Common Consent Press
4900 Penrose Dr.
Newburgh, IN 47630

Cover art and book art: Amy Bennion
Cover design: D Christian Harrison
Book design: Andrew Heiss

www.bccpress.org
ISBN-13: 978-1-948218-64-1

10 9 8 7 6 5 4 3 2 1

The very relationship with the other is the
relationship with the future.

—Emmanuel Levinas

ONE

Lily sat up in bed, unsure whether she had just experienced a dream or a memory. The pale figure stood just off the trail, watching as Lily ran past. It, he, she, they wore a coverall made of dirty white denim or canvas. Its body was half as wide as it was tall, probably because the coverall was padded underneath with newspapers or three or four sets of clothing. Its head was uncovered, except for short, hacked-off hair. Gender was indeterminate, also race and age. It had probably just risen from sleeping in the knee-tall grass next to the trail that followed the stream up canyon. Its head didn't turn, but Lily felt that its eyes followed her as she slowed. Did it want food, companionship, a different place to sleep, one where it could wake without someone staring? The face didn't disclose whether it was angry, sad, complacent, apprehensive, aggressive. Lily considered speaking to it, but she wasn't sure it would understand; instead, she ran faster, wondering whether it would retreat higher on the hill or shuffle after her, its arms forced wide by the thickness of the coverall.

Not a memory, but like one—familiar, even though she couldn't place when it had happened.

Lily swept back the sheet and blanket, swung her legs out of bed, and walked into Anne's room. Anne was awake, watching through the bars of her crib, her blonde hair mussed. Lily knelt and reached through the bars—taking hold of Anne's hands. As she did so, she felt another kind of déjà vu: she had reached through the bars of Anne's crib many times and would reach through many more times. An essential act, like the dream/vision had felt essential—eidetic.

"Breakfast, Anne?"

The child wiggled her hands loose and signed *I'm hungry.* She stood and reached her arms high for Lily to pick her up. Lily waited, filling her eyes with her daughter. She took her phone out and took a picture so she could sketch the pose later. Then, as Lily folded her child into her own body, she felt fine hair brush her cheek and small hands pat her neck.

After breakfast, the babysitter came, and Lily knelt at the door to hug her child. "Anne, I'll be back soon." She looked up at the woman Nathan had hired, not a girl but a forty-something with an unreadable face. "Before lunchtime."

Four hours later the judge mouthed the words that took Anne away, and Lily watched Nathan walk across the courtroom to lean over the table with his hand extended. She refused to touch it, but he let it hang in the air, palm open. She eyed his

FIGURE BY THE TRAIL
Automythology (USP)

---

dark suit, starched and pressed shirt, hand-painted tie, well-trimmed mustache, and smile that showed no teeth.

Then his eyes emptied, as if she were a fly he could suck dry. These same eyes had once showed desire, what she had read as love. Such a gross transmogrification, the mash-up of love and hate in the lines of his face! As if the Word, any word, meant not only itself, but also its opposite. The mangled vision of him raised gooseflesh on her arms and caused the hair on the back of her neck to stand. She managed to rasp, "I will appeal, you lying son of a bitch," but his face didn't change.

He left his open hand suspended long enough to confirm the narrative that had won him legal and physical custody of Anne—that he had no secrets, no hidden weapon, but was the constant husband with an unstable wife; he, the nurturer of her and their child, and she, the dog that unpredictably bit or licked his hand. His lawyer had designed a mélange of arguments drawn from men's rights groups, Mormon Patriarchy, and the DSM5 description of Borderline Personality Disorder. The resulting narrative had played well before the bald, self-righteous judge, who frowned down at her for being a bad woman, a bad wife, and a bad mother.

Nathan slowly lowered his hand as the judge and a few others in the courtroom watched—the center of a new drama. He lifted his left foot and shook his Italian-made shoe, tapped its toe against the floor, same with his right. She had seen him do this before when he cut relations with his sister. When she asked about the ritual, he said he had shaken the dust from his feet, using an ancient Biblical ritual to witness against his sister. *Even my God will refuse you aid.*

Watching him, Lily knew that Nathan would *not* leave her fate to God. She had to get to Anne immediately, before Nathan moved her. Lily's vision narrowed to a point of light, and she grabbed her handbag and rushed out of the courtroom, ignoring her own pink-faced lawyer, who had assured Lily again and again in the weeks before the trial that she had no reason to worry. Her primary argument had been that in Utah mothers were reverenced. No judge would take Anne from her.

Lily ran down the hallway and shoved the button to the elevator four times. Those who joined her, luckily no one from her court session, stared at her and moved away slightly. She pushed the button to the parking garage and, when the doors opened a moment later, squeezed between them, and walked to where her Audi had been. The space was empty. "Fuck!" The court agreement said it was hers, but Nathan had taken it away.

She slammed her palm against the exit door of the courthouse and used her phone to check her bank account, discovering that her password no longer worked. Then she looked up her secret account, the one set up when she decided to leave Nathan. She had skimmed a hundred here, fifty there from the money he gave her, until she had $20,000. The account had been emptied; in fact it was overdrawn by $10—the closest Nathan could come to a joke. Without doubt, he had shut down her credit card.

She tried to breathe, couldn't, as if a stone lay on her chest; an appeal required money and she had three hundred and fifty dollars in her wallet. She left the parking garage and walked out onto the street, where cars and people passed as if this were any other day. A taxi to Park City, where Anne was, would cost a fourth of her money, another fourth to get back, and she couldn't order a Lyft without a viable card, so she frantically looked for a bus stop. She saw one on the next block and ran toward it; even though it was cool for July in Utah, she had started to sweat by the time she got there. On the bus, she rocked in her seat. "Idiot!" she said. "Blind fool!" The other passengers stared at her, so she tried to calm herself. She took her sunglasses out of her handbag and put them on.

This is my hand. This is my forehead. This is my heart rooted out of my chest.

Anne's voice blossomed in her memory: "Ma." Anne laughed and patted Lily's face. "Ma."

While vision was primary for Lily, sound came first for Anne. Lily knew that Anne recognized her voice on the day of her birth because the baby had turned her head when Lily spoke, but she didn't respond to any other person. Lily believed Anne had heard her talking from inside the womb. Reacting to Lily's face came later, knowing her father's face even later. Lily had spent much of the ten months since Anne's birth speaking to her, listening to her sounds, searching her face, often sketching it. Later, when Anne was old enough, she gave her child markers and showed her how to make marks and swirls on pieces of paper.

Generally, the child sensed her watching and looked up into her face. *Tête–à–tête.* Not as looking at a cantaloupe or a hedgehog and not as looking in the mirror. Not apathetic or careless glancing, such as when people rush past each other in the grocery store or on the sidewalk, but focused, intimate vision, eye-to-eye, with the possibility of an infinity of responses, an infinity of futures with that person. During her gaze time with Anne, Lily feels a spiritual charge passing between her consciousness and that of her child, as when two metals are placed in a solution. An exchange of ions, electric. She senses an actual being before her, not merely a mannequin with eyes that might blink and surprise her or a mouth that might speak.

When she looks into Anne's eyes, she also feels doubled backward in time, as if she is the child, sitting on her mother's knees, watched by her mother's hazel eyes. Her own mother sings, "Oh, Little Hen, when when when, will you lay me an egg for my tea?" "Here go horsies trot trot trot, spilt their buttermilk every drop," and, "Blackbird, singing in the dead of night, take these broken wings and learn to fly." Whenever one of those songs surfaces in Lily's head, she swirls back to that feeling of absolute safety, swaddled by her mother's eyes, arms, and voice. Where have these songs come from? One comes from her mother's love of the Beatles, but the others? Songs about tea and buttermilk? Her great-great-grandmother, Esther Birch, was born in Wooten, Kent, England; the songs must have come into the family through her. Anne faces Lily, and Lily faces Jean, who faces Alice, Matilda, Esther—further back in time, daughter, mother, mother as daughter. *We slept in a garden, now in the dreary world.* Mothering back to Eve, to Eve's mother—that mystery.

Lily's face-to-face time with Nathan has been charged in a different way. The line of his jaw, his full lips, his voice, but especially his steel-gray eyes, which focused on her as if he had no room in his head for anything else in the universe. A neat trick. As if he knew all of her. She had seen him do it with businessmen and researchers, and with the bald judge, who would bark like a dog if Nathan had asked. *Roll over*, Lily thought, *speak, play dead.*

As the bus left the freeway and Park City came into sight, images jerked through Lily's brain: Anne's face scrunched and sad because her mother had been gone so long, the blank face of the nanny, the judge's mouth saying words that sliced Lily open, Nathan getting to Anne before her. Nathan held Anne's narrow shoulders as if he would mold her like clay to make her unable to commit the sin of her mother—rejecting him. Oh, how Lily had misread his face as he lied during mediation! She believed he had conquered his anger and reverted to the Nathan she had agreed to marry three years earlier.

She imagined telling the police or a different judge what Nathan had done, and she felt vertigo. They would think she was lying, a judgment supported by court documents which described her psychological state—borderline personality disorder. An expert witness, a psychologist hired by Nathan, proved she had no cohesive sense of identity that enabled her to judge truth and falsehood.

She got off the bus at Prospector Square and, despite the cost, took a taxi up to Deer Valley, toward the home Nathan said would be hers in the divorce settlement. After the taxi pulled into the driveway, she asked the driver to wait. Brock stepped onto the porch in front of her, 240 pounds, black-suited like Nathan, but never with as fine a cut. He was Nathan's valet and assistant but acted like a bodyguard. She smelled Brock's cologne, and it reminded her of how safe she had felt with him two years earlier in Rome when she had wanted to walk past the Coliseum at night. Nathan had work so he stayed in the hotel. Men had padded like coyotes through the shadows at her flank. They had slunk away when Brock stepped under a light and turned to face them.

"I need to get my things, Brock. Talk to Anne."

"She's not here," he said. "Your things have been donated. They were boxed, but when you didn't come get them. . . ."

"Didn't come get them?"

Brock merely shrugged. He was stiffer than he had ever looked before. His mouth pressed into a flat line.

"Where is she?"

"I can't tell you."

"To charity? All my pictures?"

He scratched his head, and then his face showed something, the hint of a frown. "Your studio, your bedroom is empty now. Even the bed is gone."

She believed him, knew that all her paintings and sketches, the photographs of her parents—the only physical link she had to them—were destroyed. Brock had always been silent when Nathan orchestrated a lie, so she didn't think he was lying to her now. Her jewelry and clothing from Nathan, perfume, the cash she'd saved in a drawer, everything—gone—all in the five hours since she had left her home that morning. Brock had been busy.

She tried to push past, but he took her by the shoulders and held her immobile until she stopped struggling. Then he opened his hands and she turned away.

The judge had said she had no rights except supervised visitation with Anne for a few hours every two weeks. It became clear, a horrid blankness in her gut, that she might not see Anne that day or even that week.

"I need to see Anne."

"Every other Wednesday."

"Brock, you have to tell me where she is."

His face didn't change. "Here's the address."

Finally, she gave up and took the card from him. "Barbara Cabel, Supervised Visit Provider." The address was in Bountiful, not far from where she'd grown up. The date and time were scrawled across the bottom. This woman would watch her play with Anne, as if the child needed to be protected from her mother.

"How will I get there?"

"I believe that's up to you. You'll need to pay half the cost of supervision, so your share is $150." He still blocked the doorway. "One more thing, Lily." He handed her a manila envelope.

"What's this?"

"I don't know," he said.

She reached inside and found two gift cards, $25 each, to Harmons Grocery and a set of keys taped to a card with an address on it—Pollyanna Apartments. The sight of these objects, after the mediation agreement said she'd get the Park City house and $10,000 a month alimony, made her dizzy with fury.

If she kept the envelope, she might not be able to appeal. She felt the wires created by Nathan connected to her hands and feet. *Triple fool!* She could extrapolate from this small allowance how it would go. His hand would arbitrarily open or close to her in the hour of her need. She felt a claustrophobic terror that was like having his thumbs on the front of her throat. On Anne's throat.

So instead of putting the envelope in her handbag, she thrust it at Brock's chest and turned away. Walking down the sidewalk, she staggered at the thought of Nathan being alone with Anne. Anne at ten months still crawled toward him when he held his arms out to her. What would that laughing child become after a year, two years, a decade in his control? "I will bring her up in the way she should," he had said to the judge, who had frowned at first but then realized Nathan was referring to scripture. Because of her youth in the Mormon church, Lily knew it was from Proverbs: "Train up a child in the way he should go, and when he is old, he will not depart from it."

Anne was an agreeable, happy child; under Nathan's control, she would become compliant.

"You all right?" said the taxi driver, standing next to his car.

"What do you think? They took my baby and gave away all my things."

He frowned as she opened the door and stepped into the taxi but didn't say anything else. As the car rolled forward, she looked at the stone walls and the tiled roof. She had brought Anne here after she was born. It had been their home. Because she knew Nathan, she knew she'd never see the inside again. She raised her phone and took a picture out the window of the moving taxi.

If she had only taken Anne to a neighbor, instead of leaving her with someone Nathan had hired. But Lily didn't know the name of the neighbor a quarter mile away. Nor the neighbor on the other side. When they had come back from a year of wandering the world, she had loved the feeling of isolation. Later, she had asked about throwing a dinner party, but he had said, "Like in the suburbs? Inviting the neighbors over for a barbecue?" Their parties had been his business parties.

She thought of him as voice and hands, open or shut, giving her gifts or taking them away. He had never touched her in anger, but his voice had several times moved her from complacency to terror in a moment. Now he would focus on Anne. Lily sobbed and saw the driver's eyes in the rearview mirror.

Anne's hands moved in Lily's memory, signing, *I'm hungry* or *I'm thirsty. I'm poopy. Mom. Dad. I want a story.* Even if she got to Anne, what could she say—"Mommy can't be with you because Mommy is fucking stupid"?

Lily took the mediation agreement out of her handbag. As soon as she could, she would talk to the mediator, but first, she had to talk to Anne.

On the bus back to Salt Lake from Park City, Lily called Nathan and got a message that said her number was blocked. So she called his office. Jill said, "He's not in."

"I need to find out where Anne is," she told Jill.

"I told you he's not in." Jill gave an edge to her voice that she had never used before with Lily—a voice that Nathan would have fired her for if she had used it on any of his associates.

"Jill."

"I don't know why you're not ashamed to call here."

Another wave of disorientation passed through Lily.

His building was not far south of Hogle Zoo, with a west view across the Salt Lake Valley. Lily got off the bus near Foothill and walked, taking about half an hour. Finally she came to his building, Sharp Cybersecurity. He was in his office on the second floor, looking down at her. She entered and crossed the lobby. Brian, the guard at the front desk, blocked her way. "I'm sorry. You can't come here."

She called Jill again. "I can see him in his damn office. I'm downstairs. I need to talk to him."

Jill hung up.

Lily stood in the parking lot, until Nathan came to the window again. He looked down at her, so she raised her middle fingers toward the window and returned inside. This time when she tried to go past Brian, he used his phone. Nathan came down. "You need to leave."

"You don't even want her. I'll take her and move away." Lily would have gone down on her knees if it would have done any good. "You'll never have to see either one of us again."

He simply extended his hand, showing her a paper. "You're violating a restraining order."

A restraining order? She asked to look at the document, at the judge's signature on the bottom. She raised her phone and took a picture of it.

"Remarkable!" She looked at the paper again. "You forged it."

He looked sad. "I didn't need to forge it."

The pity in his eyes infuriated her. She went after him with her nails reaching for his eyes. "Let me see Anne!" she screamed.

But Brian held her back as Nathan glanced at the security camera above his head. She pushed herself away from Brian, held her hands to her sides.

"Next time she comes, don't call me," Nathan said. "Call the police. Call them 30 seconds from now if she's still here." She stared at his back as he walked away. Brian folded his arms, and she left the office.

She walked down to Foothill Boulevard and sat at a bus stop. She called her lawyer and told her what Nathan had done—moving Anne, donating her things, getting a restraining order. The stupid woman told Lily that she didn't believe her. It was clear that the narrative fabricated by Nathan's lawyer had taken root in her brain. In court he had made clear that borderline people were trapped in an "I love you, I hate you" relationship with their enabler. "You can always appeal," her former lawyer said. "But with a different lawyer."

In some other universe Lily could, but not in this one.

She called the mediator and left a message to call her back. Soon her phone buzzed, and Lily explained to her that Nathan had taken the house away. "But Lily," said the woman. "You said in mediation that you didn't want the house, that you wanted him to set you up in an apartment. I'll email you a copy. It has your signature on the bottom."

"How much did he pay you?"

"That's insulting, Lily. Do you really not remember?"

Lily disconnected and found herself stumbling, so she leaned against a tree until she could stop her limbs from shaking.

She thought about going back to the courthouse. If the judge was still there she could talk to him. She got on the next bus to downtown. When she stepped into the building, the workday was ending and most of the rooms were empty. She wandered the hallway for a half hour, seeing no one she recognized, only people talking about their own concerns or hasty to get home. She felt foolish and disoriented.

At the police station the desk sergeant, a tall, thin woman, looked bored as she listened to Lily's story that seemed implausible even to her. "You need a damn good lawyer," the woman advised her, "not the police."

"I need a fucking miracle," she said.

The officer turned toward her computer. "We're fresh out."

T W O

As Lily left the building, she thought about calling the police in Deer Valley and saying that Nathan had kidnapped Anne, or the newspapers, describing what had really happened. Child Protective Services would have to follow a process, and Nathan would have time to work his magic on them. Nothing she could imagine would work.

The sun was low in the west. She fingered her money—$308, after the taxi and bus. She didn't know where she would stay that night and she wished that she'd kept the Harmons cards. She found herself at a bus stop and sat down, trying to think of a friend whose couch she could sleep on. All were from three years earlier, none of them good friends. She didn't have their numbers anymore and didn't know if the two or three she might have called were still in Salt Lake.

She thought about going to Nathan's parents, who lived 300 miles away in Entrada, near St. George, in a house he had bought them. His father had been an insurance agent and his mother a high school German teacher. Lily had only met them a few times, but she knew they wouldn't help her. When she first met them, his mother had talked about Nathan's childhood. When he was small, he had been different from her other children, more competitive. At that time Lily thought she was paying her son a compliment, but now she wondered if she'd given Lily a veiled warning.

The other person she thought of was her aunt, who had been her guardian through high school. Lily was an only child, and when she was in junior high, her parents had died from pesticides sprayed on the fruit orchard next to their house. Lily, asleep in her room on the other side of the house, had survived. Her Aunt Celia had kicked Lily out when she graduated high school, saying she was tired of Lily showing up with belongings she had no money to buy. She said she was also finished putting up with Lily's disposition, which alternated between surly and sarcastic. The worst had been when Lily refused to go to church, proclaiming to her aunt's face that she no longer believed in God. For graduation her aunt gave her $100 and a rolling duffel bag. "I have my own children and I won't have you leading them into disbelief and apostasy." Lily could never have led her cousins anywhere because they thought like their mother. Her goodbye, when Lily walked out the door with the duffel full of her things, was "I never want to see you again." It was the second-most disorienting experience of Lily's life up until then, only overshadowed by the morning she found her parents cold in their bed, not a mark on them.

With no options left, she dialed Aunt Celia from memory. When Lily identified herself, there was silence on the phone.

"It's been awhile," Lily said.

"I think about you sometimes," said her aunt.

"I think about you too," said Lily. It was true. Generally, her memory was full of anger.

"I wish it had turned out different. I mean, I wish you hadn't started stealing stuff and bringing it into my home. I wish you had stayed strong in the Church. You'd be better off now if you hadn't left the Faith."

"Better off?"

"What do you need?" her aunt said.

"I was just divorced. I don't have a place to stay tonight."

"Your ex-husband called. He said you might say that. He says it's not because you need any place to stay. He says that he rented an apartment for you."

Lily's fingers fumbled and she nearly dropped the phone. "He called you? When?"

"Yesterday. He said you refused to accept the apartment."

Her soul slipped sideways. Nathan had known exactly what she would do.

"He explained to me what borderline personality disorder is. It made sense of what happened when you lived with us."

"He gave away all my things. He cancelled my credit cards, took away my car, and he's got my child. He's trying to keep control over me."

"How am I to believe that?"

As a teenager, Lily had generally lied to her aunt, sometimes without needing to.

"It's better for you if I don't help you. That much is clear."

After she disconnected, Lily breathed her anger down. Soon she was calmer. Yesterday she'd had a home; today she didn't. She knew the Church might help her, but she didn't know who to call, finally she called her childhood bishop, also from memory, but he didn't answer.

A man walked toward the bench she sat on and held his hand out. "Spare change," he asked, and she smelled the sour alcohol on his breath. She shook her head, pressing her lips together. "Rich bitch," he said under his breath as he passed Lily.

"Poor bitch now," she said, louder than she had intended. She had the sensation of falling horizontally, that she was being pushed out before she had space and time to gather the threads of her identity.

The bus still hadn't come so she stood up and walked east with no clear destination in mind. She passed the old county courthouse and the library. The walls were glass and inside she saw a few homeless men pretending to read magazines. She knew the androgynous and amorphous figure in her dream was also homeless. *These are my people now*, she thought. But then she pulled back from that bleak vision. These men would be here next week, the week after. The thick-bodied person in her dream would never adapt to living in a house. Lily knew her mind and will were both active; she would figure out what to do next and next and next. She was not caught in an eddy of time.

Lily has been one thing to Nathan, now another—poor angel when he courted her, rich angel for two and a half years, rich bitch after she asked for a divorce, and now poor bitch. Nathan's vision of her has been so powerful that she feels the changes in her flesh.

As David Bowie sings,

Ch-ch-ch-ch-Changes
(Turn and face the strange)
Ch-ch-Changes
Time may change me, but I can't trace time.

When Lily was first with Nathan, the future seemed like a tree with infinite branches—the fractal diagram she drew in her notebook when he asked her to marry him:

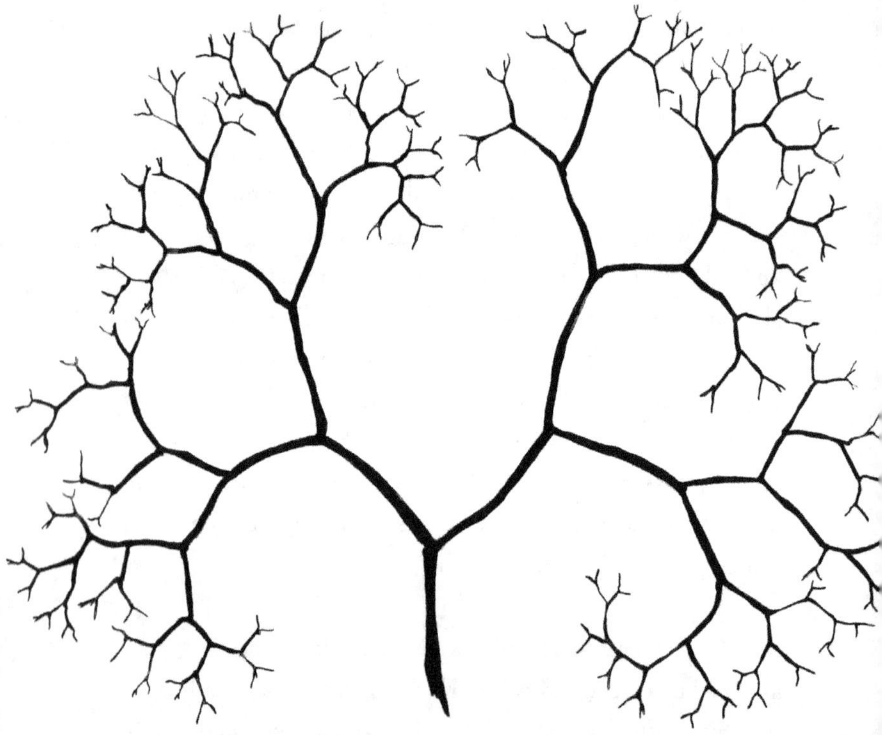

TWO-BRANCH FRACTAL
Automythology (USP)

The drawing started simple: two paths diverging, Marry Nathan or not? It reminded her of the Tree of Knowledge of Good and Evil in the Garden of Eden, a story she was taught all of her childhood and which she thinks is more about Eve than Adam. Nathan didn't have to tell her how rich he was while they had dated; he showed her. Then after they were married, traveling in Europe for a year, she discovered that money opened all doors, and she imagined time and opportunity as a sheet wide as the world, the universe, covered with branching possibilities—so unlike the twig of future she had imagined after her parents had died when she was fourteen. In Europe his total control of what they did made sense because she had never traveled before. But when they returned to Utah, his control continued quietly. She didn't see until too late what Nathan had quietly pruned from her life—until he could cover the totality of her future with his hand. Cover her with his two hands. Not a being alive with memory and hope but a mouth and a vagina. With each change of being, the shape of her future has changed. Now she can trace the ch-ch-ch-changes.

Lily watches the homeless men, a glass wall between them. Soon, she will enter or walk elsewhere along the streets, peering at the buildings as if they were transparent instead of granite or brick, and she might discover inside one of them a way to get toward the future she wants—being with Anne again. Her future is newly unsettled, but is anyone's more sure? Ministers, business executives, investment counselors, clairvoyants, insurance and loan underwriters, economists, seismologists, climate experts, political analysts, odds makers, politicians, and fashion mavens want to know what's coming, hopefully some blessed state of being, as complex and endless as looking into the face of a beloved. More likely the future is waking in the dark with a stranger's hand groping between your legs.

Lily's proximate future? Getting toiletries. She continued east, the sun lowering behind her, until she came to a Smith's where she bought deodorant and toothpaste, a toothbrush, underwear. She needed practical clothing, something other than the expensive dress she had worn to the trial, which seemed months or years ago. She could spare only a few dollars, so she looked up the closest Deseret Industries thrift store, which was on Twenty-first South.

The bus dropped her about a block from the store. Inside the racks of clothing smelled of detergent and mothballs. No one else was dressed the way she was, in a thousand-dollar dress, and she felt embarrassed, out of place. She picked out pants and shirts, a dress that didn't look too bad. She tried to think what else she might need and found a foldable, Boy Scout knife that she could use to cut bread or fruit. Then she found a charger that fit her phone, because hers had been on the stand next to her bed. While picking up a backpack, she saw a lacquered wooden wheel, mounted on a small stand. The plaque said "Executive Decision Maker," and the price tag was one dollar. She held the support in her hand and spun the wheel, which whirred as a brass arrow ticked against the small nails. Every option was blank; it didn't matter where the wheel came to rest. Lily smiled bitterly. She'd be better off if she had cast dice or spun a wheel rather than trusted a cheap lawyer. She took a picture of it as a memento of her dangerous foolishness and started toward the front to check out, but then she turned back and dropped the object into her shopping cart.

EXECUTIVE DECISION MAKER
Automythology (USP)

Outside Deseret Industries, $245 and some change left, Lily dumped everything she owned into the backpack and used her phone to find a motel for less than forty dollars, on the west side of I-15. Then she walked toward the closest Trax station, dragging her roller backpack. On the train west her phone stopped working. It wasn't out of power; Nathan had terminated her service. Her first thought was that now she couldn't get the picture of Anne off the phone.

The motel stood next to a billboard with bears and a vacation trailer on it, an ancient advertisement for Yellowstone Park. The clerk wore a bolo tie and tight pants. He wouldn't let her take a room without a credit card, but she finally convinced him to let her stay if she gave him a $100 deposit in addition to the cost of the room—$35. He gave her a handwritten receipt for the money.

When she opened the door, she knew the room was overpriced. It smelled strongly of cleaning fluid and mold and was as hot as a sauna. The air conditioner shuddered and then squealed as it pushed out frigid air smelling of oil. The weak output hardly changed the temperature of the room, so she could only get cool if she sat directly in front of it. Suddenly she couldn't stop laughing. "My life is an implausible fiction." She giggled as she took off her dress, which had certainly cost much more than the clerk made in a month. Then the giggles that shook her turned to sobs. She blubbered, "Please, God, help me find Anne." The words didn't seem to rise past the stained ceiling panels.

She dumped her handbag on the bed: wallet, nearly empty but with useless plastic inside; sunglasses, which she could maybe take to a pawn shop, along with the handbag; phone, now useless; her sketching notebook; lipstick; a couple of tampons; her passport; a candy bar, which she ate right then; a novel she was half-way through; receipts, a few loose stamps, a memo pad, a wheel of birth control pills; a small yellow duck, a toy of Anne's; some loose change which she put in her wallet; a plastic spork in cello with a napkin; a package of tissues; and a small pine cone that she couldn't remember putting in her purse. The sum of her possessions. She threw the pills and receipts away, put the rest in a pocket of her backpack, and put the handbag in the backpack as well.

While she lies on the lumpy, smelly mattress, unable to sleep, she thinks about history and her own gullibility. Three years earlier, Nathan approached her at her MFA show in the Smoot Gallery at the University of Utah. His insight into her art, that it played with the anguish of family politics, made her curious. As they dated, eating at restaurants she had never been able to afford, his conversation, his mouth and eyes, became outward emblems of a mystery she had to solve. He wouldn't have sex with her until they married, which she attributed to his sense of religious propriety. During that time of abstinence, every touch melted her, until she felt as if her core had become lava. She didn't care that he was fifteen years older. Then they married, and she rode the wave of his clear passion for her. He had business all over the world, so they traveled for a year. His wealth had also been stupefying. Before meeting him, she couldn't imagine that such freedom and power were possible. A flat high above the Thames, an apartment with a view of the Eiffel Tower, Rome, upper west-side Manhattan, finally Park City. Her ride with him had to that point been quick and heady, speeding through an atmosphere too rare for most mortals.

At first after they settled in Deer Valley, she wandered the magnificent house beset by wonder at her good fortune. With a man who was that obsessed with you—his love as hot and focused as the point of light under a magnifying glass— she believed she needed no one else. She was all-in-all to him, like a goddess. But soon she was bored. It was so different from their time abroad, where the days seemed full of adventure and romance. In Utah, Nathan left in the morning, came back in the evening. They ate and had sex. During those hours in the evening he focused on her so completely that it almost made up for the empty days. Almost.

She sees now that he had severed every one of her previous connections. Her MFA class at the U graduated and left, and he convinced her that their lives were now radically different from hers. In a flash of independence, she took an adjunct job teaching at Westminster College. The salary wasn't enough to pay their maid, so he persuaded her to quit. Her art? If she was placing pieces in exhibits, that would be one thing, but who would buy her installation work? He treasured everything she made because it was hers, but maybe she needed more time before she sent paintings to galleries. He cut each strand of her social life with a blade so sharp that she hadn't known it was gone. By the time she realized he held all the strings, it was too late.

He knew the mileage on her car, and if she went somewhere during the day, down the canyon to the university or a gallery or a bar, to a movie, or just driving eastward toward the Uinta Mountains, he pried until she told him what she'd done. At first, she thought it sweet, his slight possessiveness, but then

PUPPET LILY
Automythology (USP)

it felt ominous and tarnished the feeling of free wandering, so she tried lying to him, but that just made him still with anger. He always knew. Because that silence frightened her, she stopped going out except with him, and her days were like a blank, waiting for him to come home. She chastised herself for lack of imagination, telling herself to make art, read, write, or anything, but her efforts were tentative and unsatisfying. After a year of living in Deer Valley, she agreed to stop taking birth control and Anne was born. Then everything changed—she had purpose again.

Seven months later things changed again, a slight shift that had started an avalanche. One night Nathan had come home a little early. She wanted to tell him that Anne had started scooting herself along by reaching her arms forward, elbows out. He put his fingers on Lily's lips and told her they were going to a reception sponsored by the governor as part of an entrepreneurship conference.

"I don't have a babysitter," she said.

"We need a permanent nanny," he said, not for the first time, "then we wouldn't have this problem."

A streak of rebellious stubbornness rose in her and she told him she just couldn't go, couldn't get a sitter on such short notice. "I've told you before. I want to take care of my own child." Looking back, she knew she had never before directly contradicted him.

"Get a sitter," he said.

She shouted, "No!"

He stared at her, not speaking or allowing anger onto his face, but she became frightened, something she couldn't have imagined when they were in Europe and he fulfilled her every whim. He went by himself.

Two weeks later they had another argument and then another and the arguments became daily, her resisting his unspoken rules for her and him staying firm, her often screaming at him, and him just looking at her with the emotion of a reptile. One night he locked Anne in the closet and wouldn't let Lily free her, even though the child was wailing. Lily threatened him with a knife and he finally stood aside. But first he lifted his phone and took her picture. The next week she said she wanted a divorce. A slight look of regret passed across his face, but then he became distant, looking past her. Because she stopped believing in him, he had no use for her.

After several hours of lying in the smelly motel in a hypnagogic state, Lily seemed to leave her own body. She looked at her sorry self as if from above and felt wave after wave of hopelessness. She gave herself over to that emotion, drowning in it. She had no way of discovering where he had taken Anne. She saw that none of the methods she had used in the past to get what she wanted would help her get to her child. Ardent pleading would no longer work, neither would assertiveness, rage, dishonesty, bartering, manipulation, or appeal to authority. Prayer had also failed to connect her to a divine being who might give her reason to hope, now that Nathan had taken Anne from her. Seeing Anne every other Wednesday for a couple of hours was unacceptable. Lily felt bereft of Anne again. Like another death after the first. She felt her mind wheeling, a crow over her own carcass, pain and pain again, swoop of wings, time circling.

She didn't know what to do, but she knew she had to do something. She could not lose Anne. Would not. Finally, she dressed in the clothing she had bought at the thrift store, gathered her other belongings into the backpack, including the wheel, and waited for light. With no rational choice available that would give her Anne back, she decided to step toward an irrational future. Like Eve, she chose the apple of the unknowable over the garden of the familiar because the familiar had been made unbearable.

Sitting on the bed, she felt herself on the boundary between sanity and insanity. Her body seemed to buzz with awareness. She saw the branching of future, random possibility as both delightsome and fearsome, less like the branching of a tree with orderly branches and more like a vine, where the line of her life might divide and coil. She walked out of the room that smelled of cigarette smoke and into the office to collect her deposit.

Of course, the clerk, a small Latina with a thick accent, knew nothing of the $100. When Lily showed her the hand-written receipt, the woman peered at the signature and grinned. "*Chica*, there is no Abraham Washington that works here." Lily thought about waiting until the night shift to confront the boy who had stolen from her but dismissed that for foolishness. If Nathan had been there the motel staff would scramble to get her money back, but Nathan would never be connected to someone who had to rent such a shitty room in the first place. So she accepted the loss as the natural order of her new life.

From the cheap motel Lily walked to the Primary Children's Hospital, where, ten months earlier, she had held her new baby against her chest. She remembered the picture Nathan had taken of her and Anne. She had made a painting

EVE IN THE GARDEN
Automythology (USP)

of it, now lost with her other things. She stood in front of the doors and let one arm hang loose, her head lolling, as she took a selfie. When she had time and a place to work, she could replace the painting with a sketch of her new identity—victim of a puppet master.

Since recognizing that Nathan had put Anne beyond her reach and would anticipate and block anything she tried, she was free to think alternatively. As Janice Joplin sang, "Freedom's just another word for nothing left to lose." Emmanuel Levinas said it more positively, and probably not while wailing into a microphone: "At the very moment when everything is lost, everything is possible." Lily felt calm for the first time since leaving the courtroom. She bore in her mind the image—static, eternal—of Anne's face looking back at hers with recognition and love. Her baby would grow into a child, a girl, a young woman watching Lily's face, and that act of gazing would create Anne as a human. So preserving her natural and absolute right, to look with intimacy and clarity into Anne's face, constituted all of Lily's reality. Nothing else, no law established by God, certainly no statute established by man, mattered as much as that imagined future.

THREE

Standing with her back to the front door of the hospital, part of the University of Utah medical complex, Lily spun the wheel. It whirred in her ears and vibrated against her palms. She felt a physical and temporal vertigo. She experienced again the sensation of falling toward the future, the horizon that flees before us all. She stuck her finger in the spokes and then reoriented the wheel so the postage stamp she'd put on the wheel was north. Her finger was to the east. With the city spread below her she took a breath and walked that direction, one of sixteen the wheel could have chosen for her. To her right rose the buildings of the university. When the road turned south, she kept on straight along Fort Douglas Boulevard. She passed between the old military buildings, including the theater and the commissary, and a half-circle of small houses with signs on them that were too far away to read. Anne's face, an immaterial object Lily willed to become material, hung before her as she walked,

She came to a T in the road and spun the wheel again: south-southeast. She walked through a parking lot and down a hill covered with elm and oak brush. She knew she was heading in a good direction when she found a way through the trees, but the ground was covered with cheatgrass and soon her socks above her low shoes were full of barbs. She emerged from the grove into another parking lot, with a square, red-bricked building close by. Walking closer, she saw the sign on the front read Human Resources Building. She stepped inside and found herself in a reception area with an open office beyond, people working in cubicles. A young woman behind the desk smiled. "Can I help you?"

Lily didn't know what to say. *I'm looking for my child and a roulette wheel led me here.*

"I think this is the wrong building."

"What building are you looking for? This is U of U Human Resources."

"Sorry." Lily turned and left. She stepped out of eyesight and leaned against the building. Her hands were shaking. She had acted like a mumbling fool. She knew she had to be smarter, quicker. She spun the wheel again, following northeast along Wakara Way until she arrived at the Museum of Natural History.

Once inside the entryway of the museum, she remembered she didn't have money to spare for the entrance fee, so she digressed into the bookstore. Soon a group of elementary students came in. She joined them, and while their leader spoke to the employee at the entrance gate, she stood next to another woman at the rear. All the children stood three-by-three, holding hands.

"How long have you been a teacher?" Lily asked the woman beside her.

"I'm not a teacher. I'm just helping out today. This is my child." She pointed to a girl in the last row of three.

"Welcome to the museum," the woman at the entrance said. "I hope you have a pleasant visit."

Lily smiled as they all moved into the displays. The children turned right and walked past the glass cases into the dinosaur area. The mother Lily had spoken to looked at her oddly, so Lily moved away and climbed the stairs. From above, she looked down on the children as they stood next to the triceratops.

As it should be, Nathan stood not far from the children, propping Anne on his left hip. Lily wondered at her own lack of surprise that the wheel had led her to her child. Nathan held with his free hand the hand of a woman who could have been Lily's twin four years earlier when *she* had met Nathan— thin, wearing a sweater that hung over one shoulder, Levi's and leather clogs, ponytail—probably another art student. He smiled down at Anne, stroked his hand across her blonde hair. Yearning went down through Lily's stomach—Anne, her small head, small face. Anne.

"You're such a cute father," the girlfriend said, her voice high and flutelike. He must have been nearly twice her age. Now Nathan tried to get Anne to look at the triple claw of the dinosaur. He turned and leaned slightly toward the girl as if he was going to kiss her. But he didn't follow through, holding that tension.

Without much thought Lily knew what to do next. She took a breath and gave herself up to the flow of thought and emotion that rushed through her.

Now that the wheel has led her straight to Anne, Lily imagines herself as post-rational, freed from the conventions of not only human culture, but time and space. For primitive people, time is circular, not linear, not branching. The sun cycles overhead in the spring; rains come and go; corn or wheat grows, matures, and dies; men and women make love and women swell like squash and deliver babies, who grow into children and then into men and women who make love; the generations of people and the stories ripple like waves, advancing and retreating, circles inside circles. Even for Lily, whose mind is not primitive, the past is ever-present, but more complex than a simple cycle, maybe like a labyrinth of timespace, a pattern on the back of a turtle creeping toward the abyss. Again and again she says to Anne, "I'll be back soon," again and again she screams in Nathan's face, again and again Brock stands like a wall between her and her child, she feels the loss of Anne again and again, the rhythm of Nathan tapping his shoe against the floor; the judge's gavel seals his words, tolling in her head like the beating of her heart. But a labyrinth has a clear destination, the center of things. With patience and wit, a wanderer can get where they're going. Timespace feels less organized than that for Lily. Instead time feels like a reticulated vine ready to coil around her neck.

Lily felt a rush of adrenaline as she trotted down the stairs of the Natural History Museum to the entryway. Her voice shook as she said, loud, hysterical, "I can't find my child." A

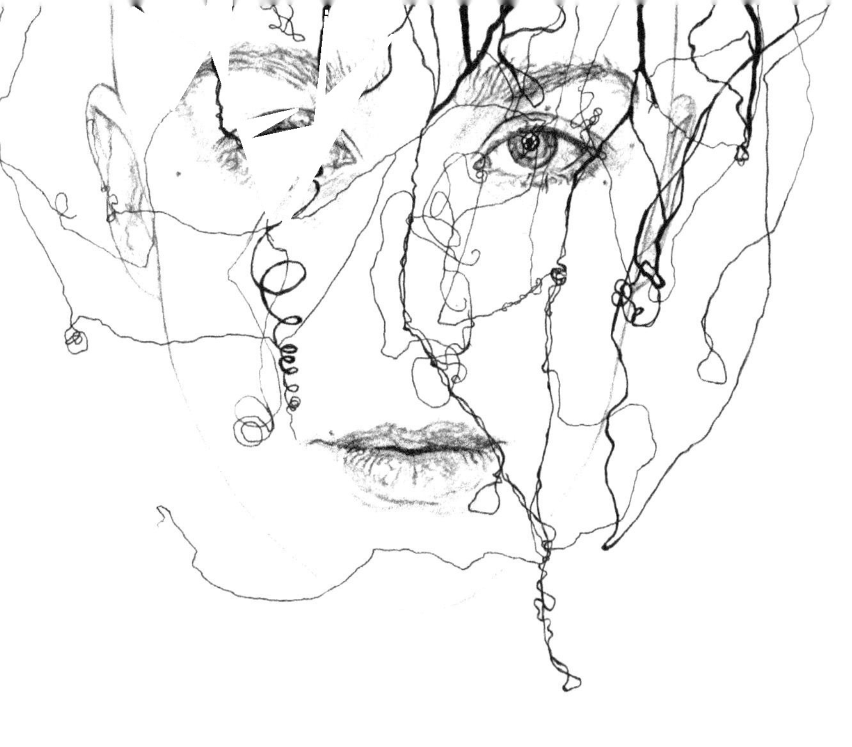

sobbing breath. "Still a baby. She can't even walk yet. I've looked everywhere. Someone took her." She worried her voice had been too loud and that Nathan would recognize her and be forewarned.

The thin woman behind the ticket desk turned from the man she was talking to. Lily focused on her eyes, which were marked heavily with blue shadow. "Let's be calm," the woman said. "I'm sure your child's still in the building. What was she wearing?"

Lily put one hand to her cheek. "A blue t-shirt and pink pants."

The woman reached for the phone and pushed a button. "I'll describe her on the loudspeaker and someone will bring her to you."

"No," said Lily. "I want you to call the police." She only needed a few seconds of confusion to get Anne away from Nathan.

Lily glanced at the glass display cases and the entrance to the dinosaur section. She knew that Nathan would soon leave that part of the museum because he didn't like children, especially clamoring crowds of them. The ticket woman held the phone in her hand and stared, first at Lily, and then at the man next to her. He shook his head.

"Please," said Lily.

Finally, Nathan walked out past the glass display cases, holding Anne who was twisting her face, getting ready to cry.

"There she is!" Lily shouted. "That man has her!" She ran toward Nathan, who saw her coming.

For an instant his face was puzzled, then he turned his back, holding both arms around Anne. "No!"

Anne saw Lily over his shoulder and started shrieking.

"Let me have my baby!" Lily screamed. She turned back to the woman at the desk. "Will you please call the damn police? Will you do it now?"

The woman started punching numbers into her phone. The man walked toward Nathan. "Put down the child."

"This woman is not stable," Nathan said, pointing at Lily. "She's—"

"Anne!" shouted Lily.

A woman and man came out of the bookstore, staring at her. A teacher came from the dinosaur section. "What's wrong?"

Anne screamed louder. "Maa, maa." She reached her arms toward Lily.

The young woman with Nathan stared at him, her brows pulled together.

"Put down the child!" said the museum employee. Several people wearing the same T-shirt came out of the bookstore. A stern woman, obviously someone with authority, strode out into the entryway.

Nathan smiled. "Please do call the police. We can easily sort this out." He actually stroked his moustache, one swipe left, the other right, just like a villain in a melodrama.

Anne continued to shriek and twist in his arms. "Maa, Maa."

"Put down the child!" said the museum employee.

"I think you better put down the child," said the stern woman.

"I will," said Nathan, "but you can't let her go with this woman."

He set Anne down, and the museum employee reached to pick her up. Anne arched her back and screamed louder. He backed away, palms toward her. Anne put her butt in the air and got to her feet. She was still shrieking. Then she saw Lily and took a step, and another, almost falling forward as she toddled toward her mother.

In some part of her brain, Lily registered that these were Anne's first steps.

Lily folded her into her arms, held her small Anne-body tight. "Oh, my baby. I have missed you so much." Anne put her hands around Lily's neck and stuck her small head in the nook between Lily's neck and her shoulder.

"I have her blanket in the car," said Lily. "It will help her calm down. I'll just go get it."

"This is my ex-wife and she's trying to kidnap my child," Nathan said. Behind him the girlfriend put her hand to her mouth and looked from Nathan to Lily.

The stern woman turned to Lily. "I can't let you take her away until the police come."

"That's fine with me." Lily tugged the band of Anne's diaper and sniffed. She swung her backpack around. "At least let me take her to the restroom to change." She pointed to the man who had made Nathan put Anne down. "He can stand at the door and you can come in with me."

"Change her here," said Nathan. He turned to the woman. "You can't let her take this child out of my sight." He took one step toward her. "We just went through a bad divorce, and I got custody because she's not stable. I tell you—she is trying to kidnap this child."

"Can we move into my office?" said the stern lady. "I want to avoid disturbing the patrons any further."

"I'm going to change her diaper," said Lily, clutching her backpack and moving toward the bathroom.

Nathan stood in front of her, blocking the way. Almost, almost, the mask came off his rage.

The stern lady tugged at Lily's sleeve. "You better change her in my office."

The girl with Nathan looked at him, and then at Lily, who met her gaze. The girl looked away.

Nathan nodded. "In her office." His public face twitched.

The office was down a short hallway behind the museum store. It had a wooden desk and a sofa. Inside Anne clung to

Lily. "Ma, Ma, my Ma Ma." Lily stroked her legs, the soft skin at the back of her neck.

"Aren't you going to change her diaper?" asked the woman—*Susan Francom*, the sign on the door said.

Lily heard a siren and knew how a criminal felt, the panic that things would soon get much, much worse. Four police officers appeared shoulder to shoulder just outside the office door, filling the hallway with their power and ego. Nathan was just behind them.

Lily felt hope drain away, but she pointed to Nathan. "He tried to kidnap my child." She put Anne's cheek against her own.

Nathan smiled and waited. "Take us both to the station. I'll call my lawyer," his smile grew even wider, "and Lily can call hers."

One of the officers reached for Anne, who looked at him and shrieked again. Lily sat on the sofa, holding her closer, wishing her child back inside her belly, where she'd be safe. Lily rocked slightly.

"If I can be alone here for a minute, she'll go to sleep."

One of the officers was a woman, and she herded the others out of the office. Lily's heart beat fast, triple fast. She had messed up. If they got her to the station, Anne would be back in Nathan's power. Everything would be worse. The officers stood in the doorway, and there was no other way out.

The stern lady, Susan, came in the door. She retrieved a folder from a cabinet. "He took your child away."

Lily nodded. "His lawyers did."

Susan held the folder in her hand, her knuckles white. She walked out into the lobby, and Lily saw her wrap her arms around herself.

Lily rocked back and forth, calming Anne—nearly white hair, pale arms and legs—and the baby gradually stopped shrieking and just cried. Then she was asleep, held against Lily's body. The policewoman opened the door. "We have to go now."

"You brought a car seat?"

The policewoman frowned. "Don't you have one?"

"We came on the bus." Lily watched as the officer left the office and talked to Nathan. Soon she returned.

"Your former husband has a seat in his car." Lily opened her mouth to speak, but the officer cut her off. "We'll put it in a squad car. You can sit next to her."

Of course Anne started crying again when they strapped her into the seat. Lily put her hands on Anne and spoke to her. Anne reached her arms toward Lily and cried, long, wrenching sobs. The policewoman helped Lily into the car, and Lily noticed that the doors had no inside handles.

They drove past the university stadium and down Fourth South. When they came to the station, the driver entered the parking garage. The policewoman took Anne out of the car seat, while her partner watched Lily. Anne was crying. "Please, let me carry her," said Lily.

"You know that it will just make it worse later." She looked directly at Lily. "Maybe you realize that you're not helping yourself. Your best tactic is to get control of yourself."

The woman carried Anne toward the elevator, with her partner behind her. He still glanced with a wary face toward Lily. Lily thought about knocking the woman down, ripping Anne from her arms and running with her. The other officer would be on her before she could take a step. And running where? Lily had no idea. She followed, her eyes on Anne's eyes, which appeared over the policewoman's shoulder. Anne's small hand reach toward her. Lily followed, struggling to keep from wailing louder than Anne.

After it became clear Lily had no lawyer she could call and after Nathan's lawyer had produced the mediation (forged), divorce, and custody documents, they put Lily in a cell. The adjoining cell had three bruised young women—prostitutes, druggies. She looked at them and saw what she might become.

She stared at the bars around her and imagined how it would go. She might get to see Anne the next week, she might not. It all was in Nathan's hands. As long as Nathan had control of Anne, he would continue to control Lily. She wished again that yesterday morning she had taken Anne to someone she could trust, someone Nathan didn't know about, then she could run with the child. But who might that trustworthy person have been?

She knew that neither she nor Anne would survive without the other. She'd have to find a job and an apartment. She was held on the tether of the court's promise that she could see Anne for a few hours every other week.

It was afternoon before Lily was let out of her cell. A police officer, a lean and hawk-nosed woman, told Lily she should be grateful that her forgiving and patient former husband had refused to press charges. They returned her backpack with her possessions inside—her sketching notebook, her wallet with $110.75, her passport, the randomizing wheel, her designer shoes, her thousand-dollar dress twisted into a ball, an extra shirt and pants. She stumbled down the steps of the station, and, unable to think where she might go, she headed back toward downtown. She was out of jail, but she knew she wasn't free. Leaving her in the cell for a few hours, making her think she was going to be booked for kidnapping, was another of Nathan's tricks to break her down, assert her dependence on him after he had taken everything from her. She passed a pawn shop and went inside, trading her sunglasses and handbag for cash, about a tenth of their value. She wanted to keep her dress, in case she had reason to present her best self to a lawyer or judge. She wished she still had her wedding ring, which she could have taken to a jeweler, but she had left it on her dresser next to her bed in the Deer Valley house.

Shaky, weak, and depleted, she realized she had not eaten since the evening before. She passed one hamburger place she knew would take too big a chunk of the money she had left, but walking farther south she soon came to a cheaper one. She ate the cardboard hamburger and then lay down in the booth, immediately asleep.

She woke to someone pushing her shoulder. "You can't sleep here," said the boy with a mop. "The manager says you have to leave." She looked out the window and saw it was dark. Another cheap motel room would take half her remaining money. Without knowing where else to go, she walked north toward the Cathedral of the Madeleine, but the doors were locked. She wouldn't be allowed to rest in Temple Square or City Creek Mall. She considered sleeping under the trees next to her parents' graves in the Salt Lake Cemetery, but that was more than a mile away. Finally, she walked up the hill toward the small park where Brigham Young was buried. She climbed over the fence, crawled under a yew tree, and lay on the ground using her backpack as a pillow. The dark branches above her tangled like the lines of her life, so she turned on the phone's flash and took a picture.

Lily had camped out before as a child with her parents, or slept on the back lawn with friends, but sleeping under a tree as a homeless person was different. Whenever she heard footsteps or voices, people walking past, going either downtown or up to the houses on the west end of the Avenues, her body tensed.

At first she thought it was fear of discovery. Then she realized that unless it was a police officer or someone with an interest in the graveyard, maybe a descendant of Brigham Young who felt it wrong that she wanted to sleep where their ancestor was buried, discovery wouldn't affect her. They'd be as embarrassed as she was. Whether they were one of the religious conservatives who wanted to live close to the temple or whether they were students or professional people who inhabited the Avenues, voting Democrat and drinking coffee—it didn't much matter. None of them could harm her.

When she had money, she walked past homeless people in alcoves, with their nests of blankets, newspaper, or cardboard. In plain view of God and everybody. Thinking about their faces, Lily recognized that most of them were from an alien culture, beyond shame, as if they were not alarmed to find themselves cast as flotsam onto the irregular shore of the street-front. Now that she was part of that vast, invisible archipelago, a new understanding of her place in the universe settled into Lily's basal ganglia, sat in her gut like lead.

But she was not yet beyond shame. She felt careless to have lost so much, ashamed for letting her identity sift through her fingers, anger at the people and institutions that had failed her. Sitting in the cemetery, she shouted, "Fuck you!" to Nathan, to the policemen, to the judge, to her aunt, to the entire city of Salt Lake, to the patriarchal father of that city, Brother Brigham. As she shouted, she felt pretentious to address the whole human structure that way, but then another wave of anger rolled through her body. Rocking, she pronounced "fuck" seven times, as if she were chanting a litany.

She imagined that the sound waves ferried away the poison that had been inside her. Her body relaxed, and she was able to calm herself further by counting her breaths from one to ten and back to one, three times, all the while focusing on each slow inhalation and exhalation. She lay back down in the small cemetery next to the Patriarch of Salt Lake and his second, fourth, tenth, and fifty-first wives, from whom he no longer got any pleasure.

In Lily's dream the ungendered, pale, thick-bodied figure stands next to the trail, maybe a little closer this time. Lily is as small as Anne as she tries to run past, but it is like slow running in water, every motion a labor. That strange creature existed before and exists now and will exist forever—outside time, never moving or adapting. Lily feels its eyes on her, and she can't breathe, a constriction in her throat.

She woke in terror and found someone's hand at her neck, his other between her legs. She swung her arms at him, but he was too close to hit with fists or elbows. His mouth pressed against her mouth, and she tried to bite his lips, so he jerked back. He dug his fingers into her flesh, pushing straight-armed against her throat, and she felt blackness coming over her. Frantic, she twisted sideways and swung her elbow against something soft, maybe his eye. He pulled his hands to his face, and she crawled forward from under the tree, gasping. She got to her feet and stumbled away, not waiting for him to grab her again. As she pulled herself over the side fence, her shirt ripped on a spike at the top, and she hit the ground with a thud. The ground was lower outside on that side of the cemetery—she had fallen about six feet. As soon as she could move, she stood, looking through the fence at the man. "Bitch!" he screamed in her face. "Cunt!" He carried her backpack out to the front fence where it was shorter and clambered over. He stood under a streetlight, throwing her clothing and other things to the ground. He finally left. She climbed up on the cement base of the fence and inched around to the front. When she came to the street, she looked up and down but saw no sign of him.

She stuffed her clothing and the wooden wheel into her backpack. Searching on her hands and knees, she found her wallet. Her money was gone, but she had her driver's license, also her phone and passport, which she had put in an inside pocket of the backpack. She still had no place to go, and hoping her attacker wouldn't come back, she climbed again into the cemetery and lay in her spot under the tree. As soon as it was light, she would use the wheel again to find Anne.

When I was Lily's age, twenty-four, I was lithe and hopeful; now at sixty-seven, I am thicker of both body and mind, much less pliable, but ironically with less of a sense of a continuous self. Sometimes my identity seems like a cluster of gnats or a murmuration of starlings.

During faculty swimming hour, I float in the corner of the diving pool at the university where I teach. My legs, more muscular and dense than my upper body, pull me down. Closing my eyes, I am rocked by the wake from a diver. Sound is erased with my ears under water. I arch my back, extending my belly upward, and lift my heavy legs higher—my body buoyed up in a manner that feels like hope.

Another exercise: I imagine that I am a pregnant woman. By the time labor starts, there's no backing out. I can't wrest control of my existence from my own body. I am to endure, merely hanging on until the pain passes, giving up my will to forces both outside and inside me.

"Abandon yourself to experience," my therapist tells me. I am to swim with the current of my life instead of fighting it. "You have control issues. You try to manage events and people that you can't possibly be responsible for." She says that when I was a child in a Mormon village, because my father was an alcoholic, unreliable, I thought that I needed to carry my mother and sisters to heaven. Through the pool exercise and imagining myself pregnant, I am to learn to release control and embrace the chaos of happenstance, the complexity of other beings, and the infinitude of intimacy.

FOUR

Lily didn't move from Brigham Young's graveyard the next morning. The previous two days swirled in her head like the flashing of a police light and she had a difficult time determining where she was and what she was doing lying on the ground. She was hungry, but she couldn't find the will to do anything.

Finally, around noon, sweaty and filthy, she crawled out from under the yew tree in the cemetery and walked down past the temple, with its spires and ten-foot wall. She stopped the first police car she saw. The officer inside told her the address of the closest women's shelter. She walked through downtown again, seeing a scattering of homeless people, more than she remembered.

After walking for half an hour she found the building. The person admitting her smiled as soon as she heard Lily's name, just as if she were expected. The woman pointed the way to the dinner room. When Lily glanced back, the woman was looking down at a paper and speaking into a phone. When she saw Lily watching, she turned her back. Inside the dinner room, women and children ate their food, some laughing, some with dead eyes. The smell of the building made her shiver with dread, the effluvium of antiseptic and despair.

After lunch, she spoke again to an intake person who asked some general questions about her situation. "Bad divorce," Lily said. "He got everything." The woman's lips pressed together as if she was going to question the truth of what Lily said. Then Lily slept all afternoon, woke up to eat, and then fell across her bed again, still weary.

She tried to make a plan but couldn't think beyond getting her arms around Anne again, being able to look in her daughter's eyes. Her own mother, if Lily had been lost, would have prayed repeatedly for her return. Lily had mouthed the words earlier, but she didn't trust a male god. She might have prayed to Mother God, but she could only imagine Her cloistered behind ranks of men in black suits—a distant face. She considered praying to one of the Hindu gods, or asking for help from Buddha or Muhammad, but she couldn't imagine the words traveling far from her mouth.

Again, she wished that she hadn't listened when her lawyer had assured her that the judge, a conservative, had never sided with the husband in a custody dispute. This simple-minded plan had backfired when Nathan's lawyer used that claim to show that she was an aberration of nature, an un-motherly woman. A Victorian Mormon argument for a Victorian Mormon judge. The diary she kept—her visits to the doctor with Anne, her care for the child—had disappeared, and it came down to her word against Nathan's. He had a handwritten log in different colors of ink that said he put Anne to bed each night. He had a pediatrician's letters forged, saying he was the one who took Anne for checkups and shots. Her tentative lawyer refused to challenge the log or the letters. Nathan described Lily's blind rages at both him and Anne, her sobbing apologies, his need to hide kitchen knives, scissors, hammers, and even screw drivers. How can Anne grow as a child should, the perfect lawyer had asked, when the one who gave birth to her moves from hen to jackal with every breath?

Because Lily couldn't stand being in the common room, she went into the bathroom. She looked in the mirror, sketched herself in her notebook—wild hair, desperate face—and then she sat on the floor and drew Nathan and Anne. Who was this caring father, this strange and unnatural woman? Lily came to wonder if she really was borderline, unable to see herself or Nathan with any measure of objectivity. The psychiatrist in court had smiled toward Nathan as if toward God and had only spent an hour with her in his office. He had discovered she was an orphan, that her aunt had kicked her out, and extrapolated her entire person-ness. He had given her a test—the Millon Clinical Multiaxial Inventory-IV—and he showed the results to the court, in graph form, showing how high she was on the capricious/borderline scale. He reduced her entire personhood to the results of a test. Just saying "Borderline Personality Disorder" convinced the asinine judge that this quack was an authority to be trusted. Then he had another chart, white with large black lettering, showing words that characterized her behavior: Instability in relationships, identity, and emotion; Impulsivity; Feelings of emptiness; Fear of abandonment. These words, when linked to Nathan's journal of her behavior and the psychologist's narration of her life, convinced the judge that he knew Lily's every dark impulse. He had nearly persuaded Lily herself that her memories of nursing Anne at her breast, holding her through colic and fever, the hours with Anne on her lap at bedtime were created out of her need to believe that she was a good mother. He had argued that these very memories proved her uncertain and destructive relationship to reality. Such a sad cycle; Lily abandoned by her own mother through death, by her aunt in life. She had such an overwhelming fear of being alone that she had forced her own abandonment. Words of self-defense tangled in her mouth, only confirming the narrative spun by Nathan's lawyer, that spider in his exquisite suit. Whenever she tried to say, "This woman you're describing is a stranger to me," they all nodded, smug and sure, believing the ten-minute lesson the psychiatrist had given them.

Nathan had enabled the narrative by making himself look vulnerable, which disoriented her as much as the identity they'd constructed for her. Somehow Nathan, who worshipped power and domination, appeared to be the victim. The lawyer told the judge that this good husband and father had finally given up on healing her. Now he needed to save himself and his child.

Lily saw herself as a lamb, lifting her white neck to the butchers. Through the past few days, she had watched amazed as Nathan's lawyer rewrote her identity. And this deceit had happened so quickly that her own lawyer couldn't articulate any rebuttal, especially since she had seemed star struck, convinced by her opponent's persuasiveness. When Lily had tried to speak for herself, the judge had silenced her.

The psychiatrist had one thing right—Lily feared abandonment. She imagined with visceral intensity that Anne was

bewildered and terrified by Lily's apparent abandonment. Lily felt this because, when she was a child, being alone felt like being swallowed by the world. Once, when she was six or eight, she and her father went camping at the geode beds in Utah's

West Desert, a hundred miles from Bountiful, west of the small desert town where he had lived as a child. Only odd twisted plants grew there, gray or gray-green.

One evening when the sun went down, her father sent her back to the foldout camper trailer to cook dinner. She had opened a can of Spam, cut and fried it, and pried the lid off a bottle of peaches or pears. She remembered standing above the stove as the meat grew hot, then cold. She watched for her father to come as dusk fell over the desert. Coyotes yelped in waves, an eerie chorus. He didn't come. She started to cry. The desert stretched forever around her. Strange creatures lived there—rattlesnakes unwound and left their holes, slithering out to hunt, ragged jackrabbits loped, coyotes wailed like tortured children.

Still her father didn't come and didn't come. She felt, without being able to articulate her fear, that sanity and identity would soon slip away into the endless desert.

When her father finally came back, he wrapped his arms around her. "I'm sorry," he said. "I took too long. I'm sorry."

When a teenager, she worried that friends would see through her, that they would leave her alone again. It felt as if nothing of substance was inside her. This made her nervous around people, especially boys. Walking the halls in school, she felt that she was balancing along a narrow path, cliffs on either side. She feared that when she was with other people, she would be absorbed, disappearing; when she was alone, that the world would devour her.

Was this all part of being borderline? She didn't know.

Lily went through her wallet, laying everything out on her bed, just as she'd done with her handbag, touching each reminder of her past. Her attacker had stolen all the cash and her two debit cards. She smiled at him trying to draw from the empty accounts. She removed her driver's license, and her insurance card, now also useless. Frequent shopper cards, her old U of U student card, an old Metro pass from Paris, the stub of a ticket to *La bohème* at the Paris Opera House. She felt the distance between then and now as a kind of nausea. Behind the tickets was a folded letter, which, as she opened it, she remembered was from Nathan from before they were married.

Teaching an undergraduate portrait class, she had been going from easel to easel looking at their work. She had taken the brush from a young man and was showing him how to be lighter in his strokes. Nathan had come in, wearing a suit that fit him better than skin. His shoulders, the narrowing of his waist, and his thighs arrested her vision. She had tactile memory of the brush of his mustache against her own upper lip, something she had thought would bother her but didn't. After dating for a month, she wanted him, was puzzled that they had not yet had sex. He put the letter in her hand, and had touched her jawbone with a forefinger and traced his fingertip across her cheek to her lips, the lightest touch. Then he turned and left. She had the most powerful urge downward through her pelvis to follow him, drag him into her shared studio and have him right then. The room was silent.

"Whew!" said one woman, and several other women tittered.

Lily looked down and saw she had marred the boy's painting, dragging his brush across the eye of the person he had painted.

"Sorry." She took a trowel and tried to scrape off the paint, but her hands were shaking.

"I can do it," he said, taking the trowel from her.

She knew the truth of the cliché "weak in the knees." Standing in the middle of her classroom, she was weak in the knees and wet.

"Read it out loud!" said the first woman, pointing to the letter.

"Not a chance!" said Lily. "Get back to work." She sat in the corner of the room and tried to calm down. Finally, she opened the letter. Now, sitting on the bed in the women's shelter, she read it again:

> Lily,
>
> I find myself enjoying my life more than I ever have before. Music sounds better, the air seems sweeter. When I'm talking to someone, a smile comes across my face, and they ask me what's so funny. They think I'm crazy, and they're right. You make me more myself than I have ever been.
>
> You are you. I mean that in the way God says, I am as I am. You seem self-existent, unique in all the earth. Your face is as lovely as your name. Your voice thrills me, as if every word enters my flesh. I love your hands, your mouth, your eyes, every part of you. Your complicated art about your parents and your aunt.
>
> I imagine a life with you as being more spectacularly unusual than any other life between man and woman since Adam and Eve. We need follow none of the tired conventions set up by people and cultures who don't understand our potential. Our love can make anything happen. We can re-enter the garden.
>
> I love you from the soles of your feet to the crown of your head.
>
> —Nathan

In class she had looked up, tears in her eyes, to find everyone watching her. She smiled, and the class applauded.

Sitting on the bed, with the old letter in her hand, she thought it had been a dream or maybe part of a movie she'd seen. The words seemed like cotton candy or lard. She had been stupid to be so affected by him, but she had been swayed, toppled, wedded, and screwed. The whole of that romantic tripe had served him well; she trusted him and gave him power over her. He had fucked her and fucked her over.

She took the letter from the sleeping room into the dining room and pushed open the door that said employees only. Entering the kitchen, where three women worked, preparing dinner, she walked to the gas stove.

"You're not allowed in here," said one of the women, walking toward her with palms forward.

Quickly Lily placed the open letter on a burner and turned it on. The gas lifted the letter half a foot into the air, the edges burning toward the center, turning black, raining fragments of ash across the stove and floor. The burning page turned in the air and dropped to the floor, black smoke rising.

As one of the women sprayed the ashes with a fire extinguisher, the other two women caught her arms and pushed her out of the kitchen. She heard the fire alarm going, and the woman who had admitted her came through the door into the dining room.

Lily thought she'd be kicked out, but the woman lectured her and let her stay.

LILITH

Automythology (USP)

Nathan invited her to reenter the garden, as if they were Adam and Eve. Now he thinks of her as Lilith or even as a beast that he had sexual congress with. A creature unmistakably Other.

The Kabbalah says that in the beginning Adam tried coupling with animals but received no joy from it. Maybe because he couldn't look into their faces during copulation. He complained, "Every creature but I has a proper mate." Then God said, "It is not good for man to be alone" and created a woman. Genesis Rabbah says that Adam watched as God built him a mate out of bones, organs, tissues. Even when her head was covered with hair and her inward parts with skin, the memory of her bones, meat, and blood disgusted him; he couldn't abide her. A later version of the story, found in The *Alphabet of ben Sirach*, named this pre-Eve woman Lilith. God created her out of the earth, similar to the way Adam was created. When they had sex, she refused to lie below him. Adam wanted to be on top because he felt superior, formed out of pure dust rather than refuse. When it became clear that Adam was intractable, Lilith became angry, spoke the Ineffable Name, and vanished. Some Muslim sources say she mated with Satan, spawning the race of Djinn.

Whether due to his distaste for Lilith's fleshiness or for her desire to be dominant, Adam was more pleased with Eve, created from Adam's rib so she was subservient, pleasingly covered with whole and perfect skin that hid her unpleasant guts and fatty tissue. She seemed simpler, more manageable. At least she seemed simple until she made the decision to seek knowledge of good and evil and got him cast out of the Garden of Eden—vastly complicating the future for both of them.

FIVE

Sunrise next day found Lily walking east toward the Natural History Museum. Her grandfather, a rancher, had told her that a cow will always return to the last place it smelled its calf, and the calf also goes back, so they find each other. Lily planned to do something similar. She'd go back to where she last saw Anne and start from there.

Standing in the entryway to the museum, where just the day before she had been pushed into a police car, she spun the wheel on the randomizing device. She held it with the base toward her, so she couldn't see the wheel. She stuck her finger in and tipped it level to see the direction she should take. West-southwest. She clambered down the hill through some oak brush, across landscaping of decorative sage to a brown, brick building, two stories with black glass—Myriad Genetics. She looked inside but could see no sign of Anne or Nathan. She felt silly because there was no reason they should be there. She spun again and walked south across the junction of Wakara

Way and Colorado Road, up to the back corner of a low building, then made her way around to the front door—Primary
Children's Hospital, back to where her search for Anne had
begun. She went inside, passing the offices and patient rooms,
but could see no sign of Anne or Nathan. She went outside,
reluctant to try randomness again. Still she spun the wheel.
Northwest. Immediately she ran again into the Myriad Genetics building. She could see no reason to go inside, so again, she
spun the wheel. North-northwest to the offices of a pipeline
construction company. Spun again. South-southwest back to
the long back of Myriad Genetics. Her third time there.

She walked once again into the building. Stephen, one of
Nathan's assistants, came out a door and stopped. "Lily?"

"Stephen." She felt too tired to be surprised at seeing him.
"What are you doing here? Is Nathan with you?"

"I—we're—I really can't tell you."

Nathan had never talked with her about his work, but she
guessed Stephen was on some secret mission having to do with
Myriad. To someone, somewhere in the world, that information would be valuable, but not to her.

"I promise you, Lily. He's not as bad as you think he is."

"He—"

"I know, I know. Here it is: you've offended his dignity.
You've rejected him, said you don't value him."

"You don't know." She turned away.

"Anyway, talking to him will do no good." He touched her
arm. "Where are you staying?"

"The women's shelter."

"The women's shelter? Why?"

"I have no money."

"That can't be true. You have your bank account, your car. He gave you alimony."

She shook her head.

"Are you being dramatic again?" He looked out the window. "Let me take you back to where you're staying. That's the only help I can give you."

Lily nodded. She didn't know how things would work out exactly, but she felt the river of spacetime carrying her.

Driving down Fourth South, Stephen asked, "Have you eaten today?"

Lily shook her head. Oatmeal didn't count.

"You should have eaten. You look shaky." Stephen pulled into the parking lot of Jimmy John's. "I don't have much time. What do you want?" She ordered and soon had her food.

Stephen looked at his watch.

"I can make it from here," said Lily.

"What are you planning?"

"I'm planning nothing," said Lily. "I'm planning on seeing Anne."

"Well do it fast. He's going to take—"

"To take her out of the city? Out of the country?"

Stephen shook his head, "You can't win in this, Lily. You have to accept what he has given you." He turned and left.

At first she couldn't eat, choking on her anger. But she knew she had to swallow and then swallow again. After she finished her sandwich, she walked out onto the road. She felt grateful for the meal Stephen had given her and for the knowledge that Nathan was soon going to take Anne away. The custody agreement stated that she could have parental time weekly, except when Anne was traveling with her father. She knew from her own experience that he was capable of traveling for a year, running his business from his phone and laptop.

The wheel pointed west, but the street went as far as she could see, so she spun for distance—9 blocks, a half-hour walk. She found herself at the southeast corner of Pioneer Park. It was the weekly farmers market, and vendors and proper people mingled with the homeless usually there. She walked toward the crowd, and there was Nathan with Anne and another young woman, but this woman was clearly not one Nathan was dating. She was too mousy, too tentative to interest him. She was also not the strong 40-year-old who had helped take Anne away. She must be someone he hired permanently to take care of Anne—a nanny. Lily looked around and soon saw Brock.

Why had Nathan brought Anne here? She suspected that the woman who had admitted Lily into the shelter had contacted him. Or maybe he had tracked Lily through her phone. She watched Anne, not far across the park from her, and she so much wanted to run and hold her. She knew that was probably what he wanted. Her throat felt tight, as if he had his hands around her neck. He wanted to show his power again. Maybe he thought she might beg him.

So far, he had predicted her actions—that she would refuse help, that she'd try her aunt but would end up at the women's shelter. He had paid the woman at the desk to call him when Lily arrived. The one thing she'd done that he hadn't expected was to show up at the Natural History Museum when he was there. She sensed one advantage—he didn't know about the wheel, so he couldn't know what she'd do next. How could his blindness help her?

She didn't know, but she knew she couldn't approach Anne now. As much as she wanted to run toward her, make another scene or maybe lie flat on her face and plead for Nathan to let her hold Anne again, Lily turned and walked away.

That night, the matron at the women's shelter handed her an envelope. It had her name, "Lily Harker," on it, even though she had not given her real name to anyone at the shelter. Inside was a key, certainly the same key that Brock had handed her in the envelope at their home in Deer Valley. The note read, "I understand your sense of pride and independence, and I recognize that Anne needs you. You can see her at the times set up by the court. I've rented an apartment for you and stocked it with food. This will help you until you can get a job."

At first, she felt a great relief, but then she felt claustrophobic because of the box he willed her to inhabit. He would control her if she started relying on him financially, if she walked into that apartment. Instead of relief it would be the beginning of hell. Nathan would maintain control through bending or breaking the rules. "Anne has a cold today, a doctor's appointment, a play date. We're in Paris. She can't see you for your supervised visit." Then he would watch for her reaction, feeding on it. "Anne said she didn't want to see you today." His eyes, his scant smile. "Your wages have been garnished for refusal to pay rent." Any idea to escape this noose, any evil thing she could imagine, he had already imagined before her. She'd become his subject, his peasant. She would watch Anne turn into a porcelain doll, a princess without a soul, a wraith. All this because Lily had said "No!" to him, "No more!"

With all her being Lily said "No!" again to what Nathan had planned for her and Anne. She didn't know what she and

Anne would become once they ran from him, but she repudiated what she knew would happen if she left her child in his hands; they would both become mannequins. She walked back to Pioneer Park and gave the key and address to the first homeless couple she met. The man was distracted, hardly inhabiting his own head and would have been unable to find the apartment, but the woman was a little sharper. They set off walking. They might have a few days, maybe a week, before they were kicked out, but they'd be no worse off than they had been.

Lily spent another night at the shelter, listening to the women and children breathing around her. She knew if she kept taking their air into her body, she would soon be as defeated as they were. She held despair back by nourishing the image she had of Anne, the small being that she'd welcomed as a precious guest into her consciousness. Finally, she dreamed that she was a polar bear and that she was swimming south, away from the melting ice. She swam for hours, days, until it seemed that she had never been elsewhere, always swimming in that endless ocean. Then she realized she had left her cub behind and that she had swum away without remembering.

She woke, wondering how she could be so careless.

I know this dream because my wife has had it several times. In her dream Karla swims under an ice floe, which frightens her until she realizes she and her cub are both polar bears, swimming in a familiar environment. She will not drown or become lost.

Karla also has had a series of dreams about polar bears migrating south, moving into American suburbs because we humans are melting their original habitat. The huge, white beasts wan-

SWIMMING POLAR BEAR

Automythology (USP)

der through yards and across streets where they don't belong. Once, a dream bear came into our house. At first Karla held out a friendly hand, but then she knew from its eyes that it was a carnivore that might eat her. My therapist, who wants me to open myself to the Other, might not approve if I got face-to-face with a bear.

I was at a conference where one speaker argued that being vulnerable to the biological universe—recognizing that we might be no more than food to some creature—could be an enlightening experience. What is vulnerability except for embracing the possibility that something extraordinary might happen—even being eaten alive by a bear or a wolf, some other apex predator? The speaker said that opening ourselves to the absolute otherness of animals and plants may help us manage our lives in the current epoch, the Anthropocene, defined by the ability of humans to wreck their own living space.

Lily knew she had to be prepared for anything. She needed a weapon, but not a gun, which she didn't know how to use. She left the women's shelter and walked across to the Rite Aid near City Creek Mall. She looked in the trash outside the store and found a plastic bag with the Rite Aid logo. Stuffing the bag into her pocket, she walked inside and asked the two clerks for some mace. The younger one, a male, unlocked the glass case and handed her the canister. "I need to get a prescription filled," Lily told him. "Can I pay for them together?" She picked up some tampons, a few pencils, another notebook, and then she waited near the pharmacist until the clerk left the front of the store to help another customer. She put the mace and the other things in her bag and walked out of the store.

She also needed a disguise. Having recognized the invisibil-
ity of homeless people, she walked back to the DI and bought a
shapeless dress and sweater. She also found a huge scarf, made
of thin cloth, that she could fold into a triangle and make a sling
to carry Anne. As she walked out, she saw a small digital camera behind a locked case. She knew she needed to get rid of her
phone. "Does that camera work?" The clerk handed it to her.
She took a selfie and turned the camera around. The picture
showed in the little window on the back. It gave her a slight
feeling of control, that she could again capture images of her
life and draw them in her sketch book.

As she walked back, she ducked inside a copy center and
got them to download and print the pictures she wanted from
her phone—the one of Anne in her crib, the restraining order,
and the picture of the branches above her when she slept next
to Brigham Young's grave. Just outside the store was a trash bin,
and she dropped her phone inside.

Her last step of preparation was to walk into Pioneer Park,
across from the women's shelter. She knelt at a flowerbed and
rubbed dirt into the clothing, as well as mud and grease she
found at the edge of the street. Later at the shelter she went
into the bathroom and peed on the dress. After it dried a little,
she put it in a plastic bag in her backpack and let it marinate.

That night in her bed, she made a list in her sketching notebook of all the ways she might escape the city once she found
Anne:

1.   Stay put (hide in the city)
2.   Walk (through mountains)
3.   Taxi

4. Car
5. Bus
6. Amtrak (North, South, East, West?)
7. Trax (only to a Salt Lake suburb)
8. Frontrunner train (South to Provo? North to Ogden?)
9. Airplane
10. Bicycle
11. Motorcycle
12. Semi-truck
13. Rideshare
14. Ambulance
15. RV
16. Skateboard

She thought a skateboard was stupid, but she couldn't think of another way to travel. She spun the randomizing device, stabbing her finger in it—the eighth gap, so the Frontrunner train. She put everything she owned into the wheeled backpack and left the women's shelter. A new woman was at the front desk so she didn't have to say anything to the one who had admitted her, the one who communicated with Nathan.

Filled with an unreasonable hope, she stood on the corner of Pioneer Park, at Third West and Fourth South, the last place she'd seen Anne. *I've found Anne twice already. Third time's a charm.*

She spun the wheel. North-northwest, the Ford Building that held a restaurant where she and Nathan once dined. Spinning again. South along Fourth West. Seven blocks. Walking through a more degraded part of town, warehouses and auto shops, she came to an overpass. Now that her life had changed, she looked at the overpass as a place she might sleep if she needed to. Next the wheel pointed northeast. Wasatch Body Shop. She could see nothing of hope in the cars being worked on, nor the men working on them. From inside the fence, she spun again and the wheel pointed north across the street—*Ventura's Custom Auto Painting*. She walked around to the gate in the fence and then back to where she could see Ventura's again. A black SUV pulled up in front of the building. Brock stepped out of the car, and Lily ducked down. He walked inside the windowless building. Lily trotted forward, seeing the top of a baby seat in the back of the vehicle. The nanny that Lily had seen in Pioneer Park also sat in the back seat. Lily opened the car door and bent over her child. "Anne," she said. "Baby."

Anne reached her arms up. "Ma, Ma."

The girl looked toward the shop and opened her mouth to scream. Lily had the mace against her face. "Not a sound. If you suck in air to scream this will fill your throat."

The girl didn't realize that Lily wouldn't spray when Anne was near.

Lily looked toward the door where Brock might emerge any second. The girl sat unmoving. "She cries all the time."

Lily unbuckled Anne, lifted her from the car seat.

The girl still hadn't moved. "All day, all night. Crying."

Clutching Anne, Lily started to run but then turned and held the mace up to the window. The girl nodded, closed her eyes, took a deep breath; Lily opened the door and sprayed a little mace in the air above the girl's head, just enough to give the smell, but not burn her face.

Then she held Anne against her chest and ran. Behind her the girl started coughing, got out of the car, and stumbled into the front seat. Lily heard the sound of the horn, loud and sustained, but she didn't stop. Anne started to cry, a thin wail of fear, because Lily jostled her as they ran. Lily ducked into a cross street. A sign above a door read *Platinum Auto Brokers*. In front of the office a car sat with its door open. There were no keys in the ignition, so it was useless to her. Without looking back to see if Brock was following, Lily opened the door and ducked inside the building.

Some people try to predict the future using the signs of the Zodiac, such as Nancy Reagan who thought that the planets held secrets that might help her husband make good choices. I would love to have a map of my destiny as I traverse my private Slough of Despond. Lily's physical journey and my spiritual one are similar in shape to Bunyan's *Pilgrim's Progress*, but in that story the spiritual and physical are mapped on one landscape.

In church I've heard the metaphor of the map many times, that the scriptures or leaders are a sure map leading us to heaven. Other groups who believe happiness comes from following a map of holy words and acts include Hindus, Muslims, Hebrews, Pentecostal Christians, Catholics, Pagans, Sikhs, Lamaists, Jainests, idol worshipers, Zoroastrians, Republicans, Democrats, Libertarians, etcetera and etcetera. A Zen master might say that there is no map, but the absence of a map is a map. Eve is courageous because she deviates from the map she has been handed. She says, "I will go in a direction that gives me experience instead of a direction that gives me received wisdom." By following the compass of her own impulse, she becomes the first rebel and the first empiricist.

In the *Book of Mormon*, the prophet Lehi and his family leave Jerusalem during the reign of King Zedekiah because Lehi, as patriarch of his family, sees visions that foretell the destruction of Jerusalem by the armies of Nebuchadnezzar, the Babylonian king. In the desert, far from their homes in the city, these pilgrims wander toward the Promised Land. On their journey they are blessed with the ability to eat meat without cooking. They are also given a guide, the Liahona, a ball of curious workmanship that helps them know where to carry their tents, so they won't become lost in the wilderness, devoured by beasts, or driven insane.

One might suppose that this decision maker restricts their choices, but another way to view the mystical ball is that it enables their survival, multiplies their possible futures. The spindle on the ball is powered by their faith in God, a physics beyond their understanding. Lily's wheel is powered by an unlikely synthesis of will and chance.

Of course, it's not strictly a wheel of chance. I cheat and let her use the randomized decision maker to find Anne. What does that show about me?

LIAHONA: SPIRITUAL COMPASS
Automythology (USP)

S I X

The office beyond the auto broker's door was small and bare, and the faces of two men turned toward her. One was thick-set and sat behind a desk, his sandy mustache curled up at the ends. He had looked up when she entered, watched while she calmed Anne. "You're safe now. It's all right." Anne stuck her thumb in her mouth and laid her head on Lily's shoulder. Another man, arms covered with tattoos, sat in a chair in front of the desk. He also turned to stare at her. She held Anne even closer and took a breath, channeling her anxiety until there was a small core of control.

"Can I help you?"

"My car broke down," she said. "Is there any way I can get a ride to the Frontrunner?"

"Did you call a tow truck?"

"My husband—" She allowed herself to sob once with fear and anger, "says it's my fault, insists he will look at it himself before he will call a tow truck. He told me to get home my own way."

The two men looked at each other. The man behind the desk stood up. He had muscled forearms, covered with hair the same color as his mustache. "Where is the car?"

"Just around the corner on American Avenue, next to that auto painting place."

"They wouldn't help you?"

"Well they wanted to just pull it inside. They wanted to work on it. My husband said—"

"Maybe we can help you get it started." The man behind the desk stood and walked toward the door.

"Please no. My husband is on his way and if he sees you he'll think—he'll be angry that I didn't do what he said."

"I'll drive you to your house," said the other man, also standing. He had long black hair, gathered in the back. He had a thin face with glasses and, except for the tattoos, looked a little like the librarian from Lily's middle school when she was a child.

She smiled. "Thank you."

"I don't have a child seat," he said.

"So drive careful," she said. "My husband is probably here by now, looking at the car. He'll be all right after he settles down, but I don't want to talk to him now."

"What does he look like?"

She described Brock to them.

The black-haired man stepped outside. Lily saw him shut the door to his car and return inside. "He's standing in the street. He's got his cell phone out and he looks pissed."

"Can I just sit here, or maybe it would be better if I waited in the back?" she said. "He'll calm down. Really he will."

"Sure," said the man behind the desk. "Or we can make sure he doesn't hurt you."

"No!" she said, on the edge of breaking down. "He'll just take it out on me later."

"Do you have someplace else to go?" asked the other man. "I mean other than home. I sure as hell wouldn't go home when he's that angry."

"My sister's. She lives in Bountiful."

Anne laid her hand on Lily's cheek, tipped her head up to look at Lily's face. "Mama," she said. "My mama."

"Yes," said Lily. "I'm your mama."

"You should go there," said the black-haired man. "Maybe you shouldn't go home ever."

Lily nodded. "I can just take the train north and the bus up to my sister's house."

"Or I could take you," said the man. "It's not that far."

Lily opened the door and peered through. Brock turned to look at the door and started their way.

She shut the door. "He's coming!"

"We won't let him hurt you."

"I don't want a fight," she said. "Can I just wait in back somewhere?" She pointed to a door behind the desk.

"Yes," said the man behind the desk. He took her through the back door into a low-ceilinged garage that stretched a hundred yards back. Parked inside were rows of used cars. She heard Brock's voice behind her. She walked toward the middle of the space to a black one with tinted windows. She opened the back door and lay across the seat with Anne. The man shut the door behind her.

"We're going to be all right," she said.

Hungry, Anne signed, moving her hand toward her mouth.

"We'll get some food soon, Anne baby. Now we play a game. Hide Anne. Hide from Brock." Anne lay across Lily's chest, both of them still. Lily could see the roof of the garage through the window, but she had to keep telling herself no one could see in. Even if the two men let Brock come back to look for her, he couldn't see her through the windows. "Sleepy time, time," sang Lily, soft as a whisper. "Sleepy time time, a-a-all the time," a song her mother had sung to her.

Soon Anne's body relaxed even more and she breathed deep a few breaths, sleeping, her soft head in the hollow of Lily's neck. Lily didn't want to move, wanted to lie there safe forever holding that small warm body. She was grateful that the two men had responded as they did, trusting her and her story, which was true in its essence even if the details were not.

Too soon, the black-haired man came back. "He's gone. I can take you now." She followed him out through the office and to the car.

Lily belted herself into the front seat, holding Anne against her.

"I can easily take you all the way to Bountiful."

"I can manage," said Lily, "once I get to the train." The wheel had said to take the Frontrunner and she didn't dare try any other way.

He drove along Fourth West along the same route she had taken south from Pioneer Park. He turned east then north again and soon pulled into the drop-off circle at the Salt Lake Central Frontrunner station.

"Now don't go home right away," he said.

"I promise," she said. "My husband will be fine once he calms down."

"I can take you to Bountiful," he said. "Twenty-minute drive."

She shook her head.

"Here," said the man, handing her a card. "Call me if you need something. Go to your sister's house. A nice woman like you doesn't have to put up with that jerk."

"Don't worry. I'm not going home until he settles down."

The man frowned and shook his head.

She got out of the car, smiled, and turned away. She passed between the concrete posts that marked the pedestrian area, her eyes toward the walkway that crossed the tracks. One of Nathan's men stood there, square in the entrance to the trains, black-suited, watching the crowd that was boarding the train. Of course, Nathan would think to have someone watch the train station. Following the wheel had led her straight into danger. Or maybe she should have randomly decided which station to board at, not merely the closest one.

She ducked into the bus station, which stood next to the entrance to the train.

"Ma, ma, ma," said Anne, starting to whimper. Lily discovered she had been clutching Anne too hard. She went inside the bathroom and into the handicapped stall. She could run the other way, chance Nathan's man not seeing her, but she had to get out of town and the wheel had said to take Frontrunner. She could go outside, walk the mile or so to the North Temple Station, but it was only with the slimmest luck that he hadn't seen her as he scanned people walking toward the train. If she left the restroom, she would be in plain sight again.

She took out the plastic bag and opened it. The dress and sweater smelled like dirt and fresh urine, not like a homeless person whose smells had blended and matured into something powerful, but there was not much she could do about that. Lily put on the dress, which was still damp, and stood in front of the mirror. She tangled her hair, rubbing it with the dirty sweater, pulling it forward around her face. Finally, she lifted Anne, who smelled like shit. She checked Anne's diaper and it was full. Anne signed, *Poopy.*

"Sorry," Lily said. She took off the diaper, dropping it into the trash, and wiped Anne's bum with toilet paper and folded hand towels around her like a diaper. She put Anne's shorts back on and folded her into the sling of fabric she'd purchased at DI. "Hiding game," she said. "Hide from everyone. Quiet. Quiet as a bunny." She could see Anne's face inside the wrap and she smiled. "Snug in your hidey hole." She pulled the sweater on over the wrap and buttoned it up. With a second thought, she grabbed the bad diaper out of the trash and dropped it into the plastic sack where her homeless clothing had been. She placed the sack inside her backpack, making sure the top was open enough that the smell was strong. Leaving the bathroom, pulling the rolling pack, she stared at the ground, developed a limp, dragging one foot behind her. She hunched forward over Anne, talking to her. "Are you snug, my baby? Are you safe in your hidey hole?"

As Lily shuffled toward the entrance to the train, Anne made a small noise. "Quiet baby," she whispered. "Hide in your bunny hole." Anne started singing softly. Lily muttered, a rasping sound she hoped wouldn't frighten Anne. "Fire will burn and God will damn me, damn you. Seek you out, bleed your insect body dry. God will come and suck your body empty. My mother is with God, my father is with God. My mother is God." She said it so low it could hardly be heard, praying for thirty more seconds of silence from Anne. Then Anne whimpered, a louder sound, and Lily prayed louder, "God of the grass and sky and trees and wheat, bless me," rasping out her pagan supplication as she shuffled past the man's polished shoe tips. Watched them step back from her. She didn't look up—step drag, step drag, until she was on the platform.

Now, she needed to figure which direction to take, north or south. She took one glance up at the monitor and saw that the first train would come from the south going north; the second, five minutes later, went south. Her brain screamed that she must get on the first train, hopefully before Nathan's man looked over and recognized her, but she forced herself quiet and smiled down at Anne, saying softly, "Quiet. Hide from Daddy. He'll be so surprised." She spun the wheel and then stuck her finger in it. North. She would take the first train. She held back until she saw the train arriving. Shuffling forward, she saw a UTA official watching her. She glanced at Nathan's man, who was also watching her. He started forward as she stepped onto the train. The doors were still open when she heard his footsteps speed up, she heard him shout, "Stop her! Don't let her on the train!"

I use various random methods, usually the Executive Decision Maker which a friend gave me as a joke, to determine Lily's pathway through the City of Saints. Sometimes I use a random number generator from the computer; occasionally I ask someone for a number between 1 and 16 if they're around when I'm writing. That determines the direction Lily goes. To decide what will happen to her now, I flip a coin.

What happens next? On one level I don't know. Randomness is a device to loosen up my mind, to help me avoid writing
ruts. But what's happening right now is that my heart is beating
a little faster than usual. I want Lily to get away. I want her to
be safe with Anne. I don't want to leave it to chance, but I will.
Heads the doors close before he can take Anne away from her,
tails the doors don't close quickly enough, and she has to face
Nathan's man.

The doors closed and the train was moving. She heard a
slap on the side of the train, saw the angry face of the man who
now had to explain his failure to Nathan. Suddenly, an official
on the train caught Lily's arm, saying something about the reg-
ulation against unclean odors on the train. She wrenched herself away from him, ducked into the toilet, and locked the door.
She took off the sweater, unwrapped Anne, and set her on the
floor. She dropped the smelly bag into the trash. The official
pounded, called for her to come out. Quick as she could, she
washed her face, her hair, pulled it back into a ponytail, put on
her dress, and stuffed the old clothing into the trash on top of
the diaper. She opened the door and pulled the backpack out
of the bathroom. She stood face to face with the UTA man.
His mouth opened a little and his eyes widened. She knew she
smelled like hand soap. Turning, she stalked past him, marched
through three cars before she felt calm enough to take a seat.
She let Anne stand on the seat next to her and they looked out
the window as the train pulled out of Salt Lake City. If the man
followed and asked for her ticket, she might shriek, she was that
close to falling to pieces.

The train stops were listed on a chart above her head. She spun the wheel, which told her to get off at the fourth stop, Layton. When the doors opened to a wave of heat, she held Anne's hand while the child toddled along, straight into a parking lot. To the east was a busy, four-lane road; to the south rose an overpass. She knew she needed to get away from the station, but she didn't relish hauling Anne along the street where there was no shade and cars sped past.

She might go north along I-15 toward Ogden and Brigham City, eventually to Idaho; east toward the mountains, roughing it with Anne until she can find a way to get out of state; west toward the marshes along the Great Salt Lake; or south, back through Salt Lake City and on toward southern Utah, Arizona. The wheel gives her sixteen branching choices at each juncture.

This fractal of Lily's future looks like the seed-head of a weed from my garden. I'm trying to see my own future as that open to possibility. Whatever she and I choose, that choice determines what we become. In "Among School Children" Yeats describes a mother who imagines her child older, as a sixty-year-old-man. She wonders about the changes and "the uncertainty of his setting forth." Later in the poem Yeats writes, "How can we know the dancer from the dance?" The act becomes the actor, a kind of metaphysical reaction, where kinetic movement transforms into flesh and personality.

Hope is predicting the best that might happen. Lily was taught by her parents that hopefulness is one of the blossoms adorning our existence. I wonder if my hopes—that my grandchildren might grow up happy, that white people might tire

SIXTEEN-BRANCHED FRACTAL
Automythology (USP)

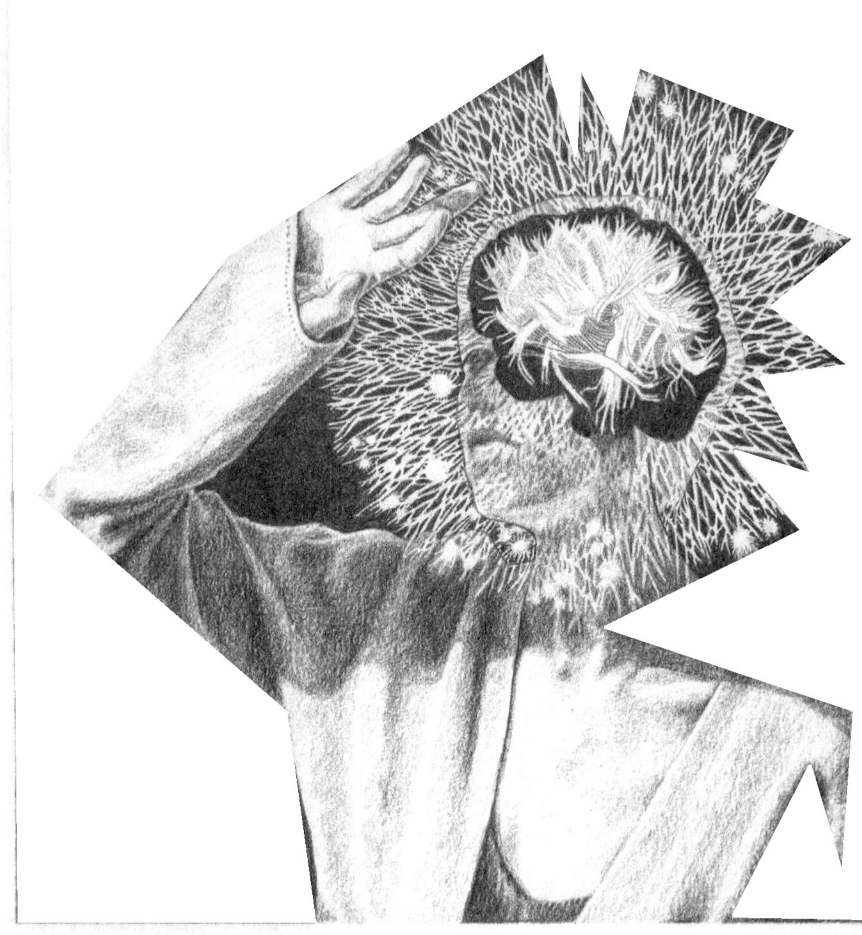

SYNAPSE NETWORK
Automythology (USP)

of violence against minorities, that we might finally think of healthcare as a right—have any influence on the future.

Lily's future is not composed of just sixteen possibilities at each node, but many more. Once we go down that path it is easy to imagine a fractal of time with 64, 128, 256, 512, 1024, 2048, 4096, 8192, or even infinite branches at each juncture. Then hope takes us beyond a two-dimensional fractal to one with ∞ number of planes, or ∞ number of dimensions in ∞ of universes. Under these conditions it is easy to imagine that time is not linear, not a pathway, certainly not a forked binary, and that causality is more complex than we can fathom.

Which is either terrifying or hopeful. But no one actually has infinite choices. My choices are limited by my knowledge of the physical universe and by my deteriorating neural pathways.

This image of Lily's brain or of her imaginable future appears as the bloom of a thistle. After nearly three years of not having to think for herself, and after Nathan has taken away her resources, Lily's choices are limited by imagination and practicality. She doesn't have the skills to escape to the desert and live like a badger or a Goshute. Her future might be a map with as many holes in it as my mother-in-law's brain after multiple mini-strokes.

SEVEN

Her heart still beating fast, Lily spun the wheel. "Are we on an adventure?" she said.

Anne looked at her earnestly, her small face framed by her blonde hair. North-northeast. Lily bound her to her belly with the sling, pulled the rolling backpack out of the parking lot, and walked along the sidewalk. When she could, she crossed the street.

She knew that for an Amber Alert, Nathan would have to prove that Anne was in physical danger. Lily had no doubt he could convince the authorities that a person with borderline personality disorder might harm her own child. First priority—she had to get off the street and find a place to stay for the night. A women's shelter, even if there was one in Layton, was the last place she wanted to go, because it was the first place Nathan would look.

She passed a tax accountant's office, a beautician's, a floral shop, and a payday loan place—all places she would have hardly noticed in her previous life. Now she looked at each one greedily, wondering what she might get from them. The window of the quick loan office said, "Make today your payday! Easy qualification!"

She stepped inside and asked for an application form, scanning it. Driver's license, which she had. "Open checking account," she read aloud. Technically she had an open account. But no proof of income. No good.

"Yes?" The woman behind the desk glanced down at her wrinkled dress and the ratty rolling pack, at Anne in the sling. Her face said, *I've seen your kind before.* The counter the woman stood behind was a barrier Lily could never cross over.

"I'll take the form and bring it back. I can't remember my account number and I don't have my pay stub."

"Right. We're open 'till six." The woman turned away. Not just a dismissal, an erasure. Lily wanted to shake the woman, shouting in her face, *I exist. I'm a being like you.*

Outside, she spun the wheel. South-southwest. The exact direction she had just come from. She knew it wasn't smart to return to the train stop. She slumped against the side of the building, nearly ready to throw the wheel in the trash. She looked up at the street sign—Main Street. Main Street in Layton, Utah. She felt pathetic standing on that pathetic street, jerked around by her habit to follow the spinning of a thrift store knick-knack.

Her brain was tired, her body tired, and she still smelled the odor of the hand soap from the train. She had no other idea of what to do, so she started back across the street, walking past the red car toward the park next to the Frontrunner station. Anne, blessedly asleep for the last half hour, opened her eyes, sighed, and went back to sleep. Lily longed in her bones for that kind of security and comfort.

If the damn wheel told her to get back on the train, she determined to break it in half.

Odds are like both hope and fear. What are the odds of this pleasant future event or that painful one? Of my mother and father meeting? Of their two DNA coils unzipping and zipping to each other exactly as they did to produce me? The constellation of his psyche and my mother's influencing me to be depressive, duty-driven, anxious about failure? Of the chance meeting of Karla and me, which led to us passing our own autoimmune, anxious, and depressive characteristics to our children, who manifest them in new ways. What are the chances of collision or influence by any other event or body? Thomas Hardy wrote "The Convergence of the Twain," a poem that imagines the Titanic and the iceberg inevitably drawn together. Rosencrantz and Guildenstern, in the Tom Stoppard play, know something is unhinged in the universe when they flip a coin and it comes up heads ninety-two times in a row. They recognize that they are subject to un-, sub-, or super-natural forces.

The odds that Lily would spin north-northeast are one in sixteen. When she spun the wheel again, the odds were one in sixteen that she would spin south-southwest. The odds of her having to retrace her steps again? One in sixteen. Yet if we ask instead, what are the odds of her spinning the wheel so that it made her walk to the cash store and back to the station, one more time to the cash store and again to the station, so that she walked past the same red car four times. The odds would be one in $16 \times 16 \times 16 \times 16 = 16^4$ or 1:65,536. Odds. Probability that this or that will happen. The branching of potential futures one link at a time—⅄ and ⅄ and ⅄ and ⅄.

Poker, similar to economics and palm reading, is not a pure science. The mathematical odds of drawing a royal flush on the first deal are 1:649,739. The odds go down when a player asks for more cards. If seven cards are available to try for a 5-card royal flush the odds become 1:30,939.

If poker were simply a game of chance, watching poker players would be as fun as watching computers or mathematicians play with probability theory. Mathematicians and the autistic may not be great poker players, because the game also depends on misleading the opponent, suggesting one thing when another is true. So the sciences of poker, investment banking, and novel writing must include not only calculations, but the ineffable inclination of the soul as read through the face. If Lily could read Nathan's soul in his face, the odds of her marrying him would have gone way down. Similarly, Tess Durbeyfield, due to her innocence and ignorance, is unable to read the intent of her rapist. Her consequent path is tragic.

Lily stood in front of the train station, where she had been just moments before. It made her realize she had no control over her destiny. *Maybe that's the first thing to learn,* she thought. She spun again—south-southeast. She angled back across Main Street and came to the entrance of a trailer court. Walking along the lane between the rows of trailers, she saw some with lawns, chimes tinkling in the breeze, lawn chairs. *Trailer trash,* she thought, but knew she was below trailer trash. She imagined herself inside one of them, living with a husband who loved her and Anne, their child. She passed one that looked abandoned and she thought of going inside. The door was locked and down the street a woman, who had been watering her lawn, looked up. She turned the water off and stood in the street, watching Lily.

She walked on past the woman. She imagined the trailer court was busy with children in the evening, but now, because of the heat, it was quiet. She imagined breaking into the empty trailer. Wherever she went, she had to get there fast. By evening her picture and Anne's would be on every television screen in Salt Lake and across the state. She felt a flash of weakness and remembered she hadn't had lunch. She and Anne needed something to eat and diapers; the paper towels were useless. She looked at the wheel. "To hell with this." She started to throw it away but then stuffed it in the backpack. She walked back up to the strip of stores, stepping inside the beautician shop. A woman sat in a barber's chair and another one stood behind her trimming with scissors.

"Where can I go to use the internet?"

The woman with the scissors looked at her as if she was from Mars, but the woman in the chair said, "The library is just across the bridge on Gentile Street."

Lily walked past the easy cash place to Gentile Street. Anne woke up and started to cry, but Lily had nothing to give her. She still wore her expensive dress, now wrinkled and useless. She looked down the street to the west, saw nothing but a bank and a costume shop. What could she wear to prompt someone to give her food? A clown suit? A matador costume? A ballerina's tutu or a prostitute's camisole? Across from her stood a Mexican café. She walked inside. An Anglo woman started toward her, smiling. "Table for one and a high chair for your cute baby?"

Lily said, "I have no food for my baby. Can you give her something?"

The woman stopped, shook her head, and pointed toward the door. Lily boiled inside, but realized how it seemed. Begging, stealing food from someone who worked for it. Glaring at the woman, she walked back to the sidewalk.

Anne made the sign for food, looking as if she would start crying, so Lily walked around the building to the back door and looked in the trash can behind the café, but there was nothing but garbage, nothing she would dare give Anne.

Lily smoothed the child's damp hair, and it stuck to her forehead. A full meal and a shower would be nice.

With Anne still whimpering "Ma, ma" and making the sign for food, Lily walked east along Gentile Street, which crossed over the freeway. Anne peed and the urine ran down Lily's arm and onto her dress. Then Anne started crying, still signing for food. Lily felt like sitting in the road and giving up, waiting for the police to come get her. She held Anne closer and walked on, scanning the street for a food store. They passed a building that had both a dance studio and medical offices, set in a large park. On the other side of the park was the library, but she needed to get food first. They passed a hamburger shop, Lily's mouth pulling saliva as if she might walk in and order one. Pizza, an insurance store, another payday loan place—all useless when she had no money. She passed a copy store, continuing down Gentile Street. A dry-cleaning place. Then a food store, but when she came closer, she saw it was out of business. Anne was really crying now, arching her back. Finally, she came to two gas stations, both with food markets. Panic was setting in and she knew she needed to do something now.

"I'm working on it, Anne," she said. "I'm going to get us some food." Anne calmed down, as if she understood her mother.

She went in the bathroom of the easternmost gas station and locked the door behind her. Her dress looked wretched, wrinkled and with a streak of pee down her hip. With Anne crying again, Lily splashed her hands in the water and rubbed them across the fabric, cleaning the pee off and wetting it just enough that she could smooth out some of the wrinkles. She put new paper towels around Anne's bottom, and, even though they were soaked, put Anne's shorts back on again to hold the paper towels in place. Lily came out of the bathroom, and a member of the store staff was waiting outside.

"Bathrooms are for customers," she said.

Lily ignored her and walked back to the other station, stashed her pack outside behind the ice machine. Inside, she moved straight toward the soft-drink and milk refrigerators. She picked up a small chocolate milk, examined the cold case as if she couldn't find what she wanted, put the milk between Anne and her own belly, and walked to the cashier. "Do you have any gallons of skim milk," she said. "I couldn't see any back there."

The woman shook her head. "We have whole but not skim." Lily made a disgusted face and left the store. She walked quickly back to the park she had passed on Wasatch Street. A wide building stood across the park; the lettering above the entrance said Davis County Library. She sat on the grass in her expensive dress and opened the chocolate milk, helping Anne drink half of it. Then she drank the other half, with Anne holding her hands out for more.

INTERNET SYNAPSES
Automythology (USP)

She regretted not thinking things through more carefully, but then she remembered what she had faced right after Nathan took everything from her. Now, she had Anne and a chance. That was worth all the trouble. She had her brain, and she would figure out what to do.

Lily pulled her bag toward the library and once inside found the computers and got a login code. She put Anne on the floor, and the child stood, holding onto Lily's leg. The act of sitting and reaching her hands to a keyboard was so familiar that she nearly had tears in her eyes, as if her fingers extended like wires, connecting her to the weave of human culture, as if there was no gap between her mind and the minds of these others.

First she checked the news. She could find nothing about her and Anne on any of the local news sites, but it had only been few hours since she'd taken Anne, so this wasn't surprising.

Even Nathan would have to take time to work his magic with the police, convincing them that Anne was in imminent danger, getting Lily's picture out.

Anne let go and stood, swaying a little. Lily rolled the chair back and held her arms out. "You're a big girl, standing all by yourself. Can you walk to Mommy?" Anne took one unsteady step, then another. Soon she was close enough that she grabbed Lily's hand, tucked her head against Lily's belly. "Sit on my lap and look at the computer with me."

She looked up bank repossessions. She found one that was still in limbo; someone had made a bid, but the bank hadn't yet accepted the offer. It was about two miles away. She started a new gmail account with her great-grandmother's name, wondering who she could write who wouldn't turn her in—no one. Soon her half hour was up. It was still early and she needed to rest before lugging the pack and carrying Anne two miles. She spent some time reading picture books with Anne. For a while she dozed in the chair, Anne sitting on her lap, turning the pages of a book. Soon Anne pushed the book away and lay across her, a position they both enjoyed. She signed for food again, her small fingers inside Lily's fingers. Lily didn't want to move, but she rose and held Anne on her hip, dragging the backpack down the stairs.

On their way out, she said to the librarian, "I'm new to town, where can I get some groceries close-by?"

The librarian pointed. "There's a Walmart not far north on Main Street. On the other side off the freeway." That would be on the way to the repossessed house. Lily walked back along Gentile Street, flipped off the Mexican restaurant, then made her way north along Main. After twenty minutes of walking she passed Home Depot, the parking lot full, all those shoppers with plastic in their pockets that gave them access to what they needed or wanted. They could all instantly gratify even an impulse. She found herself furious at them.

She walked north on Main Street. Anne was fussy again and soon was wailing, loud and dramatic. "Sshhh," she said, "Quiet, my baby." She started singing the songs, "Oh, Little Hen," "Here Go Horsies," and "Blackbird." Anne didn't stop. She needed food and rest. Neither was available.

Anne's crying, the exact pitch of her voice, made Lily's nerves feel like a bare electrical wire. She sat on the rim of a planter with a small tree in it. She held the child to her chest and rocked, and finally Anne calmed down. Panic was rising in Lily's head. Even though she had a plan, it was a temporary plan. Getting out of Utah was also short-range. All she had thought about was getting Anne and getting away from Nathan. If she had money, she could get to another country and reduce the chances of Nathan finding her.

She knew she needed help and thought again of her childhood bishop, Bishop Miller, who had probably already tried to call her on her disconnected and abandoned phone. He had been their next-door neighbor when her parents were alive. After she found their bodies he was the first person she went to, even before calling 911. He had stayed in touch. He was one contact Nathan couldn't sever.

She walked along the sidewalk until she came to a stationery store. "My cell died. Can I use your phone?"

When the girl behind the counter frowned, Lily said, "Local call, three minutes. I need to call my husband to meet me in a different place than we planned."

"I can't let you use the store phone."

"Your cell. Just for a minute."

The girl looked at the other worker, who shrugged. Once she had the phone, Lily went to a table and sat down, which made the girl nervous.

"My baby," said Lily. "I have to sit down."

Lily dialed the number, and she recognized his voice when he answered.

"This is Lily Harker," she said quietly.

"I hoped you'd call back," he said. "I heard about your trouble from your aunt."

"I talked to her as well."

"She—ah—doesn't interpret your actions kindly."

"I was foolish to call her."

"She'll call the police if you show up at her house."

"I understand that. I don't have any money. He took every-thing, even the things the court said were mine."

He was silent. His voice had a liquid quality when he spoke again. "If you return the child?"

"My husband will make it difficult for me to see her. Every time will be a battle."

"Is he such a monster?"

"He wasn't. Not until I tried to leave him."

"Still, a monster? I can hardly believe that."

"Selfish. He can't see anyone else's need. I think he's narcissistic."

"Clinically?"

"Yes."

"But you're not a psychologist."

"It would take $10,000 to go back to court and prove what he's done. I'm on the street. I have no money, no phone, no car."

"He left you nothing? That's not what—"

"He knows I have no power to make people believe what he's done."

He was silent again. "I'm so sorry this has happened to you."

"Can you—"

He cut her off again. "Where are you staying?"

"Nowhere."

"You're going to get caught," he said. "Then where will you be?"

"I couldn't let him keep Anne."

He was silent again, and she let him think through what she'd said. "You'd have to have a good lawyer to change anything. I don't have $10,000 and it might be two, three times that."

"I know."

"You can't come here. It couldn't be kept a secret. Your aunt would find out and turn you in. I can't involve my son in a crime by bringing you into our home."

"You could—"

"Helping you is a crime. I can't do it."

"Good-bye," she said.

"I'm sorry. I'm sorry."

She hung up. She tried to muster anger at him, but everything he'd said was true. She knew he was sorry, that he cared about what happened to her. She also knew that there were limits to his love for her. That was what hurt.

She hefted Anne back onto her hip, returned the phone, and left the store. Another quarter mile and she came to the Walmart. She stashed her bag again and asked the old man who greeted her whether they had any cardboard boxes she could take.

"We crush them all."

"Can I check?"

He nodded.

She went to the toilet first, not knowing when she'd find one again. She washed Anne in the sink and laid her on the counter. "We're going to get you some food and diapers." She padded new paper towels around Anne's bottom and put her shorts back on. Back in the aisles, she picked up a package of hair dye and a pair of scissors. Walking into the grocery part of the store, she found a boy restocking shelves with cans of vegetables. She begged a couple of boxes from him—a large one and a smaller one that just fit inside. Once around the corner from him, she dropped the dye into the larger box and put the smaller one on top. Then she picked up a small brick of cheese, a loaf of bread, some animal crackers, a half-gallon of milk, some bananas, and a small package of diapers. She put Anne on the floor, and arranged the items inside the larger box and put the smaller box upside down over her plunder. She balanced Anne on one hip and the two boxes on the other. "I'll have to go somewhere else for more," she said to the old man on the way out. She looked square at him, smiling so that he would focus on her face instead of what she was carrying.

"Try the liquor store. Those are the best boxes for moving. Always strong."

Lily nodded, still smiling. "Thank you."

In the parking lot she discarded the boxes and put the food in her backpack. Anne was calling out and reaching for the food, but she just kept moving. She put Anne on top, helping her straddle the extended handle as if she rode a toy horse, and they rolled across the street and sat on the grass behind a building. She put a diaper on Anne, but the shorts were too soaked to use, so she stuck them in with her other clothing. She gave Anne a piece of bread, which the small girl ate. Anne stuffed a piece in her mouth; the saliva came so strongly that it hurt. Anne ate three pieces of bread, a few banana slices, and a chunk of cheese.

"Aren't you full, baby?" she asked. "You've eaten like a horse." Anne looked at her, a slight furrow on her forehead. When Lily handed her more cheese and banana slices, she smiled and babbled. She finally stopped eating.

Lily gathered their belongings. Anne didn't want to sit on the backpack, crying "No, Ma, no" and arching her back, so Lily carried Anne on her hip and marched toward the repossessed house. They crossed a busy street and then worked their way through the neighborhoods. Anne seemed to gain weight as Lily walked. Her arm ached from holding her child, and she was so tired she could hardly shuffle her feet forward. People stared at her and she knew she had to ditch the backpack, which no normal person would drag down the street. It was a flag of her homelessness.

Finally, she came to the address from the computer. A picket fence enclosed the backyard, which would suit her fine. She walked past, looked for the steeple of a church, where she could be relatively inconspicuous, and sat under a tree. When it was fully dark, she returned to the house, went through the gate into the backyard. The sliding back door wouldn't open, so she set Anne on the grass, found a fist-sized rock and wrapped a thick shirt around it. She crawled down into the window well, tore out the screen, and smashed a hole in the window near the lock. After pushing the window to one side, she lifted Anne and the bag down, pushed the bag through the window and crawled after it. She lifted Anne inside and walked across the dark room, one arm in front of her face. She went left at the opposite wall and soon found the stairway. "This is where we're going to sleep, Baby." The house smelled musty, as if it hadn't been lived in for some time. At the kitchen counter there was enough light to see a little. She got out the bananas and cheese, along with the animal crackers. Both of them were satisfied before they finished half the food. Exhausted, she took everything downstairs and stowed it in the bag. She went to the toilet and changed Anne's diaper. Then she lay on the carpet with Anne. In the absolute dark, she took off her dress and curled around Anne, pulling the dress across her. Three slow breaths and she was asleep.

When Lily was fourteen, she and her two friends had shop-lifting contests. Lily developed tools that she wore: an elastic belt that went around her waist and her cousin's old bra, which was larger than hers. She glued two plastic bowls into the cups so the material wouldn't just collapse around her boobs. She also put other tools in her backpack: a wire with a hook on the end, a couple of books, a magnet on a string. Each girl had an hour, from start to finish; they would meet back in the parking lot with their loot. Lily started at Dillard's, trying on shoes, then when the salesperson went to get another pair, she put the shoes in her backpack, slipped the books in the shoe box so that they would be the same weight, stuck tissue paper in one end so the books wouldn't slide, and returned the box. Clothing was easy—in the dressing room she wore the stolen clothes on under her outfit. Clothing wasn't worth much so she generally went for harder stuff. Jewelry was trickiest. She once stole a diamond pen-dant. She had looked at the cases the day before, then went to Walmart to buy a cheap, glass necklace that looked like the orig-inal with the same size gem and gold chain. During the contest, she had asked to try on the diamond. She had held the eyes of the saleswoman, smiling with a grimace. "Too expensive." She had turned slightly, unlatching the necklace and letting it slip into her bra, unraveling the cheap one from her palm and quickly putting it in the box, snapping it shut. She had to leave quickly before the woman discovered the switch. Lily slipped various things into her cousin's bra—perfume, cheap jewelry, a pocket-knife, a tin of caviar. She once slipped a whole set of silverware inside the elastic belt against her skin. She stole a leather Bible, which she still had when she and Nathan had gotten together. She had slipped objects, a pair of sunglasses or a pair of gloves, into the bag behind a baby stroller, and then followed the woman out of the store, hooking the items out with her wire. She once walked out of Macy's with a microwave oven. She had waited until no one was behind the counter and had stolen a bag and a section of the red tape they used to mark a purchase. Then, shielded by rows of coffee pots and popcorn makers, she slipped the oven into the bag and walked out. She always won the contest, and she never shared her methods with friends. Wandering through a store, knowing she could figure a way to take almost any product she saw, made her feel powerful and wealthy.

When she was twenty, an undergraduate in art at the U, she did an installation where she painted a self-portrait and cut it into twenty-four pieces. On the back of each piece she wrote a single location—the steps of the Capitol building. She shoplifted twenty-four items and left a section of painting in place of each object she stole. She could still remember her haul—a wallet, a mango, a pocket mirror, a pair of gloves, a grocery-store romance novel, a tube of lipstick, a plastic-wrapped tuna sandwich, three candy bars, cross-trainers, a bag of jawbreakers, red wax lips, sunglasses, a black dress, a bag of carrots, a pair of scissors, a donkey piñata, a hymnal, a set of cutlery, a package of sushi, a rape whistle, a graham-cracker pie crust, and an English translation of *Das Kapital*. She arranged them on the steps of the Capitol Building and used a video camera with a telephoto lens to document the reactions of those who looked at her installation. She named the project "Subversion without Containment: Stolen Goods, Please Resteal." Most of the objects were gone by the evening. She saw a couple of people come to the steps carrying her cards, cut from her painting. Two of them compared pictures and fit them together, maybe part of her neck and chin.

SELF-PORTRAIT IN TWENTY-FOUR PIECES
Automythology (USP)

When she was twenty-four and in London with Nathan, she thought about her crimes again, considering the rush of adrenaline she experienced when she walked out of a store with something. She wondered if she had used shoplifting as a distraction, maybe like cutting would have been for someone else. Her college project had been personal *and* political, anti-capitalistic. Looking back, she didn't regret what she'd done, especially since the crimes seemed to have been committed by another person, not by the woman dining high above the Thames. Now she was grateful she had that old skill to fall back on. Shoplifting, taking what she must have without regard to law or the rights of the storeowner, is in her psychic genes, part of who she is becoming.

I have not shoplifted, or maybe I have, but my hyperactive conscience has repressed that memory. My daughter practiced the art during the year we lived in Hawaii; she and her gang of skinny white girls stole art supplies from the university bookstore. My former son-in-law is a master, and I've borrowed a couple of his techniques for Lily. For her it's an art that makes survival possible, but earlier it was a game—a way of flipping off prim clerks who would think her habit pernicious. For me, in this novel, it's a way of opening the future—of saying "screw this" to my habitual loyalty to institutions that have dictated how I should act—the university that puts subjects in small boxes, my church which is ardently conservative and structured on a business model, and my country, which is built on excessive consumption of natural resources. How can I undertake a spiritual journey when I'm trapped in all these boxes, like the ones made of ticky tacky in Pete Seeger's song.

EIGHT

Lily woke before it was light. Thankfully, Anne was still sleeping. She walked upstairs and looked out the kitchen window from which she could see the backyard of the next house over. Lights were on, and a man in his underwear poured cereal from a box. She stepped back even though she knew he couldn't see her standing behind the dark window.

She walked through the kitchen and living room to the front window, where she saw a couple more houses with their lights on. She wanted to get to a television to see whether her picture was on the news yet, but there was no furniture left in the musty house—no television, table, or refrigerator.

After groping her way back downstairs, she again lay next to Anne. The child's face, nearly invisible lashes and round cheeks, gradually grew lighter as dawn came. Lily sat cross-legged next to her. She wanted to touch her child's feet, pull her hair back from her face, but she also wanted to let Anne sleep. Here in the empty house they were safe, unless someone came to look at it—not likely, because the website had said an offer was being processed. She wanted never to leave this place, but she only had a little food and a few diapers. She had to get more supplies and a way out of Utah.

She thought she heard someone walking outside, but it was just the sprinklers coming on, washing against the window. Some splattered through the hole she had made.

When it was full light, Anne roused and started to cry. She put her bottom in the air and toddled toward Lily. "Good girl. Look at you walking." Lily held her and changed her diaper. They ate the rest of the food. Anne babbled as if she were talking, as she had done for a couple of months now, but Lily couldn't distinguish words yet, except for "ma" and "no."

Upstairs where there was more light, Lily used the toilet. "Let's get clean," she said to Anne, who looked up at her mother. Lily had the impression of Anne as a tiny, solemn adult. Lily turned on the shower, but it didn't heat up. She stripped her clothing and Anne's, stepping in. At first the child cried at the cold water, but soon she laughed and patted Lily's face. There was no soap, but it still felt good. Lily loved holding Anne's small, slippery body. Anne shrieked and laughed, slapping her hand at the water. Lily felt fortunate that the bank hadn't turned the water off. Maybe they didn't want the lawn to burn up. After, with Anne watching from the toilet seat, Lily cut her own hair and bleached and dyed black what was left. She put on makeup, which she hadn't done since the trial, which seemed like years ago, but it had only been a handful of days. She thought about dying Anne's hair but decided it would just upset her.

Then she sat on the floor downstairs with Anne, talking to her and singing while her hair dried.

> Oh, Little Hen, when, when, when,
> Will you lay me an egg for my tea?
> Oh, Little Hen, when, when, when
> Will you try to supply one for me?

She wondered if Eve drank tea as a comfort after she was kicked out of the Garden. She didn't want to leave the house, a place no one would think to look, but she needed food, and neighbors would notice if she came and went much. "Let's go on another adventure, baby." Anne listened intently and began to talk back, unintelligible.

She couldn't climb out the back window again, that would look too suspicious, so she watched through the front window, checking to see if anyone was on the street. Seeing nothing, she put Anne on her hip and walked out the front door, leaving it unlocked. Outside, she turned toward the Mormon church where she had waited for dark the evening before. People drove to work, children walked along the street. It felt like where she had grown up across the valley in Bountiful. While she lived with Nathan in Park City, she would have thought these houses were cheap, the people living inside plebeian. Now she just wished she had four walls around her and a supply of food.

Lily stopped next to the church, larger than the building of her youth. She had a moment of nostalgia for how safe she felt then, when God was in his Heaven and all was right with the world. Realistically, she had to recognize that, as a young person, she had been so bored when in church, bored, but unconsciously safe. Across the street was a huge, circular elementary school.

She sat Anne on top of the rolling backpack and pulled her inside the building. A woman vacuumed the foyer.

"Do you have the phone number of the bishop?"

The woman took out her phone and started reading the number.

"Oh," said Lily, "mine's dead. Can I use yours for a second?"

The woman handed her the phone. She dialed, and a woman answered. "Can I speak to the bishop?"

"He's at work. Can I help you?"

Lily started to think of some story. "Probably not."

"Let me give you his cell."

She dialed it as the woman vacuumed. "Bishop Howard? I'm a member of the Church. I grew up in the Bountiful Seventh Ward, but I haven't been to church for years." She stopped. "I—I've just become homeless. I wonder if—you could help. Just with food until I can get on my feet again."

He was silent a moment. "The closest welfare centers are in Centerville and Kaysville. Do you have a car?"

"If you could just give me a check until I can get myself organized."

"That's not the way we do it. You have to go through a welfare center. They'll give you the help you need. My wife and I can get you a ride to one when I get off work. Or my wife could give you a ride now. Call her back. Here's the number of the Kaysville center. It's closer." Lily motioned writing and the woman whose phone she was using handed her a pen. She wrote the numbers on a tithing envelope.

Lily wondered whether Nathan would have contacted the welfare center, warned them she might be coming. Probably not. He couldn't think of everything she might do. Then again, he was motivated by the hate of a rejected narcissist. He would go to great lengths.

Now the woman vacuuming was watching, frowning at Anne crawling on the carpet. Lily gave the phone back. She decided that, because of the strings attached, she would not beg for welfare from the Church. At least not yet.

She lifted Anne and dragged the backpack down the hallway. Anne waved at the woman, bye-bye. On the grass Lily spun the wheel.

South. She dragged the pack across the street, Anne prattling on top as if she was actually stringing together words. They soon came to a fence that marked the back row of houses. She spun again—northeast. They passed a park where kids played baseball, and beyond that she came to North Main Street. A billboard stood next to a grassy area, and she stood in the shade under it. Anne's face was red from the sun, and she looked grumpy. Lily looked along the road to the southeast. Somewhere in that direction was the library, where she could use the internet and see whether she was on the news. First she needed food. She began to think she'd made a mistake by not asking the bishop's wife to take her to the storehouse, which was the next town over, fifteen miles away. Passing a sandwich shop, she thought about going in, ordering something and walking out without paying, but she couldn't afford the police right now. In back she found a dumpster that had some buns in it, a little mold. She picked them up in the bag. Anne woke and reached her hand for one, but when Lily broke off a piece, it had mold inside as well, so she threw them away. Anne started to cry.

She spun the wheel again—southeast along Main Street. A muffler shop. Not much help there. On second thought, she walked in dragging the pack and lugging Anne. She found a popcorn dispenser and a soda machine. She sat in the room and ate popcorn with Anne, drank soda. Others in the waiting room stared at the television, joined by Anne, who seemed mesmerized. There was nothing about her kidnapping. After resting, she tried to put Anne back on top of their backpack, but Anne just cried and held her arms out. Lily held Anne on her hip, tried wrapping her in the scarf, but the child didn't like that either. Lily tried with the scarf again, and after a little fussing Anne lay still.

Trudging further down the street, Lily passed an auto-repair garage. She had never focused so intently on the kinds of businesses that characterized a street, and she had never looked this way at any store, *What resource can I beg or steal from you?* A desperate feeling swept over her, and she knew that if something didn't change, she'd break down like other street people she'd seen. Soon she'd come to the point where it seemed better to give up rather than to live on the edge of constant anxiety.

She passed a rent-to-own place, a closed Chinese restaurant. Layton was a town with no center, a long strip mall for a main street. She was hungry, but she had some sugar and popcorn in her stomach, and she'd survive. Anne was sleeping again, a blessing.

A pawn shop appeared, *WE BUY GOLD*. She walked inside, took her dress out of the bag. The old man with a thin mustache just shook his head. She shook it in his face. "It cost more than all this junk when it was new." His face didn't change. Anne woke and started to cry, and Lily felt her throat tighten with an even deeper level of panic.

She passed Angel Street, which she had crossed the day before. Across a wide parking lot was a big-box department store. Except for her huge backpack, she looked like any of the other people walking inside. She felt reluctant to get rid of the backpack, but it was a burden to her now. She had been seen with it, and it didn't work well for Anne to ride perched on top. Lily filled a plastic bag with diapers, the wheel, the scarf, her knife, the camera, her wallet, her extra clothing, and the folder of printed pictures. She found a ditch next to a tree and tossed the backpack.

Inside the store, the air was cool, no smell of exhaust. Someone was giving out free hotdogs and she took one for herself, one for Anne. They ate them, and then she went to the furniture section, sat in a recliner, tipped it back and with Anne on her chest, went to sleep.

She dreamed she sat at a table eating breakfast. Across the table sat another woman, an Indian. Also sitting at the table were children, three of them—Anne, longer of body and thinner of face, and a small boy, older than Anne, and a baby girl. The woman was talking, but Lily couldn't understand the words. The woman's face was full of affection toward Lily, as if they were sisters or lovers. She had the feeling of peace and safety. The small boy's face was set, as if he had a mask on. Then the mask became Nathan's face. The boy lifted his spoon toward her and light reflected off the bowl of the spoon. The baby patted her on the hand—pat, pat, another pat.

She woke to someone touching her hand.

"Ma'am, can I help you?" A male voice, a young man about her age. She closed her eyes again.

You could help me by not waking me up, she thought. The dream clung to her mind, familiar, as if it was a memory. It felt like a memory but wasn't an experience she'd had.

She opened her eyes. The man's face had become perturbed. "You can't sleep here."

"So where can I sleep?"

His face changed, and Lily knew she'd said something not normal, something a street person would have said.

She walked to the baby department, found a toy for Anne, a small doll, and a stroller that the description on the box said could fold into a small space. She got a shopping cart for it, parked it in the corner behind a circular rack of dresses. When no one was looking she used her knife to open the box. She pulled it to full height and attached the rain/sun cover. She wheeled it in to the next aisle, away from the box, and used her knife to cut off the tags. Then she looped her jacket over it, put Anne inside. She walked down the aisles and found a daypack, a burnt orange one, and put the plastic sack with her essentials inside it. Then she left the store. It was much easier with the stroller. She also felt happy that she had everything she couldn't part with in a backpack, one small enough that she could grab and run if she was threatened.

She passed a tire store, two new car lots. Car wash. Sporting goods. Hobby Lobby. Her humor was gone, as was the small hotdog she had eaten. She felt her head spinning from lack of nourishment, heat, and anxiety. Krispy Kreme. Quiznos. Cold Stone, Checksmart. McGrath's Fish House. She became angry, thinking of the food inside all those places. Check cash-ing. Staples. Loan store on the west side. Savers. Verizon, Einstein's Bagels, Taco Bell, a service station. Apartments. A strip mall—a store that sold nothing but tea, a craft shop, a maternity store, body art, a bead shop, more apartments. None of this sprawl of stores were any good to her unless she had money.

She realized that most of the people she passed looked the same as each other—and not just their mom jeans and clean fingernails. She realized they were all white, no Blacks, few Asians. She saw one Latino man, driving past in his truck. She knew all these white people weren't really all the same. After all, she walked invisible among them, but from her new perspective they all fit the same niche—the homogenous middle class she had looked down on while living with Nathan. But then as she walked farther, she saw a few others who slipped along the streets like her—a homeless woman, a man still hung over, a Latina with a child. The latter woman held a sign in front of her, her child sitting by her shadow in the dirt. Nobody saw the woman, or they glanced away. She had seen those people in Salt Lake and every other city she'd lived in while she traveled with Nathan. Now she was one of many homeless people, islands in an ocean of humanity.

Soon she was back in the area of Walmart where she had gotten food the day before. She felt desperate with hunger and couldn't think clearly enough to make a plan. Anne signed for food over and over and then started crying. Lily just pushed the stroller inside and went into the aisles. She dropped some plastic bowls and spoons into the back compartment of the stroller. Cans of pork and beans that she could open with her knife. Evaporated milk, crackers, tins of meat. Granola bars. All just dumped in the stroller. It was a stupid way to do it. It was midday and the store was not as crowded as it would be later, but she was still anxious. She was acting like a first-time shoplifter, just stuffing things in the most obvious place. She knew she'd get caught. She wheeled the cart out of the store and the greeter, an elderly woman, smiled at her. She got into the parking lot, crouched behind a car and opened the can of beans, shoveling some into her mouth, more into Anne's.

When Karla and I lived in Houston and Hawaii, cockroaches were everywhere. Adult cockroaches are difficult to kill. They can live for a month without food. They can be frozen, put underwater, kept without air for much longer than any human can stand. They can bear ten times the radiation that a

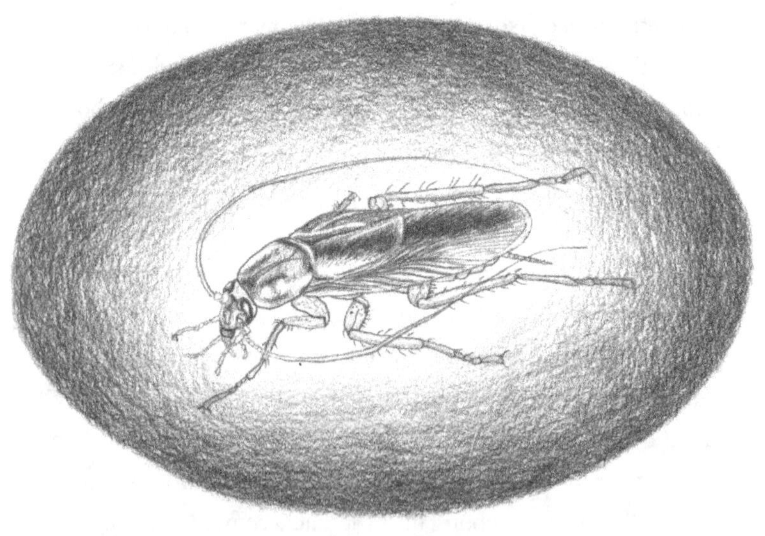

COCKROACH

Automythology (USP)

human can bear. They can eat almost anything, including the glue on the back of a postage stamp. But they are abhorrent to most people, persistently Other.

As Lily walks along that long strip of used car lots, auto repair shops, and empty asphalt, she feels like an insect, unseen. Unlike an insect, she can barely sustain herself despite all the businesses set up to trade goods for money. What sustenance she gets came by breaking one of the oldest human codes—*Thou Shalt Not Steal*. Within half a mile of where she crouches behind a car, eating out of a can, several payday loan or pawn businesses prey on the poor. Any store she walks inside, she's greeted by a show of courtesy, which disappears when they find out she isn't going to buy anything. Once it's clear Lily has no money, she becomes inhuman, a cockroach. Yet like a cockroach, she might live off them, slipping invisible down the interstices of their structures.

Her hands were shaking. She knew it wasn't the edge of hunger exactly, because she'd had the beans and a hotdog earlier and she'd gone without food when she was busy or worried about her weight. Part of it was that she couldn't bear Anne being hungry, but why hadn't she waited to get away from the store before gulping down beans without chewing? She knew it had been the feeling of desperation, the fear of having no reserve of money or food, as much as it had been hunger. She realized that shoplifting as a hobby was much less stressful than stealing food to survive.

Lily knew she was not too far from the library, so once they had eaten the whole can and scraped out the last drop of sauce, and she had put the granola bars inside her backpack in case she had to ditch the stroller, she walked across the freeway overpass and cut through the park. Inside, she logged onto the computer. She went first to the *Tribune*. The police had issued an Amber Alert. Her face was on every news site, two pictures. One was from when she had tried to stab Nathan with a knife. The other was a close-up profile that he had somehow taken in the courtroom or just outside. She had been angry and frightened when the picture was taken, but on the screen she looked insane. Her teeth drew back like an animal. In both pictures she looked ready to eat someone's liver without cutting it out of their body. Then there was a picture of Nathan holding Anne. Lily had taken that picture. Anne was happy because she was looking at Lily, but any reader would think she was happy because she was with Nathan. Lily scanned the text—*mentally ill, dangerous to herself and the child, kidnapper, erratic.* The words fit the pictures of her.

Panicked, she considered how she might steal a car. She returned to the last used car lot she had passed and walked along the cars, with Anne in her new stroller. She looked for a half an hour, then settled on an older Toyota Camry. She asked how much he could go down.

He said, "That car? I'm already as low as I can go."

She frowned. "Can I drive it?"

"Yes, I'm happy to go with you."

"Good," she said. "Then I can ask you questions." She clipped Anne into the back seat. Anne talked to the man, seriously, unintelligibly. Lily asked whether the odometer had turned over, who had owned it before, how many miles he thought were still on it. It felt so good to drive past all the car lots and empty lots where she had spent hours walking earlier.

She turned onto the freeway, drove back, passing under Gentile Street, where it had taken her a half hour to walk from. She exited and circled past the Frontrunner stop and back up Main Street, past all the restaurants and stores. She pulled into the car lot and saw that someone was waiting in the lobby.

"There's one other I'd like to drive. I'd like to take it on the same loop."

"Go ahead," he said. She traded her driver's license for the keys to a blue sedan. She clipped Anne in and drove out onto the street, where she glanced down to see how much gas there was. The needle was barely above empty, a disheartening sight. She might make it 20 miles. But then where would she be? The police would be after her, and wherever she left the car, they would find it and know she wouldn't be far. Stealing a car would be like waving a flag, "Here I am." She considered stealing gas but didn't know how to pump gas without a card.

She drove back to the car lot. "I can't make up my mind. I'll come back tomorrow."

He wanted to talk her into getting one of them, but she just said, "Give me my license. I'm just not up to this today."

"Come back when you are," he said. "I can give you a good price."

She was back near the place she'd stayed the night before and she had some food, but she still didn't have a plan. Anne was crying again, angry screaming, clearly wanting to go home and lie down, so Lily strolled her back to the church and sat in the shade under a tree where they ate all the granola bars.

She and Anne lay back, and suddenly she had a memory from her childhood of lying on the grass Easter morning, her stomach full of chocolate, the taste of it on her tongue. It was not the first warm day of spring, but her body was still hungry for the sun. On her back she looked up into the locust tree at the branches and twigs drawing lines against the sky. The branches divided in two, one thicker than the other, again and again, two and two, until the blue sky was latticed. Each leftward tend-ing twig was dark; those that reached to the right were silver, lit by the lowering sun. She looked at the negative space between the twigs—shapes made of sky or leaves with three sides, or five sides, mostly four-sided. No two were the same. She looked at a square with an angled fourth side, until it seemed that sky was a cube of blue. Then she saw the twigs again. Then the lines against the sky seemed to be drawn on a flat blue paper, two-dimensional. She had thought that the tree was magic and that the way she saw the tree was magic, her eyes seeing the shapes and then the lines that covered the reach of the sky. As a girl she had felt that this act of imagination made the sky hers, and she might go anywhere on the earth and be safe.

NINE

That afternoon Lily used a library phone to call the Tenth Ward bishop's wife who came to pick her up. "Hello," she said to Lily, smiling.

Lily said, "Thank you so much for helping me. I'm Sister Stewart." She shook the woman's hand.

"It's no trouble." She pulled onto the freeway. "That's a lovely child." It was almost a question.

Lily recognized the contract—the woman wanted to trade her service for a story she could tell her friends—a morality tale in both charity and lack of character. "I grew up in Bountiful, but when I hooked up with the singer in a local band, my parents kicked me out. I came to my senses about a month ago, but I've had trouble finding a job. I'm trying to go back home, but I have to get on my feet first. I used all my money getting here, so I don't have any food or a deposit on an apartment. I hope the welfare center can help me find a place to stay for a few days while I get a job."

"Jo," said Anne.

"Yes, Baby, job."

"I'm so sorry, and I'm proud that you're trying to come back. They're really good at helping people like you find jobs."

They pulled up to Kaysville Welfare Office. Lily got the stroller out of the back and put Anne in it. The bishop's wife walked in with her and sat in the lobby. "I'll wait here."

Lily rolled the stroller into the office of a man in a suit. "Elder Stringham," his label said. His desk had nothing on it except his cell phone and a pad of paper, a computer. She couldn't see what was on the screen. Anne climbed out of the stroller and onto Lily's lap.

"Name," he said.

"Abby Stewart."

"Bby sewt," said Anne.

"So tell me your story, ah, Abby." His face was a mixture of fear and wariness, which surprised Lily. She didn't allow herself to react as she told the same story she'd given the bishop's wife.

"Have you gone to the women's shelter?"

"One night. It's so crowded."

"But it was a place to sleep, right?"

Lily nodded. And waited.

"I can give you money for a place to stay for a couple of days while we work out a more permanent solution." Lily had trouble reading his face now, but there was no kindness.

He dialed a number and walked to a filing cabinet, the phone held against his shoulder. Lily looked at his desk again. The pad of paper had notes, names, phone numbers, other notes. The last number she could read upside down. It was Nathan's office number.

Lily grabbed her small backpack and carried Anne out of the office, leaving the stroller behind. She made her breathing calm as she walked. She smiled at the bishop's wife. "I have what I need."

"Sister Stewart," the man said behind her. "We're not finished."

She shoved open the front door and stood in the road in front of a car. She held out one hand, palm forward, and held Anne to one side with her other arm. The car screeched to a halt, and Lily stared into the wide and frightened eyes of the driver, a woman. "Emergency," Lily said. "I need to get my baby to the hospital. She stopped breathing in there. She's breathing now, but I need to go to the closest hospital. She might stop again." She held Anne close to her. Anne sensed her fear, but instead of crying, she clung to Lily.

The woman inside said, "Get in. I'll take you, but you should have called an ambulance."

Lily jumped into the back seat. "I don't have money for an ambulance. Can we just go?"

The woman drove away. Through the rear window Lily saw Elder Stringham and the bishop's wife, standing in the doorway. He spoke into his cellphone.

It took them about ten minutes on the freeway to get to the hospital, Davis County Emergency. "Thank you." Lily got out and ran inside. Once in the lobby, she turned out of sight from the doorway, sitting in the closest chair. After a minute, she stood and peered out again. The car was just pulling away.

She sat down again, holding Anne close. "Ma," said the child. "Ma." She must have sensed Lily's anxiety, so she didn't cry or babble, just sat quietly. The receptionist looked up at her, but then went back to work. Trying to think for herself, doing what seemed logical, had gotten Lily nowhere. The short-termed theft of the car had been stupid and the visit to the welfare center had been a fiasco. Anne stood between Lily's legs, watching the other people there, one who had a bloody arm, one who held his stomach, and others of the maimed or ill. Anne clung to her knee, staring at the strange people.

She thought again about how to get enough money to get out of Utah. She was at a hospital. She had sold plasma when she first started the art program at the U. She walked over to the ER nurse and asked where she could donate plasma. The nurse looked at her, then at Anne. "It's down this hallway, then turn right. Go to the other end of the hospital." She sat back down. She knew she'd have to show her ID, answer questions. As an undergraduate, she had sold her hair once online, but now she had cut it and it wasn't long enough.

She considered who had helped structure her life in the past—doctors, nurses, pharmacists, psychologists, lawyers, policemen, religious leaders, owners of stores and restaurants, waiters, plumbers, insurance agents, clothing salespeople, beauticians, travel agents, veterinarians, masseuses, bank clerks, manicurists, and personal assistants. None of them would help her now. Because Nathan was selling them his propaganda, those who should be willing to help a homeless person might think they were helping best by turning her over to the police. She thought about how to get a free ride out of state. Someone at the university in Ogden might be going home at the end of term. After the experience at the welfare center, she was sure that Nathan and the police knew she was in Layton. Police cars would have her picture on their computers.

Lily is outside the institutions that help most of us—those of us with money. It's like a spinning platform in a playground, where centrifugal force has thrown her off, separated her from the rest of the children. Yeats's poem "The Second Coming" uses the image of a falcon turning in the air around a falconer, with the bird's obedience to the trainer holding it like a tether. As the bird swings round, the "falcon cannot hear the falconer," the "centre cannot hold" and "mere anarchy is loosed upon the world." The poem describes the decay of human systems, without which the world falls into confusion. The Romantics viewed time as a rising wheel, cyclical and progressive, humanity circling toward something better. But Yeats saw reality more ambiguously. He embraced revolutionary thought that would tear down old institutions but also admired the culture that the old order had produced and preserved. Others have believed that the loss of traditional institutions might be positive. "Imagine there's no heaven," sang John Lennon. "Above us only sky. Imagine all the people, living for today." But an outsider like Lily has become finds no comfort in imagining the institutions gone.

Like everyone else, I've lived my life inside institutions—the structural manifestation of human culture. Louis Althusser, a French Marxist, described institutions and other human creations as part of the Ideological State Apparatus, structures of ideological control that are manifestations of the economic structure—the means of production. I was succored and shaped by public school from the age of five to the age of seventeen, by a decade of college, by Church from the age of consciousness until now, also by various institution-supporting narratives about love and romance, employment, family, fidelity, consumption, commerce, protection by police and insurance agents. As I write this book, I have no hope that freedom might come from dismantling confining structures. Primarily because there is no outside. There is no island where Crusoe escapes British culture and just exists, happy that he has a cave for shelter and enough food to prevent death. If I can't think my way to the outside, what can I do when the institutions I'm inside are both safe and destructive, especially for those people that these structures exclude.

The only tool or weapon I have is reflection: the ability to begin to sense the eddy of time I'm held by, the human structures that enable my consciousness, and to both accept and bend the context of my life. But I've been here before, cycled through these same thoughts before, so how will this time be different?

Lily spun the wheel to decide whether to go to the university or not. She chose the right side of the north-south axis for yes, left side for no. Sitting in her chair, she spun the wheel and stuck her finger in it.

One space west of north—no.

She slumped back. The wheel had started as a generator of randomness, but had become more than that—something she relied on and that controlled her. Maybe she should pay no attention to it, but not using it hadn't worked. There was some stubbornness inside that made her know she would do what the wheel said. She would see what would turn up.

She gathered Anne, who started to cry. "What's wrong?" she asked, but Anne wailed harder. "Are you hungry again?" All their food had been in the stroller. Lily lifted the child to her hip and let her wail. In the parking lot, she spun the wheel again—south-southwest. She walked across the parking lot at an angle until she came to the door of Wee Care Pediatrics. The sign said, "Not just an appointment, a relationship." She spun the wheel again. East.

She lugged Anne eastward to the next intersection. Beyond that the street crossed the freeway, but there was no sidewalk on her side, so she waited for the light and crossed. She walked over the freeway. Wishing was foolish, but she wished, wished, wished she was in one of those cars heading north to Idaho or Montana. Canada.

Anne was wet again and complaining loudly. They passed a motel, a drug store, a tire store, Lowe's, a credit union, and finally, a Target, where she turned and went inside. One of the clerks messed with her phone while she waited for customers. She looked up and when she saw Lily her face showed recognition and surprise. She looked down at her phone, then up again. Lily kept smiling, paying no attention to her, and walked toward the back of the store. Trying to control her breathing, she grabbed a blouse and some trousers. In the dressing room, she changed her clothing and left. As she walked toward the front of the store, she grabbed a different backpack, this time a nondescript gray one, from the back-to-school section. She dumped the wheel and her other belongings inside. Leaving her old daypack on the floor, she walked out the door on the opposite side of the clerk who had recognized her. She crossed the parking lot just as a police car pulled up. Another arrived before she left the parking lot. She walked across a connected parking lot and came to a huge building, Davis County Convention Center. She went inside and upstairs, finding an empty room. She lay on the floor with Anne in the dark. Lily took out a granola bar and shared it with her. There was a water fountain in the hall. She stayed in the dark room, and nobody bothered her that night.

T E N

Lily woke to Anne pulling her hair, trying to wrap it around her small hand. She stood next to Lily's head, bending over her. Lily imagined she was in her own bed, but because she hadn't felt safe in Nathan's house for over a year and because she was now running from the police, the feeling of peace quickly broke down. Still, she stayed in the moment with Anne, who stepped forward and plopped down, wet diaper and all, onto Lily's chest. Lily pulled her tight. Enough light came under the door that they could see.

"Where should we go today?" She knew she needed to get out of the area. Since she had been spotted twice, the police and Nathan knew where to concentrate their search.

Anne babbled steadily. The only word Lily could make out was "Da," which she said a couple of times.

Lily wondered what Anne thought of Nathan, who had only been unkind to the child once, when he shut her in the closet—and that had been to get at Lily. Mostly he was absent in his daughter's life. But Anne remembered him.

Lily heard a noise and the door opened. The lights came on. A Latina pulling a vacuum cleaner. The woman froze, staring at Lily. "Qué haces aqui?"

"Changing my baby." Lily knelt quickly and pulled a diaper out. "Bebe." She waved her hand in front of her face. "Muy malo."

The woman frowned, still watching. Lily laid Anne on her back, undid the old diaper. Luckily there was only pee, not poop. She put on the new diaper, picked up her backpack and the old diaper, walking past the woman who was still suspicious. Lily dropped the dirty diaper in a canister. Even after leaving that smell behind, she could smell her own body. She had showered yesterday morning, but without soap, and she didn't know when she could wash again. This would cause trouble. She knew that the smell and appearance of a homeless person would keep her from being invisible inside any store, and not bathing and not washing her clothing would mean the end of food.

She walked out into the parking lot of the conference center. She didn't know where she could go to be safe, so she jerked the wheel out and spun. Anne tried to reach for the wheel, but Lily held it away.

East. A random direction. Cast your bread upon the waters. She handed the wheel to Anne and carried her across a street into a parking lot. To her right a truck with a trailer full of lawn equipment was parked. A man trimmed the edge of the grass with a weed-whacker. She kept walking. To her left was a lot filled with trees.

She felt exposed, panicky, because if the Latina had watched the news, she might have called the police. Any second, squad cars might enter the parking lot. Their doors would burst open and officers with guns would spring out. It astonished her what she had come to in the past few days—that something so bizarre might actually happen to her.

Anne complained, pushing away from Lily. "Down, down," she said and signed. Lily knew that she would explode into understandable language in the next few weeks. She was right on the cusp. Lily set her down and held one hand while Anne walked, so slow it was excruciating.

She looked left again, at the trees, where she and Anne could hide. What then? The boundary of the parking lot was a white fence, beyond that extended the backyards of homes. To her right the street curved around. She could hear the sound of a television through the back window of a house directly in front of her.

Again, she wanted to chuck the wheel. She knew there was no intelligence behind it, but it had led her to Anne. How had that happened? She shook her head; trying to make logic out of it was useless. That way lay madness, the structure of the universe unraveling.

Lily spun the wheel.

North-northeast. Straight against the eight-foot-tall fence. She shook her head. "Mommy is a fool." She hooked her backpack around one of the posts, slung Anne in the scarf across her back and lifted herself up. She sat on top of the fence, looking into the back windows of the house. Nobody appeared. She heard a siren, then another; they gave her a jolt of fear as she scanned the yard for a doghouse, dropped her backpack, shifted Anne to the front and lowered them both to the ground. Slightly to her left was a small travel trailer. She walked to it and the door was locked, but when she pulled harder it popped open. She went inside. All the curtains were drawn, so she sat at the table. Then she stood up and locked the door. There was a TV on the counter, but nothing happened when she tried turning it on. In the cupboard, she found a can of chili, opened it, and opened the top drawer, which had silverware inside. Anne laughed and hit her small hand against the table. "Quiet, baby." She stopped Anne's mouth with a spoonful of chili and another. "One for me and one for you."

"Ou," said Anne.

Lily knew they couldn't stay long, but she couldn't concentrate well enough to know what to do next. Now that their stomachs were full, she held Anne in her arms and sang softly to her. "I gave my love a cherry, that had no stone." Anne lay still, a miracle. Lily peered out the window, but all she could see was the side of the garage and the back yard. Nobody came out. She sang another quiet song. The wheel had taken her, not to the university where she might logically get a ride share, but to the Target where she was nearly caught by police. She didn't trust either the wheel or her own brain, but she had to act, doing the next thing and the next and the next.

She thought about someone coming out of the house and hooking the trailer up, rolling out of Utah, maybe carrying her to Mexico or farther south. Going up or down or out of the country without effort of her will.

She turned and removed her arm from Anne, who stirred and went back to sleep. She sat at the table. She took out her notebook, which she had been too scattered to use much, and started to make a list. First was getting some money. Lily could shoplift food from a store, but she had already decided that trying to steal money would cause her serious trouble. Stealing a car and gas would bring the police even quicker. She couldn't apply for a credit card. Begging with her head down might work, but it would draw attention. She didn't look like a homeless person yet, even if she had started to smell. Because she would draw attention, she couldn't do day labor like the men she had seen waiting in a line near a big box hardware store once in Salt Lake. And she had Anne. It would be dangerous to beg door-to-door.

There was nothing else on the list. Two hundred dollars would take her out of the area.

Then she lay on the bed next to Anne, feeling so tired after a second night of sleeping on a floor. Soon she was sleep.

She woke, hungry, and saw that Anne was awake also. The child signed for food.

"Food," said Lily.

"Foo," said Anne. They had some canned fruit, drank some evaporated milk, which Anne guzzled, and more chili.

Lily looked at her transportation list, the one she had used to leave Salt Lake. She had crossed out "skateboard" as number sixteen and written in "horse," but that seemed just as impractical. She thought about where she was and wrote,

16. Trailer.

She spun the wheel and it came up, west-southwest, or about where the number eleven would be—motorcycle. She could spin the wheel for miles, but one through sixteen was not far enough. She wanted to get far away. She thought about using exponents of ten: 1, 10, 100, 1000, but that sequence would end at the sixteenth slot with 1,000,000,000,000,000, which might be a desirable distance between her and Nathan but which was not possible. So she wrote down the Fibonacci Sequence for 16 numbers. The numeral 1 was duplicated so she added a zero, for staying put:

0, 1, 2, 3, 5, 8, 13, 21, 34, 55, 89, 144, 233, 377, 610, 987

She spun the wheel, counted the spaces, and came to 21 miles. What direction? She spun and it pointed straight north. Surprisingly, it felt good to have a plan. Then she started giggling because she knew she was crazy, as if life was some kind of mystery game. *I will travel 21 miles north by motorcycle.* It seemed so funny that she fell across the bed laughing. Anne was concerned and patted her face. "Ma," she said. "Ma."

"Your mother is crazy." She realized that she was talking too loud, so she put her finger on her mouth. "Shhh, Anne. We have to be quiet."

Where to go for a motorcycle?

She decided that it would be good if she could change clothing again, just in case the cleaning woman described her to police. She looked in the closet and found some clothing that was too big for her, but she put on a pair of pants and a man's shirt. She stuffed what she had been wearing into the small backpack, along with a few more cans of chili, fruit, and milk, slung Anne across her chest and left the trailer. Instead of leaving the way she had come, over the fence to the rear of the house, she walked forward to the street, looking back at the house to see if anyone was watching. Once on the sidewalk, she spun the wheel for left or right. It said left. So she walked to the left, the east. At the intersection she stopped. Left was a dead end, no motorcycle in sight. Ahead or turn right? She spun. It said to continue on. Another intersection. Straight on. She walked down the street in this suburban neighborhood with her head high, just as if she belonged there.

What were the odds she'd find a motorcycle to steal?

In elementary school I took to math as if numbers were my first language and words my second. Numerals were symbols like words were, but what they signified seemed more like objects than abstractions. Four was balanced, two and two, whether I parted it horizontally or vertically, it was perfect. Four in my head was not four apples or horses but *four*, this and this and this and this, four concrete spiritual entities. The patterns spread in my mind: 2, 4, 6, 8; 3, 6, 9; 2 and 3 and 5. Multiplying, I found that the numbers fell into sections like a peeled orange. Three 3s is 9. Ten is 2 and 5. Twelve is rich, 2 and 6, 3 and 4, 1 and 12. The patterns seemed primal.

I like number patterns because they are trustworthy, unlike most elements of my life, which are squishy. My therapist, a prim and confident woman, helped me see that I wanted a world where everything falls into neat patterns, easily controllable, no disorder or unpredictability.

While the therapist's theory resonated with me and still does, I also love disorderly numbers, puzzles that don't add up, the chaotic elements of advanced math, which I know only a little about. For example, I adore Gödel's theorem that no logical arrangement of mathematical axioms can explain all truths about its own system; its self-consistency is indefinable.

I like the idea of irrational numbers, non-Euclidean geometry, relativity. I connect this kind of math to my idea that no system that is shaped and interpreted by humans is perfectly comprehensible—not capitalism, Mormonism, Buddhism, the scientific method, logic, or democracy. Dogma is just a way of totalizing a system, making the system seem self-consistent, easily understood.

Lily passed a postman, who didn't pay attention to her. Despite the knowledge that normal people don't have much to hide, she ducked her head as she walked past, worried that whether she looked at him or not, he might be staring at her, recognizing her from the pictures on the internet. The road curved to the right. A chain-link gate on rollers enclosed one yard and a black dog came to the fence barking at her. In the opposite yard were two plastic trikes, something like motorcycles. She thought about herself climbing on one and Anne on the other, pedaling into the sunset, but Anne couldn't ride yet.

In these houses were people with televisions, people who must have seen her picture with teeth bared. Suddenly, she snarled and grinned at Anne, who laughed. It was a release valve, that moment of joking. Still Lily felt the fracture lines in her being. The constant tension was breaking her down—to say nothing of the physical weight of Anne, who felt heavier and heavier and who today seemed perfectly happy on Lily's hip, constantly saying gibberish or singing. Several times the child twisted in Lily's arms, wanting to get down. She walked ten steps and then raised her arms to be carried again. Lily regretted not having enough time to grab the stroller when she ran from the Kaysville welfare center.

Soon it was late morning, hotter than hot. Most people were inside or at work. She passed an American flag on a pole in someone's yard. A bench under an aspen. She set Anne down and shook her weary arms, then picked her back up and started walking again. They came to an intersection. She spun fourteen, straight ahead, walked straight through the yield sign without yielding.

Snowmobiles or jet skis with plastic covers in a trailer. A cheap umbrella stroller on the other side next to a dumpster. She put Anne in the stroller, watching the front door. Nobody came out, so she pushed Anne down the street. Nobody came running after her. A boat, uncovered on her left. A large woman in a white T-shirt watched a man put a garbage can of grass clippings in a trailer. The road curved right again. She was going in circles. Basketball hoops in most driveways. The road curved right again. Intersection. She spun a four, straight on. A man in suspenders walked across his yard. He smiled at her, and she nodded and walked on, passing a cul-de-sac, no motorcycle in sight.

Soon she came back to the street she had started on and began to despair. The wheel said to turn right, the way she had just come. She hated the idea of walking down the same street she had walked down already, attracting attention. When she passed anyone, she smiled and looked straight at them. She went all the way round the circle again, getting the same choices at each intersection.

If I had an axe, she thought, *I'd smash this damn wheel*, but she obeyed and started down Foyler for the third time. She felt like an idiot, going around the same circle a third time, passing the same houses. She saw a woman in a bright blue shirt come out on her porch, turn around, and walk back inside. Lily knew the worst thing she could do was to invite people's suspicions.

Following the infernal wheel she went a fourth time around the same circle. Then the wheel took her in a left turn, another left turn, then straight, going around the same circle for the fifth time, an eternal loop.

Discovered independently in 1958 by two German mathematicians, August Ferdinand Möbius and Johan Benedict Listing, the Möbius strip is a surface with one side. You can prove it to yourself by twisting one end of a strip of paper, gluing the ends together, and tracing your finger along the paper. It is like a circle, in that you can draw a line all the way around back to the initial point, but it is clearly not your common, grocery-store circle. Because it has only one side, one boundary, it has a quality of non-orientability—you can't consistently choose a clockwise or counterclockwise, an inside or outside direction on the strip. A rectangle of sufficient length or height can be made into a Möbius band. Topologists can use imagination and computer graphics to create a three-dimensional Möbius. However, Lily is moving in spacetime, so maybe she's in a four-dimensional Möbius band.

This is how she felt, that she couldn't orient herself in space or time. I identify, I inflict on her my own confusion. Who's to say that our subjective judgment is wrong? Einstein proved mathematically that spacetime is not uniformly shaped, that it bends around gravitational mass. We conceive of time as linear, but it might be curved, looped, branched, static, accelerating or decelerating. And if time is variably shaped, how do we think about change or growth, which requires our being in one point

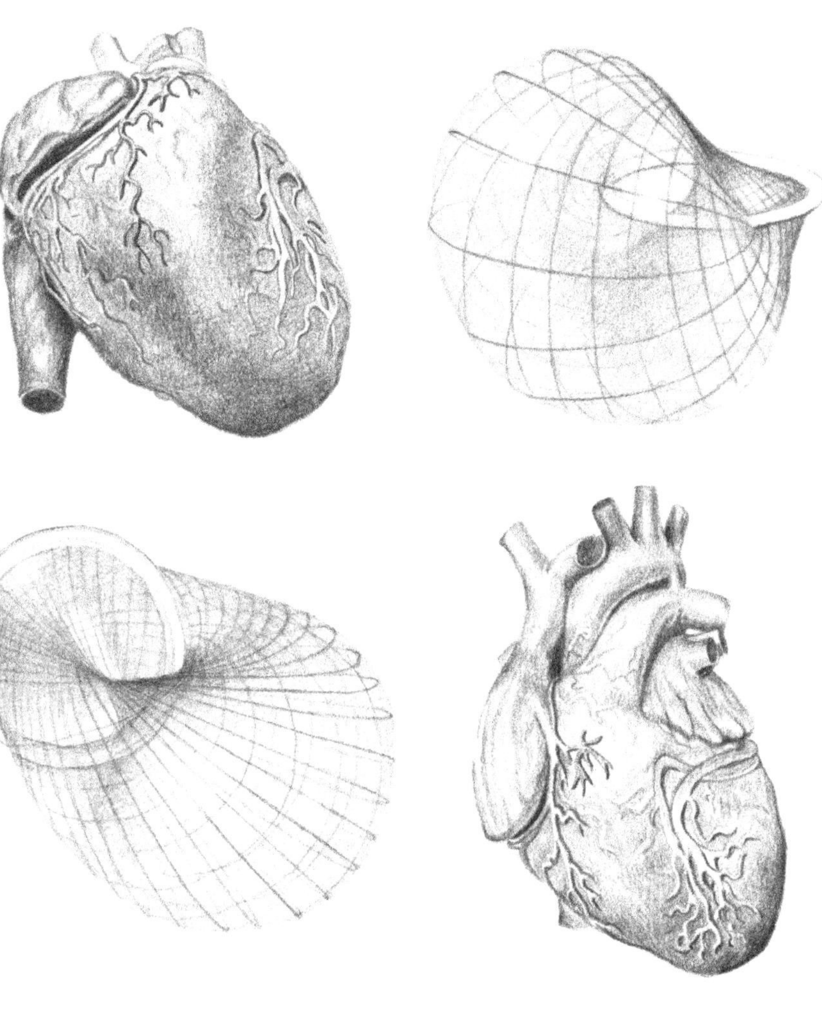

HEART MOBIUS
Automythology (USP)

in time being different than a previous point in time? This thought transforms perception of Lily's journey and mine into something like Bunyan's Slough of Despond, where forward progress is improbable. My mathematician friend says that anomalies like the Möbius band are pathologies, areas where discovered laws don't work. What happens to people when faced with loss of orientation is breakdown, identity becoming a more complex shape, which is what is happening to Lily on her physical journey, and me on my spiritual one. Or maybe that's not true for either of us, and identity is becoming simpler, a settled and unchangeable shape of being-in-time, like the pale figure next to the trail that Lily dreamed about. I can't clearly read my own nature and motion because I am the instrument that I use to read myself, I see myself through a glass darkly.

Finally, the wheel spun left. Almost immediately, at the intersection of Bennett and Paul streets, she saw a covered motorcycle sitting in a driveway, a small girl playing next to it. She wondered why the wheel hadn't led her there sooner, but she also knew that in her new universe, asking why was useless.

"Hello," Lily said.

"Hi," said the girl. Lily set Anne on the ground next to the other child.

A woman came out and sat on the back stoop. Gray streaked her hair. "Hey," she said. "New?"

Lily nodded. "Bliss Newton." She used the name of a high-school friend obsessed with athletes. She extended her hand.

"Jackie Franklin." The woman was old enough to be the baby's grandmother. "Which ward are you in?"

"I'm not sure of the number."

"Where do you live?"

Lily had noted an empty house, three streets over. She said that address. "That your husband's bike?"

"Mine. He rode his to work." The woman walked over and pulled off the cover. "We put on our tie dye and leathers and we're just like hippies," she said. "You look familiar."

Lily smiled, despite the rising panic. "I've heard that one before. I must have a generic face." She touched the handle. "Must be great. Wind in your face."

"Do you want a ride?"

Lily's heart leapt. "What about the kids?"

"Give me another hour and my daughter will be home from work. She can watch her kid, yours too."

"You'd do that? You'd give me a ride?"

"Pleasure."

Lily considered. "You could help me out another way."

"What you need?"

"I've got a sister lives north of here but Mike, my husband, is gone with our car. I wonder if you could give me a ride up."

"Where does she live?"

"I'm not from here. I can't remember the name of it. Some name invented to make people want to live there. Twenty miles north of here."

"Ogden. No, that's only ten miles. Brigham City. No, that's too far. Must be Pleasant View. About twenty minutes from here."

"That's it," said Lily. "Pleasant View."

"I can take you up there, but not on the bike. Not safe for your child."

"Never mind. I'll just get her to come get me. I'll come back another time for my ride."

Jackie paused, looking straight at Lily without blinking. As if she was seeing Lily's manipulative lie for exactly what it was. Finally, Jackie shook her head. "They're playing. Just sit awhile."

Lily wondered whether Jackie knew Lily's identity and was lying about it? Was she going to call the police?

She didn't think Jackie was lying, so she decided to chance it.

Rules for Lying:

1. Never hesitate.
2. Never try to cover up a lie with a second lie.
3. Believe your lie, or, in other words, recreate reality with each new lie. Let the lie settle in, and reorient yourself to it. Become the lie, let it transform your identity.

The concept of saying words that don't refer to someone's reality is woven into our culture—lie a blue streak, tell a white lie or a black lie, trick a lie detector, give him the lie, make a lie out of whole cloth. We are especially offended when someone stares unblinking into our eyes and deceives us. But lying can be seen as a form of rejection of traditional culture, an act of rebellion. "The Lie" is the title of a poem by Sir Walter Raleigh; he points out the way the world, the court, leaders, the church, arts, even schools are deceitful. He advises, "Give them all the lie," which means show these false systems for what they are. He lists human attributes or states of being that deceive—zeal, love, time, flesh, age, honor, beauty, favor, wit, wisdom, physic, skill, charity, law, fortune, nature, friendship, justice, faith, manhood, and virtue. He says give them all the lie.

A story that is not true, fiction, is a lie, but one that tries to tell a truth about human nature. Then there's the idea that the saying of a thing can create the truth of it. I say it, and it comes into being. Spinoza said, "In the beginning God spake the word and it came to exist." A good novel creates a believable world and at the same time gives mainstream culture the lie. Or at least that's what it pretends to do. Storytellers generally unconsciously serve the culture, agents of the lie.

In writing there are rules. In the fictional parts of this book it's expected that I'm making things up. When I essay in my own voice, as here, I'm not to lie. The problem comes with mixing the two, especially when I say that some of Lily's choices are random, but I determine what happens when she makes those choices. When am I lying and when telling the truth? Even I don't know for sure.

I confess that I admire Lily's ability to lie; distortions of reality fall out of her mouth like pearls. If I could lie in such a vigorous and unconstrained manner, I might be rich and happy. Her lies expand the potential of the universe, because lies create more axioms than truth does. *I have a husband, but he is gone. I have a sister in Pleasant View.*

But Lily has no sister and no husband. She lies to bring possibilities into being. We lie to change the past and create the future.

ELEVEN

They talked about the heat, Utah politics, the pleasure of riding a big bike. They had both read *Zen and the Art of Motorcycle Maintenance*, so they talked about looking at the surface of things versus looking at the essence, the Romantic intuitive view of the world and the rational and empirical view. When her daughter finally came home, Jackie said, "I want to ride up to Huntsville to see the monastery and this woman, ah, Bliss, wants to visit her sister. You can drive behind us with her baby and then come home."

"I'm tired. I've been on my feet all day." The girl, a little younger than Lily, had straight, blonde hair and a narrow face, a sharp nose. Lily pegged her as the last child, a whiner.

"Come on," Jackie stroked her daughter's cheek. "It'll take you forty-five minutes. Make this woman's day." She smiled in an odd way. "Make her sister's day."

The girl shrugged. "At least I'll be sitting down."

They loaded the children into the back seat of the daughter's car, Anne in an old car seat that was too small for Jackie's granddaughter. Jackie handed Lily a helmet.

On the freeway, Jackie drove a steady seventy. The wind blew Lily's short hair back. If she turned her head around, she saw the daughter driving Anne in the car.

They passed five police cars on the way, all headed back toward Kaysville.

What next, thought Lily. *What next?*

Lily had asked to use the computer just before the daughter came home and had used Google maps to determine where she wanted to be dropped off in Pleasant View. She also checked the news; Nathan had offered a $20,000 reward for information on her whereabouts. Jackie rolled to a stop in the driveway and turned off her engine. The throaty rumble had been a comfort, now Lily could hear cars on the street. She looked at Jackie.

"Good luck, Lily," Jackie said. "Whose house is this really?"

Lily wanted to run up the driveway, hide in the trees. She could see no sign of police coming along the roads. She looked back at Jackie, knowing herself to be paranoid. If Jackie wanted to turn her in for the money, she would have done so already.

"I don't know," Lily said. "I don't have a sister. No father or mother or husband, just this child. In all the world all I have is this child."

Jackie nodded.

"When?" Lily asked.

"I was watching the news when you first came up. Your face is unmistakable."

"You were testing me."

"I didn't believe what they said. You just confirmed my disbelief."

Lily turned.

"We can take you farther," Jackie said.

"No," said Lily. "This is better. You can say you don't know where I went."

"May you have bliss," Jackie said as she turned on her motorcycle.

"Let me take your picture," Lily said, taking the camera out. Jackie smiled and nodded.

Lily waited while the other two women drove away, the motorcycle toward the east, the car back toward the freeway. When they were gone, she found tears in her eyes because of Jackie's kindness. But she couldn't afford to allow tears to blind her to the danger of trusting anyone else with Anne's safety. She knew trust was useless and dangerous, and she tamped the feeling down. Anne sat down in the driveway. "Let's go, Baby," she said, but the child wouldn't crawl or walk toward her. Lily walked to the middle of the intersection near the house and spun the wheel—east.

She put the backpack in the crap stroller she'd taken from the side of the road back in Layton and hefted Anne to her hip. She pushed the stroller down the street and soon came to a wire fence. She spun the wheel again. East. She dumped the stroller over and, tying Anne across her back with the scarf, climbed the chain-link fence, hurting her hand on one of the twisted points on top. She spun again: north-northwest.

She crossed the field, carrying Anne, the backpack, and the stroller. "Ma, ma," said Anne, signing her hunger.

"Me too, baby," said Lily. "I'm hungry too." Hungry and a little dizzy. Soon she came to a piece of ground sectioned into small garden plots. In the closest plot two men picked grapes from vines on wires. They peered at her. She smiled and waved to them, so they ignored her. She walked past and into the orchard. She sat with her back to an apple tree and laid Anne, now asleep, on her big scarf in the grass.

She still needed a plan, but there was not one to be made. Soon Anne stirred, so Lily stood and kept walking, north-northwest, still carrying her backpack, the stroller, and Anne. She came through the orchard to a corrugated tin building with a half dome. No one was around so she walked across the open space and straight to a big truck with sides on the back for hauling fruit or trees or bee houses.

She climbed in the truck and set Anne on the passenger seat, her other stuff on the floor. The key was in the ignition. She twisted the key to "on" and checked the gas gauge, but it seemed to be broken. She took a deep breath, looked around, and twisted the key farther to start the truck. It ground and finally caught. She put it in reverse and backed around. Then she drove across the barnyard to the road and continued down the lane to the south, past the grapes and the two men still working. She came to the barn she had passed. Just beyond the barn the dirt road became only a track and a dead-end. There was nowhere to go but across the fields, so she backed the truck around again. Someone came out of the barn and scratched his head, so she waved at him and drove toward the original building, where she'd found the truck. She swore steadily under her breath. Anne stood on the seat, unsteady, trying to balance. "Sit down, baby," she said.

"Sit," said Anne and plopped onto the seat. Lily pushed on the brake pedal. Once the truck stopped, she pulled the dirty seatbelt across Anne and strapped her in. They passed the workers again, turned right, and came to a paved road. She pulled the wheel out of her backpack, spun and turned the way it said—left. She came to a roundabout and spun the wheel again.

It led her back along the road she had just come down. She thought how the wheel had led her to Jackie, but had also taken her to Target where she was recognized. By driving back the same way she felt that she was asking to get caught. Still she followed it. At the next intersection, the wheel instructed her to turn right. She drove toward the mountain. The horses grazed off to her left. The wheel told her to turn right again. Anne had twisted out of the old seatbelt and was standing on the seat again. Lily didn't dare stop to put her back in. "Sit down, Anne," Lily said and signed. Anne shook her head. "No, ma, no." Lily thought how, if she was still with Nathan, she would have tried to celebrate with him that their child was saying words. "No, ma, no" was almost a sentence. She smiled but also found tears standing in her eyes as she drove along the edge of the mountains until the city of Ogden came closer, with more houses to either side. She drove along the street, Harrison Boulevard, until she came to a sign that said Weber State University.

She thought about her haphazard, random pathway to get to the university, and she felt frustrated. It would have been easier to get a ride straight to here from the hospital. She turned into a parking lot, stopped the truck, lifted Anne and the stroller down, and walked toward the buildings. In front of the first building was a map, and she found the student center—where she might find out about a student going north at the end of the semester. She was desperate enough, that instead of going directly there, she turned and walked the other direction to a grocery store. She took a bagel and a banana, a small bottle of milk. Then she sat on the floor in the back and gave part of the food to Anne and shoveled part in her own mouth.

A couple of customers saw her and went another direction, but none of them turned her in. *Never again,* she promised herself, *will I be so stupid.* She knew it was an empty promise.

Back at the student center Lily asked the information desk about a rideshare board. Behind the desk sat a girl, who managed to look both chipper and bored as she said, "It's online now." She told Lily how to find the webpage. Lily walked to the library and went to a computer, where she called up Google Maps. She took a breath, looked at Anne, her white and pink face. "Here we go, Baby Peach."

She spun the wheel. North. So her destination was Idaho, Montana, Canada, or Alaska. She spun the wheel for distance. This time she didn't write down zero. It came up on the sixteenth spot, 987 miles. She used the online map and took a minute to determine that 987 miles was just north of Maskwacis, Alberta. A little more research showed her it was a town between two Cree reserves, a site of gang violence and suicide.

"Maybe we'll be invisible there," she said to Anne, who said a whole string of sounds that Lily couldn't translate.

Within a minute, Lily found someone online who was going to Edmonton about 44 miles farther north than Maskwacis. She asked to use the reference-desk phone and called the number. A young man answered, "Chris here."

"It's about the rideshare. I'm Amy Monson. I'll pay half the gas."

"Good. That's about $125. I'm glad you called, because I'm leaving tonight after my last final."

She knew that amount was more than half the cost of gas, unless he was driving an old tank of a Cadillac.

"It's just me, my daughter, only going to Butte." She was going all the way into Alberta, but she didn't want anyone to know where she was going, so she'd stop in Butte and try to take a train or a bus the rest of the way.

"The cost is the same."

"Of course," she said.

"Deal," he gave her details and hung up.

Now she just needed to find a way to get $125. She walked out of the library and someone stopped, staring at her. She looked straight at them and smiled. She didn't think it worked this time, so she just kept walking. She pushed the stroller through the bookstore, past short lines of people selling their books back after the end of summer classes. She just wanted to find a place where she could be alone with Anne and think. Upstairs in the student building was a series of conference rooms, most of them empty. She sat on the floor and played with Anne's toes, while she sang "This Little Piggy." Then she lay on her back and lifted the child above her, face-to-face. Anne giggled and babbled. After hearing Anne say actual words, Lily listened carefully, but she still couldn't understand.

Lily didn't know how she'd get from Butte to Canada, but she'd worry about that later. Now she had to get money.

She spun the wheel and went west from the university. It was easy to shoplift, stores counted it into the cost of their merchandise, but it wasn't so easy to get cash. She put Anne on her hip and walked along the street. She thought about Nathan's face in the courtroom, about the way she'd felt when her cash card didn't work, when her car was gone, when Brock wouldn't let her in the house. The anger and hurt made her weep. She stopped the first person.

"My car just ran out of gas and the cash machine ate my debit card. I don't know why." She sobbed, bewildered and washed over with sorrow at the state of her life. As she let herself go into that sorrow, she wondered if she'd be able to pull back out when she needed to. "I'm just trying to get to Salt Lake to my sister's house. Then I'll be safe."

"No," the man said. "I've heard that scam before." He turned his back on her. She kept the tears coming out of her eyes. Anne looked at her and started crying also. A woman approached. "My car ran out of gas I just need enough to get to Salt Lake. I'll be safe at my sister's."

The person ducked her head and walked on.

But the third person gave her $10. Then she had four more rejections. Then $20, $10, $5. A mother with a child the same age as Anne. A businessman in a suit, and a street person, which she was proud of, because she fooled even him. She walked into a shop but left when they lifted the phone. After an hour she was tired to her core, but she had $150.

She walked back to the university. One man stopped and stared at her as she went past. She wanted to flip him off, shove her finger in his face, but she smiled and looked away.

She started toward the library but went another direction because the library had only one entrance and exit. She headed for another building, a science building, and got onto the second floor. She put Anne down, and she toddled to a display case where there were rows of insects displayed. Above the cases were drawings of butterflies and moths. Anne stood with her hand on the glass. She laughed and pointed, turned her head to look at Lily. "Ma." Lily looked out the window and back at her daughter, out again. About fifteen minutes later two police cars drove up with a third, unmarked car following. Two men and a woman got out—plainclothes. Anne walked back, babbling in a whiny tone. Lily held Anne close to keep her from fussing.

She knew she had to change the meeting place of her ride north, which had been planned for the front of the student union, which is where all the policemen headed. She grabbed Anne and walked to the other end of the science building. An office door was open with a receptionist and a phone. Lily slowed herself, calmed her breathing. "Can I use your phone?" She smiled. The secretary turned her phone around and Lily dialed the number.

"Chris here."

She spoke slowly, trying to keep her voice from shaking. "I need to meet you at my cousin's house instead. Can you come to get me there?"

"What's wrong with the student building?"

"It's not a good place to give my baby a nap. My sister's is. We don't want to drive with a cranky baby."

"Okay. Give me the address."

"I—I don't have it, because I have never been there. I was going to stay there overnight, but now that you're giving me a ride, I don't need to. I still want to see her, I just have a phone number."

Lame, lame, lame.

Pause. "Whatever."

"I'll call you with the address at seven, just before we leave."

Another pause. "Okay. Just as long as you help pay for gas I don't care what you do. Pay it up front."

"Fine," said Lily.

She walked out the back of the building, circling away from the student union and then turning west toward the commercial streets. She went into the first department store she could find. She went up the escalator to the clothing level in the middle of people. "We're going to play hidey hole," she said to Anne, who wanted to get down. She toddled toward a rack of dresses and stood behind them, only her feet showing.

"Good job, Baby." Lily lifted her, and they sat against a shirt bin. Then she rocked Anne in the stroller until she fell asleep. Every few minutes she moved to another place, standing and rocking Anne, through the afternoon. Every second she thought someone would recognize her, but nobody did.

At six she left the store and stood in the front entrance, where she spun the wheel—west-northwest. Walking in that direction, she crossed Harrison Boulevard. She passed the stores on that street and entered the neighborhoods. After a few more minutes of walking, she came to a house with no cars in the driveway. She went in the backyard and tried the rear door. Locked. With a rock she broke the back window and opened the door. She cursed herself for taking the chance of breaking into a house where someone could come back any second. Even if they didn't recognize her, they would call the police. Or Chris might get suspicious and call the police. Too many chances.

She checked the address of the house on the opposite side of the street. Luckily the house had a landline, which she used to phone Chris. She hoped that he wasn't watching the news, that he wasn't going to turn her in for a reward. No student would be like Jackie, who thought that letting Lily and Anne continue on their way was more important than what $20,000 could buy. That was a rare woman.

She got some food out of the fridge and cupboards, made a package of apples, carrots, yoghurt, bread, and other food she could eat on the long trip, and put it in a couple of plastic grocery bags.

Will Chris come alone? What are the chances that a university student from Canada taking finals and packing to leave has watched the news sometime in the past two days? Not a huge chance, but he doesn't have to have watched the news himself. When Elizabeth Smart was taken, people couldn't talk about anything else. Someone might have told him about the crazy person, the criminal, who had kidnapped her own child. I estimate it's probably about equal chances. The coin spins in the air and falls to the ground.

TWELVE

At five minutes to eight, someone pulled up to the front of the house she was hiding in. She could only see a man in the driver's seat, and two smaller heads in the back. She gathered Anne and fled out the back door. The gate on the far side of the house was stuck, so she ran back across the backyard and waited until the car doors slammed and the door to the house swung shut. Finally, she dared walk out through the carport and down the street. She walked about a hundred yards before she turned and came back, wheeling Anne in the cheap stroller. She stopped when she came to the house with the address she'd given Chris. It was a split level, with weathered wood around the doors and some kind of siding on the walls, an ugly house. She passed it and ducked to the blind side of the next house, where there was only a bathroom window high above her head. From there she could see the street clearly. Before long a car pulled up and stopped. A young man got out and started walking toward the front door. He was a little taller than Lily, with slight build. She looked up and down the street and saw no one suspicious. She walked around the side of the house to the back of the car. "Chris," she said. "Chris Druby? I'm already out here. We were waiting for you."

She looked at the house across the street, where she'd broken in. The lights were on, but the drapes drawn, so she couldn't see inside. She expected that any second the man with the two children would see the broken door window and would call the police. She hoped he would look around a minute to see what was missing—just food.

Chris frowned and walked back to the car.

"Where's your stuff?"

She spread her arms wide. "This is it."

He shook his head, but walked back and climbed in the driver's seat.

"It's a long story," she said.

"No child seat? I'm not driving her without a child seat."

At first she didn't know what to say. *I've been so busy begging and breaking into a house that I just haven't had space to think of every damn thing.* But finally she found the words: "I'm planning on buying one as we leave Ogden." She climbed into the car, holding Anne on her lap.

The man across the street was peering out his blinds, talking on the phone.

Chris stared at her, clearly unhappy about breaking even this small law. "Okay, so long as we don't drive on a busy road. Where to?"

"What's close?"

He looked at his phone and then started driving. "You have money for your share of the gas?"

"Yes," she said. She put $125 in the space below the CD player.

He pulled in to the parking lot of a Target, which made her nervous because of her close call in the one in Layton. She went inside. Some of the car seats were in boxes, some were out for display, with price tags on them. She set one on the floor. A man came up and said, "Can I help you?"

"Is this one certified to be safe?" she said.

He bent and read the tag. "Yes," he said. "The American Pediatrics Society and the American Safety Association."

"Okay," she said. "I don't want to get it unless it's safe."

"It's safe," he said. "It seems to fit her all right, but you can adjust the straps when she gets bigger."

"I don't know," Lily said. "Are you sure this plastic is strong?" She bent the back of the seat.

"Strong *and* flexible," he said.

"I want to look at these others."

"Fine," he said. She took Anne out of that one and put her in another chair. She spent some time adjusting the straps. "I'll be over here if you need anything." He walked the next aisle over and started fiddling with the cribs. She thought he was keeping his eye on her.

She took Anne out and smiled at the man, waving toward him. "Thanks."

As soon as he turned away, she picked up the first chair and walked into the next aisle. She tore off the price tag, put Anne back in the chair, noticing it was one that could be carried by a handle. She walked toward the exit. "I can ring you up over here," said a cashier.

"I didn't find what I wanted," said Lily. She just kept walking. The cashier started toward her, then turned to lift the phone. Lily turned the corner of the building and ran toward the car. She knocked on the window, and Chris opened the back door. She climbed in with Anne, put the seatbelt around the chair, forcing herself to move slowly, with smooth motions. She said, "All set," as she buckled herself in. The cashier and a man in a white shirt and tie walked down the sidewalk, peering into the parked cars. "I'll ride back here for a while, if that's all right." Maybe they had Chris's car on camera, her getting inside. She couldn't worry about that now.

"Fine with me," he said. "I'll drive two hours, then it's your turn."

He pulled out of the parking lot. She ducked down as they passed the two people from the store.

Anne sang a song with a wandering tune and indistinguishable language. Lily thought the sound was lovely beyond words. She hoped Anne's song wouldn't bother Chris.

In fifteen minutes they were on the freeway going north. Lily peered up over the seat and saw that Chris was going only five miles over the speed limit; she didn't need to worry about being stopped by the police. She let the air in her lungs out with a long sigh. Flying north at 75 miles an hour felt like heaven. For the first time she felt like she might make it. And she had a place to be, a car. For at least fifteen hours, she wouldn't have to drag Anne back and forth from one street to another.

After about an hour, they crossed the boundary into Idaho, leaving Utah behind. She smiled and leaned back. She shut her eyes and felt herself drifting from any waking reality. She woke when Chris pulled off the freeway on one of the Idaho Falls

Exits. "Your turn. I'll stay up here so I don't disturb—what's her name, your baby?"

"Val. Short for Valerie."

He sat in the front, passenger seat. "Really?" He leaned back and went immediately to sleep. She was too weary to care if he believed her or not. She talked in a soft voice to Anne, who fussed for a while and then went to sleep as well. Lily hoped she'd sleep the whole night. To keep herself awake she crunched carrots.

She worried about how to get into Canada. Nathan would certainly have gotten some kind of alert put on her driver's license and passport. It would not help after all the trouble to get stopped at the border and carried back to Salt Lake. It probably wasn't possible to walk around the border station, so the crossing worried her.

Finally, about midnight, it was Chris's turn to drive. Lily stayed in the front seat, which she could recline. When they were rushing toward Canada again, she made herself relax. She looked across at Chris and thought about how long it had been since she'd just chatted with a person—a week, a month? "Are you Mormon?"

He shook his head.

"A lot of Mormons live near Calgary, right?"

"Mostly over by Cardston."

"Why Weber State?" Lily asked.

"They have a good nursing program. I got a scholarship there."

"Do you have a girlfriend?"

He looked at her. "Do you have a husband?"

She shrugged. "Will you graduate soon?"

"This is my last year. I'm just going home for a couple of weeks before school starts in fall."

"What kind of nursing do you want to do?"

"Geriatric," he said. "I want to be a hospice nurse."

She was silent a while. "That seems like a hard job, watching people die."

He shrugged. "A time to be useful. People face the unknown and are terrified."

She watched the lights flash on the lines on the freeway. "Do you think there's something beyond?"

"No," he said.

"So you're not even agnostic," she said.

"No," he said. "There'd be some pattern, I mean an empirical pattern, something observable. Some order that is external to us. I think we impose order on a universe that has no order."

"So you give order to the last months of someone's life?"

He nodded.

"I can't think of anything more important."

"Who are you really?" he said.

She glanced at his face and felt like telling him the truth. But what part of the truth?

He frowned.

"I am trying to get away from my husband," she said.

"You're going to cause me trouble," he said.

"It could happen." She nodded.

"Damn," he said. "I can't afford this."

"I know." Her heart was beating too fast for her to think straight. "But I'm just going to Butte."

"Would be good for you to have medical care," he said. "You'd have it in Canada. You could get false ID in Calgary or Edmonton."

"I could get false ID in Montana. I'm frightened to cross the border."

He nodded.

She leaned back and pretended to sleep. Should she change her plan? She didn't know, but the thought of asking him to stop in the middle of the night and let her out terrified her. If he used his phone, she'd act. To help herself relax she counted to ten, back down, three times.

She didn't know about God. Every piece of scripture she knew of showed God as a patriarch, someone vested in his own authority, someone who could get jealous and angry and hated sin. The New Testament Christ was much like a mother, but he had been crucified for preaching the revolution. They thought he was power hungry. The Islamic God didn't like women much. Maybe physical and psychic matter was recycled like the Hindus thought. *Whatever*, she thought, mimicking Chris, a brisk but apparently good-hearted atheist, who seemed disinclined to turn her over to the police. That was a comfort, the strongest comfort she'd had since leaving Jackie. Had it just been that afternoon? Now she was headed to a place far from Utah. Nathan wouldn't know for sure which direction she had gone. From Ogden, she could have gone northeast to Logan and into Wyoming, east toward Cheyenne or Denver, southeast to Albuquerque, south to Phoenix, southwest to Los Angeles, west to Reno or San Francisco, northwest toward Oregon.

Nathan might think that, because she went north to Ogden, she'd continue northward, but he'd still have to consider the other directions she might go. She fell asleep and dreamed about Canada, which she'd never been to and which she imagined as a great flat land.

THIRTEEN

It was pale dawn by the time they got to Butte. Lily had seen a glow in the night sky for some time as the freeway wound through the mountains. Chris exited onto another freeway, but she still couldn't see many houses. Suddenly the freeway ended, right in what seemed to be a residential neighborhood. "Where do you want to be dropped off?"

She didn't know. "Right," she said. "Turn right." Before long they came to a Safeway and just across from it was a low, official-looking building. "Here." She pointed to the building. "This is where I'm going."

"You're going to a Safeway? It's probably not open yet. It isn't even open."

She pointed to someone who had gotten out of her car and was opening the doors. "Will be soon. I need to get a few things and then I'll wait on the steps."

"You don't trust me," he said.

She looked at him, but didn't say anything.

Chris handed her back her money. "You need this more than I do." She considered staying in the car and driving into Canada with him, but she had to figure out how to cross without using her passport. Also, it was her principle now not to follow her trust in anyone as a guide for decisions.

She got out of the car and unstrapped the car seat from the back, gently so that Anne wouldn't wake. "Thank you." She turned away and took the handle of the seat, carrying Anne toward the front doors of the Safeway. She heard the car pull away behind her. She wanted to turn and wave goodbye, but she shut it down.

She thought of where she might go, a woman's shelter, straight to the bus station, to the train station, or to the university to get a different rideshare. She was too tired to think of other options, so she spun the wheel to decide. She stuck her finger in the wheel—woman's shelter.

Unable to see the woman who had already gone in, Lily waited until someone else came, a young man, a little younger than Chris. He wore a goatee and a bland face.

"We're not open yet."

"I'm trying to find the women's shelter."

"I don't know anything about that." He turned away.

The woman who had first opened the door came back. She had silver hair at her temples, the rest the darkest brown. "What's the problem? We're not open yet." Her mouth was flat. Clearly, she had so much work to do that she didn't have time for Lily.

Lily smiled and explained that she had left her husband. Finally, the woman's face softened. "Let's look up the closest one." To the young man, she said, "You have something you should be doing. Do you need me to tell you what it is?" The young man shook his head. Since Lily had first seen him, his face had showed no emotion. What would it be like to pass through day stacked on day without being ruffled, passing through the water of time unaffected? It seemed inviting to Lily.

The woman took Lily to the customer service counter and showed her the map on the computer. "We are here. The shelter is here. Safe Haven, about a mile away, straight up Montana Street."

"Thank you."

"If you give me a minute, I'll drive you."

"I've been sitting all night. I need to walk." Lily looked down at Anne, who still slept, a blessing for which she was grateful. She tried to balance the car seat on top of the small stroller, but it kept tipping off, so she had to carry both. By the time she had passed four side streets, Lily's arms ached, and she wished she'd accepted the woman's offer.

The shelter was in a small house with no sign. She checked the number above the door and the street sign, confirming that she was in the right place. A red brick building overshadowed the small house on one side. The front door was locked and instead of knocking, Lily sat on the doorstep and waited for the shelter to open. Even though she was warm enough and weary enough, she couldn't go to sleep. She worried that Nathan had called every women's shelter in every direction from Ogden. How many calls would that be if he just called cities big enough to have a shelter? Maybe hundreds. She knew he couldn't do it all himself, but he could have had his secretarial employees make the calls. Could he get the police to contact shelters? When the door opened, what could she say to the managers of the shelter, what explanation could she give that would make them not think of the woman who had taken her child from Salt Lake City?

She calmed herself with the wonderful thought of breakfast and a bed with walls around her that were made for someone like her, someone escaping a bad husband. She had gone in a random direction and her pathway away from Nathan was clear only to herself. If they started questioning her or if she caught the faintest hint of suspicion from anyone, she would escape again. She believed that as a committed and inveterate liar, she had the ability to sense any subterfuge from another person. She also knew that such a belief, based on nothing but her own certitude, could be untrustworthy.

She woke to the sound of the door being unlocked from the inside. "What are you doing?" a woman said, surprised.

Anne woke and looked around, ready to cry, so Lily took her into her arms.

"I left my husband last night. I walked here from across the city that way." She pointed toward where the sun was rising. "I'd be dead if I stayed home."

"How long have you been here?"

"Just an hour."

"You should have pounded on the door. My room is right here and I would have let you in. Come in now. We're just having breakfast."

Lily made the sign for food. "Do you want some breakfast?" Anne nodded her head. "Yes," she said distinctly. She didn't make the sign back and started walking into the house, but Lily picked her up. The child squirmed and shouted until Lily put her down. She took Anne's hand and led her into the hallway.

"I'm Mary," said the woman, who was blonde-haired, fading to gray. She had a round and friendly face.

Lily smiled. "Bridget, ah—"

Mary held up her hand. "No last names. We don't need to know where you're coming from."

"Val." Lily nodded toward Anne. "I'm Bridget."

She and Anne sat at a table with a few other women, but she didn't look at their faces and hoped they wouldn't look at hers. Mary found a highchair for Anne, who slapped her hands against its tray and shouted "yes" in a high pitch until they put food in front of her, a banana, cut up, and some oatmeal. Lily kept waiting for the police to come in the door, but she forced herself still until they had both eaten.

When she finished a great weariness overwhelmed her.

She found Mary. "Can I have a bed? I've hardly slept."

"It won't be very quiet, we have people coming in and out."

"Won't matter," said Lily.

She was led to the corner of a large room full of beds; she lay down with Anne sitting next to her and was out within a few seconds.

Emmanuel Levinas, who is my Virgil on this journey of self-exploration, hopefully not into the depths of hell, built many of his ideas on Hebraic traditions of hospitality. When the stranger comes to the door, the human obligation is to let them enter, as Mary does with Lily.

From the mouth of his tent Abraham sees three men approaching, so he rushes inside and asks Sarah to make bread; he kills a calf and tells a servant to dress it. In examining this story, Levinas points to the fact that Abraham welcomes the guests without conditions—not knowing they are heavenly visitors—even though the visit interrupts his routine. The host willingly opens the home to potential danger: Are these three visitors murderers or is Lily an insane kidnapper? Neither Abraham nor Mary demanded to know. By inviting in the stranger, the homeowner relinquishes a measure of sovereignty and identity. The host invites the Other inside, and the nature of the home is changed. Similarly, if we open ourselves to strangers, even those we don't invite inside our homes, their presence affects who we are. For Levinas ethics is becoming vulnerable to other people, generally through searching the face of the Other and responding with hospitality and love. This act causes the boundaries between the home and the world to become less defined, more permeable, and the home becomes a place open to risk. When this happens a greater diversity of futures is possible. But the idea of opening to everyone unnerves me. If I avoid opening myself completely to my own family, how can I manage when I meet a stranger? So I'm as stuck in my own identity as the thick-bodied woman Lily dreamed about, standing eternally to the side of the trail—hopeless. I didn't invent that woman. Last year when it was early spring and the nights were still bitter cold, I rode my bike up the canyon and was startled by this inscrutable and ambiguous person standing not far off the trail. The image still haunts me. They were homeless, but it isn't just my lack of doing much about homelessness that makes me unable to forget the person. It was their eternal changelessness that still affects me. The idea that nothing will ever change for that person means that it could be also true of me—a terrifying vision.

When she woke, disoriented, Anne was gone—a fist around her heart. "Anne," she called, before remembering she'd said her name was Val. She ran into the hallway and found Mary. "My child. Where is she?" Mary took her elbow and led her to a room where a group of children played with toys. Lily lifted Anne into her arms. "Mamm," said Anne in words and signs, both at once. "Ma, ma, mamm." She patted Lily's face.

"You should have told me you were taking her," said Lily.

"I looked up and she was standing in the door to my office. I tried to talk to her, but she didn't respond to her name, so I just put her in here to play. I didn't mean to scare you."

Lily nodded, still panicked, still breathing hard.

After lunch, Lily sat in the doorway of the playroom, while Anne played with five other children. One girl had gathered all the toys she could reach and held them on her lap. Anne played by herself with a ball that made a musical noise when she turned it over in her hands. A boy sat next to her and put his hand on the ball. Anne gave it to him, and he gave it back.

Lily considered what to do next. The wheel had directed her to go north into Canada, but she didn't know how to cross the border without being caught. She didn't know whether she needed a passport or just a driver's license. Soon Anne came back to her, leaving the ball behind.

Lily found a drawer with paper and markers inside, so she took them to the table with Anne. Lily made a swirl of shapes and colors. She wasn't sure how Anne would react, but soon the girl started drawing her own clumsy swirls on the paper in front of her. Lily was suddenly jerked back to a memory, one that had happened maybe a dozen times, of sitting on the floor of their Park City house, drawing with Anne on her lap.

Mid-morning Lily pushed Anne in the stroller to the city library and got picture books for her. She found the computers and spread the books on the carpet next to her. Anne turned over the first book and opened it. After finishing, she put the book back. She started to get up, but Lily said, "Just sit there. Mommy has work to do." Anne looked at her and went back to looking at the books.

Lily got on the US customs web site and the Canadian one. She also looked up the specific process for going through customs and immigration at Sweet Grass, where I-15 crossed the border. Anne stood at her leg and started pulling at her sleeve. "Yes, Mama, yes." Then she signed her hunger.

"I've got to teach you more words." Anne kept pulling at her. "In a minute, Baby. Val."

"Babb," said Anne, looking proud.

"Oh, all grown up," said Lily. "Let Mommy work."

She got more books, which occupied Anne for a while longer. Soon Anne was pulling on her sleeve and shouting, "Yes, Mama, yes." Lily left the library, pushing Anne in the stroller back to the women's center. She didn't like to do it, but she left Anne in the playroom, while she sat in the dining room where she could be alone and think.

Trying to cross into Canada would be dangerous. She had learned she couldn't cross with just a driver's license. She would need a passport or some other document such as a Permanent Resident Card. She would face an immigration agent, who would probably scan her passport in the computer and search the National Crime Information Center database. She might not be in that database yet, but she had to assume that an Amber alert would notify border officials. She also needed documents for Anne, which she hadn't realized before.

She decided she had three options—figure out how to forge documents herself, hire a forger to make documents, or sneak across the border, either by hiding in the trunk of a car or the back of a truck or by trying to walk across in another location. She read about some Canadian kids hiking who had crossed into the US without knowing and had been picked up by US border patrol. All the options seemed dangerous. A criminal forger would be untrustworthy by definition. Such a person might look her up and turn her in for the reward Nathan had offered. So what could she do? She finally decided to use the randomizing device. She spun the wheel, closed her eyes, and stuck her finger in the spoke. Her finger lay in the eighth slot, a good sign because the number eight signified to her calmness and continuation. Maybe she got the idea from the sign for infinity, an 8 on its side. Sometimes when counting backward and forward didn't calm her, that it helped to chant eight, eight, eight, eight, eight. Eight was in the second section of the wheel, so she would find a forger.

At dinner she looked around and saw a Latina, who ate with her two children across the room. Lily sat next to her and smiled but didn't try to talk. She had seen the same woman in the playroom. After a half hour, Lily scooted close to the woman. "Have you been here long?" The woman just stared at her. Finally, she shook her head. Lily thought she probably didn't speak much English, and she clearly didn't trust Lily.

The next morning early, Lily left Anne in the play room of the women's shelter. Warnings went off in her blood and brain, but she ignored them. She took the bus to Home Depot and found where men waited who hoped to get hired for the day. They all wore working clothes, most carried leather gloves. Most were minorities, Asians or Latinos. She tried talking to several of the men, but they ignored her. Finally, a tall, dark-skinned man said, "We want to work. We don't want trouble."

Walking back to the bus stop, she saw a taxi, and thinking that taxi drivers knew a lot about what went on in a town, she flagged it down, giving him the address of the women's center. The driver was not Anglo, probably a Middle-easterner, so she leaned forward from the back seat. "I need help getting documents so I can cross the border into Canada. Do you know where I can go?"

He shrugged his shoulders. Either he didn't know, or something about the way she asked made him suspicious. She felt foolish at profiling people, but she didn't know how to get in touch with someone who helped get documents for people.

She had the taxi let her off a block away from the center. She trotted to the center and strode quickly through the hallway to the playroom. When she saw Anne still there, playing happily, she let her breath out. She picked Anne up, who tried to twist away and continue playing, but she held her close and left the shelter. She held Anne close to her, but Anne said, "No," clearly wanting to walk again, so Lily held her hand. Anne wanted to stop every few steps and give a small oration, but strain as she might, Lily couldn't understand her. She felt the urge to hurry Anne, but quieted that and let herself relax into walking slow with her child.

"You have a new name because you're in a new place. It's Val." She knelt on one knee and looked into Anne's face. "Val." She pointed to Anne. "Mommy." She put her hand flat on her own chest. "Val. Mama. Val, Mama. Val, Val, Val, Val, Val."

She stopped at the library and looked up immigration lawyers on the internet, called one up. "I'm writing an article on undocumented immigration to the US vs undocumented immigration to Canada. Where can I go to find people to interview?"

He would tell her nothing. He probably assumed she was from ICE.

Leaving the library, she got Anne some candy because she needed to focus. They sat on a bench off Main Street. Anne ate the candy and got it all over her hands. She then tried to climb onto Lily's lap, but her hands were sticky so Lily held her away. "Yes, Ma," said Anne. "Yes."

"Your hands aren't clean."

"Han," she said.

Anne was tired now, so Lily put her in the old stroller. In the center, she washed Anne's hands and sat rocking her baby, who lay against Lily's chest, sucking her small thumb. Lily had wasted a whole day and was no closer to finding someone who could forge documents for her. She could have done it herself in that time, she thought. She could scrape the numbers off her passport and laminate new numbers on. But what numbers? How could she duplicate the bar across the bottom of numbers and symbols?

At dinner the Latina finally smiled back.

"I am trying to immigrate to Canada," Lily said, "but I can't get a legal passport."

The woman shook her head. "No hablo Inglés."

Later when Lily got up to leave, the woman touched her on the arm. "Bus station."

"Who? Who should I contact at the bus station?"

The woman just shook her head, lips pressed together.

Lily spent the next day sitting at the bus station. She watched the people. Soon she noticed a man, an Anglo who sat across the room from her. Occasionally he got up and went out. Once she followed him and observed him talking to a group of Latinos.

Later, after they had both returned to the waiting room, she walked over to him. "I want to emigrate to Canada, but I can't do it legally. Can you help me?"

"I don't know about that. I have nothing to do with that."

She went back to her seat, holding Anne on her lap. But at the end of the day, he came over. He was small, slender, confident. He looked straight into her eyes as he spoke to her.

"Why not just apply if you want to immigrate to Canada?"

"Two reasons," she said. "I need to get there quickly. And second I have a criminal record. As a teenager, I was a shoplifter. I was with a friend who was careless, and I was caught as well." She shrugged.

"It could work. Canada wants immigrants, the United States does not." He stared at her. "I am a fool to deal with you."

She took a breath. "You think I'm ICE because I'm not the right color?"

"No. If you were an ICE agent, you'd be Latino."

"So you have a rule against helping white people?"

"No. I'm just—ah—curious." He stood. "Walk with me."

They walked half a block to a large public building; "Civic Center" said a sign above the front door. They sat on a bench and he took a laptop out of his backpack.

"A thousand dollars," he said.

"You think that because I'm white I have that much money?"

He didn't answer, so she got up to leave.

"What do you have?" She took out her dress and shoes.

He shook his head. "No."

She thrust the dress at him. "Neiman Marcus. $1700."

"It's not worth that to me."

"Feel the fabric." He did so and looked back at her. "The shoes were $1200."

She found herself sweating. If he looked carefully at the news from Salt Lake, he would know he could get much more money by turning her in.

"Give me your passport," he said. "I'll change it to a number that will get you through."

She took it out of her pack and handed it to him.

"So let's plan your strategy. What skills do you have?"

"Skills?"

"Like for the skilled worker program. Something you know about so you could answer questions if the border agent asks."

"I make art."

"Useless," he said.

"Teaching art."

"Just as useless."

"Shoplifting," she said.

He glared at her. "Be serious." He looked at Anne. "Childcare. You have a job offer to do childcare in Edmonton and you need Permanent Resident Travel Documents to get there. You want to live in Canada, and you will use the time to apply for a Permanent Resident Card and eventually citizenship. Can you remember those terms?"

She nodded.

"Where should you be from?"

"Arizona."

"Why do you want to go to Canada?"

"I have this job, and I want to have better healthcare, and I'm tired of the racist and sexist politics of the US."

"Don't overdo it. Just healthcare. Forget those other things. Politics doesn't help convince a border agent." He stood. "Meet me here tomorrow morning at nine. In the meantime find a ride to Canada."

"I was going to travel by bus."

He shook his head. "Go by car. Cross between four and six in the afternoon. The agents just pass people through."

"Do you mean your documents won't pass examination?"

"They will pass. This is just extra insurance. I will have your travel document, a Montana birth certificate for your child, and a letter from your husband saying you have his permission to take your daughter to Canada."

"Wouldn't it be better to say I don't have a husband?"

He shook his head. "But don't show the letter unless you need to."

After she left the forger, she walked back to the city bus stop. They only had to wait a minute. "We're going to have food now," she told Anne.

"Food."

"Yes, Baby."

"Yes. Food."

They walked into the center, which had come to feel a little like home. They were just finishing dinner when Mary sat next to her. "A productive day?"

Lily shrugged.

"Your husband has custody of your child," said Mary.

Lily nodded.

"I received a bulletin yesterday and looked up the story. I think he sent one to every woman's center in Utah and every surrounding state."

Lily waited.

"You're not crazy," Mary said. "And you're not hurting your child." She stood and left the room.

Lily had to wait for nearly half an hour before her hands stopped shaking. She lay on her bed, listening to Anne breathe and imagining that at any minute the police would come through the door. Anne lay next to her, a small warm body. As soon as the room was quiet, she rose, took her backpack and Anne, and let herself quietly out the front door. It took her two hours to walk to the bus station, where she bought a ticket, for ten the next morning. It took all her money, except for change. She wanted to dye her hair again, but didn't want to walk to find a store, didn't want to face the hassle and mess of dying it in a bus station bathroom.

She found a bench and tried to sleep. At about eight in the morning Anne started crying and wouldn't stop. Lily used her last coins to get a candy bar, which she fed to Anne. Lily pushed Anne, twisting in the stroller and screaming, to the Civic Center. She started to believe that Anne would never stop shrieking. Intellectually she knew that wasn't true, but emotionally, she could imagine shaking the child to make her stop. She felt her intellect taking over. *Men shake children, not me.* She knew it wasn't even men, but impatient men. Not all men but just those who couldn't use intellect to control emotion.

Holding the child, who arched her back and flailed with her arms, Lily day-dreamed of the day, about a month before the divorce trial, that she had taken Anne to the Uinta mountains. She had stopped in Kamas to buy a fishing pole, some worms, and a license; she also asked them for directions to a lake she could try. She had gone fishing once when she'd lived with her aunt, and her cousin had showed her how to set up the pole, so she knew at least that much. She spread a quilt on the ground and then got the pole ready and cast it out about twenty yards, the farthest she could manage. Anne wouldn't stay on the quilt and kept crawling toward the edge of the lake, patting her hand on the mud, dipping it into the cold water. Lily didn't catch any fish, even though people all around her were pulling them in. But it had been a sunlit July day, cool because they were in the mountains. The green of the pines, the blue of the sky, the white and gray of the rocks were all burned into her memory, as was the sound of the small waves lapping on the shore, the pat pat of Anne's hand against the mud.

Finally, Anne stopped screaming and fell asleep, and Lily was left with her own thoughts. The memory of being with Anne in the mountains was so different from her memories of Nathan at the end of their marriage—him locking Anne in the closet, his calm, dead face. Without Nathan, she would never have gotten Anne, so was marrying him a mistake? In her life, it was about half and half—mindful acts and foolish mistakes had about the same success rate.

Her judgment of Nathan was one of the mistakes. After they had separated, while they waited for the divorce trial and he was living in an apartment near his work, Lily felt so disoriented about his transformation from knight to devil that she went to therapy. She had time for only a couple of sessions. The therapist was good, and, as if she were a deft masseuse, she quickly found a knot in Lily's psyche. As the tangle rose to the surface of Lily's mind through her conversation with Allison, the therapist, it seemed more and more bewildering. Why, if Lily was so fixed on independence, did she allow her life to be taken over by Nathan? She had felt abandoned by her father and mother, and her aunt's love was conditional. Was Nathan a replacement for her father—although more wealthy, confident, righteous? Was this why she let him control her life, take her out of her network of friends so she was alone? She never unraveled this distracting knot and, on the run with Anne, she still couldn't fathom why she had trusted him when he said the house was hers and that he wouldn't try to take Anne from her. Knowing she had believed him still sapped her self-confidence.

I hate making mistakes or taking risks, unnatural son of Eve that I am. Despite my therapist's efforts, I still hate screwing up or doing something that doesn't fit my vision of myself as a competent person. I would rather inhabit a universe where learning doesn't depend on making mistakes. I'm talking about how I feel, not how I think. Intellectually, I admire Heidegger's stuckness, accepting our rough and uncertain state of being. Plato was fixated on ideal objects and a heaven-like state we can hardly imagine. I both desire and abhor the idea of passing through life as Adam would have, forever in an ideal Garden. I've made mistakes—convincing Karla to leave school and a wonderful scholarship when we first married so I could work a job I hated, shouting at my children before I found an anti-depressant that could work, letting junior-high-school students bring chaos into my classroom when I first started teaching, losing contact with people I once treasured, and not telling nearly enough people who were selling bad ideas to go to hell. I wish for a life without these errors, but through them I've been forced to examine how I might balance my control and lack of control, my will to power and recognition that, as George Eliot put it, others have an "equivalent centre of self."

With someone else the same experiences would have resulted in a different psyche. This is the mystery—the ways Experience creates Being. Lily is a different being as a result of her choice to steal Anne than she would be if she took Nathan's offer of an apartment, becoming his vassal. Experience is encountering spacetime and Being is a function of Experience: $B = E^\infty$. Sensory experience transforms us in ways that abstraction doesn't. The poet Lance Larsen wrote, "This is thy errand tongue, to savor the world's flesh. Then translate beyond it." Sensations from fingertips, small bones of the ear, hairs of the nostril, cells at the back of the eyeball, taste buds. All these electrochemical processes establish pathways through the neurons. The brain sparks this way or that and all these motions create patterns. Somehow experience becomes flesh.

A branched stick Y is the smallest unit of binary experience, the smallest engine of possibility and the smallest machine of fiction. It's also the shape of the Hebrew letter ע, *ayin*—the eyes or the tears that spring from the eyes. The eyes are the brain's tongue and, with them, like worms, we devour timespace. The Hebrews, grand explicators, can unpack the shape of *ayin* as the will being shaped by the good or evil eye—two pathways. Lily would abhor this whole discussion of pseudo spirit-physics. She has only two criteria to judge the morality of an act: it must keep her and Anne together and it must help them survive.

FOURTEEN

At nine she was at the Civic Center, and soon the man walked to her bench and handed her a manila envelope. She looked through the documents. "Thank you."

He nodded and walked away, the dress over his arm, the shoes in his hand.

Back at the station, she sat waiting for the bus and watching the doorway. She knew she should obey the forger's advice and get a ride in a car, but she was too tired to do the work of looking for a rideshare, trying to connect with someone. She just wanted to get out of Butte.

Finally, it was time for the bus to load. She found a seat and stood Anne next to her so she could look out the window. Anne put both hands against the glass and watched the people passing. Lily scanned for policemen running through the bus station. She relaxed some when the driver backed up the bus and pulled out. She smelled the diesel through closed windows. They drove through downtown and joined the freeway in a few minutes. The woman across the aisle on the left crossed over and looked through the window. "What is it?" asked Lily.

"Whasit?" said Anne.

The other woman said, "Our Lady of the Rockies."

She pointed to a finger of white on top of the mountain to the east. It was an enormous statue, far away.

The coming sun lit Anne's hair.

"It's Mary, Mother of Jesus," said the woman.

Lily thought of Mary at the shelter. She, Chris, and Jackie had stirred something inside Lily that she thought was dead: faith in the ethical sense of another human being, the intuition to know when obeying the law was wrong.

The bus drove between mountains, through pine forests. The other people on the bus sat in their seats, not looking at each other. There was a pair of teenage girls, an old man with earbuds listening to music on his phone. A woman and two children, who played with matchbox cars in the aisle. Anne climbed down and tried to get past Lily's legs to join them.

"You'll fall," said Lily.

"Fa."

Anne crawled under the seat and came up in the next seat. She took one step and the moving bus toppled her so she fell on her bum. She tried again and made it up to the others. They looked at each other and then the older of the two children handed Anne one of the cars. Lily worried she'd put it in her mouth, but she didn't. She watched and then moved it back and forth on the floor. Soon the older child decided they should all march up and down the aisle, and then the bus driver asked Lily and the other woman to keep their children in their seats.

The woman in the next seat said to Lily, "It's hard for them to be still for so long. They need to be on grass where they can run around."

"Yes, she misses our backyard in Par—" Lily coughed. "Parowan."

"You Mormon?" the woman said. "I'm from Phoenix. On my way to Calgary."

"Used to be," Lily said. "My husband was a Mormon. More like a moron."

The other woman laughed. "My husband was a drunk. They all need something to believe in."

"Mean drunk?" asked Lily.

"Yes. Alternating sad and angry. Worst kind."

"Worst is a vain and self-centered man who worships himself," said Lily.

"But that's every man," said the woman, laughing.

When Anne wanted to sleep, Lily laid her across her lap. When she woke, Lily took her to a seat in the back, where, because of the smell of the toilet and the roar of the diesel engine, there were no other people sitting. She opened the documents and read her name. "We are going to a new place," said Lily. Anne searched her face, listening. "I need to tell you again. In this new place we are going to have new names. My name is Alice." She pointed to herself and signed "Mom." She placed her hand on her chest. "Alice, Alice, Alice."

Anne said, "Lice," and other words, babbling, which was probably how Lily's words seemed to her—sounds that only had meaning through inflection.

"Your name is—" Anne made more sounds, as if they were words and sentences. Lily hugged her. "Val. Still Val." It was a dangerous name, but it was useless to try to change to a new name for her everytime they moved to a new place. The child couldn't understand the need.

Eventually the mountains pulled back and the bus came out into a wide valley. Soon Lily realized it wasn't just a valley, but high plains. To the east were farms retreating in the distance, to the west were the Rockies. Now that she was within an hour of Canada, her worry increased about crossing the border. She was weary of watching for police cars every minute of the day. Twice that vigilance had paid off—when she had escaped from Target and the student center.

At the border the bus stopped in front of a building. Everyone unloaded and walked inside. She waited in line and soon came to the front, where the official glanced at her passport. "Where are you going?"

"Visiting my friend from college. She lives in Edmonton, and she needs a nanny."

"How long will you stay?"

"As long as she needs me. Maybe I'll apply for immigration and stay forever. That's what she wants me to do."

He stared at it, scanned it, and then handed it back to her. She walked away. At the door she glanced back to see if anyone was watching her. Nobody was. Still it was petrifying.

"You're paranoid," she told herself, but then remembered the saying that even the paranoid sometimes have real reason to fear.

Soon they were back on the bus and rolling away from the building. She smiled out the window; the forged documents had worked. Even though the officer had scanned her passport. She wondered how the forger could find numbers that wouldn't set off an alarm.

Lily had never trusted police, church leaders (except for her childhood bishop), school administrators, and others whose existence depended on enforcing abstract Law. Since she'd taken Anne, the people who helped her did so by contradicting legality and obeying some other sense of rightness.

How does someone determine right from wrong? Some readers of early drafts of this novel wanted me to have Lily punished for shoplifting, but these same readers didn't worry much about a much more serious violation of law—kidnapping. Also, they were not bothered by Jackie, Chris, and Mary aiding a criminal. These readers responded to something they felt about Lily's actions and decisions, which is the way most people make ethical decisions.

Some might say that ethics is primarily based not on emotion but on rationality, on deducing what will promote the most good for the most people; others say that we should rely more on experience, discovering what increases happiness for self and others. These ways of gaining knowledge of right and wrong also fit the general ways we gain any kind of knowledge—through reason or empiricism. Reasoned truth is definitional truth, which is not conditional on experience and is less subject to doubt. Adam may have been perfectly happy forever organizing the animals and plants in Eden. He named an animal and it was so, and he knew for certain that it was both true and good. Eve embraced something else entirely: experiential knowledge gained through trial and error. Of course, my comparison to Adam and Eve is bunk because both men and women use emotion, reason, and evidence from experience. In my life these three mingle, difficult to distinguish.

Before his work on ethics, Kant strove to move beyond the conflict between the disciples of Descartes (reasoned or definitional truth—a baby is a human) and the disciples of Bacon and Newton (experiential truth—having sex can produce babies). Kant searched for kinds of knowledge that condition how we view the world but are not discovered through experience. Our understanding of time and space, for example, is an aspect of our minds and does not come from either reason or experience. He wrote, "Space is not something objective and real, nor a substance, nor an accident, nor a relation; instead, it is subjective and ideal, and originates from the mind's nature in accord with a stable law as a scheme, as it were, for coordinating everything sensed externally." One implication of his thinking is that all our ways of knowing are limited; abstract reason is playing with meaning without much regard to things as they are in the world, and empiricism is gaining knowledge of the world through our senses and processed by our brains. Empirical truth is probable truth, true most of the time. We can't know the world independent of our subjective perception of it. One of my teachers said that Kant's ideas eventually resulted in the Romantic revolution, to the belief that the patterning of our minds is innate and subjective.

Kant determined that our conception of ethics is similar to our perception of time and space; knowing that it's wrong to hurt someone is different from either knowing "I am a human" or "That stove is hot." While both reason and experience might influence our decisions, the aptitude and propensity for making ethical judgment, Kant said, is built into the human psyche, hardwired. We are creatures who make ethical judgments, and these judgments are subjective, which doesn't mean that they are arbitrary. He also postulated that, because reason can only restate what is already known and because we can only apprehend the universe through our senses, we can't know scientifically whether there is pattern in the universe, ethical, divine, or otherwise. However, Kant thought that our pattern-creating, ethical nature implies that we were created by a pattern-creating, ethical entity—God.

He wrote two hundred and fifty years ago, but his questions still seem relevant to my exploration of how to walk mindfully into the future. As my eyes create good or evil, am I discovering order or imposing it? Who is wiser, asks Frank Waters in *The Man who Killed the Deer*, the shaman who observed the order behind the surface chaos or the one who sees chaos behind that order? Intellectually I embrace the idea of an ordered disorder in both ethics and reality, but as I drag my pilgrim flesh along my journey, I long for a simple pathway, where decisions are clear and life is free from obstacles and mishaps.

Before long the bus passed through Lethbridge and then drove on to Calgary, where Lily left the bus and the station. She walked with Anne across to a big supermarket on the far side of town and bought a poster board and marker. She was desperate to change her appearance, so she bought some dye, cut her hair even shorter, and dyed her hair auburn in the supermarket bathroom. She stripped the excess dye and water out of her hair with paper towels and then walked around outside until it was dry. She wrote "Edmonton" on the poster board and walked into the parking lot where she held up her sign. Soon someone stopped, a beefy man, and said, "I got my truck over here."

Lily shook her head.

"Ungrateful bitch."

She just shook her head again. Bastard, she thought, but didn't say. She couldn't afford to offend him more than she already had.

Then there was a woman and a child who stopped. Lily smiled and lifted Anne and followed the mother and child to a minivan. "I have no money to pay you."

The woman shrugged. "That's all right."

Lily buckled Anne's car seat in. Soon they drove north out of Calgary. The landscape looked the same as Montana.

"Where are you going in Edmonton?"

"I'm not. That's just the direction I want to go. I'm stopping in Maskwacis."

"Oh, yeah. The reserve town. Why there?"

"Found it on a map."

A pause.

"Not a safe place. There's gangs. They shot a child a couple years ago. They drove past this house where they thought somebody was staying. Shot up the whole front. The child was hit through the door. Not a good place to stop."

Lily thought about taking Anne to this place. Whether it was stupid or not, the wheel had helped her find Anne, Jackie, had gotten her across the border. "That's still where I'm going."

The woman stared at Lily's face and then turned to look at the road again. Lily thought about how hard it was to disappear on this earth. If someone from Edmonton had a friend in Salt

Lake and shared a picture on Facebook with this woman, she would remember because she had dropped Lily in the rough First Nation town, where no sensible Anglo went.

The woman pulled over at the sign for Maskwacis and dropped Lily and Anne off on the highway. Across the road was a shopping center, including a gas station, a post office, and a grocery store. Inside, Lily picked up a small bundle of grapes and glanced at the cashier, who watched her closely as she put them back down. Anne reached for her hand and patted it, talking all the while, and this time Lily recognized the word "want." Finally Anne signed for food. She pulled Anne out of the store. She felt her face burning and regretted going inside.

She pulled carrots from her backpack, but Anne chewed on one for a few seconds and spit it out. Lily looked around at the other buildings, a law office, a bank, a café, and an employment center, all in the same strip mall. It didn't seem like a rough town, just poor. The people in the store laughed and greeted each other.

She walked further away from the highway and soon came to a community center. Four women came out. They were early middle-aged, about forty with thick ankles and bellies. From their gloves and helmets, Lily figured they worked some kind of construction.

"I'm looking for a place to stay," said Lily. "Do you know anyone with a room to rent?" Anne reached her arms up and Lily lifted her.

The women looked at her. Two of them turned their backs.

One woman pushed through the others. "You lost?"

"No," Lily said. "I hitched here. This was as far as my ride went."

"Who did you hitch with? We would know them," one woman said.

"You going to keep hitching," said one of the other women. "You'd better get back out on the highway."

"I plan on staying here," said Lily.

They all looked at each other.

"So you are lost," said the woman with the phone. Her face was weathered, her skin a beautiful coffee color. "You must not care where you are."

"I just care where I'm not," said Lily. "Lost is good."

At this the women laughed.

"There's no place to rent here," said another woman. "It's the reserve, only Crees can live here."

"That's not hospitable," said the first woman. "Come to my place, I'm Suzanne Wolf. We'll figure out what to do." She walked across the street, and Lily followed her along a long curve of houses. They came to a lane, and Suzanne walked down it to her house, which was alone, next to a big grove of trees. It was tan stucco, no carport, only a rectangular box. The closest house was two hundred yards away. Lily felt herself hoping that this woman would take her in. Immediately, she shut it down. Hope produced disappointment. There might not be room for her in such a small house.

"Come in." Lily went inside and sat on the sofa. Two children, a boy of four and a girl of two, stood in the doorway. A truck dangled from the girl's hand and a car from the boy's. Lily felt déjà vu and immediately remembered her dream of

a woman and two children. She didn't trust that it meant anything other than a random loop of time. It certainly didn't mean
she could safely stay with this woman.

Anne jumped down and joined the other children but soon
came back and leaned against Lily's thigh, as if to make sure
her mother wouldn't leave.

"I'm going to be here," said Lily. "I'm not leaving without you."

The woman watched. "A little unsettled."

"You don't know the worst of it." Lily knew that if she
wasn't careful, she'd let the whole story out. Not something she
could afford.

"You can tell me your name when you feel like it," said
Suzanne.

"Alice Jenkins."

Suzanne looked at her and smiled, as if she knew it wasn't
her real name. Another woman, a little older than Suzanne,
came from the kitchen. She didn't look happy. "I'm done. I've
got my own family, and I can't be watching yours."

"All you do is sit on your fat butt," said Suzanne. "They're
yours as well."

"I'm finished," said the woman. "I wash my hands of them."

"Just like your son did," said Suzanne.

"Just like your daughter did," said the other woman without
turning. She slammed the door behind her.

"These your children?" asked Lily.

Suzanne smiled. "You think I'm that young? I'm forty-five.
These are my grandkids. A year ago my daughter ran off with a
summer cowboy from the rodeo in Calgary. Guess she wanted
to play cowboys and Indians."

"I'm sorry," said Lily.

"Their father, that woman's son," Suzanne said, her lips pointing at the door, "was a little more responsible, or maybe his mother just threatened him. He lasted until a few days ago. Since he's run off, she has come over to help me out." She shook her head. "Somebody's got to take care of these kids, make sure they don't grow up and join a gang. Gangs all around here. A little boy, a teenage girl, shot." She looked at Lily. "Why you want to be here? Why don't you just keep going? This is not a good place to live."

Lily considered what to say. "I don't know how to tell you why, but I'm staying. I'm going to find work and stay here."

"This a First Nation reserve. Samson Cree land. No work for a white woman here. Nothing. Nobody would rent."

"I'm not leaving town."

The woman nodded. "You want to talk over dinner?"

Lily smiled.

Suzanne called the two children. "Mikey and Mia, come for dinner." She pointed toward Lily. "This is Alice and her daughter—?"

"Valerie. I call her Val for short."

Suzanne set two more plates. She swarmed up potatoes and gravy, home food for Lily, food that her aunt had made all the time.

Mikey started talking to his grandmother. "Mia and me found a toad in the yard, down by the ditch. We tried to catch it, but we couldn't get close."

Mia said nothing, just nodded, touching her grandmother's arm.

Anne used her hand to put more food in her mouth. The little girl beside her laughed. She jumped down and handed

Anne a spoon. "Use this to eat." Anne looked at the spoon sitting on her plate. Lily showed her how to use it.

"What kind of work can you do?"

"Anything," said Lily. "I work hard, and I can figure out anything."

"You could watch these kids for me. I couldn't pay you much. I started a job two weeks ago, driving a bulldozer to knock down old houses here on the reserve. Burnt-out houses. I got their other grandmother to watch these two, but you heard what she said. She's tired out."

Lily looked at her. Hope and stubbornness had produced a blossom. "You'd trust me with your grandchildren? You don't know the first thing about me."

"What I need to know I can read straight from that child." She indicated Anne with her thumb.

Lily felt tears come to her eyes.

"Bad husband?" the woman asked.

"The worst," said Lily. "I was a damn fool."

"Mine left when I was about your age. That was eighteen years ago. I turned into a drunk. Lost two of my children to the government. Now I've lost the third, mother of these two kids." She paused. "Tell me as much as you want about yourself."

"I have an MFA in art. Useless to me now."

"Why useless? You might be able to get a job at the university in Edmonton."

"Yes, I could, I guess," said Lily, knowing she couldn't prove to anyone she had a degree. "I want to do nothing but spend time with Anne."

"Yes, but you might not have the luxury to be with her all the time."

Lily knew she had to be careful; she couldn't afford to be seen as someone who didn't want to work because she was lazy. "I'll take care of your children as if they were my own."

"Let me show you where you and Val can stay. I have a crib out in the garage that we can bring in. It will do her for a while."

"Thank you," said Lily. "Thank you."

"Tan ou," parroted Anne.

Suzanne bent toward the child. "You're welcome." She led them into a room that had two narrow beds. "Where our daughters slept," she said. "Now I don't know where either one of them is. Don't care where their father is."

The room had a window out on the back, a bare stretch of ground that led to some trees on a small hill. The bathroom was next door. "We just have the one bathroom," Suzanne said, "but it will do for us."

There was a chair and a few books on the shelf, stuff read by teenagers. "I have the children's books in a box in the other room," Suzanne said.

There was a small desk for a girl and a soft chair, where she could sit with Anne. Lily sat on the bed. A smile rose through her body and broke out on her face.

She heard tapping and walked into the hallway. The crib was standing in the kitchen, a small, white bed with railing around it. Suzanne had a huge butcher knife. She used a hammer to drive the knife into the back doorframe to hold it shut. Suzanne turned to look at her. "What you're running from must be bad, bad news." She sat in a chair, her hands, one holding the hammer, dangled between her legs. "I had a man living here until about five years ago," she said. "I thought I was safer.

Then he ran off with the neighbor's daughter, twenty years younger than him. Last was my daughter's boyfriend, father of these kids. Now it's just me and the kids. So far nobody's bothered us."

Anne called out, "Ma, ma."

Lily stood, and they both pushed the crib into her room. They took one of the beds apart and leaned the pieces and the mattress in the hallway. Suzanne smiled and left. Lily shut the door, put Anne in the crib, and lay down on the bed. The crib was angled so she could face Anne. Just enough light came in the window from a yard light that they could see each other. Anne put her hand out through the bars and Lily held it. Soon Anne let go, asleep.

Lily lay on her back, thinking about the shut door, the house around her, the space around that, the distance from her trouble in Utah. So damn good that she thought she might float off the bed. Not even the danger in the village dampened her good spirits. She had hidden herself where Nathan might never find her.

It pleases me to put Lily in a place where she has the possibility of happiness, a place where she can spend time with Anne without intense fear of the police showing up. With Suzanne she had a conversation like the one she had with Jackie, two women searching each other's faces and responding with some understanding and love. Levinas wrote, "the face speaks to me and thereby invites me to a relation." But it is a hazardous invitation: "the Other manifests itself by the absolute resistance of its defenseless eyes. . . . The infinite in the face . . . brings into question my freedom, which is discovered to be murderous and usurpatory." I take this to mean that as I make myself vulnerable to the Other, their infinite nature challenges my assumption that I can constitute my identity independent of them. Consequently, at least a part of me wants to usurp their infinite nature, murder them by reducing them to a being I can comfortably comprehend.

Which is why it's much easier to imagine human feelings about Lily than it is to imagine intimacy with my wife, children, and grandchildren. I'm a little like Mikey, who wants his household to stay the same. He will certainly view Lily as a stranger who took the place of his father.

The next morning Suzanne was already up when Lily went out into the kitchen. They sat at the table, drinking coffee.

"I don't know what you're running from," said Suzanne. "And I don't need to know, but people here will know that you're here. They'll talk about it."

"I left a bad husband."

"Why did you come here?"

"I put my finger on a map."

Suzanne thought about that.

"Tell them I wanted to live like an Indian—I mean First Nation person."

Suzanne looked at her sharply. "I sure as hell won't tell anybody that. I'll tell them that you were my niece's friend from college."

Lily nodded, and Suzanne left for work.

Soon Mikey woke. He stumbled into the kitchen and asked, "Where's Grammy?"

Lily knelt on the floor but didn't try to get too close. "She went back to work."

"I want Daddy to take care of me," he said.

"He's not here, but I'm going to be here."

She watched him, this small human standing with uncertain dignity before her; she thought he might cry, but he didn't this time.

"Do you want some breakfast?"

"Not now," he said. "I eat with Mia." He started back toward his room. "And with Dad." He turned to face her. "We eat with Dad."

She walked into the room and watched him get his trucks out. He made two lines of blocks and drove the truck along the road he'd made. Mia slept with her mouth open, a line of drool going from her lip to the pillow, a curl of black hair over her cheek. Lily walked into the other room to watch Anne sleeping, a pleasure she couldn't get enough of. Anne's mouth was closed. She sighed, but didn't wake. "Sleep on, my precious child," said Lily.

Anne opened her eyes and stretched her arms up. She saw Lily and didn't smile, but seemed to relax. Lily wondered if she would ever ask for Daddy. She had never experienced his meanness, his quiet maliciousness. He had mostly ignored her. When Anne was tiny, Lily had noted that he never wanted to hold her. This was before Lily knew him as unable to focus on another person for longer than it took him to bend that person to his will.

She picked Anne up, and she arched her back and cried out, "No!" Lily laid her back down and changed her diaper. Anne talked and talked, using a linguistic structure with words that sounded like things and acts. For Lily it was like the taste before her tongue touched food.

Lily carried Anne into the other room, and together they waited for Mia to wake up. When she did, Lily changed her diaper, cleaned her up, and put on ointment where she might rash. The girl didn't talk, and Lily wondered why, because she was older than Anne. Then Lily moved them all to the kitchen.

"What do you want to eat?" she said.

Mikey gave her a hard look. "We always have orange juice." She looked in the freezer and couldn't see any frozen juice.

"Not there," Mikey said, exasperated. "In there." He pointed to the cupboard, where she saw a hand orange juicer. He opened the fridge and took out an orange, handing it to her. She cut it in half and pushed the juice from four oranges before she had enough to satisfy Mikey.

She handed a drink to Mikey and another to Mia, who knelt on her chair. "No," said Mikey. "Sippy cup."

Mia dumped her cup on the floor. "I want a sippy cup."

"So you can talk," Lily said. "Sippy cup. Where are they?"

Mikey pointed.

She squeezed two more oranges and handed the cup to Mia, who drank happily.

Anne, who had been trained in disruption, was anxious, signing drink again and again, and calling out. Lily squeezed more juice, while Anne shouted louder and louder.

"She's a baby," said Mikey. "She's too loud."

"Yes, she is loud." Lily gave her juice, and Anne tipped it too far, pouring it into her mouth and down her neck. She shouted for more. Lily helped her drink a second batch.

"I'm hungry," said Mikey. Mia banged her cup on the table.

Lily found three bowls.

"Not those," said Mikey. He pointed again. She took out a plastic bowl.

"No," said Mikey. He was not whining, Lily noticed. Their father had taken care of them. Suzanne thought of him as a bad father, but the children had a steady ritual. Mikey didn't find it necessary to whine or cry. Lily had to think that whatever their father had done wrong, he had been good with the children. Or good until he wasn't good and left.

She found the right bowl, and all the children had cereal. Anne ate hers with her hand. Lily ate an orange and some cereal. When the coffee was ready, she drank a cup and watched the children eat. She felt the strong liquid drive her slight headache away.

When Mikey was done, he got down.

"What do we do now?" Lily asked.

He waited a second. "We watch television," he said finally.

"What do we do really?"

He looked at her. "We get dressed and go outside to play before it gets too hot."

"Can you get your clothes on, or do you need help?" Lily asked.

"I always get myself dressed."

She waited for Anne and Mia to finish. "Today we will play, Val. Today we will go nowhere."

Anne pointed at Mia and said a long sentence.

"She can't talk yet," said Mia.

Soon Mikey came out, wearing a dark green shirt and red shorts. He looked like a small elf. The day before he had been dressed in clothing that made sense together, so Lily doubted that he always picked his own clothing. Today that didn't matter.

Lily sat on the back porch with a second cup of coffee, watching the children play in the dirt. Mikey had brought his trucks out, including some that were older for Anne and Mia to play with. "We're sharing," he said.

Again Lily thought that the father could not be some order of universal bastard.

One Christmas Lily's father gave her a sweater. It was nothing she could ever wear to school—heavy sea-green wool. It was the only gift he had ever given her. In their three-person family, the mother was the gift-giver. Despite their relative poverty, she bought discontinued or second-hand toys for Lily's birthday and Christmas. Lily kept the sweater in a drawer and wore it sometimes when they went camping. When her father smiled at her or brushed his hand across the sleeve, she felt pleased to honor his gift.

One camping trip she sat too close to the fire. When a log popped, three burning fragments landed on the sweater. One on her arm and two in her lap. One burned a hole in the sweater, and the smoke from the wool smelled like burning hair. Her father stood from across the fire, but when she brushed the ember off, he sat back down. She poured a little water on the burned place, and then stuck her finger through the hole. She looked up at him, and he gave her a wry look, neither a smile or frown.

When she moved in with her aunt, she didn't take the sweater with her. Her aunt would only let her bring two laundry baskets of clothing and two boxes of books. Lily supposed the sweater went in the trash. Without her father, the sweater didn't mean anything to her.

Her life in general had been one of reduction; now she had so few possessions that they fit in a small backpack. When living with Nathan, she had swaddled herself with a hundred thousand dollars of stuff. She had felt more secure then, but it had been an illusion.

That night, Lily cooked a dinner that was ready when Suzanne came home—chicken roasted with small potatoes. After dinner, while the children watched a video, the two women talked. "We haven't made a formal arrangement," said Suzanne.

Lily shrugged.

"Board and room and what?"

Lily considered how difficult it had been without money. She had to have a cash reserve, so she could move on if she needed.

"A hundred dollars a week."

"That's not enough," said Suzanne, "but I can't afford it."

"Twenty-five, then," said Lily. "Cash."

"Deal," said Suzanne.

They took a pair of beers onto the back porch, watching the sun lower across the plains.

"So what kind of art did you do?"

"Mostly conceptual. I did things with corndogs."

"You're kidding!"

"No. I thought it was socially revealing. I also did installations, kind of performance art. The best thing I did was to hang empty picture frames in Liberty Park. Then I took pictures of people looking through the frames. They'd pose different ways and have their friends take pictures of them."

Suzanne leaned back, eyebrows raised, as if to get a better look at Lily. "Sounds—ah—interesting."

"I was not a good artist. I just messed around." She chose not to tell Suzanne about the shoplifting art project.

"How did you meet Val's father?"

Lily shook her head. "Not yet. Maybe someday, but not yet."

Suzanne has the right, as an employer screening a childcare provider, to ask for references, past experience, qualifications. But she is also host, and her sense of rightness allows her to push a little but not require Lily to answer. Nobody, especially me, wants uncertain relationships with others. But I have two opposing tendencies—to avoid people I don't understand, who have an edge of mystery to them, and to be curious about such people. Last year I had a student from the South who called me sir, which was a bit unnerving, but she also had a subtle, ironic, sometimes even bitter wit. I could never tell what she really thought of me.

To take a leap from the personal to the public, I note that Suzanne is subverting the convention dictating that First Peoples live on a reserve and Europeans live off the reserve. She's modifying the definition of public space. Levinas thinks that community, national, and international ethics require that anyone in the world should be welcome into the public space of someone else's homeland. But politics is more about power than vulnerability, and nationalism totalizes the foreigner, so for a country to become ethical the nature of public space must be transformed. My son, a lawyer, started a non-profit, The

Free Migration Project, whose mission is to "support immigrant communities and to advocate for the right of all people
to freely migrate." He considers free movement a basic human
right, which he defines as the "right to migrate, the right to
remain, and full political and economic inclusion." What
remarkable changes would have to occur in the United States
to make that possible!

The next morning was not so smooth. After Lily squeezed
his juice and handed it to him, Mikey held his cup out and
opened his hand. Juice splattered across the floor. He watched
her, waiting to see what she would do.

"Help me clean it up," she said.

"No!"

"Time out for you," she said.

"No!" he kicked and kicked as she carried him to the living
room.

"Stay here," she said.

Anne and Mia watched, waiting to see what would happen.

"No." He left the chair and ran out to the back of the house,
where he started playing with his truck. Lily felt the anger rising, so she turned away from him. She cleaned up the juice and
had breakfast with the two girls. She stood at the sink, where
she could watch him while she ate her cereal. Anne was silent,
watching Lily, knowing something was up, some tension in
her mother. Lily breathed. *I can do this*, she said to herself, *I
can do this the right way. I can.* She breathed, smiled at Anne,
breathed again, breathed peace into the air.

She went out and knelt about six feet from Mikey. "I am
not your father. I'm just taking care of you."

"I want him to come back."

"I understand," Lily said. "I can't make him come back."

"I want you to leave. Maybe then he will come back."

"I can't make him do anything. I told your grandmother that I'd take care of you."

"You are supposed to go away. I hate you."

"I understand." She rose and walked back toward the house.

Soon he came in. "I want some cereal," he said.

"I'll get you some if you say please. That's your dad's rule and your grandmother's."

He thought about it. "Please, can I have some cereal? And orange juice."

She set him out a bowl of cereal and squeezed him some orange juice.

"Please say thank you," she said.

His mouth was full, and he took some time chewing. Then he said, "Thank you," as if it was his idea.

All the children had naps in the afternoon, and Lily sat in the living room. There were books on the shelves she could read. But she just wanted to sit and feel time stretching out in front of her. Soon she dozed off. She woke later, feeling anxious, but couldn't remember her dream.

She knew there was internet at the local community center, but she didn't want to go out of the house and she didn't want to encourage questions from Suzanne, who would certainly wonder what Lily was looking for. She knew Suzanne would be tempted by the $20,000 reward, if it was still only $20,000, but she didn't know whether Suzanne would give in to that temptation. Lily couldn't take the chance, not yet, maybe never.

That night Suzanne came home with a few art supplies, mostly for the children, but some pastels and acrylic paints, brushes. "You need something to do," she said. "In the evenings when I'm with my children."

Lily looked at the materials. "Thank you. You spent too much."

"They were in a house we were set to demolish. I couldn't believe it."

Lily didn't touch them for a week, but then she did some studies of the children playing in the dirt out back. Anne liked playing with the others, but sometimes she wanted to make pictures, like Lily. Then all the children wanted to draw.

"These are our crayons," said Mikey when Anne reached for them.

"Your gram gave them to all of you kids," said Lily, "including Val."

"Val," said Anne. "Cayon." She grabbed the crayon in her fist and moved it on the paper.

After that Lily figured ways how to show that they were one family. For one thing, she had Mikey and Mia call her Auntie and had Anne do the same for Suzanne. She knew that early Mormon polygamists had the children call the sister wives that, as a protection against anti-polygamy laws. Suzanne liked it because it was also a First People tradition.

Evenings she sat at the kitchen table or on the back step with Suzanne, and they talked. One night she asked Suzanne about the Cree reserve.

Suzanne had been looking into her coffee cup, but she looked up at the question. "What do you want to know?"

"Anything. You never talk about your people."

"My people? I'm Canadian. Who are your people?"

Lily shrugged. "I used to be Mormon."

Suzanne watched her for a minute.

"I've offended you," said Lily.

"I'm used to it. So you're from Utah?"

"I don't have to be from Utah to be a Mormon."

"Right," said Suzanne. They both waited. "No pressure."

"Not hardly."

Suzanne took a breath. "My people. It's complicated. But people who ask about it don't usually want a complicated answer. Like that cowboy who wanted to screw my daughter because she was Indian."

Lily felt her face heating up. "Sorry. I asked a dumbass question."

"It's funny. I usually don't get offended so easily. I guess you caught me off guard. My grandmother taught me some stuff about Cree traditions. My sister really got into it: the trickster god, what's his name? Wisakedjak. What the stars mean. How the animals used to talk." She looked at Lily. "My parents didn't have much use for that, and neither do I. Some people do. Keeping the stories going helps some people."

Lily nodded.

"Canada pretends to be different. First Nation and all that. But do you know that this town used to be called Hobbema, after a fucking Dutch painter. It was because of the railroad that Anglos built between Edmonton and Calgary, somebody in charge liked that painter so he named the railway station Hobbema, instead of

Maskwacis—Bear Hills." Suzanne took another drink. "I want to move away. When I can I will. Mikey and Mia need to grow up in a safer place. For now I'm stuck, like everybody else. All these kids," she waved her hand in a circle above her head, "they don't have a plan, nobody makes a plan for them. I mean everybody makes schemes. The council, the government all make schemes for what to do with us, but it's not like there's any real plan. It's expected the kids are stuck here. Kids you grew up with, there was an expectation, a community expectation, right?"

Lily nodded.

"Not here. The expectation is violence and alcoholism, so that's all people think about. It shapes the whole discussion." She hesitated. "Well that's not right either. There are a lot of good things, like there's this prison that's not a prison where they try to use traditional healing methods to help people solve their core problems. That's a good thing. Other things also. But how will all this help my two grandkids? Maybe it would. But I'm not going to take a chance, so I'm going to get out of here when I can."

Lily felt an undertow of fear. "When do you think that will be?"

Suzanne looked at her. "I don't know. Maybe if I make enough money from this job I can move to some racist city, where the white kids will pick on Mikey and Mia. Maybe that will be an improvement." Her mouth turned up in a wry twist. "There are no good options."

Lily wanted to say something to this woman who had given her a place to live, but all she could think about was how frightened she was that Suzanne might leave and Lily would have to move on. She had tried to avoid thinking about the wheel, but

Suzanne's talk had unsettled her. She decided she shouldn't wait any longer.

That night in her room she chose three sectors: 1–5 for days, 6–10 for weeks, 11–16 for months. She decided it was useless to measure time from when she had arrived, but from the current moment. She spun the wheel: 12 for months. She spun it—12 again. She would stay with Suzanne for a full year longer. Did that mean that it would take Suzanne that long to get enough money saved up to leave? Lily didn't know how to think about that. She also feared that Nathan would find her before that much time had passed, but she also thought that staying in one place was staying invisible. Then she just let herself feel joy because maybe she, Anne, Suzanne, Mikey, and Mia could have that long a stretch of undisturbed peace.

Many days she spent drawing with the children or making drawings in the dirt in the backyard, lines and sticks and rocks, sometimes water in splashes across their creations. They also read stories and played with toys and ate food together. Every day Lily felt herself relax a little more.

SIXTEEN

It took six weeks before Suzanne came to Lily's bed. "I'm so lonely," she whispered, standing in the doorway. "I just want to have someone next to me while I'm sleeping." Lily rose from her narrow bed, checked to make sure Anne was asleep, and followed.

Suzanne lay on her bed and Lily spooned her, holding her arms around the other woman. They lay without moving. Lily was sensitive to the warmth of her employer. She held her close and touched her face with her palm. "I'm here."

Suzanne released a long sigh, as if exhaling muscular tension. "It's been five years, dammit, but I still miss him. I miss him more than I can bear."

Soon she was asleep. By morning they had both turned and Lily woke with Suzanne's arms around her.

She disentangled herself. Suzanne opened her eyes, but apparently was still asleep, unseeing, so Lily left the room without speaking. She checked on Mikey and Mia as she passed their room and saw that Anne was still sleeping. She turned on the coffee machine and sat on the back porch, waiting for it to get hot and percolate.

She felt a deep and pervasive contentment, and she recognized it had come from sustained touch. Like babies, both she and Suzanne would wither without human contact.

She considered the ardent, sweaty encounters with Nathan, before desire for him died. She had been shaken to her bones, her soul tugged in a primal manner, as if the Neanderthal in her was waking and moving against Nathan's hardness. She had thought she was making intimate contact with him. Eventually his face and motions mystified her. She began to suspect that for him their encounters were like making love to a mirror. For him sex was connected in a perverse way to his hunger for power, a forcing of subservience, reducing her to a thing that was less important to him than his own hand. Rapacious. Even toward the end, he sometimes still put on the look, staring at her face as if he cared about her. It became disorienting. But even more disorienting was that sitting on the back step, a thousand miles from him, she felt a stirring low in her belly and crotch, a memory of heat and pleasure, and she became angry at her body's betrayal.

Soon Suzanne joined her on the back step, handed her a cup, and they both drank. Lily anticipated the waking that would flow into every vein. They sat, shoulder to shoulder.

"Sometimes I see their father in their faces," said Suzanne, "sometimes their mother. His nose on Mikey, a little hooked. Her eyebrows on him also more peaked than arched. His jaw, her cheekbone."

"I can't see it," said Lily, "because I didn't know them."

"It's like that picture that looks either like an old witch or a young, dressed-up woman. You know, that optical illusion."

"I know that picture, but I think it's more like it's synthesized, two chins, two noses, eyes, in the same place, not just pressed against each other. Can you see them both at once?"

"In the witch picture or in these kids?"

"Either one."

"That's hard," said Suzanne, squinting at Mikey. "It's either one or the other."

"What do you see in Val?"

"I see your bottom lip in her, fuller than the top one. The shape of your face, how it drops from your head to your chin in a smooth line. Some people have wider cheekbones. The color of your skin. But there's a difference. The mystery man that you won't show me a picture of."

Lily just grunted, as if to say, back off, but she didn't move away, didn't release the touch of skin, shoulder to shoulder, arm to arm.

"She's an amalgam of you two," Suzanne said, "whether you want it or not."

Lily grunted again, and Suzanne grinned as she stood to go inside and get ready for work.

After Anne's birth Nathan's mother came up from St. George to help Lily, because her own mother was dead. His mother played the game that Lily and Suzanne just played—seeing the parent's face in the child. The game pleased Lily, but Nathan just said, "She's not really formed into a person yet, not really a face you can read." His mother chided him, "Oh, you men, blind to what's right in front of you." Lily couldn't think about the blurred overlay of her face and Nathan's in Anne, without thinking of the strands of DNA that unzipped and cross-zipped, splicing her genes and Nathan's genes together to create the being known as Anne. How would Nathan's genes manifest, how would hers? Would Anne be manipulative or passive, self-absorbed like an artist or self-absorbed like a power broker, a rebel or a master of conformity? She doodled a picture of the mystery of Anne, Lily and Nathan in one, woman and man, yin and yang.

xyxyxyxyxyxyxyxyxyxyxyxyxyxyxyxyxyxyxyxyxyxyxyx
yxyxyxyxyxyxyxyxyxyxyxyxyxyxyxyxyxyxyxyxyxyxyxy
xyxyxyxyxyxyxyxyxyxyxyxyxyxyxyxyxyxyxyxyxyxyxyx
yxyxyxyxyxyxyxyxyxyxyxyxyxyxyxyxyxyxyxyxyxyxyxy

Watching the children play, she doodled images of strands joining and unzipping, whipping like snakes, coiling in double helixes, which looked a little like the decision path she had sketched—the letter y, stacked head to foot.

She considered the grand tapestry made by all these strands, the mysterious weave of x and y. Choice and accident created being, and she felt as if she had touched the face of a god she didn't believe in.

That day Mikey peed his pants, once in the morning, again in the afternoon. Then he pooped in them. Lily knew he had trained himself, or his father had been there to urge him and help him know how to use the toilet. Each time Lily handed him the wet wipes and encouraged him to select new clothing. Each time he was weepy and ashamed. Lily was curious about why this was happening now, more than two months after his father had left.

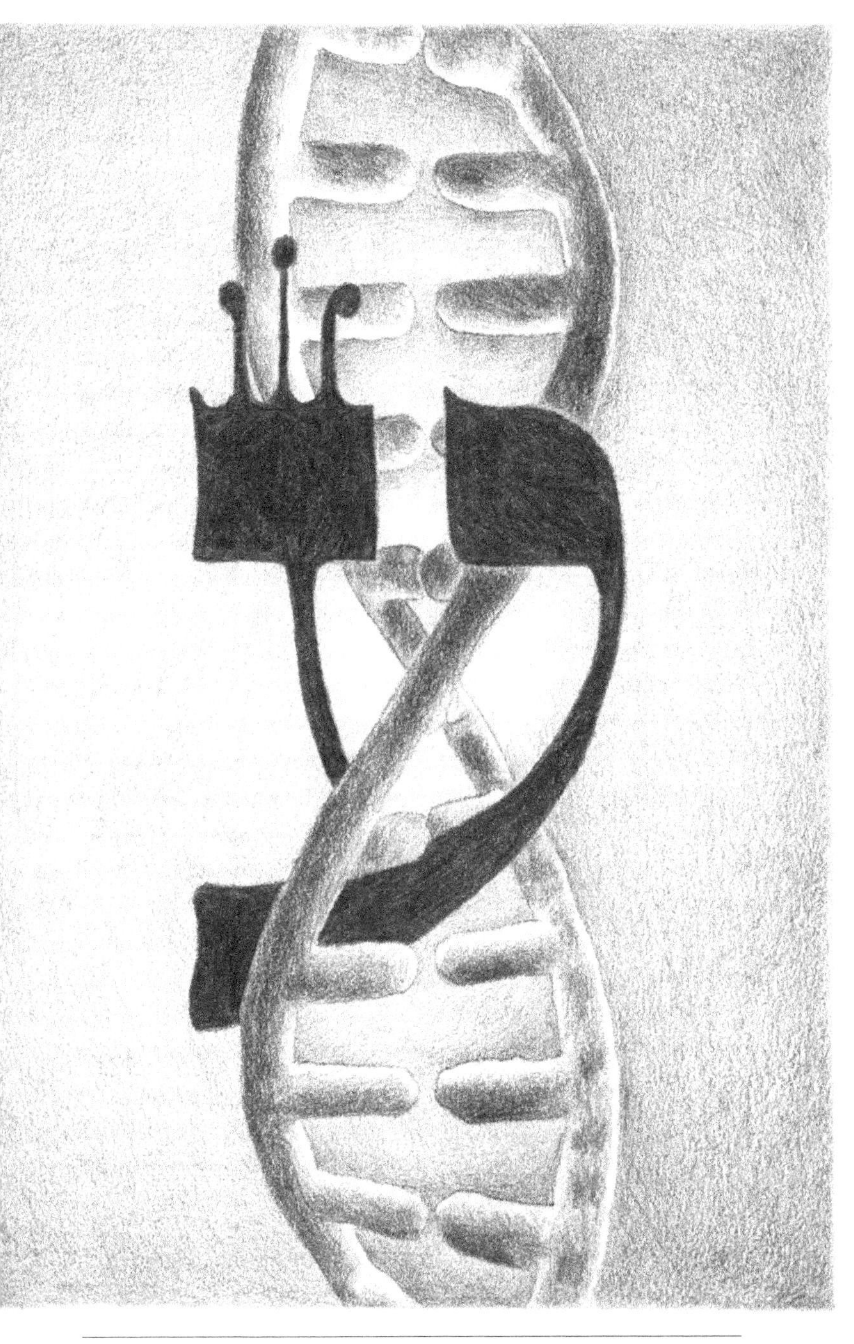

AYIN, DOUBLE HELIX

Automythology (USP)

"Mikey peed," said Anne, who at a year of age was making small sentences. She seemed to have figured out that speech wasn't just any sound, but specific sounds that made words.

Lily watched the three children playing in back. They had the hose out and had made a puddle, were putting mud on their skin. The three of them stood before her, small and naked. She made them stand on the back step and washed them with the hose. They shrieked and danced, laughing.

In the evening, on the back porch, after the children were in bed, Lily raised the question of Mikey's accidents with Suzanne, who asked, "What do you think?"

Lily thought for a moment. "He still misses his father."

After a moment, Suzanne nodded. "They were close. Actually he was close to both of them."

Lily tapped a weed stem against the ground between her feet. "Where is he?"

"He was in Calgary. Now I don't know."

"Are you keeping him from them?"

Suzanne's head whipped around, her lips white from being pressed together. "I'm not keeping him from them. He told me in his note that it's better this way, that part-time parenting is no parenting at all. He believes a clean break is better."

"Better for him, maybe."

"Not even that. Not good for him either. Just cleaner, just more logical." She gave a wry smile. "That's what makes me so angry. If only he were a true bastard, I could get over it. He was a damn good father to these kids, but only up to a point. He decided he wanted freedom more. I think it had to do with a woman he met. She didn't want any children, and he wanted to screw her."

"Mormons used polygamy," said Lily. "When the men's eyes and dicks wanted someone new, there was a socially acceptable way for them to find another woman."

"Anyway, polygamy's no solution or it's a damned hellish one."

"Right," said Lily. "The Bible says woman becomes one flesh with a man, but the reality is that, as soon as they're one, he gets her pregnant and then her flesh sags and she has to accept him taking a younger woman. Sometimes in the same house. Bedrooms in a row, first wife, second wife, third wife." Lily snorted. "Always a younger woman, or nearly always."

"It's a damned efficient method to keep the species going."

"Yes. A man might sire a couple of dozen children."

"You are not helping me at all," Suzanne said. "I wanted you to talk me out of my anger."

"Reality sucks," said Lily.

"I don't want a perpetually young man," said Suzanne. "I want a smart man, one who appreciates me."

Lily put one arm around her friend. She nodded toward the mud pool. "I'll make a man for us. I'll bake him in the sun and breathe life into him."

"You better make two if you want to get any yourself. We'd wear one man out."

Lily smiled. "Especially a mud man. I'll carve you one out of a cottonwood root. More durable."

Suzanne laughed. "Get started. It'll take you a while, and I'm ready now."

"Won't take long. Forget about a face and arms. I'll just carve the necessary part. Make two round handles."

Suzanne leaned over laughing, spilling her coffee. "You'd make me into an idol worshiper."

"An idol wouldn't run off, wouldn't try to own you."

The next few days Lily was curious, but not anxiously so, about whether Suzanne would appear again in her doorway. She didn't, at least not while Lily was awake. After a couple of weeks, Lily followed her own inclination and folded herself against Suzanne, knee to back of knee, belly to back, mouth and nose to back of head, arms curved around.

When they cooked together, they often diced shoulder to shoulder, or Lily found Suzanne's hand on her shoulder. She wouldn't have even noticed it, except that it increased when they didn't sleep in the same bed.

"We're like sisters," said Suzanne. "When I was young, I slept with my sister. I know it made me happy. One of the offshoots of poverty."

Lily hadn't grown up with a sister, so she could only imagine that kind of closeness. For her, Suzanne was still Other, an unfamiliar being, undiscovered country. So it was comforting, but still interesting to sleep with that other body, warm against hers.

She had never had that kind of companionship with Nathan, and she wondered whether it was possible with a man. Like brushing hair, which she'd done in girl's camp or college; a circle of girls, or a pair of girls, stroked each other's hair. She remembered the sensuous pleasure of the massage and pull of the brush. She'd had a boyfriend who, when she tried to describe it to him, immediately wanted to brush her hair. She'd even let him once, but for him it was foreplay, an intimacy that turned immediately to sex play. Not that she didn't want to mess around with him, but girls brushing each other's hair was something else. Something a man couldn't share.

She and Suzanne didn't ever really talk about it. They just slept against each other when they felt the need. Or when they felt cold. She had noticed that when the nights became more bitter as they passed through fall into winter, they found themselves in the same bed more often.

One night, after Suzanne came home and the children were all in bed, Lily heard gunshots. She rushed to the crib and lifted Anne to the floor. Soon Suzanne came in and crouched with them.

"They went the other way," she said. "They don't usually come down this lane. Our neighbor through the trees is a woman everyone respects, so they leave her and us alone."

Lily finally calmed herself and went back to bed, but not to sleep.

The next morning they found out that the shooting had been between two rival gangs. A boy had been shot, but it hadn't been serious enough to go to the hospital. After a week nothing more happened, but Lily's fear about the gunshots waked her fear about being discovered. It had been months since she had last gotten on the internet. It surprised her that she hadn't felt desperate to find out what Nathan was doing. She knew he was doing something, because he hated losing any kind of battle; he would not give up until he had punished Lily for thwarting him.

She talked to Suzanne. "I want to get on the internet. How can I do that?"

"All these houses are wired for internet." Suzanne went into her bedroom and returned with an old laptop.

The next afternoon, Lily logged on. It felt odd typing in her own name and Nathan's. She checked the *Tribune* first and found reference in the Utah section: "Nathan Sharp has not given up on finding his daughter, kidnapped on August 15 by his former wife, Lily Harker. 'Despite Lily's instability,' he said. 'I feel in my soul that Anne is still alive. In what condition, I'm frightened to imagine. Lily is not a bad person, she's just mentally unstable, so she could hurt Anne without meaning to." The article went on to describe his efforts to work with the police. "I want our child to be safe. I've raised the reward to $40,000."

Lily wondered if he knew she had passed through Butte. She couldn't imagine how he could have found out, unless Mary had regretted her decision. If so, he knew the direction she had traveled. Lily found her breathing had sped up at the thought of her narrow escape.

She read more, but she knew that he was not disclosing all the ways he was trying to find her. She knew he'd pressure every police department in every town or city. Of course they might reject or disregard his pressure, or they might be too busy to spend time looking for her, but she had to assume the worst. It unsettled her, like a snake in the garden, this inability to control her destiny, this inability to ever be safe from him.

The summer Lily was pregnant with Anne, Nathan wanted to take her to his high school reunion in St. George. His mother, Barbara, met Lily at the door and beamed at her. It made Lily feel odd, like a brood mare. This woman, thinner even than Nathan, but wearing long gray hair, was just pleased because Lily was giving her a grandchild. That didn't help Lily because she was still not sure that she wanted to have a child, still resented Nathan's pressure for her to get pregnant. But talking with his mother that afternoon, while Nathan took his father golfing, she discovered that Barbara was also pleased that Nathan had found someone to love him. "He has such high ideals for a woman that he always ends it after a couple of dates." That puzzled Lily because she knew she wasn't his perfect ideal. Even when they were in Europe she was constantly bumping against his expectations—wearing a dress that wasn't right for a specific social event, suggesting sights they needed to see that he wasn't interested in, talking about subjects he knew nothing about. "He's lucky he's found the perfect woman." She smiled and folded her hands in her lap, as if she had completed a difficult task. "It's good for him to learn how to love another person." Now she realized that he had known she wasn't perfect but had thought she was pliable.

That night she dreamed about Nathan, a sexual dream, not abstract. He was inside her, pushing with a steady rhythm. The thought of it made her melt, low and deep inside. His face was above her, and his eyes were on hers; she knew he was focused on giving and taking pleasure. The hard core of intensity built, and she woke, her body shaking to a wave of ecstasy and release. The second wave was of fear and disgust. Her body and the undertow of her subconscious had betrayed her.

Nathan was not the first man she had sex play with, but he was the first man she had allowed to put his penis inside her vagina. Twelve years earlier than that event, when she was nine, she had asked her mother about how children were made. Her friends had been telling her stories that didn't make sense. *He puts his what where?* Her mother told her she'd answer when she was older. When she was eleven and she had her first period, her mother told her that the blood didn't mean she had cancer, but that it was the normal plague of women. She told her about Eve and her sin, that women were still being punished. She talked about women's cycles having to do with the way babies were made, so Lily should be careful with boys. Her mother, who was so open and clear about most things, stumbled over words and equivocated when talking about sex. The sex portion of her health class lasted only a few days, and the teacher didn't allow any questions. At the school library Lily looked for books that could help her understand, but she couldn't find any. At a bookstore downtown, she found teen and women's magazines but the articles were either all about how to appeal to boys, or they had titles like, "Twenty-five Creative Pickup Lines" or "How to Give and Get Great Orgasms." She read them with interest but felt that they were only giving part of the picture. She knew about an Internet café next to the U, and she went there and looked up the word "sex." What came up was a mix—ranging from pornography to clinical information. She found an article from *Psychology Today* which led her to the public library to a copy of *Masters and Johnson on Sex and Human Loving*, which she didn't dare check out. Sitting in the library, she read it and other books and decided that her friends' ideas were composed of myths and misunderstandings and that church lessons on chastity were so limited—so full of "not" with so little about "what," "how," "when," and "why"—that she stopped going to church until her mother and father confronted her. Instead of telling them about what she'd learned, she just went back to church. Later she endured a couple of lessons on female morality that made her cringe. On the western edge of their ward was a man who had a milk cow and the young women's leader had him come in one day with a bucket of sloppy, stinky cow shit. The teacher didn't call it that; she called it "manure." The teacher had a sack full of pastry—maple bars—and she asked the girls if they wanted one. "Raise your hands," she said. Every girl stuck her hand in the air, even Lily's friend who was anorexic. Then the teacher had the very serious farmer, dressed in a suit and tie, bring his bucket forward. She dipped one of the maple bars halfway into the shit and held it up, dripping brownish-green. "Now who wants to eat it?" One girl's hand shot up. She said that she could break off the part with manure on it. The others laughed at her. The teacher ignored the girl's response and said to the class, "This is the same as with men. No righteous man will marry a woman who is dirty. No man will marry a woman who has sinned with another man." Later in her life, Lily tried to figure out exactly what the parts of the parable stood for. The maple bar was supposedly a woman, but it was in the shape of a wide penis, and what was the bucket of shit the solemn farmer had thrust the maple bar into?

This happened in her aunt's church, after her parents were dead. After that she refused to go to church again. It was such a narrow and bitter view of a woman's sexuality that it disgusted her. On the one hand they said she was a goddess in embryo, on the other, if she made one mistake, they said she was shit.

After her extensive reading, Lily experimented with her-self, her own thumb and fingers, finally achieving orgasm. As a teenager, she played with a couple of boys, one of them the president of the chess club who seemed astonished at his good fortune. However, fear of pregnancy held her back. She had been unable to get birth control pills while living in her aunt's house, and she didn't trust that the boys she let touch her could get a condom on correctly. They were so horny that their hands shook like delirium tremens when they palmed her breast or thrust their hand between her legs. She had to take control and give them pleasure with her hand, which was fine with her, and apparently with them also. When they had calmed down enough, she was able to show them how to return the service, but she didn't have intercourse. In college she found that birth control made her gain weight, so she stopped. After a bundle of short relationships that ended when she made it clear she wasn't going to let them penetrate her, she met Nathan. She was twenty-one and ready for a more permanent relationship.

She believed that he embodied the perfect balance of restraint and desire. His Mormon background made him respect women, she thought, and she hadn't known a man could be so courteous when he clearly had a passion for her. She believed that he would always treat her that way, and after they married, he had been good at sex, oh so good. Later she figured out that his focus on her was a trick to get her to respond.

Don't worry, I'm not going to talk about my own sex life in these pages, except to say that my culture's objectification of women, especially our fetish with female youth, my own aversion to deep emotional conversation, and my reluctance to talk about significant issues have made true intimacy difficult, or even frightening. I'm sure I'm not alone. Levinas writes, "the face is present in its refusal to be contained." Many of us, men and women, survive through refusing to see infinity in our partner's face. We contain the other, like Nathan, who reduced Lily to a fixture of his home, a bed mate.

After Christmas, Anne talked more, making sentences that Lily could make out, but that no one else other than Mikey could understand, "I hungry," "I love Mommy," "I want outside," "I want that toy."

Each night the women put their children to bed, telling stories. Lily and Anne also spent time drawing. She taught Anne the drawing game. "Draw on this page." After Anne drew a circle and a line, Lily took the sheet back and drew more circles and lines. She handed the paper back to Anne. "Now add to my drawing." Back and forth, they drew until the page was full. The drawing looked like a new universe.

Lily sometimes made illustrations of stories she told Anne. One was of the mommy princess and the baby princess. She told Anne that baby princess was captured by ogres and kept in an evil land, in the City of Ogres. The mommy princess found a magic mirror that was like a compass and she found the baby princess and they flew away together.

She settled again into an even more profound happiness. She gradually allowed her fear of discovery to relax. Occasionally, she tried to rouse herself into watchfulness, but somehow she didn't have the energy. She knew her lack of vigilance was dangerous, but she couldn't seem to make herself do anything. She put off again and again her occasional thoughts about moving, of finding another place to live that wasn't on the extended line that passed through Weber State, Butte, and Edmonton. Any fool could check every place along that line. And Nathan was no fool. Her efforts also failed when she tried to convince herself that Nathan didn't know what she knew, that his ignorance was greater than she supposed. That first week after losing Anne had broken something inside her. Intellectually she knew there was danger, but she had a blanket of apathy that continued to swaddle her.

Every day with Anne and the other children seemed a blessing. Even the past seemed less horrific. Memories of being in the Deer Valley house with Anne rose to the surface. Nathan was absent from these memories, because he had been gone working, and then he moved out when they separated. They were scattered fragments of light that her mind wouldn't gather into discrete experiences: sitting on the hearth watching the flames with Anne, keeping her from touching the hot glass; feeding her in her high chair, the small child waving her fat arms like an orchestra conductor as she swallowed the food; walking in Park City with Anne in a stroller, singing some wordless song. Sometimes, if Anne was crying, Lily took her into bed, curling her arms around her child. When Nathan came home, he'd start to get into bed and then move to another room. He didn't think it was proper that the child didn't get used to sleeping alone.

Lily thought about when Anne was born. They had known the child would be a girl, and Nathan had seemed interested, but after she was born, he didn't try to hold her. He glanced at Anne's face resting on Lily's breast, and his face registered no curiosity, just a kind of puzzlement. Looking back, Lily believed he was wondering who this interloper was. He thought of the baby as merely a threat to his command of Lily's attention.

Lily marked that experience as the start of change in Nathan, or rather the point she started seeing his true nature. The child seemed invisible to him, or if he was forced to notice her, she became an irritant. He wanted to go out like they had before, didn't want her spending too much time with the child. He said, "That's why we should have a nanny."

So he had never watched Anne, never tried to discover whether she was cheerful or sad, introverted or extroverted, self-sufficient or needy. Lily had discovered Anne to be quiet in public, but she babbled when alone with Lily. She didn't laugh often, but her face was expressive. She didn't get to know other children much, because Nathan refused to have her in daycare. When Lily had insisted on spending most days and evenings with Anne, he had commanded her, and when that didn't work, he shut Anne in the closet. Then, he used the court system to take Anne away so Lily could not contradict him. She believed the only reason he wanted Anne was to thwart Lily, to show her wrong.

SEVENTEEN

"I've met a man," Suzanne said early in the spring.

Lily stopped stirring a pot of creamy soup and turned to stare at Suzanne. Then she worried about the soup burning and started stirring again. It was still bitter cold outside, and she felt like something warm and liquid. She had also made bread, which she could smell because it was almost done. She didn't know how it would turn out.

"How did you meet him? Have you had him checked out?"

Suzanne laughed. "Like a car?"

"No. Like a horse. Does he have good teeth?"

"His teeth will do," Suzanne said. "But really, when it comes down to it, I don't care much about his teeth."

Lily arched one eyebrow. "You're in a bad way."

"You think? He's not from here. Every so often, we drivers go up to Edmonton to eat out. He owns this restaurant we like. He's an Anglo like you. I asked him out."

Lily didn't think her apprehension had to do with jealousy, but more to do with fear of Suzanne talking about her situation at home. "A white woman on the run watches my children." But why would she do that after Lily asked her not to talk about it?

"We're going out this weekend."

Lily waited.

"We're going for dinner and country dancing." Suzanne spoke carefully. "I hope this isn't a one-night stand. That's not what I want."

If another person entered their household, she might become redundant. *Yes,* she thought. *It is jealousy.*

"I won't bring him here. At least not yet."

"I have nowhere else to go."

"I understand."

Lily nodded. Her heart told her that this was the end of her peace.

"James," Suzanne said. "His name is James Stringham." Lily thought it a bad omen that his last name was the same as the welfare man who had called Nathan while she sat in his office. She tried to dismiss the thought but the name stuck in her mind, making her pay attention—a cosmic coincidence, when she didn't believe in coincidences.

Lily had some trouble getting Mikey to sleep. "Gram always helps me pick my pajamas." He stood next to the toy box. Something about his mouth and the way he held his body, let Lily know that he had made himself immovable. He would not forego this bit of tradition, of stability.

Mia stood in her crib, silent, watching.

"She's on a date."

"What's a date?"

"It's when she goes out with a man."

"Daddy is a man."

Lily watched him. "Yes. But Daddy left. And he was much younger than your Gram."

Mikey tried to keep his face immobile. "Maybe he'll come tonight. Maybe he'll come soon?" He made it into a question.

"I don't know," Lily said, "but I don't think he'll come soon."

He looked at Lily. "I hate you."

"I don't hate you."

"I hate you."

"Do you want to go to bed with pajamas on or without pajamas."

"Daddy puts me in bed. Daddy reads me a story. Daddy or Gram, not you."

Lily rose from the floor. "I'll check on you again in a minute." She turned to Mia. "Bedtime."

"I want a book," said Mia, which surprised Lily because Mia usually let Mikey talk for her.

Lily handed her one, and she sat up and started turning the pages, looking at the pictures.

In their own room, she pulled Anne out of her crib and sat with her. "Which book should we read?"

"Butterflies," said Anne.

"Do you like butterflies, Valentino Peach?"

Anne shook her head. "Val. Not Valemno."

"I know. You're just small and round like a peach."

"I'm Val," she said in a stern voice. "Not a peach."

Lily took down the book and read it.

"Again!"

Lily read it again and then laid her back in bed, covered her with a blanket. She looked down at the small head, small fingers curled around the edge of the blanket. "Precious Peach."

"No. I'm Val," she said, sleep heavy in her voice.

When she went to see what Mikey had done, she found him asleep on the floor. She lifted him into bed. The weight of his small, warm body seemed like the weight of sorrow.

Lily found herself unable to sleep without Suzanne in the other room. She tried to talk herself out of anxiety. Suzanne was not a teenager; she would pick a good man. She would not do something dangerous or foolish. Whether these were true or not, Lily was not Suzanne's mother.

About two in the morning, she finally heard the door open. She walked down the hall and stood in the doorway. Suzanne turned and hugged her.

"I needed that," she said. "Since Troy left I've been wondering what's wrong with me. I didn't need to wonder. Nothing's wrong with me."

Lily said, "You don't—"

Suzanne put her hand across Lily's mouth. "I know I don't need a man to tell me I'm all right, but don't take this confirmation away from me. It's been too damn long since I felt a man inside me. Too damn long. Especially since you never did make me that dildo out of a cottonwood root."

Lily laughed and then hugged her back. "I won't take anything away from you." She went back to her bed, still frightened about Suzanne bringing a man to their house. Even though she told herself again and again that it wasn't her house, she couldn't quiet the longing that it be her place as well.

In the morning Suzanne spent time with Mikey. They walked to the store, and when they came back, Mikey's mouth was rimmed with ice cream. "I want to go too," Mia said. So Suzanne took her to the store.

"Mama," said Anne. "I want to go with them. Let's go."

"No, Val, we can't go with them."

"I want to go."

"No," said Lily.

Anne started screaming. Lily lifted her and put her in her bed. She could hear the shrieking from the kitchen.

"She wants ice cream," said Mikey.

"I know," said Lily. "You don't have to tell me that."

Suzanne came back with a bag, from which she took an ice-cream bar.

Lily brought Anne back out, and the child took the bar, sitting on the floor to eat.

Then Suzanne helped Mikey make ramps of picture books in the front room for his trucks. Lily played with Mia and Anne in the bedroom. Mia took Anne's ball and Lily's hand reached to take it away from her. Instead, she said, "We share." Mia gave Anne a smaller ball.

Anne wasn't happy with the little ball. "I want that one."

Lily reached toward the large ball, but she didn't take it. "You can have a turn. Then Anne can have a turn again."

"Mine," said Mia. "Mine, mine, mine."

The next weekend, Suzanne stayed overnight in Edmonton. Mikey asked about her at breakfast, but he seemed to accept what Lily said, that she'd be home soon. Lily let them watch television as she cleaned up. Suzanne came home before she finished. She was smiling.

"I didn't think I'd find someone again so soon."

It was almost warm enough for the kids to play outside, but not quite, so they played in the living room while the two women sat at the table and drank coffee.

"What's he like?"

"I told you he's a cook. So—" she smiled in a sly manner, "he has these long, deft fingers." Suzanne smiled. "He's also in a part-time band, guitar."

Lily nudged Suzanne on the elbow. "That's what he does. What is he like?"

"He's a strummer." She held her thumb out as if she was stroking a guitar.

"You are focused," said Lily. "You are a damn horny woman. What does he look like?"

"He's a little taller than I am, but not much. He's solid, but not fat. He laughs at my jokes."

"Has he been married before?"

"Yes. He has two grown children."

"Is he older than you?"

"Yes, mother, he's older than I am. He's five years older, fifty." She touched Lily's arm. "Are you through grilling me."

"I don't trust men."

"Are you jealous?"

Lily paused. "I don't think that's it. I'm terrified."

"You have a home here."

"A seven-month home."

"Bad stuff happened to you where you came from, Utah, wasn't it?"

"Montana. A bad divorce. I got nothing, and I couldn't get far enough away."

Suzanne watched her. "Montana. A bad divorce. That's not a reason for such secrecy."

"Reason enough." Lily went into the other room to check on Anne, to hold her on her lap for a while. The child patted Lily's face, which she loved. She smiled and held Anne's hand against her cheek.

"Mommy," said Anne. "Mommy has a sad face."

"Mommy's happy to be with you," said Lily. "Very happy."

The next weekend Suzanne brought James home with her. They didn't arrive until after the kids were asleep in bed. Lily heard the keys in the door and walked to greet Suzanne. He was just behind her.

"Alice, this is James Stringham. James, Alice Jenkins."

He was wide and a little taller than Suzanne. He wore cowboy boots and a shirt with western style pockets. He had a crew cut, which Lily thought was the worst kind of haircut.

He had thick eyebrows, and his body was heavier than she'd imagined. Slightly sweaty face. She didn't like him, but she didn't trust that emotion. He might be fine. She didn't know what to say or do next, so she went to bed. She still heard their voices low, from across the house. She put the pillow over her head and tried to sleep.

Lily looks James Stringham in the face and mistrusts him. Part of it is the name. But through talking to Suzanne and also to him, she will construct a version of his personality that is based on both mistrust of him and trust in Suzanne's judgment. This construct will be much like fiction. This is silly for me to say, because they're all fiction, but the process of finding out about living people is like building a character in fiction.

As might be expected, Levinas also applies the idea of hospitality to the act of writing and reading. I invited Lily into my mind, and she is both like and unlike me. As people read novels, this one for example, they invite something foreign into their consciousnesses—virtual practice for encountering the Other in the real world. In this novel that means Lily being used as a tool to explore my culture and my mind. In Levinas's words, I've totalized her, made her into an implement. Maybe I can make her human enough to fool myself and readers that she possesses infinity, but I'm lying to myself and to you, because she is still a creation, one whose being is created as I describe her. She is composed of glimpses, never a whole person.

All the children were at the table eating when Suzanne and James came out of the bedroom.

"Mikey and Mia," said Suzanne. "This is James."

"Hello, Mikey. Hello, Mia." He made a show of shaking their hands, as if they were grownups. Eating was awkward, with Mikey staring at his cereal, refusing to look up. Suzanne was falsely cheerful.

"And this is Valerie. Val."

"Hello, Val." He held his hand for Anne to shake it. "Valerie is a fine name." Anne looked at Lily then back at his face. She frowned, nearly ready to cry.

"It's all right," he said. "It will take time."

"This is Auntie's friend," said Lily. "Sometimes people shake hands." She took Anne's hand. "Like this."

Anne looked at her mother. "Okay." Her face solemn, she held her hand out to James, who shook it.

"I'm glad to meet you," he said.

"I meet you," Anne said.

He and Suzanne went on a long walk. All Mikey wanted to do was watch television. When Lily turned off the device, he had a screaming, kicking tantrum. She unplugged the TV, and he tried to tip it over. She carried him to bed and held him close on her lap until he stopped kicking.

He slept through lunch.

James was curious about Lily, asked her why she was visiting Canada.

"I'm thinking of immigrating," she said. "I like what I've seen of the place and the people. I may just choose to live here forever." She examined his face, not wanting to tell him anything.

"You have a nice deal here," he said.

Suzanne looked at him. "What do you mean?"

"Nothing," he said. "Just that you two are good for each other."

"Where does your ex-wife live?" Lily asked.

"Saskatoon," said Suzanne.

"My kids are in school at UBC. I make it over there about once a month."

"Good," said Lily. "That's good of you."

"She's screening you," said Suzanne. "Making sure you're up to my level. She thinks she's my mother."

"I think I'm your friend," said Lily.

"Then we should get along fine," said James, but something in the way he said it made Lily think of a cartographer, making sure the landscapes aligned the way he wanted them to.

After lunch Suzanne drove James back to Edmonton. She planned on staying overnight again. Mia clung to her, didn't want to see her go. "Gram will be back," Suzanne said.

"Please don't go," said Mia.

"Auntie will be with you. You like Auntie, don't you?"

"Yes," said Mia. "But I like it more with both you and Auntie."

Lily took Mia in her arms as Suzanne left. She sang a song as she cradled Mia. "Grammy will be back. Grammy will be back tomorrow. Grammy will be back. Grammy will be back to stay."

Mikey was indrawn and quiet. He lay on the couch with his blanket.

Lily thought he was processing it all. Despite her mistrust of James, she thought Mikey would adjust. Despite the many changes, he would manage.

She thought about her own dislike of James. Her mother would have called it a sign that he was not a good man, would have told Lily to trust the inner voice, but then her mother would have condemned the whole lot of them for drinking coffee. She would have thought Suzanne the rankest sinner for sleeping with a man she wasn't married to. Lily knew her own misgiving wasn't based on anything real, that it was constructed out of her own experience and based on her mistrust of Nathan.

She thought of Suzanne's need for touch, her eagerness to be with a man. Lily had isolated herself in this house for more than half a year, seeing no one but her small group face-to-face, only seeing people who walked in front of the house. She felt no need to get out. She thought of men she had known, their shoulders, hands, butts, thighs. She liked thinking of them, and she still felt a perverse warmth when she remembered lovemaking with Nathan, but she didn't feel the anxious need that had driven Suzanne.

The next weekend Suzanne and James wanted to take everyone to dinner. Lily refused. "I have no desire to leave here."

"You're afraid to be seen," said James. "You've committed some crime."

She saw he was only partly joking.

"But we don't care about that," said Suzanne. "We don't care what you've done."

So they gave up on getting Lily and Anne to go with them. Mikey walked down the driveway, holding his grandmother's hand, and James carried Mia. Lily shut the door behind them and locked it. The space felt strange, empty without the other children, who seemed to fill the whole house. She sat on the floor with Anne, who played with a doll. She occasionally looked up and signed "mother" again and again. Lily wondered why she had regressed, why she didn't speak the word.

Anne ran to sit on her lap, but Lily couldn't sit, couldn't get what James had said out of her head, "You've committed some crime."

"Maybe I'm just running away from someone, and I don't want him to find me," she wished she had said to him. "Who do you think you are, calling me a criminal?"

Unnerving.

She stood and walked back and forth through the empty house, cradling Anne and singing to her. Anne lay still, watching Lily, her eyes wide. The child picked up all her anxiety,

Lily knew. She tried to keep her voice cheerful, but Anne remained quiet and silent.

Criminal. If James was suspicious and if Suzanne believed she was from Utah and if any internet notice came to their attention, their suspicions would make them focus on her. If their suspicions crawled southward like vermin, how could they not encounter her description? If James searched for "mother," "child," "crime," "Utah," or some variation of those four words, the story might come up. It was likely he would. Too slim a chance he wouldn't.

She could leave right then, while they were gone. She could take the computer. She had only four hundred Canadian dollars saved. That much money had melted in two days when Nathan made her *persona non grata*. She was committed to the wheel. It said she had another five months here. It had taken her straight to Anne three times, had taken her to Jackie and Suzanne. She was hooked to it, needed it. Still, she wished she was free of it.

But she wanted the 12 months here that it had promised her. She didn't want to go without a bed, no food except what she could shoplift. Their escape from Nathan and Utah had been no good for Anne, dragging her store to store, place to place.

She would learn to know James, as she had learned to know Suzanne.

After that, when she talked with him, she watched his eyes. He didn't take chances; was this because he was insecure or just conservative? Anne came to sit on her lap and grabbed at the pen in her hand. She let her play with it, still watching his eyes.

"You're still keeping me out," he said.

"The one who matters is Suzanne. She took right to you. I trust her."

"She made me feel as if I didn't need defenses. She opened me up with affection."

"As she did me."

"So we have that in common."

Lily looked at him. "Do I threaten you?"

"I feel wary of you."

"Likewise," she said. "You said I must be a criminal."

"And that was something you couldn't just shake off. It affected you."

"I'm no threat to you," she said.

"So I can invite Suzanne to come and live with me?"

"That's up to her."

"I don't know whether she'll come live with me, but I know that you are part of that consideration."

"I've only known her for eight months."

"But the trust between you is palpable."

Lily felt odd because, as much as she felt safe with Suzanne, she didn't trust her with information.

"So we'll see what will happen," he said.

EIGHTEEN

The beginning of the next month, Lily asked if she and Suzanne could go out to dinner while James watched the children.

Lily could see Suzanne was considering what she clearly knew was a test. "All right. I'll ask him," she said. "You haven't left this house since you came here. Are you sure you're ready for this?"

Lily couldn't imagine any reason to answer the question.

The night of the dinner, Lily knelt in front of Anne. "Mommy is going out and having dinner with Auntie. Okay?"

Anne reached for her. "You'll be back."

"James will stay with you. Soon I'll be back."

Anne nodded. "Yes, you'll be back."

"James will watch you, Mikey, and Mia."

She nodded.

Lily felt exposed as she walked to Suzanne's truck. She opened the door and looked back at the house. Suzanne started the engine, but Lily stood, one hand on the door. She could see James through the window, but not the children.

"You all right?" Suzanne asked from the driver's seat.

"No," she said. "I'm scared as hell."

"She's going to be all right. You have to be able to leave her."

"Tell that to my body. It's sending alarms to my brain."

Suzanne laughed, and Lily climbed in the truck.

In Calgary, as they walked along the street in the warm evening, Lily found herself still anxious, ready to jump in any direction. The restaurant advertised itself as a public house or pub, but it was just a loud bar as far as Lily could see. They got a booth as far from the noise as they could get. When they leaned forward they could understand each other, despite the din of conversation at the bar.

Suzanne said, "When I was a teenager I loved to go to dinner with my mother, just the two of us women."

Lily knew she was supposed to say something similar about her relationship with her mother. "My mother died when I was fourteen."

"It's strange that I seem to know you intimately, but I know nothing about you, none of your history."

Lily said, "Does that make you nervous?"

"It didn't, but I have started to think of it as a trust issue. You don't trust me enough to tell me about your past."

"I don't know what's going to happen with you and James."

"You just changed the subject."

Lily nodded slowly. "Partly, that's true. What we have created will end."

Suzanne nodded, her lips tight. "Mikey is calmer and happier than before you came."

"Val is happy here."

Suzanne folded her hands.

Lily went on, "My husband would have taken my child."

"So your running was illegal."

"He would have made her life miserable. She loves me and needs me."

"But he wants to find you."

Lily nodded. "I considered leaving the other day, when you and James took your kids to town."

Suzanne leaned back. "Why didn't you?'

"I don't have enough money yet."

"When you have money you'll leave? I should stop paying you."

"I want to stay," said Lily. "For a long time."

"But—"

"If I am threatened, I'm gone."

"Threatened by?"

"Anything that would lead to my former husband taking my child away from me."

"So James is threatening to you."

"I don't know yet." She shrugged. "I don't have any reason to feel threatened."

"But that doesn't help. You came up with this idea of dinner to see how the children are when we get back. You didn't really want to be with me."

"You know that's not all the truth. My mother died and I had no sister." Lily shrugged. "You are important to me."

"I've never seen anyone so good with children as you."

"Thank you." Lily waited for the "but."

"Such focus on them."

Lily scanned the room, watching for anyone who was watching back. She knew it was paranoid, thinking that someone in Calgary would recognize her. What she'd disclosed to Suzanne was much more dangerous.

"Will you ever be able to fully rest?"

"I don't know," said Lily. "I've forgotten what that's like. Or rather I'm made anxious because I'm so relaxed now. Does that make sense?"

"Yes. It makes me sad."

"You have helped. You have helped so much."

When they came back, James had the children in the living room. They all had capes on and were marching around the room. They seemed happy. When James stopped, Mikey reached up and held his hand.

A good sign.

Lily wondered if he had sat them in front of a movie, then gotten them up and done the parade just before the women came home. Or he might be able to put up an act for a couple of hours and wouldn't be so good with them over a long period of time. All this judgment was useless, because Suzanne hadn't chosen him for his abilities with children. But Mikey trusted him. That hadn't happened easily.

James looked at her. "Do I pass?"

She smiled. "The first test out of a hundred."

"Bring it on," he said, grinning. "Move and countermove."

This surprised and discomfited her. His likening of chess to their relationship, a contest, seemed to be a reading of her mind. Yet it made sense that they would both see the connection. He seemed trustworthy, but she kept reminding herself that she had trusted Nathan. She was warier now, maybe smarter, but perhaps not wary enough. She thought about the four months stretching in front of her before she would leave Maskwacis. What would happen in that time? She felt herself relaxing, but then she caught herself. She might never be able to completely relax again, not for the rest of her life.

After reading with Anne and putting her to bed, she lay down. She felt nostalgic for a sense of security. For when? Before her parents died? That might be the last time she had felt sure of the playing board. Even more than the game between her and James, her escape from Nathan felt deadly, winner take all.

As full summer came, James adopted the habit of staying in Maskwacis two or three nights a week. Most evenings he spent with Suzanne and her grandchildren. He was friendly with Anne, but she walked away from him when he invaded her zone.

At dinnertime much of the conversation was between Suzanne and James. They both made efforts to include her, but it was different than it had been when she and Suzanne had talked on the back stoop during her first months in Canada.

Lily began staying in her bedroom more when he was there. She and Anne cycled through all the children's books in the house about every week. Each Sunday Lily made a computer search for information on Nathan's hunt for her and Anne. She knew he wouldn't give up. The reward was now $60,000, enough to make any number of people give up work and look for her. He was recruiting a public army.

She started painting in her room. At first they were pictures of Anne. She took a photograph with Suzanne's phone of Anne holding a doll and put it on her computer. It took her two weeks to finish. With private access to the world through the computer, she thought of who she might email with the fictitious account she had opened in Layton, but she couldn't think of who might be sympathetic. She thought about posting a picture of Anne laughing with her. Of them all having dinner together, one of the pictures James took of them. Posting them to Facebook so the world could see that she wasn't a deranged monster. That would be foolish, a trail of electrons that could be traced back to Maskwacis.

She dreamed again about the pale, stocky person standing by the path. In this dream she thought it was female. The woman raised her hand as if in greeting, as if Lily was a fellow creature. Then the figure lumbered after her, mouth slightly open, and Lily knew the being wanted to swallow her, eat her like a small fish. She backed away from it, unable to turn and run.

Lily sat up in bed, trying to calm her breathing. She knew that part of the dream was the fear of losing what had become her home, being put outside again—homeless. Her other reaction to the dream made no sense. She remembered all the times James had his eyes on her. Before she thought he was genuinely trying to get to know her, because she was Suzanne's friend. Now he seemed similar to Nathan; they both thought of her as an object he might use or cast off, whichever he pleased.

She told herself it was just a dream and that she shouldn't let it affect her judgment of him, but it did.

James, Suzanne, Lily, and all the children went on a picnic. The kids were playing next to the stream, and James was showing them how to skip rocks. They were too young to do it, but they liked the sound it made as a rock plopped into the water.

Anne clasped her hands together and shouted, "Too much fun." They all laughed. She looked up at her mother, embarrassed, and shy. She picked up a rock that was almost too big for her and dumped it in the water.

Lily watched Suzanne's face, and it seemed lit from inside.

James was still a puzzle to Lily. He seemed too perfect to be true. She thought, a man wanting sex will become whoever the woman needs him to be—at least temporarily.

Soon they all got down in the water and waded. James threw water on Suzanne, and she chased him. Lily helped Mikey build a mud-drip sand castle. The two girls threw mud at their feet and sometimes on each other. James and Suzanne came back a half hour later. Suzanne gave her a shy, sly smile.

"Teenagers." Lily searched for malice in her heart toward either of them, but couldn't find any, certainly not for having sex while she watched the children. Still she felt insecure.

Suzanne showed the kids how to make whistles out of reeds. Anne was leaning toward the woman, one hand on her leg, so excited that she lifted herself up on her toes. "This is like magic," she said.

She tried to blow on the reed Suzanne gave her, but no sound came out.

"Like this," Suzanne said, holding the child's fingers.

James sat next to Lily, stretching his legs out toward the water.

"Tell me about your life," he said.

"I was orphaned at fourteen by a car accident. I finished high school living with my aunt, and I went to college in Phoenix, grad school at the University of Utah." As soon as she said it, she remembered she had told Suzanne she was from Montana. She knew that she hadn't given everything away because people could go to school in another state. But it still worried her. Either one of them could discover with only a little research that she was lying.

"In art."

"Painting. Installations."

"What kinds of things?"

"A picture of myself cut into pieces and put in—odd places. I hung empty frames in a park. I painted seat covers with my face and put them on the train. Then I ate only mac and cheese for a month and made a series of before and after paintings of my plates."

He raised his eyebrows.

"Fine art," she said. "Repetition and personal obsession. Conceptual."

"Then what?" asked James.

"With my art?"

"With your life."

"I had a bad marriage, and I ran away."

He watched her with total focus. She felt like an insect under a microscope.

She asked, "Tell me about your work."

"I managed a restaurant. Now I own it."

"So you're ambitious. A climber."

He twitched his head toward her, a flash of emotion, quickly buried.

"I got tired of working for someone else, so I figured out how to buy my own." He shook his head. "But that's enough. I'm not really ambitious. Certainly not a climber."

"And you're good with children. A perfect man."

"My first wife didn't think so."

"What happened?"

"She didn't find me romantic."

"That's what she told you?"

"Not in those words. She said that the fire had gone out. She wanted someone who held a permanent, all-consuming passion for her."

"Impossible."

"I'm going to take care of the flame this time," he said. "I'm trying to be better at love."

"I hope for your success," said Lily.

"How about you? You don't seem interested in a new relationship."

"You mean I never leave the house."

"You did today, and you did when you and Suzanne went out. You overcame your—ah—agoraphobia."

"I have no interest in a relationship right now."

Lily looked across at Suzanne. The kids were seated next to her on the bank, listening to her talk. Lily assumed it was a story. Anne stared up at her auntie, her mouth open, rapt.

Oh, how Lily didn't want to lose all this.

James stood, and Suzanne did also. "Time to head home." Mikey started crying, and Suzanne put her arm around him and spoke to him until he stopped. Lily watched James's face and saw the shadow of a frown appear. Then he turned and smiled when he saw her watching.

On the way home, Suzanne drove and James sat in the passenger seat. Lily sat between the children in the back. Lily could see that there was an unfinished conversation between the two of them.

He turned and looked at Suzanne.

"Not now," Suzanne said. "I'm not finished thinking it through."

The rest of the way home their shoulders were stiff with whatever needed to be said.

Levinas writes that truly recognizing the Other as transcendent and infinite is impossible, and that this failing is the origin of ethics. We continually reach for something we can't reach. Or we give up or we follow a set of rules to manage relationships. Levinas also says that erotic love is partially this reaching for an infinite other—keeping open the idea that the other is an unreachable mystery. But it's also a selfish act—satisfying one's own need. Suzanne hopes this relationship with James will last. People who are together for decades find that their mundane lives challenge their romantic feelings; working with the other to shop, clean the house, nurture children, and make decisions requires knowing how the other will respond. To get along we reduce the other to a manageable concept: the one who likes to shop (which I do, much more than Karla, who hates it) or the one who backs away from conflict (which we both do, so there are things we rarely talk about). After living together for a long time, many married people can no longer sense the infinite mystery of the other person. Interesting sex requires mystery and difference, and it's easy for that to also become perfunctory. James seems sincere, but courtship is an unnatural phase. In *Middlemarch* George Eliot wrote, "Has any one ever pinched into its pilulous smallness the cobweb of pre-matrimonial acquaintanceship?" Meaning that the knowledge one has of the beloved may seem as expansive as a spiderweb, but if you roll that web, it compresses into a small pill of actual knowledge. This is true not just of courtships but marriages and other long-term relationships. How much do we really know about each other?

That night James went back to his house in Edmonton. After the children were all asleep, Suzanne came to stand in Lily's doorway.

Lily set her book down and followed her friend into the kitchen.

Suzanne held her hands folded in front of her, as if she was praying.

"It's not sensible to keep two houses," said Lily.

Suzanne looked up from her hands. "That's what we've been discussing."

Lily waited.

"He thinks of my hesitance as a lack of faith in him."

Lily remembered that from Nathan. *You don't trust me anymore.* With him it meant that he wanted Lily to give up another freedom. By the time she realized what was going on, she hardly dared leave the bedroom, which was the only place he paid attention to her. What did it mean with James? She reminded herself repeatedly that men were a diverse class.

Suzanne said, "I want to know what you think."

"He doesn't want me to move to the new house with you."

"He hasn't said anything about you. I think he understands that you are valuable to us both if we are to keep working. He wants me to get a job in Edmonton. I don't think he understands how difficult that is for a First Nation woman. He wants me to work at his restaurant."

"As a waitress?" Lily said. "That's a step down from heavy-equipment operator."

"No, not waiting tables. I'd be keeping the finances, managing the restaurant while he opens another one." She unfolded her hands. "But yes, he doesn't see the need to keep paying rent on this house."

"What do *you* think?"

"I think that if I hold back, I fail him for sure. I have to let go of a safety net."

"Let go of a safety net?"

"You think that's foolish."

"I think it's insane. I had every safety net taken away. One by one."

Suzanne pursed her lips.

Lily stood. "You think I'm exaggerating. I'm not."

"I don't know whether you're exaggerating, because I know so little about what happened."

Lily opened her mouth. Shut it. "I'm frightened to leave this house. I'm frightened to be in the city. Before I came here I was on the reserve even before I knew what a reserve was."

Suzanne and James planned to take their time getting everything ready. First, he would train Suzanne in the operation of the old restaurant. Then they would buy a new property, and she would quit her heavy-equipment job to manage the restaurant while he got the new one running. Somewhere during these moves, they would get married and combine households.

Lily felt that she stood on crumbling ground. The wheel said she had almost two months left in Maskwacis, but Suzanne would certainly move out sooner than that. Should she try to stay on the reserve without Suzanne? That might be illegal but it was also certainly unwise. She wondered if Suzanne would try to take her with them. She might pay Lily to continue watching the children while she and James worked. Lily didn't think James would go for that.

She looked at the website Nathan had set up for finding Anne and saw that he had upped the reward to $75,000.

NINETEEN

One day, after lunch, when the children were having a nap, the doorbell rang. Lily looked through the side window, straight in the face of a Royal policeman. After he saw her, she couldn't pretend not to be home, so she opened the door. Her heart thudded, but she forced herself to smile.

"Have you seen this woman?" He held up the picture of her that Nathan had posted on the internet.

"No." It was the one Nathan took when she went after him with the knife. Only it didn't show the knife, just the face of an insane woman. "What has she done?" She took the picture from him and studied it.

"She kidnapped a child." He waited.

Her other hand started to move toward the base of her skull, because she hadn't died her hair for a month and knew the roots were coming out in her natural color. Luckily, she caught herself and held her hand still. "That's horrible. Whose child did she kidnap? And why?" She handed the photo back to him. "She looks like me."

"Yes, she does," he said. "Where are you from?"

"Montana," she said. "Where did she kidnap the child?"

"Salt Lake City."

"I lived there before I lived in Montana."

"Can I see some identification?"

She went back inside and showed him her papers.

He scrutinized them and handed them back. "This is set to expire."

"I know. I need to apply for PR papers."

"Yes. Why did you come here?"

"To nanny for Suzanne Wolf. She owns this house. She has three children and I take care of them while she works."

"You came from Montana to nanny for a First Nation woman?"

Lily took a breath, fighting for control of her panic. "My brother is a cowboy and he married Suzanne's daughter. That's why I knew she needed help. But now that I'm here, I'm thinking of immigrating because of the healthcare situation in the US."

He looked at her, weighing what she said. She had lost her edge, lost the ability to lie convincingly. Dread overwhelmed her panic and rose like bile from her stomach to her throat.

"She has three kids?"

"Two. Do you need to see them? They're asleep now."

He looked at her face again. "You do look a little like her. Not much, though." He thanked her and turned from the door, walking to his car.

Her head felt like it might burst from blood pressure, so she sat quickly on the couch because she was disoriented and unable to see clearly. She knew she needed to leave, but she had foolishly made no advance plan for when something like this happened. She needed to gather her wits and decide what to do.

When Suzanne came home, she saw Lily's face and asked what happened. Lily had been unable to pull herself together enough to pretend before her friend.

"Where's James?"

"He's gone to Saskatoon to see his children."

"My name isn't Alice. It's Lily Harker. I kidnapped Anne, when my former husband got custody of her. He's dangerous."

"Dangerous."

"So self-centered that he can hardly see anyone else."

"Hmm."

She told Suzanne the whole story. When she finished, she watched Suzanne's face.

"So why tell me now?" said Suzanne.

"Because—because a policeman came today. He had pictures of me. I don't think he recognized me, but I've been shaking all day."

"What are you going to do?"

"I considered leaving, but I couldn't bring myself to go again. It was so hard on Anne being homeless." She looked at Suzanne. "What do you want me to do?"

"I don't know. I could get into trouble from keeping you here."

"I didn't want to tell you."

Suzanne put her arms around Lily. "It's okay. You did the right thing."

Lily wondered if she could trust the hug.

"We'll wait until James comes back."

"I have enough money to get to Vancouver, or some other city, but I don't know what I'll do when I get there."

"We can afford to wait a few days."

Lily wasn't sure she could afford to wait. If the police came back, they would be in interrogation mode, but she was too tired to leave that night.

Too tired to leave this home.

It seemed clear that James had directed the police toward her. Her stomach sank. That meant they would come back. He could get everything he wanted if she disappeared. Suzanne would no longer hesitate to move in with him. They'd have $75,000 more to put into the new restaurant. He might have searched the internet and figured out who she was, especially since he already knew she was on the run from something.

The other, less likely option was that the police or Nathan had talked to the women's shelter in Butte and figured out that she had gone through there. They were looking into every town along that direction. She searched for news about her in Butte, but she could find nothing. She wished she could hack into the police computer and learn what they knew, but she didn't have that ability. She couldn't afford to stay as long as the wheel said she should stay.

When she saw Suzanne again, she said, "When you leave, I'm leaving."

"Where will you go?"

Lily shrugged.

"You won't tell me where you're going."

"If someone asks you, then you can honestly say you don't know."

"But who will take care of Mikey and Mia?"

"That was not a sustainable plan anyway," said Lily. "Not after you move to Edmonton. James wants you, not me."

"How will you survive?"

"I have over a thousand dollars. Before I had nothing. I'm better off now."

Lily decided not to wait. She quietly put on the backpack and lifted Anne into her arms. In the kitchen, she stood next to the back door and stared at the kitchen knife. She heard loud music and shouting from the direction of the co-op. Where would she go? How would she get a ride to Calgary or Edmonton?

She heard a noise and, turning, found Suzanne standing near the table. "The policeman already checked you out. Why would they come back?"

"It's so dangerous to stay here. He had a picture of me. I was saved this time only because it was a shitty picture."

"Don't answer the door. Don't go outside."

"Drive me to Calgary tomorrow," said Lily.

"I have to work, and what would you do there anyway?"

Follow the wheel. Which told her to stay in Maskwacis.

She took Anne back to her bed. She lay down but couldn't sleep.

The days, full of tension, moved from one to the next. She started at every noise, kept the curtains closed. She couldn't draw, couldn't relax. The time was both tedious and excruciating.

Three weeks later James and Suzanne took the kids to live in Edmonton. They planned on coming back a week later to get rid of stuff they didn't need right away, put it in storage or sell it. Lily said she'd stay that long, to clean the house, watch over things.

"Thanks," said Suzanne. "Soon as those boys know nobody's living here, they'll rip everything up."

The first thing Lily did after they left was to make a place for her and Anne in the attic. There was a trapdoor in the hallway ceiling. She put a step-ladder under the trapdoor and climbed up. It was dark up there, but some light came through a slatted vent to each end of the attic space. The dust was thick, but it would be a good hiding place. She tied a rope to the top of the ladder so she could pull it up after her. In the garage where Suzanne stored stuff she claimed from the houses she demolished, Lily found some thin boards that were about a foot wide. With Suzanne's old saw she cut a few of them into six-foot lengths, lifted them into the attic, and laid them together across the trusses next to the access hole. She found a length of carpet, which she laid across the boards. She hauled up a couple of old sleeping bags from the garage and a sheet, which she laid across the whole thing to guard against dust. She practiced lifting the stepladder up into the hole. She also practiced taking Anne to sit on the boards, telling her it was a game of hiding and quiet. Anne seemed to like the game and at odd times she'd say, "Let's hide, Mommy," and they'd slip up the ladder with Lily carrying her, placing her on the blanket and pulling the ladder up. They practiced enough that they could do it sound-lessly in 30 seconds. Anne's face was bright and happy when they sat together on the boards, the light coming in through the slats at each end of the attic. She was always quiet up there.

A few days later someone rang the doorbell. "Now we hide, Valerie," she said. They were up the ladder and crouched in the dark before the doorbell rang again. Lily whispered for Anne to stay on the blanket. She stepped on the rafters as she crossed the attic and peered out of the slats above the driveway, seeing two men in Levi's and t-shirts walk toward their car and drive away.

A week later the same thing happened. A car pulled up, so she peered through the window and saw James and a couple of men walking toward the house. Instead of going into the attic, a place James knew about because he had put a satellite TV receiver up there once, she headed out the back door and was gone with her pack and Anne into the trees. From the grove of trees, she watched James come out onto the back porch. He shrugged his shoulders, and soon she heard the sound of a car again. "Son of a bitch," she whispered. "That bastard." She had suspected him, but knowing for sure still hurt. She feared for Suzanne, who was binding herself permanently to him. Then she wondered if Suzanne knew, and that was an icy hand on her heart.

"What, Mommy?" said Anne.

"I'm mad at James," she said. "He's a bad man."

Anne frowned. "Is Auntie bad?"

"No, my Peach." *I hope not.*

"I'm not a peach. I'm Val." She put her arm on her mom's arm. "Is Auntie in trouble?"

"Maybe," said Lily. "I don't know."

They waited, playing in the dirt under the trees, until well after dark. Then Lily carried Anne back to the house. She lifted Anne into her crib and lay on her own bed.

Against all reason, she felt relaxed. Within minutes, she was sound asleep.

The morning of the move, when James and Suzanne had planned to come back with a rental truck, Lily worried that he'd bring the police with him. She told herself that Suzanne wouldn't let that happen, but $75,000 was a lot of money. She arranged to be in the trees when they arrived, and she watched from there. Nobody else was around. No police cars drove up. He might be waiting to call them, but she spun the wheel and it told her to go back to the house.

"Hey," said Suzanne. "Where were you?"

"Playing with Anne in the trees," she said.

She watched James, and he smiled back, and she couldn't see any benefit of making a scene in front of Suzanne, who would probably side with James.

Some of the furniture belonged to the house, to the local band of Crees, but they took everything else. Lily watched them loading the truck.

"Who's going to move in here?"

"The council is going to decide what to do with it. They'll allot it to someone. Probably in a few weeks."

Lily told them she would take a bus to Calgary, and from there back to the U.S.

After the truck was full, they all stood in the front yard. Lily hugged Mikey and Mia. She felt tears coming as Suzanne knelt in front of Anne and put her arms around the child. "Goodbye, Val. I'll miss you."

"Miss you, Auntie."

Lily hugged her friend. "You saved me," she said in Suzanne's ear. "Saved my life and soul."

"I hope you'll be all right," said Suzanne.

"I'll be fine except for this big hole in my heart."

James climbed in the truck, and Suzanne got her grandkids in the car.

As they pulled out with the truck, Lily and Anne waved. Suzanne looked back, a frown on her face that Lily couldn't read. Her first thought, one she tried to tamp down, was that Suzanne knew about the $75,000 and the policemen who had come. It felt as if the blood had drained from her body and she was just a shell of flesh. Worried about passing out, she went inside and sat down.

When she felt better, she told herself she was wrong, and she and Anne walked to the grocery store, bought cans of meat, vegetables, and fruit. They sat in front of the store, eating candy, as if they were waiting for the bus. They waited until dark, walked back to the house, and let themselves in with the key.

It was still strange being in the house without Suzanne. All the good memories seemed wiped out, as if they were just a fantasy.

"We staying here, Mommy?"

"We're staying here, yes."

"Will Auntie come home?"

"No, Auntie will live with James now. She's not coming back." Lily felt tears spring to her eyes. She blinked them away. She didn't, didn't, didn't want to have her last image of Suzanne be that face and that ambiguous frown. She realized the police might return.

"I want to play with Mikey and Mia."

For a minute she couldn't speak. "They live in a different place now. Soon we're going to leave and move to another town."

"What other town?"

"I don't know yet."

"I want to live in this house with Mikey and Mia and Auntie and you."

"I know you do, Baby. So do I."

They didn't use the electricity, even though it was still on, so that people in the row of houses to the north and the people to the west, on the other side of the grove of trees, wouldn't see lights.

That night some boys broke in. She had worried about that, but when she first heard their voices, she went up the ladder with Anne. She worried that they might set the place on fire, but they just sat on the couch and drank. Soon they left. She told herself again and again that she should just leave, but she didn't. She stayed in the house and spent all her days with Anne.

She painted a canvas, a portrait of Suzanne as they said goodbye. Then she scraped all the paint off and painted another, a picture of James, which showed him bent over a chessboard, his face perplexed. She liked the ambiguity. Was he perplexed about her move on the chessboard, or was he thinking about how he might get rid of her or how he might profit from the reward on her head? Whatever he might be thinking, she knew he saw her as an object, a piece to be moved here or there. She scraped off the paint and painted a portrait of Nathan from memory. He had dark, dark hair and a pale face and she made his face look lustful, then angry, then sly. She thought of the painting as if it was actually him looking out from the canvas at her. She gave his mouth a sneer of distaste, as if he was looking at a slug or a parasitic worm. He had cut people out of her life until no one but him was left.

Earlier, I described Adam's reaction to Lilith's fleshiness and desire to be in control. Repulsed and slighted, he repudiated her. Abandoned by Adam and banished by God, what would Lilith do? Some myths say she is not subject to death, being created before the Fall. She still wanders the earth, an eternal outsider, strangling infants and seducing dreaming men. Isaiah connected Lilith to demons of the desert, where strange and unnatural creatures dwell—those who might refuse to follow the pathway laid down for them by God: "Wildcats shall meet with hyenas, goat-demons shall call to each other; there too Lilith shall repose, and find her resting place. There shall the owl nest and lay and hatch and brood in its shadow; there too the buzzards shall gather, each one with its mate."

Nebuchadnezzar, like Lilith, was driven into the wilderness, where his heart became like that of a beast; he "did eat grass as oxen, and his body was wet with the dew of heaven, till his hairs were grown like eagles' feathers, and his nails like birds' claws." He escaped human culture and its confining structures. Free of his previous life.

According to my uncles, my grandfather forgot what it meant to be human after living alone for thirty years in the desert. He forgot how to have intimate relationships. When Marilyn Monroe died, my grandfather imagined that the wind whining through the cliffs sounded like her and her sirens moaning. He had hired someone to irrigate and build fences, but this man was an alcoholic and a pedophile, a man who feared adult women and felt revulsion toward them. These two named the moaning cliffs Whorehouse Rock. Bureau of Land Management mapmakers changed the title to Warehouse Rock. Until now, I've only seen humor in my grandfather's story, but it is sad to think of those lonely, complicated men dreaming about a woman whose real name was Norma Jean.

Those two weeks were some of the strangest Lily had spent in her strange life. She missed Suzanne. Despite the ambiguous look as they parted, she was Lily's only friend. She worried what she might become if she had no other adult in her life. The boys came often to the empty house, so she retreated to the grove, to a room-sized meadow with white-barked birches for walls. She felt like a feral animal, a deer or goat keeping away from the predators, which added to her concern that she might forget how to be a human.

She spread a blanket and they sat or lay under the dappled shade. It was cool and pleasant there, even though it was late July. She put half of her money and everything essential in a backpack. She kept the rest of the money in a pocket of her trousers.

She brought her drawing and painting supplies and painted her mother and father, Suzanne and James and the two children. She did two more portraits of Anne. Each time she scraped the paint off, erasing what she had done. Anne drew as well—swirls of color and form that Lily thought were lovely. They built small statues out of twigs and stones. She told Anne long stories, and it gladdened her heart to see Anne listening with rapt attention. She had worried about bugs, but they never got bad. After dark, if the lights were on in Suzanne's house, she wrapped herself and Anne in the blanket and stayed out all night. She never slept well, hearing every rustle in the underbrush as a threat. When it was daylight and they were still safe, she felt happy. They ate breakfast early and ate two lunches in the grove of trees. In between they played or napped.

Anne told her more stories. "There was a mommy fairy and a girl fairy, and they had a big sword, and they used it to hurt all the bad guys." Another story: "The fairy and her mommy lived in space on a planet and nobody else lived there. They were alone all the time."

"Good stories," she said to Anne, but they also made her long for the time when the house seemed full. Mikey, Mia, and Anne, playing and laughing; she and Suzanne sitting on the back step. Now, even that face seemed ambiguous, untrustworthy. The two versions of Suzanne seemed to rip her heart in two.

Lily cleared a patch of sand from debris and made art there—sticks, stones, leaves, and lines in the sand. She drew more pictures in the sand for the stories she told Anne.

She followed a whim and tried to teach Anne letters, but the child was not interested, she put heads on all the As and Bs, then added legs and arms. She sang,

> "Mikey, Mia, mommy me.
> Playing in the sand.
> Drawing in the sand."

Once Lily had flown to New York to shop for a dress for Nathan's sister's wedding. The memory seemed like something she had seen on television or in a movie. Lily had tried

ANNE MAKING ART IN THE DIRT
Automythology (USP)

on dress after dress, but then she had realized Anne was gone. She couldn't see her anywhere. Then the saleslady pointed to a rack of gowns. The faint sound of singing came from the rack. Bending low, Lily saw Anne's two feet. She had been stroking her hand across the fabric, singing her pleasure. Lily had picked her up and hugged her, but Anne arched her back, trying to get out of Lily's arms. The saleslady gave Anne a ring of swatches to play with and she had sat happily, touching one and then another of the textures of cloth. Now as Lily tried to picture herself in that store, she realized that every dress had been different, every gown on those racks didn't have a duplicate. And each one was worth many times the money she had earned for tending Mikey and Mia.

In the afternoons when Anne napped, her face dappled by leaf shadow, Lily watched her, the curve of her forehead, with Lily's mother's blonde hair falling across. The two curves of her lips, her cheeks. Her tiny nose, her legs and arms, which were thinning out after being pudgy her whole life—a precious child.

She avoided thinking about what she would do next, planning immediate escape routes. Beyond that, she tried to inhabit the current moment, sufficient unto itself. Time seemed to slow and nearly stop, her whole world a child on a blanket. Despite missing Suzanne, the old Suzanne, she thought this was sufficient. All the universe folded into its simplest whole as she waited for the days to pass that the wheel had given her in this place.

TWENTY

A couple of weeks later, Lily heard someone walking in the grove of trees. She gathered her things and walked to Suzanne's old house, slipping behind it, so that it was unlikely that anyone in the row of houses to the north saw her. Again, she felt like a doe and fawn, slipping here and there, trying to be invisible.

Then one day she heard footsteps, but before she could gather her things, a young man, probably eighteen, and a girl, maybe thirteen came to the grove. He looked at Lily and his eyes showed no emotion, not even humor. Lily looked at the girl. He held her arm above her elbow. Her face was complex, fear and an odd kind of triumph. Lily was drawn to the girl, couldn't take her eyes away. It was like looking into the face of a virgin sacrifice.

"What are you doing in our grove, our town, white woman?"

"I've lived here for a year."

"A year in this little clump of trees? I've never seen you. You're lying."

"I lived in that house with Suzanne Wolf. I have nowhere else to go. So when she moved out, I stayed on."

"Leave," he said. He worked out, she could tell—his arms were sculpted. His face was angular, very handsome. The scars on his face might have been the scars of a Cree from a hundred and fifty years earlier. If he had been born then, he might have been a chief's son, because he possessed the arrogance of a young warrior. Looking at him was disorienting because he wore the clothing of a city gang member, low trousers, shirt too big, chains from his pocket, tattoos with gang symbols. She started gathering the blanket.

"Leave that," he said. "It will make it nicer for her." His face was not even arrogant, just flat. He took the blanket because he could. He took it to demonstrate power over Lily and the girl, not for any concern over the girl's comfort.

Lily looked at her. Would he be gentle with her? Lily had no hope for that. The girl wanted this, wanted the status it would bring. She gathered her backpack and Anne and left. After that threat, she carried the mace in her pocket.

Lily was in the attic the next evening when he came to her house with four younger boys, all with thick arms. She couldn't see if they carried guns. They went inside and called for her, "White woman! You don't belong in our town." Frightened that they would shoot up the house, she held Anne, held her hand to Anne's mouth.

When they didn't find her inside, they left.

They were right: she didn't belong in their town. In most towns across Canada and the United States, they would be in the minority, but here she was the one who had no power. She also knew that nowhere was as dangerous as the house. She imagined her picture in the post office, in every police car in Edmonton and Calgary, and all the towns between. Hopefully James thought she was gone, so there would be no reason for the police to return for her.

Also, the wheel had told her to stay. She berated herself, swore at her own stubbornness, a kind of willed stupidity. Deciding again to leave, she grabbed the backpack and started toward the community center and grocery store. She saw a car crossing the road ahead of her, boys' arms hanging out the windows. Rather than facing them, she turned around and walked back to the house. The next day she made it out to the highway. The bus was supposed to pass at three o'clock, but it didn't come. She held her thumb out, raised high, and seven cars passed without slowing down. People coming out of the store or stopping at the gas station looked at her, unsmiling. When she still didn't have a ride after dusk, she crept along the streets back to the house.

As a thought experiment, I want to explore the similarity between the society I live inside in Utah and the social structure of gangs. Gang members think of themselves as a community, or even a family. Gang communities are dispersed, not continuous like the dominant patriarchal and racist culture in which I live and breathe. Gang society is more of an archipelago. According to the FBI, 30,000 gangs are active in the

United States—1.4 million people. Gangs are groups of people who associate with each other, have common interests, clear organization, and strong leadership—punishing those who disobey or leave. Just like my culture in Utah. They act as a group in pursuit of common goals and they claim a specific area. People in Utah and gang members draw identity from the name of their groups—not Bloods and Crips but conservative Christians and Republicans. Gangs have common hand signs and graffiti instead of hand shaking and street numbers. The gang, again like my state's dominant culture, is based on masculine hierarchy, where status is essential. A woman's sexuality is capital, and it is the property of the community. Loss of dignity to the leader/father is dangerous for everyone in both cultures—similar to packs of wolves.

Gangs seem like any other group, except that most religious, community, and social communities don't focus on committing crime, at least not openly. Among my own people, especially among Utah Mormons, fraud is high, as are pyramid businesses selling soap, cosmetics, or nutrition supplements. Another difference between gangs and the dominant culture is participation in traditional institutions—family, church, school, and business. Disintegration of these mainstream support systems invites the growth of gangs.

Not all Mormons fit my description, but many do. And it's not just Utah that is patriarchal, racist, and homophobic. Across the country, the sexist, racist system values social identity above ability. It may be empirically true that a woman, a Black, a Latino, a gay person could be as productive or effective as a white man, but many people believe that women, gays, and people of color are weaker, less rational, less industrious.

Consequently, it doesn't make sense to view them as equals or reward them as equals, and many men don't risk making the empirical tests that might help them question this view. In the U.S. women make eighty percent of what men make. Blacks and Latinos make seventy-five percent of what whites earn. It's a matter of not seeing potential. In Levinas's terms, the racist or sexist viewer totalizes the Other rather than seeing them as an infinite being.

Going back to gang members: they can be Latino, Black, Native American, or White, but they are all totalized by middle class people who fear the violent unknown—so the image of them for the white middle class is that they are marked by foreignness. Even Lily, who is not particularly racist, fears them and is unable to see their faces as human.

Lily and Anne were in the grove, and the boys came so quietly that she didn't hear them coming. She looked up, and they were already inside her small clearing. The boy she'd seen before was in the center, the three others moved smoothly and quickly to surround her and Anne. She stood. Anne looked up, silent.

They had guns stuck into the waists of their pants, but the youngest one didn't even have one, so maybe their intent was just to rape her. The youngest one stepped forward, and Lily focused on his face. He was frightened, she could tell. Whatever they planned, this was his rite of passage. Panic rose in her, but also a feeling of disorientation—a century and a half earlier he might have been on a quest to prove his manhood by raiding an enemy band. Their faces shifted between boy and man, and she didn't know how to convince them to let her go.

"Do you want to know my story?" she asked the leader. She took steps away from Anne, and the circle shifted slightly. The leader stepped past Anne.

Lily stepped toward the youngest boy. "I'll tell *you* my story."

The frightened boy looked puzzled. He looked toward the other one, the leader.

"I come from Salt Lake. My husband was a cruel, cruel man, and he took my child from me. I stole her back, and I've been running ever since. I have escaped him and the police by moving in random directions, not knowing where to go next. I spin a wheel and follow it."

The boy looked nervously from her to his leader. He didn't know what to do.

"So following that random path, I came here and I lived with Suzanne Wolf. I am a fugitive from the police."

She looked from face to face. The only emotion showing was in the boy, the one who was supposed to rape her first. She wanted to shout, "Why? Why do you need to do this?" But she knew there was no reason, or a reason that was internal to their group. The others, the three who had already been through what the boy was going through, stood impassive, just waiting. They stood in a half circle, within arm's length of her.

Fear rose and kept rising in Lily. She knew she couldn't pay any attention to that or she wouldn't be able to think.

She kept talking. "There is a $75,000 reward on my head."

The leader shook his head slightly, but she kept talking, "Suzanne and I had a good relationship, but she found a man who wanted her to move with him to Edmonton. So she abandoned me."

She knew it was a mistake, but she turned toward him. He was slightly taller, so she had to look up into his face. "I've been living on canned meat and vegetables, a little fruit. I'm going to leave next week and go someplace else, someplace random." Anne started to cry, wailing, and Lily saw the youngest one glance at the child.

She knew words wouldn't change anything, but still she continued, filling the air with them because they were all she had. "My girl played with Suzanne's kids. We had a good household until that man came and ruined it all. He tried to turn me in to the police, but they couldn't find me."

She could see he was losing patience. He took half a step toward her, and all the others did also. He was about a foot away from her. The half circle had maybe two yards of space inside. She thought about running, but that would probably provoke them to shoot her, not just rape her. Or she could go ahead and let the youngest one have sex with her, but they would probably all rape her afterward. She could never outrun them, especially not with Anne, and not when they had guns. She stepped toward the leader. She knew it wasn't logical, but she looked him in the eyes, feeling as if she was staring into the eyes of a wolf. He didn't back down, she didn't back down. She knew there was no way to talk past this one.

Then one of the boys said, "Jason." The leader turned and looked. The boy pointed toward Suzanne's house, where an SUV had parked. Two Mounties and a plain clothes detective stood at the front of the house. One went around to the back door. They went inside and soon emerged.

Lily pushed between two of the boys, grabbed Anne and the backpack, and stumbled out of the clearing. She looked back and the boys had disappeared. She walked through the trees to the opposite end of the grove. She didn't dare stay there because of the pathway worn in the weeds between Suzanne's house and the grove, so she walked toward the closest house, keeping the grove between her and the Mounties. She tried the front door but it was locked. She lowered her shoulder and drove it into the door. The door didn't budge, so she ran around to the back door, slammed her shoulder into it. Three tries before the deadbolt splintered the wood of the frame and she was inside. Walking through the orderly kitchen, she regretted ruining the doorframe. The table had four chairs and a high chair pushed against it. She jammed a chair against the door.

Off the kitchen, in the center of the house, was a bathroom. She shut the door and sat on the floor and held Anne, letting the tension go. Anne wailed and Lily sobbed from fear and the rush of adrenaline, stronger than she'd ever felt. Anne's crying seemed impossibly loud, and she thought the Mounties would certainly hear. She put a towel under the door, sat on the toilet lid, and rocked Anne until she calmed. She expected the door to burst open, but nothing happened.

Soon, she washed Anne's face and her own with soap. She had told Suzanne she was leaving, so why had the Mounties come? If someone had seen her, the tribal police would have come. Unless that person had told Suzanne, who might have said to James, "Oh, my friend told me that Lily's still living in the old house. I wonder why she hasn't left. It's not safe for her there." Then he might have told the officers. Lily thought, *Maybe that's the way it happened.* But her image of Suzanne as her sister was still made ambiguous. That and Suzanne's frown as she left created a new image of her friend in Lily's fearful mind—one that made her feel as if her own soul was torn in half.

Neither the grove nor the house was safe now. Suzanne had told her the name of the oldest woman in town, an elder that even the gangs left alone. This woman's house was not far away, just on the other side of Suzanne's house from where she hid, but she didn't dare go there in daylight. She waited with Anne in the bathroom until she heard someone drive up, then she went out the back door and walked along the street, watching for the boys. She cut across to the grocery and sat inside in the back next to the bakery until they closed. Then she trotted back along the street to the woman's house.

She knocked on the door. Soon the curtain parted, and she heard an old and shaky voice say, "Who is there? Who are you?"

"I'm Alice Jenkins, I've been living with Suzanne Wolf. I was attacked by a gang of boys. I need to get off the street. I'm worried they'll come back." The door didn't move. "I know you're Belinda Bobtail, and that the boys leave you alone."

The door opened, and Lily stepped inside. The woman was bent with age, her face wrinkled. "Sit down," she said. "Tell me what happened."

Lily told her about her encounters with the gang, but she didn't tell about the police who had come. Then she had to tell her what she was doing in Maskwacis, so she told her the whole story from the beginning. Then she waited.

"You want me to keep you, a criminal?"

"Yes," said Lily. "In a week I'll leave."

"Why in a week?"

Lily told her about the wheel, about trusting chance.

"You think it's chance?"

"I don't believe in God."

"I believe in something," said the woman. "I'm not sure it's God, but there's something. Some pull toward good."

"Not in those boys," said Lily.

"I don't think that's true," said the old woman. "There is a sense of loyalty to each other. There is pride. They will look for you."

"I will leave this town in five days," said Lily.

The woman turned away from her, and Lily thought she was going to open the door and ask her to leave. The woman stood with her hand on the door. Then she turned and looked out the front window. After a few minutes she walked back toward Lily.

"I have a room that was my son's," the woman said. "You can stay there."

Lily stayed inside, only leaving the bedroom to eat or use the toilet. The old woman let her shower, which was a pleasure—holding Anne's slick, small body. Anne seemed to accept their new life all right, but she became more silent, which she always did when she was anxious. Lily tried talking to her about the encounter with the gang because it must have terrified her, but Anne wouldn't say anything back. Lily held her every night, told her stories. Sometimes Anne told one back. Generally her stories were about a princess, kitten, rabbit, or owl. Living together in a tower. Outside somewhere was a dragon, a coyote, wolf, or bad man.

Finally, it was the night before the end of her time in Maskwacis. She would leave in the morning. Nobody, not even God, knew where she'd go.

Despite this realization, she slept well, already mourning as she left this town where she had spent a happy year. It hadn't been without trouble, and she'd learned again not to trust anyone, but she and Suzanne had been happy for a long time. She would try to remember that and not that James, and maybe Suzanne, had tried to turn her in for the reward.

The next morning, she ate breakfast with Anne and Belinda. "My son will take you as far as Calgary."

With Belinda watching and with a map of the surrounding area, shaded to show the three reserves, spread on the kitchen table, Lily spun the wheel twice: southwest, 55 miles. The only town close to that point was Stettler, which Belinda didn't know much about. It was off the reserve. The old woman called her son, who must have been reluctant to get involved at first. Belinda spoke sharply into the phone and hung up. Within five minutes he was parked in front of her house. Lily shouldered her backpack, took Anne's hand, and rushed from the door to the car. He asked her to duck down until they were away from town.

"I don't want this coming back on me or my mother."

T W E N T Y - O N E

Belinda's son said he'd take her all the way to Stettler. She was happy for the ride, but not happy about anyone knowing which way she'd gone. He let her off at the city library.

She thanked him and gave him $50. He held his hand up. "No," he said. "My mother would not be happy."

"Then buy something for her and give it to her for me, okay?"

He still shook his head. Lily felt stupid, trying to give money to pay for the woman's generous blessing.

Inside the library that looked like the convention center in Layton where she and Anne had slept that one night, she got on the computer and surveyed the web for news. The reward was higher, $90,000. Nothing else had changed. She leaned back in her chair, happy that she had almost $1,000.

Anne climbed onto her lap. "I want to go to our new house."

"I don't know where it is yet."

"Why don't you?" Her voice was whiny.

"That is a good question. Let's go get some lunch." They went to a hamburger shop, and Anne sat on a booster chair in a booth. Lily handed her a child's menu and talked about the options. Anne seemed very pleased when her food came.

She walked downtown with Anne, bought some hair dye, and went to the bathroom in the city park and cut her hair short. She also cut Anne's hair short. Nobody had come in during the cutting so she bent over the sink and started dying her own hair. Halfway through a girl came in, but left again. The stink was bad enough to drive anyone away. She changed her hair color to auburn and bleached Anne's to blonde. After cleaning up as well as she could, she went to the Salvation Army and bought men's clothing. She already had a long piece of fabric to bind her breasts. She also bought boy's clothing for Anne. She practiced walking and moving like a young man.

She didn't know how long she should stay, whether to spin the wheel for time or for a new destination. She was a little frightened of spinning the wheel, which could take her straight back to Maskwacis. So she did nothing. Picking up a newspaper, she looked at the want ads. Someone wanted a gardener, a house cleaner, someone for childcare, an assistant painter. She liked the idea of childcare, because she could keep Anne with her, but she didn't want to get attached again. When she thought about never seeing Mikey and Mia, she felt the loss as if it had just happened.

She prepared a story, to explain why she wanted to be paid in cash. "I have left the U.S. because of our wars in Iraq and Afghanistan, and because of our immigration policy. Also we don't take care of our own in terms of welfare or medical needs, and fundamentalists are dismantling our society." She decided her best bet was house cleaning. If she charged by the job, not by the hour, she could take Anne with her and have breaks when she needed to. She rented a motel room for one night and planned to look for an apartment the next day.

She sat on the bed and looked at the wheel. She paced back and forth but finally gave up. She spun the wheel for days, weeks, and months and it came up days. Then she spun it for the number of days and it came up one.

She threw it across the room. "To hell with you," she said.

Anne woke up from her nap and stared at Lily with huge eyes.

"You scared me, Mommy," said Anne. "I don't like it."

"Sorry, Baby," she said. Then she smiled and soon they were both laughing.

She decided not to do anything until she'd eaten. She walked to the grocery store, carrying her backpack with the wheel inside. She bought some bread, cheese, and grapes for dinner, which she took back to the motel room. After Anne was asleep, she lay down but couldn't stop turning and twitching. Finally, she got up and spun the wheel for direction—southwest.

The next morning as she left the motel room, she saw a semi driver standing next to his rig. It was backed up to the store where workers unloaded it. Lily walked over and talked to him, found out he was headed toward Calgary and then Banff.

"Take us with you," she said in her deepest voice. "I'll pay you $100."

He looked at her, gave a half smile. "$200."

She frowned, pursed her lips. "Deal."

He extended his hand and gripped hers so hard it hurt. He pointed and she climbed up into the passenger's seat with

Anne. She had food in her pack and a truck that would take her far from where the police had most recently looked.

She held Anne on her lap so the girl could see out the window. The driver pulled out onto the highway. "My name is John Hansen. You would have gone with me anywhere I was going, wouldn't you?"

"Steven Place." She started to say that she would only go southwest, but that meant she'd have to explain. "Anywhere but here."

"I wouldn't have thought that a young, ah, guy with a kid would be so—"

"Flexible? The kid's mother ran off, and I just need to get out of here, take a chance on where to go next. I have no heart for making a plan, but I'll make one."

"The kid's mother." He rolled his head in a circle, and she heard his neck crack. "I used to travel with my wife. Our home was this truck, but she got tired of it."

"Of not having a home?"

"We're going to a new home," said Anne.

"Good," he said to Anne. "My wife was always looking. Never satisfied."

"Your wife?" said Anne. "Auntie?"

John smiled at the child. "What do you plan to do in Banff?"

"I'll find something."

"Probably not a good time. Slack time. Summer tourists are leaving and the skiers won't come until there's snow."

"If I can't find something I'll move on."

They pulled into Calgary, and he drove to a warehouse—Canada Food Group.

Anne said she was hungry, so Lily opened the sack and gave her a cheese sandwich and some grapes. Soon John climbed back into the truck, and he pulled out of the yard.

"Do you want some food?" she asked him. "I have cheese, bread, and grapes."

"I'll have some grapes."

Anne took them out of the pack and passed him the bunch.

"Thanks, but not that many."

Lily broke a small cluster off and handed them across.

"Delicate hands," John said.

Lily had no response. She didn't know why she kept up the charade; clearly he knew she was not a man. They started across the flat toward the distant mountains. Anne went to sleep on her lap, and she pretended to sleep as well.

She thought about her year with Suzanne, how good it had been. Then a snake had entered the garden, not for the first time in her life.

She opened one eye.

"What do you do?" asked John, who had apparently been watching her.

Anne sat up also.

"What is my trade? I'm an artist, so I don't know how to do anything practical."

"Artists make pictures," said Anne. "She made a picture of me."

"I'm sure it's great." He smiled. "Banff is full of people who don't know how to do anything practical."

"But I can work hard, so I'll find something."

"I've got something for you to read," said John. He reached into a shelf behind his head and brought down a blue-colored book. A Book of Mormon. Lily hesitated before reaching for it. It was so unexpected, and her own reaction was even more unexpected. It looked like the one her parents had given her when she turned eight. It was nostalgic, but not for a time she wanted to go back to.

"You don't have to take it," he said. "I can tell you're already acquainted with the book."

"Yes," she said. "I was born Mormon."

"I'll bet you don't have one anymore."

She shook her head. "No, not for a long time now." She took the book because he wanted her to. Opening the pages to the pictures, she showed them to Anne. She remembered from childhood the prophets, all men with unnatural muscles—like young Arnold Schwarzenegger.

The road headed arrow-straight across a plane with farms spread across it; in the distance were mountains, tall and dark, like the ones east of Salt Lake. As they drove, she thought about what she believed, not in a male god, for sure not that. A gendered god was invested in power, and she'd had enough of male power. She remembered the scriptures from her childhood. "For I am a jealous god, my wrath is kindled, I will not turn my fierce anger away." A being who required the worship of lower beings and who grew angry when they didn't glory in his name was not a being she could respect. At the same time, she couldn't imagine a powerful being who wouldn't be full of his own power. She was also confused about God's decision to stand back and leave humans alone. Mormons believe a father takes care of his children, but God doesn't interfere with human action. So if Lily prayed for Anne's safety, but there was a drunk driver on the road, would God intervene? She thought not. Otherwise God would step in and stop pedophiles from harming children.

Lily believed a Mother God wouldn't be so heartless. Eliza Snow, an early Mormon poet, wrote, "In the Heavens are parents single? No, the thought makes reason stare! Truth is reason; truth eternal tells me I've a mother there." Later in the lyric she writes, "When I leave this frail existence, when I lay this mortal by, Father, Mother, may I meet you in your royal courts on high?" Mormons don't talk much about Mother in Heaven, praying to her in public could get a person disciplined. Despite this, many Mormon women pray to Mother in Heaven in secret.

"You think you'll ever come back to the Church?"

"I don't trust God."

"Maybe someday you'll feel different," he said. "Maybe someday you'll feel the need to come back."

She slowly shook her head. No. Not ever.

They finally drove into Banff, and he turned, backed up to the dock behind a grocery store.

"This is it," he said. "In an hour I'm headed back toward Calgary."

He offered his hand, and she shook it, trying to grip as hard as he did. He held the grip a few seconds too long, so she pulled free.

"You're lucky you happened upon me. Some drivers would have taken advantage of you, and dropped you and your kid in the middle of nowhere."

She shrugged. "I'm glad you're one of the good ones." She turned and carried Anne away, walking fast. She believed that most truck drivers would have been all right. John seemed to want to think and talk about what he could have done to her but wouldn't, because of his religion. Getting his kicks vicariously.

"I can walk, Mommy," said Anne. "Put me down."

"In a minute, Valentino Peach."

"You know I don't like that name."

Lily clung to her and kept walking, hoping to get the bad taste out of her mind.

John, who I've named for myself, is not a good host, and unless some significant sorrow knocks him out of his inflexible world view, he never will be one. He stands as a lesson in humility for me. How should we respond to ungracious hosts? Lily has confronted many who didn't welcome her freely: her aunt, the women who managed the shelter in Salt Lake, the supervisor of the welfare center in Kaysville, James, and of course Nathan.

At a creative writing convention, I heard George Saunders speak. He is Buddhist and spoke about the conflicts between literary writers, who are often liberals, and the conservative political and social structure we live in. He said that while he might be a mediocre person, sometimes acting mindfully and sometimes not, when he is writing he is focused and mindful. I've thought about this myself. While writing, I try to be my best self, I can't overtly boast, complain, whine, pity myself, hold forth dogmatically, judge others too harshly or express hatred of them. Literary traditions of balance, empiricism, rationality, and a general love of people make personal failings obvious. Saunders suggested that he and his audience try to transfer those writerly restraints to their lives—treating even enemies with respect. He said that this doesn't mean anyone should allow others to harm them. We may respectfully remove ourselves from their homes or respectfully ask an ungracious guest to leave. The same is true of virtual hospitality in public relations.

However, someone in a position of weakness—Lily and those who are repressed because of gender, race, class, or some other characteristic—might not have a margin of safety in being generous with those who enjoy power and use it to harm others. Lily and others may have to fight back.

Lily walked for fifteen minutes before she was calm enough to stop and put Anne down. She breathed the crisp, piney air and it tasted like freedom. She went into a store and bought a stroller.

"We live here?" asked Anne.

"Yes," she said. "For a while."

She found a daycare center where they allowed drop-ins. She left Anne playing with the other children but stayed in the building, watching her child through a window they had in the office. Finally, she shrugged and forced herself away from the window and out of the building. She walked to every restaurant near the center of town, many of them similar in style to the restaurants in Park City—mountain rustic. None of the restaurants would have her. The lodges were the same. She asked about cleaning rooms, and they said they were full up with maids. So she went to a bathroom, unbound her breasts, put on clothing that would fit a woman, thinking that they might no longer think it strange that she would descend to cleaning rooms. Introducing herself as Susan Carson, she got a job in the third place she tried. She said she wanted to just work part-time; the manager said that, since she was from the States, she could work for cash. She could have a room in a building behind the lodge for half of her wage, which was fine with her.

The manager, whose name was Todd, said she'd start the first of September. He gave her the number of a daycare close by, so she called to confirm a space for Anne. This would take the bigger part of the salary she had left after paying for her room. That night she explained to Anne what would happen, that she would play with children, learn her letters, and then Lily would come and get her. Anne's face looked frightened, but then she asked, "Will Mikey and Mia be there?"

Lily shook her head. "No, but kids like them will be there."

Anne frowned, clearly not satisfied with that answer.

The next day Lily walked Anne to daycare. The building was an old house, with the downstairs for the children. The woman in charge was brisk and quick with Lily, asking her to leave because hanging around would just prolong the separation. Lily shook her head. "Fifteen minutes. I'll sit in the corner and watch."

The woman looked more intently at Lily, and then nodded. Lily put Anne down, and the woman knelt in front of the child. Her entire demeanor changed from brisk to soft.

She smiled. "Welcome to our school, Val. Do you want to play with the other children?"

Anne nodded.

"Can you use your words?"

"I want to play with my friends."

"Go play." Anne smiled and touched the woman on the cheek before running to play with toys and other children.

Lily sat in the corner. The room was big, twenty by twenty, had books and beanbags in one corner, toys in another, tables, cupboards, and a refrigerator. In another room was a rubber floor with a small slide and other things to climb on. The woman had two assistants who sat on the floor and played with the children. The first woman, June, sat and watched. Lily had the impression that she listened to every word spoken. Anne ran to Lily twice, both times she stood between her knees for a moment, just making sure she was there, and then ran back to the other children.

When Lily's time was almost over, the woman said, "Circle up." All the children made a circle on the floor. The two assistants were part of the circle. Anne looked up, but kept playing with her toy, a board that made animal noises when she pulled a string. The woman knelt in front of Anne. "Sometimes we need to talk, all of us together. Do you understand?"

"Yes." She left the toy and sat in the circle.

"When we share, how do we do it?" said the woman.

"If someone wants my toy, I give them another one," said a boy, bigger than the others.

"What if that doesn't make them happy?"

"Then they're not sharing," said the boy. "They just want my toy."

June didn't argue with him. "Is there a way you can make it so both are happy?"

"No," said the boy.

"Take turns," said another child.

"Tell the teacher to make them share," said another.

The woman never corrected the children, but she talked with them.

"Both people can't always be happy," said the boy, "but both can be partly happy."

The next time Anne ran to her, Lily lifted her and said, "I'm leaving now. I'll come back after you have lunch, and we'll do something fun."

At first Anne seemed worried, but then she turned to the other children, who were playing with toys. She nodded, jumped down, and ran to join in.

Lily felt peace blossom inside her. Later, she put the wheel in the back of a drawer in their apartment, not wanting to know how long she would have in this new place.

Her work was easy on the brain, but strenuous on her body. She had to clean five rooms in an hour, but during her first hour, she could only do two. Her trainer said, "You have to be quicker. You have to make it a habit you don't think about." After four hours she was a little more efficient, having cleaned thirteen rooms.

One of the other maids told her about a hot-spring swimming pool, built on a flat spot on the mountainside above Banff. From the pool, the swimmers could look over the valley, the high granite peaks, the pine forests, the cleared ski runs, snowless for now. On her day off, Wednesday, she took a bus up and played in the warm water with Anne, showing her how to float. Their first time in the pool it started snowing, the first of the season, huge flakes falling on their faces and wet heads. Lily and Anne watched the waves of flakes falling across the valley.

"I'm swimming," Anne said, moving her hands like fish wriggling in the water.

"Yes. Now hold to the side and kick your feet."

"I'm floating."

"Yes, you certainly are."

"Is my skin coming off?" She held up her hand.

"No, the water makes your fingers crinkly."

They went to eat at a diner, and when the meal was over, Lily didn't want to go home, shut up in their small apartment again. Anne was bored in the diner, so Lily opened a napkin and drew a picture of a butterfly on it. She used her knife to cut out the wings. Then she put a bit of honey on the end of a straw and glued the straw to the body of the butterfly. She showed Anne how to make the paper insect flap its wings. It wasn't perfect, both wings kept clinging to each other so the wings wouldn't flap like a real butterfly. For a few minutes Anne went up and down between the tables, waving the butterfly, grinning as if it was a real toy.

When Lily was young, her family had enough money, but she got it in her head that they were poor. She wanted a drawing case, one with colored pencils, markers, watercolor, scissors, and clay, a complete art set. Her mother put one together by buying materials, some used, and put it all in a shoe box, but her aunt gave her a complete set, brand new. Lily looked at the two sets and became angry with her mother. "You shouldn't give gifts that are bad gifts, you should only give the best gifts." Her mother didn't respond, but a line in her jaw tightened. Even as a child Lily noticed that tightening. After her parents died she remembered this and felt bad, but there was nothing she could do about it.

While Anne was at daycare, Lily worked a four-hour shift, all she wanted. She made beds for the guests who would stay another day. For the others she tore off the sheets and replaced them. She replaced soap, vacuumed, cleaned the toilets and the bathtub. She thought about the fact that this was work for the marginalized—the old, the foreign, and the female. It seemed like a joke because that's where she wanted to be, poor enough to be invisible; not in anybody's database, trackless on the internet. She was grateful not to be in jail. She still had Anne with her, and she could make money to save for when she had to move again.

They settled into a routine, Anne and Lily. First they had work and day school, and then they spent time together in the library, apartment, or at the mountainside swimming pool, talking about what they'd done that day. Every evening she cooked in the room, where there was a small stove and a microwave, a tiny fridge. Then they ate together and drew. Anne was making stick figures, but Lily also had her trace her small hand and fill in the lines and wrinkles. They did blind drawings together, where they sat face to face and drew what they saw, without looking down at the paper.

Anne loved school. It was clear to Lily that she felt safe there, and that she was happier without the boundaries she'd had in Maskwacis, when she couldn't leave the house or yard. Lily recognized that she felt safe and happy as well. She enjoyed the physical part of the work, touching the fabric, flipping out the sheets, making a room clean. She didn't like the attitude Todd, the supervisor, had toward most of the maids—that they were lazy and always trying to cheat him or the lodge. He treated her differently, and she wondered when he'd try to get her to have sex.

It's probably past time to confront an issue. Why would a man in his late sixties write a novel about a lovely, young woman? Hardy was probably infatuated with his own character, Tess. He had close friendships with several young women, including the country actress who played Tess in the stage version of his novel. Tess's story questions the Victorian belief that even a raped woman is guilty. That problematic idea persists a hundred and thirty years later. I hope that Lily's story might engage readers but also do something similar, question why Victorian-style patriarchy still persists, a patriarchy that totalizes not just women, but people of color, people with a non-binary gender, and others.

The question remains: do I replicate the problem by being a voyeur of my own character? I admire Lily's intelligence, will, determination, and devotion to her child, but I don't spend time describing her face or body the way Hardy did with Tess.

Instead of Lily, I could write about someone I know better—a man my own age, possibly a computer programmer who failed to keep up with the light-speed changes in his industry and who is fired just before retirement. He loses his home, his kids have their own lives and difficulties, his wife is dead, and he is homeless in Salt Lake City. Or I could have written about someone like my grandfather, estranged from his wife, who moves farther and farther west until he's living alone in a cabin in the desert. But these stories about dis-enfranchised white males seem self-absorbed and don't get at the feminist issues I'm interested in.

Just before I started writing this book, I read about Susa Young Gates, daughter of Brigham Young. She entered university at age thirteen and after one year became the editor of the college newspaper. When she was sixteen, she married a man and had two children with him. After their divorce, she got custody of her son but not the baby, a girl; however, the agreement stated that she'd keep her daughter until the child was older. Soon Susa married again, and she and her new husband were called on a mission. At the train station, when she hoped to take her daughter with her, the former husband came with police and took her child away. As I started writing, I also thought about my sister, who after her divorce ran to Vermont with her children, and about a former student, whose husband shot her when she asked for a divorce. These were the three core stories that prompted this one.

Writing, I feel a tension between myself and Lily, that of a host and guest. I've invited her into my head, but as host I am obligated to care for her. This tension evaporates if author and character are too much alike—there must be similarities and differences. It feels like any other relationship with the Other, but it isn't really the same. Because it's virtual, it's safer, and it's also idealized, so I can pretend to be a better person than I am. I can freely criticize Nathan and the system that oppresses Lily, when in my actual life, I participate in oppressive systems. I know these systems manifest themselves in my narratives in ways that are invisible to me. For example, I'm bossy and stubborn with my wife and children, who generally just laugh at me when I try those tricks. Of course I'm bossy with Lily; despite the trick of random choices, I control her life, make it not her own—a paradox because she's not real.

TWENTY-TWO

Lily and Anne ate dinner together every evening, mother and daughter talking across the table. Lily missed Suzanne and wondered whether she had stayed with James or whether his subtle desire for control had manifested itself in unsubtle ways.

Being with Anne in such a beautiful place was a profound pleasure. Bundled up, they sat in an empty playground. They crawled inside the tunnel of a slippery slide, pretending to be dire wolves inside a cave. They growled at each other as they ate animal crackers.

"Is this a gorilla or a lion?" Anne asked.

Lily shone the flashlight on the cracker. "Dire wolves don't care what they eat."

Anne picked up another cracker. "This one is a lion, so that one is a gorilla." She growled and ate them both.

"We're like Eskimos in an igloo," said Lily.

"And a zoo."

"When have you been to a zoo?"

"We talk about zoos at school," said Anne.

"We will go to a zoo, sometime," said Lily.

Anne was silent for a minute. "I think I went to a zoo once."

"You remember that? Your dad and I took you when you were still a baby."

"Maybe I don't remember," said Anne. "Who's Dad?"

As they crawled out from under the table, Lily said, "We left him."

"We left him alone?"

"He's not alone," said Lily. "He was mean to me, and we left him."

Anne frowned. "A mean daddy?"

"Mostly he was mean to me."

They walked home, and she put Anne to bed. Even though Lily had no nostalgia for the kind of authoritarian security Nathan would have given her, after Anne went to sleep, Lily felt alone—not just lonely, but frightened. None of the people she had met in her life knew where she was. She had no one to phone or contact; she certainly didn't dare to call Suzanne. If she perished no one would know, except for her boss. Certainly no one would take care of Anne.

Toward the middle of October, when enough snow had fallen that they opened a few runs, she and Anne took a shuttle up to Lake Louise, passed through the huge Victorian hotel, and walked around the turquoise lake. There she met two men, brothers, who stopped and talked with her. One worked as a ski instructor, and his brother had come across from Vancouver to visit. "Susan Carson. This is Valerie."

"I'm Val," said Anne.

They found out she was working, living alone, so after chatting about the snow, the blueness of the lake, the pleasure of skiing, the advantage of the healthcare system in Canada, and the ideas of John Ruskin, they invited her to have dinner with them at a restaurant the ski-instructor brother liked—a grill with steaks and seafood.

At first she said, "No," but the ski instructor, Sam, said they would insist because they hadn't met other intelligent people in Banff, and they were tired of talking to each other.

"What a bad line," Alan said to Sam.

Lily said, "Two men should look for two women to have dinner with."

"I'm not a dater," said Alan. "I'm married."

"This is not a date," said Sam. "I want to talk to you about the connection between John Ruskin and Wendell Berry."

"They lived a hundred years apart. What connection could they have?"

He bent to talk to Anne. "Then the connection between Thing 1 and Thing 2. Why is your mother being so difficult?"

"I don't know," said Anne. "But she *is* difficult."

They laughed, and Lily said she would come. That afternoon she purchased nice trousers and a blouse, when generally she only had the shirt on her back and one to wash. While dressing for dinner, she kept telling herself that she could afford to eat at a restaurant once every year.

They met inside the front door and soon were taken to their table. Anne sat up on a booster chair, looking from Sam to Lily to Alan. Lily could tell from the way she held her hands and shoulders that she was happy in her own importance.

"You're American," said Sam. "I can tell from your vowels."

"Pretentious," said Alan.

"The West," said Sam.

Because someone was trying to uncover her origins, she felt the shadow of fear again.

"Montana," she said.

"I was going to guess Utah. I worked in Brighton for five winters."

"He thinks he's that professor from *My Fair Lady*," said Alan.

"I have an MA in linguistics," he said. "I might as well put it to some use."

"My parents were from Utah," said Lily.

"So, Susan," said Sam. "Everyone who works in Banff has come here to escape something."

"So what are you escaping?" she asked Sam.

"A career as a college professor," he said. "I started a PhD but couldn't finish."

"You told me you came here because it's the most beautiful place on earth," said Alan.

"What better place to run away to," said Sam, "than the most beautiful place on earth?"

"That's why I came here," said Lily. "I heard about it and thought I could afford to spend a winter here."

"Are you independently wealthy?" said Sam.

"Beware the male ski instructor," said Alan. "He's always looking for a rich snow bunny."

"Wrong on all three counts," said Lily. "Not rich, not a skier, and certainly not a bunny. I clean rooms at the Fox and Bear Hotel." She felt unnatural, a little manic, way too talkative.

Sam was still.

Alan looked at him and laughed. "I thought I was joking, but when he finds out that you're working for a maid's wages, he's struck dumb—no longer interested."

"No, that's not it at all," said Sam. "I was just thinking how unfair it was to invite you to dinner where it's going to cost $40 a plate."

"It's all right," said Lily. "I'm generally frugal, so I can afford to splurge once in a great while." Then she realized it was how she felt, before Nathan, while still in grad school. Talking with friends, not worrying about what she was saying.

"You have to let us pay for your dinner," said Sam.

Lily liked it that he had assumed they'd each pay their own way. "I can pay for myself."

"At least let us pay for Val's," said Alan. "Is that all right with you, Val?"

The girl looked at her mother.

"Big spender," said Lily. Anne had eaten a small bit of meat and a couple of steak fries from her plate.

Anne pointed at Sam. "That's a silly man."

"Yes, two silly men," said Lily.

"How long are you here for?" she asked Alan.

He looked at his brother. Something passed between them, the hint of a smile on Alan's face. "Another few days," he said. "Then I have to get back to work."

"She wants to get me alone," said Sam.

Lily pointed her fork at him. "I'm not interested in romance. I'm interested in intelligent conversation."

"Well," said Sam. "At least one of us is intelligent."

"I'm intelligent," said Anne.

"Precocious child."

Anne hesitated, but then nodded.

At the end of the meal, Lily put money in the payment folder. Alan stared at it, but Sam picked the folder up and put his credit card inside and put it out for the waitress.

"We're skiing tomorrow," said Alan, "but the two of us would like you to come over for drinks."

Lily smiled and looked at Anne. "Hot chocolate," said Alan.

She wondered when they had communicated this to each other.

"We're just doing this because it's clear you're lonely," said Sam.

They dropped her and Anne off at her apartment behind the hotel. She put Anne to bed and lay down, filled with warmth in her head and heart. She tested her feelings—not merely attraction to men, although they were both good looking. It was just that it had been months since she had seen Suzanne, and going that long without affectionate human conversation had withered her heart.

She knew she had to be careful or she'd make it mean more than it should, which could be dangerous.

It's probably clear that I want her to have love in her life. I want her to have a friendship of the heart that will last a decade or a lifetime. I have been in love only twice, once in high school with a somewhat frail, thin girl, who liked her religion to be both fundamental and mystical, and once during my last year of college, when I met my wife, whose eyes flashed when she engaged in conversation and who is passionate about ideas— the smartest person I know. Those two couldn't be more opposite. Of course, I've had many infatuations and crushes, before and after marriage, but none of them measure up to love.

Love of all kinds, including sexual and romantic varieties, is central to the philosophy of Levinas: "Love is not a possibility, is not due to our initiative, is without reason; it invades and wounds us, and nevertheless the I survives." As I balance on the fulcrum between control and chaos, love seems to be the unpredictable force that might loosen my grip on my own soul, but also open me to wounding.

This chaotic element is part of the pleasure of love, but scientists and slick magazines want to make it quantifiable. Love begins with attraction, which is based on physical qualities. Some are visual, such as proportions of face, shape of body, clarity of skin, whiteness of teeth. Other have to do with smell, taste, touch. Finally attraction has to do with non-physical attributes such as type of personality, common interests, level of confidence or aggressiveness—all read in a cultural context. What mathematician could write a function for this complexity? It would be much easier to work out the math for how a tree grows.

As a criminal and a nomad, Lily must resist being bound to anyone, but the longing for intimate connection pushes her toward Sam and his brother. As an aging man married to an aging woman, I too have difficulty balancing friendship and desire. But our age isn't really the problem. As are most people, I am frightened by emotional intimacy, allowing another being unlike myself to enter the house of my soul—perhaps taking residency there, leaving me no place to hide.

The next evening, after she and Anne ate, they walked to Sam's place. Alan opened the door, smiled, and motioned her in. His face was red from snow burn.

"Ouch," she said.

"I forgot to put more sunscreen on after lunch."

"He only listened to me once," said Sam. He was brown, maybe a little deeper brown, or maybe she just noticed it. They played some kind of rock music that also sounded Celtic—an odd fusion, she thought. She walked over to see what the band was and didn't recognize it.

"It's a local band," said Sam. "Local, meaning here and in Calgary."

"Calgary is a cowboy city. I thought the only music here was country and western." She looked through Sam's books. E. O. Wilson and S. I. Hayakawa.

"A linguistic environmentalist."

"He's an elitist slacker," said Alan. He was down on the floor, playing with Anne, helping her put on his ski gloves and his mask.

"What did you study at the U of Utah?" Sam asked.

"Art," she said. "Painting, installations."

"Now he's going to ask if you were any good," Alan said. "Like I said, elitist slacker."

"I wasn't good," she said. "I mean I was all right, but I could never have made a living painting."

"What is your work in Vancouver?" she asked Alan.

"I coordinate high school visits to the museum of natural history."

"You like it?"

"Yes," he said. "It's important to help young people find out about the earth we live on. Especially with the environmental crisis."

She wondered whether they had imperfections. She didn't trust people who didn't. But then she didn't trust anyone.

"You're more responsible than your brother."

Sam smiled. "I haven't grown up yet."

"Kids?" she asked Alan.

"Three. The full catastrophe."

Sam laughed.

Lily saw Alan was serious. "Why do you say that?"

Alan said, "It's a quote."

"But you weren't joking."

Sam's smile faded and returned. "Our parents' marriage was the catastrophe. They fought every minute. They finally got divorced about eight years ago. It should have happened years earlier."

"You two have turned out all right."

"Thank you," said Alan. "We helped each other through it. We were—are—close."

"When it got loud, we'd get out of the house."

"Where was this?

"Ontario."

"We got as far away from them as we could."

"They can die lonely," said Sam.

"Harsh," said Lily.

"You know nothing of it," Sam said. "They deserve to die alone."

"Sorry," she said. "We should talk about something else."

"How about your parents?" asked Sam.

"They died when I was fourteen. I lived with my aunt. Then I went to college and grad school. Made a bad marriage. Here I am."

The tone in the room was much more somber.

"We're a bunch of misfits," said Alan.

"Let's go for a walk," said Sam.

"Have you looked outside? It's a blizzard."

"Yes, let's go." Lily started to dress Anne. "We're going to play in the snow."

Anne said, "Yay!" As soon as she got her snow pants, boots, and coat on, she wanted to leave. She shouted, "Let's go! Let's go! Let's go!"

"Wait until I get my stuff on," said Lily.

Because of the snow that swirled in their faces, they could hardly see. They walked down from Sam's apartment into town and along the street to the east. At the edge of a park they turned past a tree and came face to face with a moose. Everyone froze, but Lily picked up Anne.

"Back up slowly," said Sam.

He hadn't yet lost his antlers, and they seemed as wide as a snowplow. Lily knew his feet were the most dangerous; being stomped by a creature as big as a fat horse would not be pleasant. She backed up with Anne, and soon they were far enough away that he stopped looking at them.

"Doesn't he know humans have taken over this part of the world?" said Alan.

"He's reclaiming it," said Sam. Out of the apartment his good spirits had returned. "I saw someone who had been trampled by a moose. Both legs broken, one in three places. A broken arm. A concussion. Broken ribs, injured kidney, backbone cracked."

"Did he survive?"

"Yes, until he moved to Florida and got hit by a car."

"You're kidding."

"Yes, I am. But just about the car accident, He did move away from Banff."

"Where does that name come from, Banff?"

"It's a First Nation word for the sound someone makes when they're being trampled by a moose," said Alan.

Lily snorted.

"I don't know," said Sam.

They walked back toward the apartment. "We didn't have our hot chocolate," said Alan. "I bought supplies."

Lily smiled, she put Anne down again and the girl spread her arms and watched snowflakes settle on her gloves.

They had different flavors of chocolate mix, canned whipped cream, and marshmallows. Anne picked hers out of her cup with her fingers, and Alan sprayed a little mound of cream on her hand. As she licked off her hand, half of the cream got on her face.

Lily felt a long sigh shudder through her. She decided being alone, without friends or family, was not for humans, not for her. Because she was worried that Sam would want to be romantic, she wished Alan would never go home. She hadn't imagined she could be so close to people after only a couple of days, but then the same had happened with Suzanne. She now knew that the first two years of their marriage, Nathan was isolating her. Not just by helping her think that her friends weren't loyal or the best kinds of friends, but by convincing her that she was not a social person, that he was sufficient for her needs. It had been one of many manipulative lies he had made her believe. He was older and, when she was twenty-two, she thought he was the smartest person in the world and that he would lead her to some kind of enlightenment.

Suzanne had been desperate for a man. Lily couldn't afford that luxury. She couldn't trust either a temporary or permanent man while she was off the grid with Anne.

She didn't see Sam and Alan again for a couple of days, and she wondered if Sam thought that the conversation about their parents had been too heavy for their superficial friendship.

The night before Alan was to leave, she walked over with Anne. They were not home but came up just as she walked away.

"Alan," said Anne. "I want to put on your gloves and boots."

"Come in," said Sam.

"I came to say goodbye to Alan, since he's leaving tomorrow."

Alan knelt on the floor and put his gloves on Anne's hands.

"So he's made quite an impression," said Sam. She wasn't sure of his tone.

"He is a gem," said Lily.

"Yes, I am a gem, that's what my wife Karen always tells me, 'You are such a gem, such a prize.'"

Lily looked at him. "I don't know what you mean."

He didn't answer.

Sam got out the mix, and they had hot chocolate again.

Lily had brought paper and markers, and she made the four of them sit at the table to draw. Sam sketched Lily. Alan drew a picture of himself with his red face and Lily and Anne drew their abstract lines and shapes. Anne's were all vertical, a little like mountains and valleys.

After that, Alan hugged her, and she and Anne walked home. Because she didn't know how things would change, Lily felt odd.

She took Anne to the YWCA where they showed old movies for children, this time the cartoon *Robin Hood*. Lily didn't know if Anne would sit through the whole thing, but she was entranced, sat with her arms up on the armrests, so focused she hardly moved her head.

They still went swimming in the hot springs above the valley; it was pleasant on a winter afternoon, to sit in the water and watch the lifts go up the mountain and the skiers go down, the whole valley covered with snow.

When they went at night, the lights of Banff spread below them, with the lifts like moving threads of light. Back in their room, she heard the music from bars in town. She thought about Nathan when he took her dancing in Salt Lake. Then they had lived in Paris, Delhi, London, São Paulo. When they came back, everything changed.

She shopped and brought the food back to their apartment. While she cooked, Anne told her about the other children. She told Lily about the letters she had learned. "Soon I'll be able to read."

"Maybe," said Lily. The most important thing to her—the staff worked to keep the space safe, and Anne was happy playing with the other children.

The wheel stayed in the drawer, but she was always aware of it. She lasted a week, but then she couldn't bear it anymore. She took out the wheel and spun it for days, weeks, and months. It came up months. She sat with the thing on her lap, wondering who had made it and for what office party it was given. Executive Decision Maker. She spun it again, but when she looked away and put her finger in the spokes, the screw came loose and the wheel part rolled across the floor. She took out her knife and put the screw back in, but she stuffed the thing back in the drawer, refusing to spin it again.

One day, when she came to pick Anne up, the leader frowned. "I was in the bathroom while the aide was watching them, and when I came back Val wasn't around. I thought that you'd come a half hour early to get her."

Lily felt her vision focus to a pinpoint. "Get the aide!" she barked.

The other woman came over; she was as young as Lily.

"Did someonecome to get Val?"

The aide shook her head.

"Where is she then?"

The two women looked at each other. "I don't know," said the older one. "I don't know how she could have gotten out with the doors locked."

Lily darted outside, but the playground was deep in snow and there were no small footprints. She rushed back inside.

"Call the children together," said Lily.

"Children," said the woman, "Gather round." She blew the whistle she used when attention was important. They all looked up, except for one boy who kept playing.

"Ask them!" said Lily.

"Have any of you seen Val?"

Lily looked in their faces as they shook their heads.

"We haven't seen her," said one of the larger children.

The boy who had continued playing pointed toward the cupboard, which was swinging open. Anne crawled out, sat up, and rubbed her eyes. Lily lifted her, clutched her close.

"I'm so sorry," said the older woman.

"You should have talked to each other when you first knew she was gone. You should have done that."

The woman was going to say something in reply, but then she seemed to deflate. "You're right. We messed up. We'll be more careful."

"Damn right," said Lily. She left with Anne. While they ate, she held her child on her lap, even though Anne kept asking to sit in her own chair.

"I need you on my lap," she said. "Please let me hold you on my lap."

"My chair," whined Anne. "You're smushing me."

Lily let Anne sit in her own chair. She still felt shaky, still felt dread like poison in her heart. She wished there was another daycare center, but the other one was across town and was just as expensive. She thought about taking Anne out of daycare; most her pay went for a half-day at the center. Finally, Lily told herself that the two women were generally responsible, and this was a freak accident. They would pay more attention now. They'd better.

The next morning she dropped Anne off. The women brought her into the room with the other children, fawning over her.

"She is my treasure," said Lily. "Please watch her carefully."

"I'm sorry," said the older woman. "We gave you a scare."

The next night, Sam came to her door. "Alan made it back all right. He asked about you, so I thought I'd come check on you, so I could give him a detailed answer."

"Come in," she said. "I'm glad to see you."

He sat on one of the two chairs.

"Where's Val?"

Lily pointed to the bed.

"Oh," he said. "Sorry."

"She'll be all right, so long as we don't shout. I guess you said this before, but I don't know whether you're a teacher or a guide."

"Both," he said. "I teach the beginners and then I guide people in the backcountry."

"Keep them from killing themselves."

"I'd rather teach beginners. They have a sense of proportion about themselves. They don't have egos the size of a mountain. They appreciate what I teach them."

"So why not do just that?"

"Variety. Being on the bunny slope all day can get boring. I get in the backcountry even if I have idiots with a death wish." He looked at her. "Making beds. All day."

"Your brother is right. You are an elitist."

He shook his head. "That's not what I meant. Or maybe that's part of it. I couldn't do the same thing all day."

"I don't do it all day, just for four hours."

"So after daycare, what do you make?"

"About fifteen dollars a day."

"Man," he said. "Are you a Buddhist? Reducing your wants."

She smiled. "I get to live here. I don't pay rent for this room. My wants are naturally reduced. Being with Val is all my desire. Conversation with a grownup human every once in a while. They don't want us talking much at work."

"You could be anywhere, but you're here. I mean, you could live simply anywhere, maybe much easier, but you're here."

"I went where the wind blew."

"What kind of wind was that? A hurricane at your back."

"That's pretty much it."

"I keep trying to imagine that strong a wind."

"Like the one that blew you away from your parents."

He lifted his head slowly. "That bad, eh?"

"Worse."

"I can't imagine you getting in a fight," he said.

"I didn't fight much," she said. "Not nearly enough."

"It frightens me—what people do to each other. I wish it was different, but I just keep skiing. I don't do anything to fix the way the world is."

"Maybe teaching how to ski helps. Showing people how to do something that helps them relax, helps them feel something they don't feel in the city. Makes them feel competent."

Talking with Sam, she felt a strange kind of future nostalgia—the longing for a state that she hadn't yet left. She knew their friendship was temporary. Something would happen, and she and Anne would run again. She realized she hadn't taken any pictures with her small camera for months, but as she got ready to leave, she took out her camera, but the battery was dead.

"Next time," Sam said.

Lily watched his back as he walked away through the snow. She felt a surge of happiness rising through her. Safety, work, a place to live, a friend—she couldn't think of anything else she wanted.

TWENTY-THREE

Lily and Anne were walking along the main downtown street, passing all the ski shops and restaurants, to get groceries, when they came up behind a couple holding hands. The couple turned, and she saw it was Sam. She felt an immediate upwelling of good cheer because she was free to be his friend, without fearing complications. She called his name, and he turned. His face registered surprise, not a pleasant surprise. Anne ran toward him, but Lily came up more slowly.

"This is Becca," he said. "Becca, meet Susan, Val." He was hesitant, as if he wasn't sure he wanted them to meet. He hugged Anne and nodded at Lily, but then stood there like a post.

Becca smiled and bent to pat Anne on the head, as if she was a dog.

Anne looked up.

"Say hello to Sam and his friend," Lily said to Anne.

"Hello, Sam. Hello, friend," said Anne. "Becca."

"She remembered my name. So cute."

Sam stood awkwardly, so Lily said, "Let's go, Val, we have to get our groceries for dinner."

She walked on, wondering about Sam's awkwardness. She felt as if she were back in high school.

The next day she and Anne dropped by his house. Sam stood in the doorway.

She said, "Are you going to invite us in?"

He nodded. "Sure."

"I was glad to see you yesterday. I was glad to meet your girlfriend."

He nodded. "Maybe not girlfriend."

Anne ran for the cupboard where Alan had put the blocks he had gotten Sam to make her in the lift repair shop. She pulled them out, spilling them across the floor, and Lily felt happy that Sam had saved them. Anne carried them a few at a time into the room where Lily and Sam sat.

"How's your work been?" she asked.

"I took a group of three doctors into the backcountry. I should have checked out their skill level before I agreed to guide them. They skied like shit. Well, one of them was all right." He paused. "How's the sheet folding?"

"I don't fold sheets," she said. "I unfold them. What was the nature of your thesis?"

"The difference in dialect between the Canadian Ojibway and the American Chippewa."

"They're the same tribe? I didn't know that. So what are the differences?"

"Very slight. It was a sociolinguistic study, seeing how many American English words each tribe had incorporated. We Canadians pride ourselves on being inclusive of the First Peoples and look down on the US for the melting-pot analogy blending everyone into one soup. So the idea, not a great one, was to see if Ojibway had less linguistic pollution."

"Pollution" said Lily. "That doesn't sound like a neutral term."

"Anyway, Canadians think they're more accepting of diversity, so I wanted to see if it's true, at least from this one measurement."

"More like a light stir-fry, keeping all the original flavors distinct."

"Yes. Look at the names—First People and Indians. Neither is a name that has anything to do with their heritage, but in reality, I found little linguistic evidence to suggest that there is any less prejudice north of the border."

"Still that's something to discover."

"It is interesting," he said, "but my readership was three members of the faculty. Oh, and five undergraduates in Atlanta writing term papers for an English class. They found it through ProQuest and wrote me."

"Fans."

"It was a drop in a little pond that didn't even create a ripple."

She looked at him. "You would only think that if you think it's possible for the world to become better. I don't think it is. You and your brother are idealists. I'm not."

"Alan is an idealist. Bringing young minds to blossom. I just take people's money."

"Whatever," she said. "I think it's remarkable what you two did for each other. You made yourselves into good people in the absence of responsible parents."

"They were responsible. They kept a house for us and bought food. Made sure our school expenses were paid. They just used up all their emotional capital on fighting, instead of paying attention to us."

"Admit it," she said. "You two are remarkable."

Sam smiled at her. "I admit it. Alan is remarkable. In fact, I think it's his shadow or reflection that made you come here tonight."

"You have a dour turn of mind."

"Why do you want to know me?"

"Maybe you're right. Alan made friends with Val, so he's remarkable. Me, I'm so desperate for talk that I have elevated your quality."

He stared at her. "Desperate."

"I'm like a wolf, not a lone wolf. Not a herd animal either. I just need another intelligent person. Even if he's second tier."

He gave her another hard look. "You think I'm second tier?"

"Of course I don't. That's what you were saying about yourself."

"You are the most confusing—"

"Not confusing." She sang, "I don't want a lover, I don't want a sister. I don't want a brother. I just want a friend."

"You're serious, aren't you? If that statement came from anybody else, I'd think that you were playing a woman's game."

"Getting you off your guard, so I can swoop in for the romantic kill. No. Not during this part of my life. No." She frowned. "Why do you say a woman's game? That kind of subterfuge is a human thing. A trait that belongs to all genders."

"Mommy, where is Alan? I want him to put that glove on me."

"Can you pretend that I'm Alan," said Sam, "and let me put gloves on you?"

She frowned at him. "If it's just for pretend."

He went into the other room and came back with his gloves, boots, and goggles. He lifted her and stood her in the boots. The tops made her pants bunch up. Then he put the gloves on her arms, the goggles on her head. "Stay right there." He grabbed his phone and took her picture. While he was punching the buttons to send it to Alan, Anne tried to walk and fell over.

Lily lifted her back up. "These are too heavy for walking in," she said. "You can hardly move your legs."

"They're too big," Anne said.

"Way too big," said Sam.

Anne fell forward and crawled out of the boots. She marched into the kitchen with the gloves held high, and soon she marched back. She went back into the kitchen and didn't come out. Soon they heard the clash of metal bowls. They both went into the kitchen and the bowls were all over the floor.

"Let's put them away," said Lily.

"I want to play with them."

"For a little while. Three minutes."

"Five minutes," said Anne.

"Okay," said Lily.

They watched her put the bowls together and separate them, put them together again.

"Time for us to go home," said Lily.

"I don't want to go home," whined Anne.

"It's time."

"Maybe we'll come back again." Anne looked at Sam.

"Yes," said Sam.

She bundled Anne up and led her to the door.

Sam stood in the door behind them. "Thanks," he said. "See you soon."

Becca Sam Lily. Anne Sam Lily. Alan Anne Sam. Alan Lily Sam. Alan Lily Sam Anne Except for the last, it's a game of triangles, which are a stable form, in building construction and in fiction. In stories, the triangle produces tension based on the probability that one of the three bonds between these three people will grow stronger and the other two will weaken. In the case of a romantic relationship, one of the three will lose out, and in this case, it's probably not Sam. He will choose love with Becca or the possibility of love with Lily; he wins either way he turns.

These tensions are manifested as a series of comparisons: Sam compares Becca and Lily, one for love, one for friendship. Sam likes both Lily and Anne, but the liking is different with the mother than with the daughter. Anne decides Alan is fun and Sam is silly. We define a quality by its opposite, not just young and old, but the urge to be domestic or ambitious, compassionate or aggressive, emotional or logical. We know what these terms mean because of their opposite. One example is binary gender differentiation; at least since the Victorian Age, we know masculine traits because feminine traits are supposedly opposite. As I try to loosen tradition's hold on me (a project rife with delusion), I have to view our binary systems as traps.

I imagine a universe where both computers and human behavior, especially as pertaining to love, run on a ternary system. The aliens who thrive there probably think that lovers must possess qualities in oppositions of three. I can hardly imagine what qualities those might be, because we're so used to defining by binary difference. What kind of novel would be written on a planet where sex and traditional gender traits came in threes, or fours, or more? In such a world a love triangle would be the normal pathway to sex—a problematic love would require four, five, or six beings. But oh, what possibility for stories!

My youngest son and his friend, formerly his wife, define themselves as gender neutral, hoping to further disrupt the idea of gender binaries that define people through opposition. They are familiar with gender terms, such as Agender, Bigender, Cisgender, FTM, MTF, Non-binary, Neither, Other, Pangender, Transgender, Trans, Two-spirit, and others. The terms are fluid. In 2014 ABC News published a list of fifty-eight such terms. My son and his wife and others hope to achieve actual change by changing the language we use to describe gender, including using plural pronouns rather than gendered pronouns.

What does that have to do with me, a cisgender male in his late sixties? It has everything to do with openness to the Other, with welcoming guests into the house of my mind, and becoming respectful of how they perceive themselves. I have come to believe that my own emotional health depends on my ability to open myself to the Other. That act with people distant from me is easy, especially when they're characters I've made up. What's much more difficult is being open with people close to me; their ungainly, impulsive, rough-edged, complex personness often feels like an affront. My leap to emotional intimacy is made easier because I love them, my wife, children, and grandchildren, my close relatives and neighbors (at least most of them), but it's still difficult to continually make conversations exploratory and vital.

TWENTY-FOUR

Toward the end of January, Lily pushed her cart of cleaning and restocking supplies down the hall at the lodge, when a door opened and the truck driver who had carried her to Banff came out. She smiled at him and just kept going, wheeling her cart down the hallway. If he followed her, she would run. When she unlocked her next room, she turned and he was staring at her. *Shit!* She knew that looking at him had been a mistake. She entered the room and started working.

Bad luck.

Soon he leaned against the doorway. "Did you read the book?"

"What do you mean?"

"You did as well as you could, but a delicate woman has a difficult time pretending to be a man."

She tried to push past him, but he didn't move and the doorway was too narrow.

"Not a normal cross dresser. What are you running from?"

"Let me go past," she said.

"Mother and a child, running from something."

She stepped to the room phone and dialed security. "Room 348. A man is blocking my way. He's being aggressive with me." She hung up.

"I can't believe how lucky I am. Of all the trucks you could have hitched with, you chose mine. Of all the trucks you could have gotten a ride with, you had to find one with family in Salt Lake. My sister sent me this." He opened a printout from a newspaper, the same picture of her and Anne that she'd seen on the internet. "Because she thought that as a trucker on the road all the time I'd have a chance at the reward. A slim chance but my prayers were answered. "

"You have me mixed up with somebody else," she said.

"So we'll wait for security." He opened his phone and dialed three numbers. "Police," he said. "Banff Inn. Room 348. I've found a woman who kidnapped a child in Salt Lake." He said more into the phone while he watched her, but her head started buzzing with anger and fear. She went into the bathroom and ripped down the shower-curtain rod. When he appeared in the bathroom doorway, she hit him in the throat with the end of the rod. He stumbled backward onto the bed, the plastic curtain covering him. She darted past him, and when he came at her she threw a chair at him. She wedged the cart crossways in the hall and ran down the stairs. She heard him thundering on the steps after her. She slipped into the employees' locker room and grabbed the backpack from her locker.

She walked out through the lobby, turned the corner, and once out of sight of anyone, sprinted toward the daycare center. She controlled her breathing and asked for Valerie. They brought her out.

"I don't want to go home yet." Anne folded her arms and looked up at her mother. The woman went back to the other children.

"We're not going home. We're going on an adventure."

"I don't want to go."

Lily knelt. "Remember when we had to run from those boys in our summer place in the trees by Suzanne's house?"

Anne nodded.

"We have to run again. Somebody is after us."

"Are they an ogre?"

"Something like that."

"Are you going to fight the ogre?"

Lily shook her head. "No, no, I can't."

She took Lily's hand and they walked out the door. Then she picked Anne up and walked fast to another lodge, where there was always a taxi. She helped Anne into the taxi.

"Where to?"

"Just a sec." She opened her backpack and took out the wheel. She had two choices, eastward toward Calgary or westward toward Lake Louise. She spun the wheel and it pointed westward. She could see the driver's eyes watching her in the rearview mirror.

"Lake Louise," she said.

He pulled out onto the street. Lily craned her neck to look behind and couldn't see anyone following. The driver let her off at the huge Victorian hotel, where she could hide if the wheel told her to; it was like a small city. After paying him, she walked inside and checked with the concierge, who told her that she'd have to wait until evening for the next bus. In the hotel she bought different clothing. After changing in a bathroom stall, and spinning the wheel, which still pointed west, she walked through the parking lot looking for BC or US license plates. When she found a pickup truck with BC plates, she opened the tailgate and sat in the sun while Anne played in the back. If the owner came up, he'd probably be upset at them using his truck, but it would give her the chance to talk to him.

"Going on adventure." Anne stopped walking. "Will Sam come?"

Lily shook her head. "No, Sam's staying in Banff."

"I don't want to go."

"But we have to." She had to look away from Anne's face.

People came out of the lodge and got in their vehicles, but none of them came to the cars she had marked on a piece of paper. She stood in the bed where she could see better. A man and a woman, both with white hair, started loading luggage in a car with BC plates. She lifted Anne and carried her toward the couple. "Are you going to Vancouver?"

"Kamloops," said the woman.

"No," said the man. "Don't talk to her."

"Can I get a ride that far? I've been working in the Fox and Bear. My sister had a car accident, and I'm trying to get to her, but the bus doesn't come until eight hours from now. It would save me a day."

"No," said the man.

"I'll pay you $200."

The woman got in the car, and the man did as well, both ignoring her. He backed out quickly and pulled away.

"Bad man," she said to Anne. "Stinky man."

"Really?" said Anne. "Are they chasing after us?"

"No. That's a different bad man." She had to remember that Anne was still only two; despite her language there was so much she didn't understand.

They returned to the truck.

Soon a woman came out and got into a car with US plates. She pulled out before Lily and Anne could get close, but she pulled up to the lodge entrance, where another woman with skis stood. They clipped their skis to the roof and loaded their luggage in back.

Lily walked up to them. "You're headed back to the States?"

"Spokane," said the woman on the far side of the car.

"Can I get a ride?" She told the women the same story. "I'll pay you $400."

The driver looked at her and Anne and then at the other woman. They both nodded and moved some luggage to the trunk. "Get in."

They drove west. "I'm Mary," said Lily. "My daughter is Val."

"Kris and Charlotte."

"Is your sister going to be all right?"

"Yes. She broke both her legs and arm. Two hundred stitches. She'll be all right, I just need to take care of her for a while."

"What were you doing in Banff?"

"Working as a maid. It was okay through the winter, but I was ready to leave anyway."

"If you've been working as a maid, you don't have $400 to spare."

"It's fine," said Lily. "I'm just ready to move on." She wished she'd had time to say goodbye to Sam, who would wonder about her disappearance. Maybe she could send him an email.

She thought about the truck driver, who was much smarter and more perceptive than he had looked. He was so pleased with himself for discovering her identity. *The bastard!*

They drove through small towns on the river—Revelstoke, Arrowhead, Gerrard, Nakusp, New Denver, Slocane. She thought about taking the wheel out and spinning for how far she should go with them, but she decided just to let herself be carried to Spokane. Part of her was anxious about that decision, but she refused to take out the wheel. When they came to the border, she handed her lapsed documents to the guard. "I stayed too long, but now I'm going home." He looked at her, and looked at Anne, but finally he handed it back and let her through.

Toward evening they came to Spokane. She had them let her off at the hospital, just so they wouldn't think about it. In the end they just asked her for $200, about twice the cost of their gas.

She thanked them and walked toward the hospital doors. After they drove away, she asked a woman who sat behind an information booth where the closest hotel was. She helped Lily look it up—a half mile away. She considered hiring a taxi, but she was still in the mode of conserving every penny, so she decided to walk. When she finally got there and went inside, she saw it wasn't that great a hotel—grungy furnishings. But it would do.

The clerk would only accept American money, so she said she'd sit in the lobby until she could get to a bank.

"You can't sit here all night," he said.

"Then give me a room," she said.

"You don't have a credit card. You only have Canadian money. I can't."

Lily sat on the sofa in the lobby, leaning back.

"I'll call security."

"Go ahead," said Lily. "But he'll have to drag me out. My girl will cry and there will be a big scene. I'm not a homeless person just off the street. I've just been in Canada for a year and I'm damn tired and cranky."

The manager finally let her have a room with a $200 Canadian deposit. She made him sign a receipt and had the two clerks witness that he had signed. She walked up to the third floor, got inside the room, helped Anne get undressed, and then she collapsed next to her child on the bed.

T W E N T Y - F I V E

Lily woke, her hip and back sore from the bad mattress, and wished she had found a better hotel. Anne still slept, so Lily lay thinking, something she hadn't had time to do since the truck driver had found her. Even traveling with the two women she couldn't focus, couldn't think past getting to Spokane. Now she had to find work and a place to stay. Anne couldn't be put through homelessness again; the stress of not having a home after Nathan had taken all her money made her fear that kind of powerlessness. She had found work and a place to live in a new town twice before, but she wondered about this city— whether she'd have a better time finding work as a man or as a woman. She looked at her money, $1,800 Canadian. She had hoped to save more, but she didn't regret eating out or buying clothes for herself and Anne. She'd get her money back from the hotel, unless they cheated her.

Anne woke. Lily saw the child's eyes open and shut. Her breathing was awake breathing, and her eyes moved unlike they did in sleep.

"I wonder when Valentino Peach is going to wake up. We're going to have breakfast in a restaurant, maybe pancakes with strawberries on them. If she's asleep, I'm going to call her Valentino Peach all I want because she can't hear me when she's asleep."

Anne's lips bent slightly into a smile. "That's not my name." She sat up. "I don't like it when you make me smile when I'm mad."

"Why are you mad?"

"Because I don't like sleeping in this room. Let's go back to our own room tonight."

"We can't. We're far away from our room. We're far away from Banff. Don't you remember traveling?"

Anne considered. "We were in a car with two women. That's where I slept. Can I go to daycare?"

Lily shook her head.

"Come on. Let's shower and get dressed."

During the shower and while Lily pulled her same clothing back on, the girl was too quiet. Lily wished she'd ask more questions about where they were and why they had left. Lily considered leaving the backpack in the room until they came back, but she felt too insecure without it. They had breakfast at a café. Anne ordered a waffle and scrambled eggs.

Lily followed the clerk's directions to find a bank and changed her money. She lost some to the fee and more to the bank's shitty exchange rate, but she came out with $1,530 US dollars. She paid her bill at the hotel, took the $200 Canadian back to the bank and got more change. Then she and Anne walked to the library and read the newspaper ads while Anne looked at books. Only a few jobs for house cleaners, waiters, hotel maids—not much work in the city.

She walked with Anne or carried her, as they wandered past the hotels. She asked in each whether they needed maids. Unlike in Banff, where it made sense for someone to do menial work just to live there, for skiing or the landscape, Spokane wasn't the same kind of destination. She suspected that if she appeared to be a foreigner, someone from Mexico or farther south, she might have gotten a job. They suspected an Anglo woman who would work for almost nothing. That afternoon, she played with Anne in a park, walked with her along the river, a developed area with landscaping and cobbled pathways.

She imagined having a good job, maybe a family, two women living together as she and Suzanne had. She couldn't imagine living with Sam without the relationship turning competitive. She considered sex with Sam, moving from touch to arousal, helping him inside her, and her body ached for that movement, heat, and climax. She shook her head—a dangerous daydream.

She would have to find daycare, a cheap place to live. She knew she needed to spin the wheel to determine how long she would stay. Her semi-random movements had protected her so far, but the uncertainty made her weary. Whether she wanted it or not, she knew her life was going to be always uncertain. She could look for an opportunity to go somewhere else, but Spokane was as good as anywhere. In a city she had greater anonymity.

So, while Anne played, she spun the wheel, once for days or weeks or months, once for a number. Weeks. Three of them. She didn't want to pay a deposit on an apartment, plus first and last month's rent. She wanted to find a hotel that would arrange a rate for three weeks. On the way to the library she passed a department store and went in to buy a stroller. Stealing one was an unnecessary risk when she had money.

Back at the library, she picked some books for Anne and took them to the public computers. The website offered the reward for information, now $100,000. Then she looked for a hotel where she could stay, settled on one farthest from the river. Finally, she looked up daycare centers, choosing one not far from the hotel. While Anne slept, she pushed the stroller to their new home. The manager she talked to at the front desk wanted her to pay in advance and give him a $200 deposit, which took more than half her money. She made him give her a receipt and asked him to look over the room with her, writing down what was broken. It was basically clean, the carpet worn, with a sink, small fridge, microwave, television. After the manager left, she considered the location of the elevator and the stairs, one at each end of the hallway.

"This is our new home for now," she said to Anne as they sat on the bed. "When we're in a new place, Mommy has a new name—Rachelle."

"So I'll have a new name also? Not Val?"

"Not Val. Brooke."

"I like Val best."

"That's a secret name. Just between us. What's my name for other people?"

"Rachelle."

"Right. Rachelle. What's your name?"

"I'm Val."

"Yes, that's your secret name. What's your name for other people?"

She frowned. "Brooke," she said in an irritated voice.

"Good job." She gave Anne a hug.

"This is our house?"

"Yes, for a while."

"I want to go back to Sam."

"That would be nice. That was good to have a friend."

"Do I have a new school?"

Lily nodded.

"Is it a nice school?"

"Yes."

"Will I have new friends there?"

"Yes."

"Good." She gave Lily a hug.

Lily considered sending Sam an email, but she wondered what the use was. She thought it would provide closure for her, but what would she say? "Had to run"? "Had to get out of town to escape imprisonment"? "Goodbye forever"? He would wonder about the meaning of any of the things she could say. He deserved better than just wondering, but she didn't know how to avoid saying everything to him.

The next morning, she took Anne to the day school, which was a square, cinderblock building with a small yard, a dingy playset. The women inside were friendly, and the children seemed happy. Anne ran to play, for which Lily was grateful. "I'll be back at lunchtime," she said, holding Anne's cheeks between her palms. She was beset by the sudden memory of saying that to Anne before the divorce hearing.

Shopping for food, Lily went to the vegetables and fruit. She found a woman who picked up a cantaloupe and put it down again, frowning. Lily walked up to her, started examining the melons. "Hello, are you a native?"

"Yes," said the woman, still holding a melon.

"My husband's company moved us here, and we are looking for where in town to live."

The woman looked at her and clearly didn't approve of her, something about her, her clothing or her hair, made the woman shut down, shake her head.

She talked to a younger woman and found out the financial scale of the suburbs and bought a week's groceries. She walked through the closest suburb, houses with two stories and a basement. She knocked on every one, saying she was a college student and that she would clean houses for $10 a room, deep cleaning; $15 for a huge room, $20 for the kitchen.

She found three places and arranged dates for cleaning. She was pleased that in just a day she had reestablished herself. Before getting Anne, she sent Sam a note using the email account in her grandmother's name. "This is Susan. I'm not what I seemed. I broke a law a year ago, and someone found me in Banff, and we had to run again. Valerie misses you. I do also. We're safe in another place." She pushed send before she could reconsider.

That afternoon she played with Anne in the park, went back to the library, found a Target and let Anne pick a toy: a small truck and a small stuffed dog to ride in the truck. Watching Anne playing with the truck on the carpet of their apartment, she felt time slipping past. She thought how much Anne had grown since they had left Utah. Another year and she'd be a different person. She took a dozen pictures, some with her alone and some with her sitting on Lily's lap. When she had time, she'd make drawings from the best of the photos.

Lily, like all of us, knows she cannot find an eddy where time slows and circles. Instead the river of timespace bullies us forward. Still she and I both fondly imagine that time might somehow freeze, or at least move more slowly, circle lazily—a perpetual Eden. But that stasis might also bring the death of desire. I imagine this timeless place, sealed off from the world, where I can sit and write forever, never interrupted by practical reality. My grandfather came close to this in his lonesome cabin in the desert. Science fiction writers imagine that we might subvert time, traveling backward or forward along time's riverbed, changing human or personal history, preventing the Great Fire of London, assassinating Hitler, or delaying death.

Newton saw time and space as absolutes, independent of specific objects and relationships. We are players on the stage of space and time. According to this theory, time marches forward independent of an observer. Leibniz thought time was relational; without an observer time could not exist. Kant asks, "What is time?" He proposes that it's neither an independent entity nor merely a relationship between entities. Rather, time is an aspect of the constitution of our minds, intuitive. He calls time a predicate, by this I assume he means a predicate of our minds. We time, meaning that the time function in our beings manifests the universe as timed; we time the universe. Einstein, rather than using pure logic, analyzed empirical evidence, processing the evidence through mathematical models. He theorized that space and time are inextricably connected and that gravitational mass affects spacetime. Stephen Hawking explains this through the metaphor of a ball dropped onto a rubber sheet; the rubber bends around the ball. Time is not a backdrop to the play, it is the play. Time is relative to space and to observers. A clock on a speeding spaceship runs slower than a clock on earth, which is also speeding but at a slower rate. This phenomenon is measured by particle accelerators. The formula is

$$t' = \frac{t\sqrt{t - V^2}}{c^2}$$

where t' = dilated time

t = stationary time

V = velocity

c = speed of light

A few years ago the theory that spacetime is not uniform was supported when scientists at the Laser Interferometer Gravitational-Wave Observatory heard a chirp, the sound of two black holes colliding. This sound confirmed Einstein's prediction that when black holes collide a part of their mass would be released as energy so powerful that it would cause a ripple in the fabric of spacetime. The LIGO is like a pair of huge microphones, one in Livingston, Louisiana, the other in Hanford, Washington, that can hear the sound of gravitational waves as they pass through spacetime. When the holes collided the increase in frequency entered the range of what humans can hear.

Still people believe what they will about time. Is it cyclical as ancient peoples thought? Does it exist at all or is it an illusion as the ancient Jews believed? In his book, *Einstein's Dreams*, Alan Lightman imagines Einstein dreaming about time as he worked on formulating his Theory of Relativity. One dream is of a world where time is a circle, like a snake with its tail in its mouth:

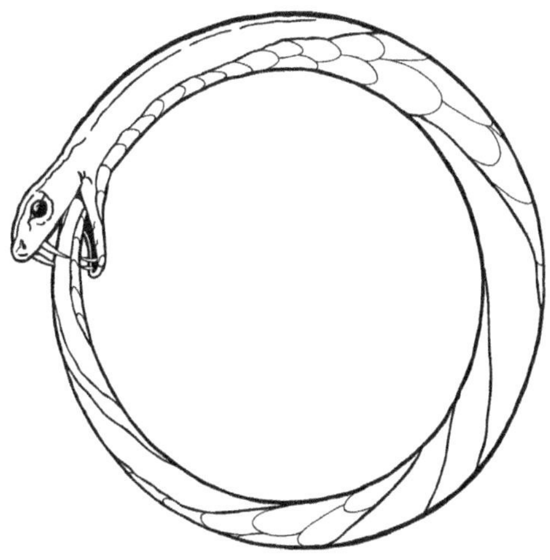

People aren't conscious of being in an eternal loop, but some of them dream the reality that they are doomed forever to repeat their mistakes and relive their misery, so every night the sound of these people moaning drifts through the streets. In another, time is like a river, with occasional dead spots or back currents, where someone is carried into the past. So in every city there are people who know the future, but because most don't want to know what they face, these people are shunned. In another world time is branched, but the branches coexist; people are indistinctly aware of their doubled lives. In another universe there are two times, a predetermined time and a flexible time, a mechanical time and a body time. Each is true, so the problem occurs when someone inhabits both ways of apprehending being, and desperation results. In another dream of time, the past doesn't exist. In another, time is visible and people can look into the distance and see either the past or the future. In another, time doesn't flow smoothly but fitfully.

What became clear as I read this book was that all these times exist, or could exist, in the minds of people who inhabit our own reality. People apprehend time and space in different manners, and their lives are shaped by their vision. I choose to imagine time as an infinite fractal, the branches curling back on themselves, so I am doomed to a cycle of stasis and movement. I break a crack in the shell of my existence and then become complacent.

Mormons think about time in two ways: that the eternities are outside time. Beings were never created, but originated as intelligences that God organized into a higher state. Or Mormons imagine sidereal time. Human time is relative to the orbit of the earth around the sun. Time for God is relative to the distant star Kolob, which is the system where God lives. God's planet takes a thousand years to orbit Kolob, so a year to God is a thousand years to humans. Mormons hold both these ideas about time in their heads without contradiction, in part because they're similar—a thousand years is eternity. Also, the main point about earthtime is that it's for testing, for working toward perfection, with the knowledge that we will always fail. For Mormons, Christ's atonement can bridge that gap between the highest state of organization we can attain and a perfect state of organization. We accommodate ourselves to our imperfections in different manners—denial, mindful acceptance of our imperfections (embracing Eve's quest for experience), empathy for ourselves and other people, self-delusion, and my personal favorite, guilt. Guilt is mostly what I want to shed as I try to reinvent myself.

Another metaphor for time and being—water bubbling and flowing from one space and form to diverse other forms, becoming something new. I like this image of time, but it implies perpetual instability, continuous change. How painful the transition from one form to another, one face to another, from one sack of skin to another!

The next day Lily took Anne to daycare and cleaned the first house. She found that she could clean a whole house in four hours, about $25 an hour. It was enough.

She felt that this place might be different and that she might live there in a less random manner. She vowed to give up on the wheel and spend the next two weeks figuring a permanent place to live. If she had no identification, she could only get the worst-paying jobs. She figured the first step was getting a social security number. She thought of several ideas that she immediately rejected—pretending to be an illegal immigrant from a country where there was danger, getting a number off the black market, making up a number, stealing someone's identity. It was dangerous to steal a living person's identity. The next logical thought was to steal a dead person's social security number. That seemed to be her best bet, but she didn't know how to go about doing that.

While Anne was at day school, she went to the library. On the internet she looked at the obituaries published earlier in the week. She looked up the addresses of the deceased.

She used $10 and got a bike from the Salvation Army and rode to the houses. There were people in the first two, but the fourth seemed empty, and the garage door was open. She made sure no one was on the street. She put her shoulder against the door inside, and on the third try, the wood splintered and she was in. Luckily the children had not yet cleaned out the house, so she looked for an office, and found the place where bills were paid. She finally found the old income tax forms and took the last two year's forms. She picked up a few utility bills.

She left the house and went to the bank closest to her apartment. She sat at the desk after giving the numbers to the bank clerk. He put the numbers in his computer. He looked at it and frowned. "We already have an account in that name, but it was just closed by the executor of her will, her son."

Lily walked out of the bank. The clerk called for her to stop, but she just kept going, not running, just walking as if she had someplace important to go.

She decided that the chances of that happening again were minimal, so she got online and looked again at the obituaries. She picked a few where the funeral was not for several days. She made sure that she found women who were widows when they died. At the first few houses cars were parked in front. The next was in a condominium and the door was visible, so she didn't want to try to break in. The next had doors that she couldn't just push open, substantial doors. She went through the whole list riding hard for two hours and found nothing, so she had to go back and pick up Anne.

"Did you have fun today?" she asked her.

"Yes. I have a friend. She wants me to come to her house for a play—a play something."

"A play date."

"Yes! A play date."

"Did she talk to her mom?"

Anne shook her head. "But she will. She will talk to her. And then we can have a play date."

"I hope so."

Lily wondered whether she could take the chance and apply for a social security number for Anne, then use it herself, but she discovered she needed a birth certificate, which she'd have to have mailed to her current address—not a good idea. She regretted not having computer-hacking skills. She supposed that social security numbers were kept behind significant security.

The next day she looked up a new set of obituaries, this time of women who died but the husband survived. She had decided it would be easier to talk her way past an old man than it would be to break a door down. She found eight that fit the criteria. She spun the wheel. The wheel told her the sixth one. When she read it again, she noticed that the wife was preceded in death by a daughter. She rode her bike to it, five miles. There was a car parked in front, so she knocked on the door. An old man using a walker came to the door.

"Are you here for the car?" he said.

"No," she said.

"They said they'd come get it today. The kidney foundation."

"I'm here from the Social Security Administration. We have some money for you that we can't distribute, because we don't have your wife's information. I wonder if you could give it to me?"

"My wife is dead. I can't drive anymore so that's why I donated the car."

"Yes, we know she's dead. That's why I've come, so we can give you this payment."

"What do you want?"

"Her social security number. I have your address. I need her birthdate."

"Her birthdate?"

"Look. I'm just trying to do my job, but if you don't want the payment, I'm sure the government can put it to good use." She turned to leave.

"Wait! She was born on 5 October 1943, but I don't know her social security number."

"Can I look at your papers, your tax returns, maybe?"

"They're here somewhere. The person from the tax service always gives them back to me."

"Good. If I can look at the papers briefly, I can get on my way. I still have five people to talk to today."

He led her to an office and opened a filing cabinet drawer. She looked inside and pulled out a few of the tax forms. They went back twenty years. She looked at the oldest one, and it had a daughter on it. She pulled out the next one and the daughter was not there.

"Was Ellie your daughter?"

"Granddaughter. We took care of her when her mother couldn't. She was retarded. She died some time ago." Lily jotted down the social security number.

"When was she born?"

"I can't remember. Oh, it was on Pearl Harbor Day in 1979."

"That's too bad. But all I need is your wife's information." She jotted down Ellie's birthday. "Thank you. That's all I need."

"I wish they'd come for the car. The title and keys are right there. I can't drive anymore so I have no use for it." He frowned. "I wish they'd come when they say they'll come."

"What's wrong with it?"

"It's just old. It was working fine when I last drove it." He followed her to the door. "Aren't you going to take it? I've been recharging the battery."

"Yes. I'll take care of it for you."

He shuffled out to the carport and unhooked the battery charger.

"It's all yours. I'm just glad to be rid of it."

"Thank you." She took his hand and patted it. "You have helped me so much." She found she had tears in her eyes, which surprised her. She was grateful to him, and having a car would make it so she could clean houses all over the city, not just in one neighborhood.

Lily put her bike in the trunk, then she climbed in and started the engine. She didn't want to be stopped by a policeman, so when she drove past a movie theater, she parked next to another old car and used her knife which had a screw-driver attachment, to switch license plates. Then she drove it to pick up Anne.

When Anne saw the car, she was excited to sit in the passenger seat and have the seat belt put around her. Lily knew she needed to buy a car seat, but she drove carefully to the hotel. The next day she went to a different bank. The application went through without a problem. Within an hour, she had a debit card in hand.

Levinas would not approve. The old man invited Lily into his home, trusting her, and she stole from him. Part of what she took was only a number, and using what she stole probably won't harm him or his deceased granddaughter. The car? He was going to donate it anyway and was happy to have her take it. Still these two thefts were a violation of love, which is an obligation and an invitation from the Other.

What interests me is that, when I wrote the scene, I knew she wouldn't feel guilty. She had a moment of gratitude toward him and I don't find reason to think it wasn't sincere. I have thought of her as a good person, one capable of love for Anne, Suzanne, Sam, others. Still, I had her do something that bothers me. Some readers of drafts of this novel think she engages in behavior that risks her child—basically agreeing with Nathan's version of her. She either has borderline personality disorder or she's a sociopath, who doesn't see that what she did to Anne was harmful. Lily is a dangerous woman to these readers. I can see that, but I disagree. I think she is a survivor, who does what's necessary to protect herself and her child.

How to balance love and self-preservation—the need of the host and the needs of the guest? The two will always come to conflict. Levinas says this failure is not a mistake, but the machinery of learning to love. And how does this balance work when I am reflecting on myself, when I am both host and guest? I've decided that shedding some of my baggage may enable a better future, but if I love myself, there is a limit to what I can sacrifice.

Walking away from the bank, Lily felt happy, a lift of spirits that could only be attributed to the card. It made her feel secure, normal even. It had been a year and a half since she had a credit card. Was it a liberating device or a captivating one?

For her it was liberating, the gain of some stability. She had given the bank her new address instead of the old man's.

The next day she cleaned a house. She worked hard and did a good enough job that the woman gave her a tip. Total, she earned $120, which made her feel like a proper capitalist. She deposited the cash on the way to the daycare center.

She took Anne to the library, where they looked at books. Then Lily checked her email and found a message from Sam: "What you wrote scared me. I wondered where you had gone. I also wonder what threatened you. I hope that you and Val are all right. If I can help, let me know."

The email tugged at her, but she knew nothing good could come from enlisting his help. Still she let herself daydream: one day Nathan would give up. Or she would discover a way to kill him. Or she would find a lawyer good enough to get a judge to give her Anne. She had zero hope for any of those. She knew her identity would change every so often, or that she'd find a corner of the world where nobody could find her, where she might be able to give Anne a semi-normal life. She had the most hope in that prospect.

She wrote him back: "Sorry about leaving without saying goodbye. We had to leave so quickly that there wasn't time to do anything. Thank you for not asking what I did, but I want to tell you. I kidnapped Valerie." Then she looked at it. How could she know Sam wouldn't turn her in for the reward? She believed he wouldn't. Also, he didn't know where she was. Still it was dangerous. More than that, she didn't want to put him into a position where he might hurt her—that would break her. She deleted the confessional lines, ending with, "You are a good friend." There was no one else who would care where she was, except for Nathan, but it was good to know there was someone who cared about her.

She found that the library downtown also showed children's movies, just like the one in Banff. She spent an hour with Anne on her lap. As was their permanent habit during the evening, they talked, read stories, and drew.

The next day she cleaned two houses in five hours. She figured she needed a phone that she could make calls on, not just take pictures, so she got a cheap one. She made a flier with her phone number on it and taped the flier to two hundred doors in the same neighborhood where she'd already had work.

Two days later she got a call from a woman who said she needed deep cleaning in the whole house, that it was an emergency. Lily arranged for Anne to be at daycare all day. The next morning, Lily drove to the address. The woman met Lily at the door and motioned for her to come in. "The moving truck is coming tomorrow, and this place is filthy." She was maybe fifty. She had a wide face, but her body was thin, which made her look a little like a bobble-head doll. She had a decades-old hairstyle. "My husband got a job here." She paused. "It was so sudden that we had to find a house to buy without having seen it." She smiled at Lily. "I've forgotten my manners. I'm Esther." She shook Lily's hand.

"I'm Lily."

"I can pay you $500 if you can finish today." Then she said she had to go pick out different drapes. "The carpet's all right, but I can't stand those drapes."

Lily couldn't see anything wrong with them. Esther had bought cleaning supplies, and Lily worked hard, dusting off the walls, then wiping them down, vacuuming the carpets, cleaning the windows, wiping the walls and wall boards with ammonia. She wondered if Esther really planned on paying her that much money.

She was on her hands and knees scrubbing the wall boards of the living room, when she turned, and a man was standing in the door. As soon as she looked, he smiled. "I'm Frank." He was heavier than his wife, and he wore a mustache that looked just like Nathan's. Immediately, Lily didn't trust him. She wondered how long he had been watching her.

She finished mid-afternoon, about a half hour before she had to pick up Anne. Together Esther and Lily walked through the house as Esther looked everything over. Back in the kitchen she smiled and nodded, her head bobbing. She then lifted her hand to give Lily high five. She grabbed her handbag, "Is a check all right?"

Lily hesitated, but then looked at the woman's broad, innocent face and nodded.

Two days later the check was rejected, and Lily's bank charged her twenty-five dollars.

After dropping Anne at daycare, she drove back to the woman's house. Esther met her at the door, and Frank was there as well, sitting on the couch.

"You're lying," Esther said to Lily. "The money went out of my account. You're trying to get paid twice."

Frank looked at Lily. "How much did she say she'd pay you?"

Lily said, "Five hundred dollars."

"That's too much." He turned to his wife. "You wrote her a check out of our old account, didn't you?"

Esther didn't look at him but kept her eyes on Lily. "Please leave."

"I'll go to the police."

"No, you won't," said Esther. "They'll believe me, not you."

Lily examined Esther's face and decided she was right.

Frank took his wallet out. "I only have a hundred."

Esther said, "That's probably about right."

Lily took the money and left quickly before she did something that would cause her trouble. She drove to the daycare center slowly, and by the time she got there her frustration and anger were mostly spent. It seemed like karma. The offer was a mirage, and she got half of what she would have charged for a deep cleaning. On the other hand, she had recently gotten a car without paying for it. It more than balanced out.

That night, after Anne was asleep, Lily thought about Frank and Esther. She wondered if Esther had shoplifted when she was young. With an apartment, a credit card, a car, a way to make money, and a phone, she felt secure again, but she had felt the same way with Suzanne and in Banff. Her security had melted then and could melt again. Even though she was tempted not to leave at the end of three weeks, she would do what the wheel said.

TWENTY-SIX

Anne didn't want to go. She sat on the bed watching as Lily packed their few belongings into a duffel she'd bought for the move.

When Lily said, "Come on! It's time to go," Anne didn't respond. "I don't want to either, Val, Baby, but we have to."

"I'm not a baby. Why do we have to?" She said this in a loud voice.

"This is our life," she said. "This is the way we live."

"I don't like it." She turned away and looked out the window.

Lily sat on the bed next to Anne. "We have to go."

"Why?"

Lily shrugged. "Because we do."

"That's not a reason."

Anne held her body stiff as Lily carried her out to the car.

She clipped Anne into a seatbelt in back. She drove to a store and bought a new child seat and fastened her into it. Sitting in the driver's seat, she spun the Executive Decision Maker.

The wheel pointed east-southeast. She spun again for distance—233 miles. On an atlas she found in the glove compartment, she determined that the closest large town to that was Missoula, which she had passed through on her way north to Canada. She wanted a large town, so she could sustain her cleaning business. She had 200 miles to drive.

With $1,400 in her bank account and $200 in cash, she crossed the neck of Idaho, passing through Coeur d'Alene and into Montana. Even though it was still February and snow covered most of the fields, she looked forward to spring and to being outside more with Anne. Within four hours they were in Missoula.

She drove through the streets, discovering on one side of the river a moderate-sized Montana town with truck stops, cafés, and stores containing cowboy hats and boots. On the other side was a university town, with ordered lawns and chic restaurants. She considered how she might take advantage of that difference. She and Anne ate at a fast-food place with an indoor playground. She felt tired at the thought of finding an apartment, work, and daycare. She daydreamed for the hundredth time about finding a place she could stay with Anne for years.

At the library, her home away from home, she found books for Anne and checked the local newspaper's want ads. She had considered teaching private art lessons but found the university had an MFA in studio art, so that niche would be flooded.

Missoula was small enough that many of the students would take the bottom-feeder jobs, the ones she was qualified to do. She saw a couple of waitress positions, but she didn't want to be that public, especially not in one of the several restaurants that catered to truckers. She knew that if she went to neighbor-hoods far from the university, she could always make money cleaning houses. She looked up daycare and apartments for rent. Those close to the university were more expensive than those that were across town.

There was a note from Sam. "Hope you're still all right. Wish I knew where you were, but it's also neat to have known a real criminal. I've been imagining crimes: murder, armed bank robbery, investment fraud, cheating on your MFA final (if there is such a thing). Miss you."

She sent a note back saying only, "You're still way off. Val-erie and I miss you too." She thought he might know what she'd done but was too polite to invade her privacy.

While at the library she spun the wheel and felt a settling when it turned to months. The next spin was for thirteen of them. She found an apartment that was mid-range, not so cheap that it would be a dump, but not so expensive that it would take all her money for a deposit plus first and last month's rent. She looked at the apartment—it was clean and fairly new.

"This is our new place," she told Anne.

Anne walked into the bedroom, the kitchen, the bathroom. "It's bigger than our last house, but we should still go back to live with Sam."

"We can't go back to live with Sam. This will do just fine."

The deposit took most of the money she had, but that was acceptable. She and Anne asked around and found a daycare center that wasn't far. At Salvation Army she bought more clothing for her and Anne. They had a rack of children's books, and she bought twenty. She also bought pillows, sheets, and blankets. Then she went to a mall and spent money on new shoes and a new jacket. She also bought new shoes for Anne. Back at the library, she considered putting an ad online to sell the car. If she priced it so that it would sell quickly, but not so low that it would make someone suspicious, she could take the money and buy another. It was unlikely that the old man's children would accuse her of stealing it, but she didn't think they could find her. Then she realized that if she got a car she'd need to get new license plates, unless the seller left the old ones on. To get new plates she'd have to have some id, and she didn't dare use her forged passport or her old driver's license. The thought of trying to steal someone's driver's license number filled her with dread, and she knew she'd screw it up. She decided to put off worrying until the next day.

With the books around them on the bed, Anne seemed happier. "We're going to be here for a long time," she told the child.

"Yay!" said Anne. "I'll have a new school."

"And you'll make new friends. Val. In this new place we need new names again. Sarah. I am Sarah. What do you want your name to be?"

"Not Brooke."

"Not Brooke and not Val."

"Sam," she said.

"That's a boy's name."

"Sam," said Anne.

"But that's Sam's name, our friend. Do you want to steal his name?"

"My name is Sam. Sam. Sam. Sam."

"Okay. Sam. Short for Samantha."

"Sam."

She helped Anne write her name. Then they drew pictures of each other and wrote their new names on the bottom of the pictures. Sam and Sarah.

The next day she took Anne to the daycare. "I'd like to start my daughter here, but can I look around first?" April, the head caregiver, a plump woman with white hair, walked around with her. Lily noted the rows of books, and Anne pulled at her hand to go look at them.

"We alternate learning and play. They learn their shapes, or letters if they're older. They paint and look at books." There were two women inside painting with the children. They looked happy. Nobody was off in a corner, ignored.

"Looks good." She went back and talked to Anne, who had already made friends with another girl.

"I'm going to leave you here."

Anne nodded and turned back to her friend.

When Lily woke the next morning, she knew what to do about the car. It worried her that it hadn't come to her sooner, that maybe she was losing her edge. She didn't need a new car, she just needed new license plates, a set the police wouldn't be looking for. She couldn't just steal another set, replacing them with the ones she had already stolen, because the owner might notice the changed plates and contact the police. She had to find plates that nobody would miss.

She went to a Walmart and bought some superglue. She drove to a junkyard and walked inside the front office. A bald man with a greasy T-shirt sat behind the counter, typing into an ancient computer. She told him she was an art major and wanted to do paintings of old cars. "I'll just take pictures of them and paint them in my studio." She held up her camera.

"An artist," he said.

"Yes." She showed him her sketchbook.

"Go ahead."

He went back to picking at the computer keys with one finger.

She walked through the rows of junkers until she found a car that still had license plates on it. The tags were from only the year before. She took the plates off with the screwdriver tool on her pocketknife, stuffed them in her backpack and walked out, smiling her thanks to the bald man. That night, after Anne was asleep, she stepped outside and used her exacto knife to slice the tags off a car not far down the street. The tags had been glued on top of each other year-by-year, so they came off in a wafer. Back inside, she glued the tags to the plates she'd gotten from the junkyard and walked down to put them on her car. She put the stolen plates deep in a dumpster. She couldn't change the VIN number of the car, so she couldn't afford to be stopped by the police.

The next day, after walking Anne to her new daycare, she went to the library and looked at a map of the town, her home for the next year. On the south of the river was the university. The rest of the town spread in two directions, northeast and southwest. She rode the bike through the streets, which was a better way of getting a sense of the place than in her car. She examined each business—hotels, restaurants, a bookstore, stores that sold jewelry, cruises, clothing, alcohol. She didn't mind becoming a thief, but the steeper the profits, the greater the risk.

She parked her bike and walked across campus, thinking about her time at the University of Utah, studying art. She'd had a ring of acquaintances and work to do, a pleasant time in her life.

She found the employment center and got a printout of secretarial jobs. She wished she could teach art as an adjunct, but she had no way of proving she had an MFA, and she wanted more money than that. Most of the other jobs required her to be a student.

While she was leaving, she overheard a woman asking if she could place an off-campus job on their university listing. Lily paused in the doorway, listening. The young woman behind the counter told the other woman that she couldn't place that kind of ad. "We're having a campus career fair for employers to talk to students. You could get a table."

"I just need some help for a while. It's not a career person I'm looking for." The woman wore Levi's and a sweater. Her auburn hair was pinned behind her ears, and, as Lily approached, she looked at her through square glasses.

"What kind of help?" asked Lily.

"Farm work. Planting hops rhizomes mostly. That's what's urgent right now. I used to hire people from Mexico, but the damn government has everything in a log jam. Maybe driving a tractor if the person learns fast, planting barley next month. Helping dig out the footings for a cement pour. All kinds of stuff. Are you looking for work?"

"Yes," she said.

"What skills do you have?"

"I can work hard," said Lily.

"You're not very—ah—substantial," said the woman.

"Where's your farm? Try me out."

"Between Lolo and Florence." When Lily frowned, she said 20 miles.

"I have a car," said Lily. "I could drive out there."

The woman eyed Lily.

"Are we having an interview?"

"I guess we are," said the woman. "Let's go outside."

They sat on the lawn in front of the building.

"I'm Frances Markham."

"Sarah Jackson."

"Any background in agriculture?"

Lily grimaced. "MFA in visual art. Pretty useless."

The woman looked at her over her glasses. "Maybe, maybe not. Where did you go to school?"

"University of Utah."

"You a Mormon?"

"Does it matter?"

"Probably not."

"What do I need?"

"Good work boots, leather gloves, a hat, long-sleeved shirt, thick pants.

"What are you doing?"

"Running a farm."

"What kind of farm?"

"Barley."

"And you said hops."

"Yes. I'm doing what men have done forever with water, barley, and hops."

"Making beer?"

"Yes. Water comes first. I have a spring on my farm between Lolo and Florence. It's not a big spring, but I got the main brewer here in Missoula to run a batch with it. All other ingredients are the same, but this water made spectacular beer. The water has just the right mix of sulfates, calcium, magnesium, sodium, chloride carbonates. The perfect blend."

Frances was excited, as passionate as a visionary. Lily distrusted that kind of idealism, so she just nodded.

"Since my husband died, I've been working with a genetic engineer from Montana State, Bozeman. Laura Stuart. She's invented a system of mathematical derivatives to craft the perfect balance of uniqueness and general traits. And hops. I have a gardener who engineers dirt. She creates the perfect silty and sandy loam. Perfect for growing hops."

"All these experts. And me. The laborer."

Frances looked at her. "Do you want the job or not?"

"Twenty hours a week?" said Lily.

"That's about what I was hoping," said Frances. "$15 an hour."

Lily knew she could earn more than that cleaning houses, but something about the way this woman moved, confident in her own body, and talked with a relaxed and wry smile intrigued Lily.

"Yes," said Lily, "I'll take the job." But she wasn't sure she meant it. "If I work hard enough to earn $20 an hour is there the possibility of a raise?"

Frances frowned. "Sure, but first things first. You have to show you're strong enough." She gave Lily her card and drew a rough map on the back of it.

Lily rode toward the daycare with the backpack that she always carried with her, the wheel, her passport, her driver's license that was still in her birth name, her Canadian documents, some money. She sat on her bike outside the daycare and spun the wheel to decide whether to take the job, left side, yes, right side, no.

I spun the wheel that Lily spun, a single wheel in two dimensions. It came up, "Yes."

That afternoon Lily and Anne went shopping again, this time for work clothes. She bought some of what she needed at the thrift store and the rest new. Through the evening, she played with Anne, taught her letters, took her for a walk to a playground.

"How is your new school?"

"Good."

"Have you made new friends?"

"Yes. My new best friend is named Anne."

Lily smiled but didn't feel like smiling. Her daughter didn't even know her real name.

"How long will we be here?" Anne asked. '

"More than a year."

"Really? I don't like moving. I like being in one place."

"We talked about this."

"We move all the time. The kids at daycare don't move all the time."

"Sam, we've talked about this before."

"My name is Valerie, Mom. You don't have to use my pretend name."

"Listen to me! I take care of you. Even when we've moved around a lot, I've taken care of you. There are people who don't want me to do this. They want to take you away, so we have to be careful."

Anne nodded.

"Does this scare you?"

"A little."

"You know I'll watch out for you."

"Yes." She frowned. "Mom, what is your real name?"

"Alice," she said. "Alice Jenkins."

After Anne was asleep, Lily considered what she'd told her daughter—a necessary lie. One she hardly felt guilty about. Who was she? Anne's mother. That was the anchor of her being.

Then she thought carefully about working for Frances. She couldn't afford to work very long for such low wages, but the farm woman was offering what could be long-term employment. Lily had wanted to get out of the cycle of living hand-to-mouth. She wanted to get to where she didn't have to break new laws. When she had stolen the first social security number and gotten caught immediately, she knew she couldn't afford that kind of risk.

One of my readers of early drafts of this book said that somewhere around this point in the story the book becomes episodic as Lily repeats the same process in Banff, Spokane, Missoula—moving, setting up an apartment and day school, finding employment. He implied that I should disrupt disruption. I'm struck with the idea that this is how Anne feels; she wants her life to hold still for a while. She wants the physical constellation of her life—home, bedroom, books, toys, daycare, friends, even her mother—to stop changing so often. Lily believes that Anne would be better off without the fear of disruption. Still she doesn't regret taking her away from Nathan, who would have forced all of Anne's experiences into an inflexible pattern, one of his choosing. Anne loses both ways; being with her mother her life is unsteady, being with her father it would be rigid.

My next thought about disrupting disruption and giving her permanent relationships was to have Lily invite Sam back. She will be frightened, anxious that he will betray her, but she will do it anyway. Because I don't have a coin in my pocket, I walk out of my office to the copy center in my building and ask if someone has a coin. I flip the borrowed penny on the shelf next to the mailboxes—tails. Sam will not come back. If it had come up heads, I would have had him visit her in Missoula. They would certainly have had sex; they like each other and there would be no reason not to. What would happen next? I don't know. With his money and hers, maybe she could buy a new identity. They might live in Banff or Aspen, or at a ski slope in Europe. Nathan might still find her, but her life would be less furtive.

One of the aspects of the novel *Tess of the d'Urbervilles* is the relentlessness of fate that grinds her down. At any point her creator, Thomas Hardy, could have let her off the hook: she doesn't doze off and the mail cart doesn't run into her horse and kill it causing her to have to look for work, her false cousin is not a sexual predator, her husband Angel allows himself to have sex with her on their wedding night even after his discovery that she is not a virgin. There are a hundred places in the book where her life could branch differently, but to make a social and philosophical point, Hardy is relentless with her.

Am I doing the same thing? I can say it was chance; the coin could have come up heads, the wheel could have spun differently all those times. But I freely admit to manipulating the story. My intent is to explore how vulnerable life is and how tenuous our relationships to others. The social fabric that separated Lily's life in Deer Valley from homelessness was thin to the point of transparency even though she thought it was as solid as love. I want to imagine that what happened to Lily could happen to me or anyone, even if it feels like a fantasy. For millions of people it is no fantasy; the social tether that keeps them from the street is like a single thread of cotton.

Even after a year and a half, Nathan still maintained the website, and she knew from her experience in Canada that he spread her picture with police everywhere. He had certainly hired detectives to search for her. The Mounties had found her, and the truck driver would probably have communicated with Nathan about seeing her in Banff. It was unlikely, but possible, that Nathan could have found the women who had taken her to Spokane. She felt herself hoping that she was safe, but she distrusted that emotion. Complacency would get her caught.

The next morning, she and Anne had breakfast, and then she dropped her off at daycare before driving south out of Missoula through Lolo and then east, toward the hills. The sky was blue and she felt happy going to her first day on this new job. She found the ranch house, and about a half mile from it, a cluster of vehicles on the edge of a barley field. There were four women standing next to a backhoe parked next to what looked like an old Baptist church and a huge greenhouse. The air was colder outside than she thought it would be. She hoped her coat was warm enough. Frances walked over. "You've been promoted. Can you drive a tractor?"

"Give me five minutes."

Another woman taught her the clutch, brakes, hydraulic, and turning. The tractor would pull a disk harrow, which was about six feet wide. She was to pull the disk down the rows between the hop trellises. Frances already had an acre of hops, but she wanted Lily to prepare the ground for another acre. The poles that would hold the trellises were already put in the new ground, but nothing had been planted. The ground had been spread with manure from a neighboring dairy. She drove the harrow between the rows of poles, which were seven feet apart. At first she drove slowly, wary of the machine. Soon she was driving faster, keeping the wheels straight. At first she had to stop the tractor to lift the harrow with the hydraulic to make her turn and go back down the next row. Soon she got into a rhythm, hitting the hydraulic just as she cleared the trellis and turning in a partial figure-eight to go down the next row.

Even though it was cold sitting on the tractor, she loved the smell of the newly opened earth, the swarms of gulls and other birds that followed the tractor, looking for insects and mice turned up by the circular blades of the harrow. She finished the acre of hops in about two hours.

Frances smiled when she finished. "Good work for your first time." Then Frances had her disk between the trellises where hops were already established, about a half-acre. The buds had started to grow out from the bines, a few yellow-green shoots along each woody stalk. She drove down the rows, disk-

FRANCES WARMING HER HANDS
Automythology (USP)

ing up the rhizomes that grew from the roots, cutting up weeds, and turning the brown manure under.

At lunch all the women sat around a table in the big kitchen in Frances's house. In the other room was a wood stove that heated the house. Frances sat in front of it, warming her hands and her body. Lily took her picture; Frances looked up but didn't smile.

Lily looked around the room—traditional western couches, a painting of a sentimental mountain scene with a bugling elk, and a Georgia O'Keeffe painting. Everyone talked over each other. There was Sophie, the mechanic and heavy equipment operator, Blaire, who would be in charge of the cement pour, Frances the owner, a carpenter and electrician named Ellie, and two college students from Montana State studying agribusiness.

"She'd never driven tractor before," Frances said. "But she drove perfectly straight down those narrow rows."

"That probably kept her hopping," said Sophie.

It was a dumb joke, but everyone laughed, and she smiled at the circle of women. She felt her body relax, some of the tension she always carried draining away.

TWENTY-SEVEN

The next morning Lily and Bess, one of the college students, planted rhizomes in the greenhouse, which they would later replant under the trellises. Frances said, "Buds up, one inch of dirt over the bud."

They sat at a big table under the sun-warmed half dome and filled plastic pots with soil. The rhizomes looked like dead sticks, so the green buds sprouting from each one seemed unnatural or even miraculous. Lily took her gloves off so she could feel the dirt on her hands, under her fingernails.

Her parents had planted a garden when she was young, but later they stopped—she didn't know why. When she was six, she had helped her father plant beans, squash, carrots, chard, and lettuce. He had made her count the squash seeds and showed her how to put the bean seeds one inch apart. He didn't let her try to plant the tinier seeds, like lettuce and carrots. She remembered watching for the plants and asking her father over and over when they'd come up. She remembered the rush of pleasure she felt when he showed her the small, yellow-green bean leaves, and later the squash and other vegetables. She knew she was manufacturing nostalgia from a time when she was safe, but it gave her pleasure to be planting again.

Lily looked around at the orderly farm of about three hundred acres in the corner of the Beartooth River valley. It was gently sloping land. She watched the spreader whirling out the manure that Frances had hauled from a dairy across the river. After that, the same woman drove the tractor, plowing the fields for planting with barley. Frances said she wanted to get the barley all planted by the first of March. The builder and her assistant measured the ground next to the church, planning the location of the cement pads that would support the brewing tanks. The two scientists Frances had talked about when she and Lily first met weren't out that day, they only came out once a week. Another woman worked in an area of the farm with close rows—Lily assumed it was where vegetables would be planted later in the spring. The outdoor hop bines had started budding out, and only a few days after planting the barley would sprout. That fall water would run into the tanks and brewing would begin, all things that came from the earth. It all gave her more pleasure than she had imagined feeling again— much better than cleaning someone else's house.

It took them two days, but eventually they had all the rhizomes planted. Bess smiled and laid her hand on Lily's arm. "We did a good job." Bess was an agricultural science student, finishing her last year, and worked with Frances as a paid intern, so she knew what she was talking about.

Lily felt again the rush of pleasure. "Yes, it was good work."

She treasured her afternoons and evenings with Anne. They read books, wrote and read stories to each other, drew pictures, and talked. They drew each other objects in their apartment, or magical pictures of whatever came into their minds.

"I remember a man," said Anne. "He was tall, and he had a mustache." She showed Lily a rough picture of someone who might have been Nathan—a round blotch of a head, a dark line for a mustache.

"He was your father," said Lily. "What do you remember about him?"

"Nothing. I remember him talking to you, but I don't remember playing with him."

"I don't think he did. I never saw him paying attention to you."

"Why?"

"I don't think he loved either one of us," said Lily. "I think he loved himself more."

"I love myself. Don't I?"

"Yes. We love each other and we love ourselves. We are survivors."

"Survivors? What does that mean—survivor?"

"It means I take care of you. I make sure we have food and a place to live."

"How long will we live here?"

Lily waited. "At least a year. I hope for longer than that. We may someday get a house with a yard for you to play in, but wherever you and I are together, that is our home."

"Will I have a sister to play with in the yard?"

Lily shook her head. "Probably not. We need a man for that."

"I want a man. I want it to be Sam."

Lily smiled. "I like Sam too." She thought again about Sam and their talks about language and philosophy. That had been a good part of her life, though so short.

"Let's get him to move in so I can have a sister."

"Probably not."

"You are mean to not let Sam move in," said Anne.

"Yes, I'm a mean, wicked mother, but I'm a survivor!"

Anne touched her palm on Lily's face, Lily's favorite thing in the world.

That was a sleepless night for Lily. Being on the farm had made her think of elemental, earthy things, like taking a man's seed inside her, making a zygote that would grow. She felt a pull toward that kind of primitive thinking, but she also felt an undertow of horror, of becoming trapped by her body. When Nathan had started talking about stopping the pill, she had vacillated between wanting to have nothing to do with getting pregnant and wanting to make a baby with this man she loved. Now she saw that getting her pregnant had been Nathan's way of entrapping her. Anne had meant nothing else to him. She knew someone like Sam might do the same thing unconsciously, trap her, hold her to him. Contraceptives made it so she could have sex, follow her natural instincts, and not be trapped. It would be so nice to be with Sam. She thought it stupid to long for impossibilities, but that didn't mean she could keep herself from imagining Sam as a surrogate father to Anne, as a friend, as a lover.

"I want to meet your daughter," Frances said. "How can I know you if I don't meet your daughter?"

Lily brought Anne to work that Saturday.

"Sam, this is my boss, Frances. This is my daughter Samantha."

"Sam," said Anne. "I like to be called Sam."

Frances knelt before the girl, holding out her hand. Anne took it. "I'm pleased to meet you, Sam. Your mother is a hard worker."

"I'm a hard worker," said Anne.

Lily smiled.

"Can I show her around?" asked Frances.

"Of course."

Frances held Anne on her lap on the four-wheeler as they drove around the farm. From a distance, Lily watched them get off the vehicle and walk to the brewery site. Frances bent low and pointed across the valley.

"Smart kid," said Frances when they came back. "Smarter than either one of us."

At lunch, Anne sat with the other women, eating.

"I want to be a farmer," she said, "like Frances."

The women laughed.

"Good girl," Bess said.

Lily beamed.

On the way home, she asked, "Do you like Frances?"

"Yes! She's going to be my grandma."

"You have another grandma," said Lily, without thinking.

"Where?"

"In Ut—in another state."

"I want to go see her."

"That probably won't work."

Anne fell silent. "Sometimes you're just mean."

"Yes, I suppose I am."

One day as Lily finished checking the irrigation system, she drove the tractor up to the farm buildings and saw cars all around the old church. The women were inside, looking down at blueprints they had spread across the floor.

It was time for lunch, but nobody was paying any attention to the clock. There was a new woman, one who spoke with a German accent—the brewer. Lily knew she'd have to leave soon to get Anne. She stood on the stairway and examined the huge drawing. From the back Bess pointed to each part and whispered to Lily the stages of the brewing of beer. First, the barley is sprouted and then dried in an oven to stop the growth. The result is malt, which is milled to break apart the kernels and then mixed with water to produce mash. The mash is heated to break down the starches into soluble sugars. The liquid or wort is strained out of the mash and hops are added. It is boiled to remove water and provide sterilization. The wort is cooled rapidly in a heat exchanger, then yeast is added to ferment. "With a process thousands of years old," she said, "there's a lot of knowledge accumulated."

Lily looked at the diagrams of the brewing equipment, the flow of water, barley, and hops. She also saw that Bess had a religious feeling about the process.

"There are byproducts," said Bess. "Frances will sell the barley mash and extra yeast. It goes to the dairy she gets her manure from. Fed back to the cattle. So it's a cycle—spent barley turns into manure that's put on the land to create more barley."

Another woman said, "We'll use some of the spent barley mixed with cow manure to grow mushrooms."

Looking at the plan, Lily had a feeling of awe at the perfect system, the transfer of heated water that would be used in other parts of the process. The equipment had an order and a shape, like a poem.

The brewer said, "I've seen a system like this in Germany, but it just used heat from the kiln to sprout the wheat. This uses water from the heat exchange to supply heat to the kiln and to generate part of the electricity that runs the system."

"Hardly any waste energy," Frances said. "The water is right, the barley is good, the hops can be just strong enough, but all of this doesn't do any good if the beer doesn't taste right. Any accident can bring in strange bacteria that changes the taste, so good breweries have every worker taste the beer several times a day."

Bess gave a wide grin.

"Taste," said the brewer, "not guzzle. It's a scientific process, but it's also an art, where we as artists must be sensitive to the slightest changes."

Lily liked looking at the blueprints—the images of what would become substantial.

Everything is material and material has shape—a mother with a daughter on her lap, the balance of water and barley and hops, the design of the brewery. When I was on my Mormon mission learning the Navajo language, I discovered the concept of *behgha*, meaning rightness or proportion of something made or some act performed. Adding a negative, as in *do behgha da*, changes the meaning to disproportionate to itself. Balance and proportion enable traditional Navajos to walk the beautiful path, pilgrims on the earth in balance with all organisms, which is essential, because each organism is a lesser form of a god.

Their dwellings, called *hogans* are traditionally placed with the doorway to the east. The making of a hogan is like the making of the Earth, part of the same creation. This is not an abstract or symbolic relationship for the traditional Navajo. The last time I went down to the reservation, I could see hardly any hogans, except for those at tourist stops, designed to entice *bilagaanas* to stop and spend money. Building the traditional hogan is a prayer, an act of creation.

I gather that the concept of *feng shui* is similar. In ancient China architects used the stars to orient buildings in space according to metaphysical principles, so that the building would be compatible with its surroundings. More precisely they paid attention to the invisible forces in a place and used those forces to situate their buildings in time and space. They considered not only the immediate orientation, but orientation on the planet. They used formulas and calculations, as well as astrolabes to track the movement of the stars. Eventually they used magnetic compasses to orient buildings. As a result, the buildings were established for maximum solar gain. The system is partly mathematical and partly practical, partly mystical, just like the brewing of beer.

A recipe for a small batch of beer (say five gallons, fifty, or five hundred) will not be a good recipe for a 5,000-gallon batch of beer. It has to do with porousness of the malt and the mash, the ability of enzymes to communicate with every pocket and every grain, so the recipe for beer changes non-proportionally given the size of the batch.

Proportion, scale, balance. Sitting in harmony with the universe. My great-grandfather wrote that he wanted only the amount of cattle and property that he could manage well. This art/science of proportion, which Wendell Berry often writes about, has little to do with hierarchical, greed-controlled capitalism, and has much to do with the feeling a craftsperson has about being good at something. It's also about what happens in a community, like the one that Frances has formed to run her farm and brewery. Her operation involves science, luck, human feeling, pride of work, experience, innovation. It is a good community because everyone in it is important and has respect. A society that rides on the backs of the poor and dispossessed—think about what we've done to the tribes that lived here before Europeans arrived—is dysfunctional and disproportionate: *do begha da*.

For me, my most ideal personal balance is related to uncertainty, because when I'm able to hold my many tensions in proportion—faith and doubt, intimacy and distance, possibility and impossibility—I am in a position where I don't have to rely on dogmatic certitude and can instead innovate in my own life.

Hopefully. Gradually, day by day, I feel it happening, but there are always reversals, where I return to the ruts I've already made for myself. Today, I think, that even ruts can lead somewhere and since the ruts are permanent, I should work with them, not try to get them to vanish like magic.

Twice a week Lily went to the library, checking out books for Anne and trying to see what Nathan was up to. One night there was an email from Sam waiting for her. "I want to visit you. I don't want to never see you and Val again."

At first Lily felt a rush of emotion, then more. Her whole body felt enlivened. Then she remembered the size of the reward.

$100,000 could warp anybody—just as the smaller reward had warped James and maybe Suzanne.

"I would love to see you," she wrote, "but I can't."

He was on his computer apparently so a message came back in a few seconds. "You don't trust me. I would never do anything to harm you or Val."

He knew. She felt it deep in her gut. He had guessed why she was running, and he had found out who she was. He probably knew about the reward.

"I can't risk it," she wrote back. "Please don't pressure me."

She thought about trusting Sam, telling him everything. Maybe he'd be an ally and her life wouldn't be solitary. She thought about it for a while, but instead of writing him, she bought a sheath knife, six inches long, and put it on the floor under the bed next to the wooden baseball bat she had bought the week before.

TWENTY-EIGHT

Bess and Lily worked on digging the foundations for the brewery next to the spring. One of the women had already done the rough work with a backhoe and a bobcat, but the two younger women cleaned loose dirt from where the builder had put in stakes and strung twine.

"You have a husband?" asked Bess.

"Used to."

"What happened to him?"

"He's ex now."

"Ex or exed?" Bess laughed, "You ex-ed him."

"If only. He ex-ed me. Exed, axed, excised, exorcised."

Bess laughed again.

"How about you?" asked Lily

"I'm never getting married," Bess said.

"Good girl."

"Well, maybe someday," she said. "When I'm about thirty. Maybe I'll want a kid by then. Now it would be a burden."

"Boyfriend?"

"Of course. I like men. I just don't want to live with one. Like horses. Good for a ride but I don't want one living in my apartment."

Lily smiled. "I would be happier now if I'd had that philosophy. Did you grow up in Missoula?"

"My mother moved here when I was five. After her divorce."

"What does she do?"

"Newspaper editor." Bess asked, "What do you want to become, eventually?"

"What I am now. Mother. Protector of my child."

"That's your only goal?"

"The main one. I also hope Frances's dream happens. And I hope for world peace, but I only have control over one of those three wishes."

And maybe not that one, she thought, maybe I can't protect her, although that worry seemed something of the past—the anxious, unsettling, fearful past. She thought she could live in Missoula forever.

Lily had a neighbor in her apartment building, a man who sat on his balcony each evening, drinking beer. The first time he saw her, he lifted his beer can and said, "Hey." He nodded toward Anne. "Cute kid." When she didn't answer him, he went back to staring at the trees. He tried a couple more times to talk when she and Anne went out there to draw or read or just watch people walk past. After she ignored him he seemed to give up on trying to talk. Still, his presence bothered her. The space was not hers when he was there, because he could stare at her whenever he wanted. She didn't look at him, but it felt as if his eyes were always on her. One night he was more drunk than usual and every time she glanced his way, she found him staring at her.

The next night, she woke. A sound. She heard some low noise from the other room. She couldn't recognize it. She reached under her bed and grasped her bat. She strode straight to Anne's room. She didn't turn on the light, but she stood inside the door, waiting. She heard Anne breathing, and she heard the sound of slow steps coming down the hall. She waited until she saw a shadow opposite the door, and she swung the bat, and as she swung the bat, she saw it was a man in her apartment, just raising his arm to block the bat.

She hit him on the forearm, but in the narrow doorway she couldn't get a good swing. He fell against the wall, but then grabbed the end of the bat, wrenched it free, and threw it behind him. She grabbed the door and tried to shut it against him, but he pushed through and came at her. He grabbed her arm and slugged her in the face with his free hand, a solid blow that knocked her over. She couldn't think, and her mind nearly went to black. She fought to stay conscious. He pulled her up and hit her with the other hand.

By then Anne was awake and crying. The man took Lily in a bear hug and carried her through the door, but she twisted loose and fell to the floor. He kicked at her, and then he grabbed her feet and jerked them back so her face slammed down.

She reached for anything to hold onto, but there was nothing but carpet. Then her hand caught the bat, she pulled it in and got her hands around the handle. She held it under one arm, against her side, so he couldn't see it. She let her body go limp, as if she'd passed out. He dragged her into the living room, bent over her and flopped her across the end of the couch, her butt toward him.

She felt him pulling her panties down, so she twisted again, got on the other side of the couch from him and took a step back, where there was swinging room. The streetlight outside the window was shining, and she could see his silhouette but not his face. She thought he might not be able to see her clearly. He came over the couch, his arms reaching for her. She swung the bat, sideways and down, smacking the top of his head. He dropped to the floor, but then he groaned and lifted himself to his hands and knees, so she hit him again.

By then she heard the siren. Someone must have heard the screaming and thumps. She followed the sound of Anne's shrieking and picked up her child, holding her close. She got the emergency backpack and headed out the door. Anne still cried in a shrill voice. Lily said into her ear, "It's going to be all right."

Several neighbors stood in their doorways, the woman from across the hall in her pajamas, her cell phone still to her mouth. "She's coming out," the woman said.

Another neighbor, a young husband, left his wife in the doorway and came toward her. "Come in our apartment," he said. "You can sit there until the police come."

"No," said Lily, "I'm fine. I have to get out of here." She still felt wobbly.

"Your face," the man said.

"You need to sit down," said the woman who still had the cell pressed to her ear.

The man caught Lily's arm.

"No. Let me go." She freed herself and went down the hall-way. By the time she got to the ground floor, the police were coming through the front door, four of them. She walked into the lobby, waiting for them to pass, so she could leave. Anne was still crying, loud, and the same woman, with her damnable cell phone, came down the stairs and pointed to them.

"There she is. She's disoriented, and she shouldn't be left alone."

Lily slumped into a chair, and a policewoman knelt in front of her. "You're safe now."

The hell I am, thought Lily.

"Is your child hurt?"

"No."

"You need to get to the hospital," the policewoman said.

"Is he—is he dead?" asked Lily.

"Is who dead?"

"The man who attacked me."

"I don't know," said the policewoman. "We'll know in a minute. Whether he's dead or alive, you're safe now."

The obtuse woman misunderstood what she wanted. She wanted him alive. Dead he meant a lot of trouble to her.

Sometime later the police came down the stairs with a stretcher. It was not covered with a body bag. She tried to see his face but the policewoman was in the way.

Anne had finally quieted, clinging to Lily's neck.

The policewoman spoke to Lily, "I need to ask you a few questions. Then you can go to the hospital."

"I don't need to go to the hospital," said Lily.

"Did he rape you?"

"No," said Lily. "That's what he was trying to do. I hit him with a bat."

"Did he hit you?"

"Yes," said Lily. "He hit me in the face, twice."

"Did he hit you anywhere except for your face?"

"He kicked me in the ribs."

"But you're sure he didn't rape you? You didn't pass out?"

"No. I didn't lose consciousness." She clutched Anne tighter. "Are you finished now?"

"Can I ask just a couple more questions?"

"I don't have a choice, do I?"

"What is your name?"

Lily paused, trying to think. "Sarah. Sarah Jackson."

"Was that your apartment?"

"Yes."

"Do you know the man?"

Lily believed it was her neighbor. "Yes. I mean, I don't know. It was dark and I didn't get a good look at him just now. Maybe it was the guy in the next apartment. When we go out on the balcony to sit, he's always staring at me."

"The apartment to the left of yours?"

"Yes."

"We'll know soon if it was him." The policewoman bent and looked at Lily's face. "Your attacker hit you?"

"Twice. And kicked me. I already told you."

"Tell me again what happened."

"I woke to some sound. I got to Ann—my baby's room and he grabbed me when I tried to hit him with my bat. He hit me twice and dragged me down the hall. Somehow I grabbed the bat. He tried to get my underwear down, and I twisted away. I hit him twice with the bat."

A policeman standing nearby said, "He seems to have come in the sliding door. The lock was broken."

"One more question. You didn't invite him in?"

"I already told you," said Lily. "He tried to rape me, and I hit him with a bat."

"Thank you."

They took Lily to the hospital in the ambulance. "I can't afford an ambulance," she told them.

"It will be all right," said the policewoman.

Lily wanted to ask her how the fuck she knew it was going to be all right.

They also tried to take Anne away from her, but she refused.

"I want to stay with you, Mommy," Anne said.

"You heard her," said Lily. "Where I go, she goes."

"We'd take—"

"No! Dammit, no! How many times do I have to tell you?"

"Okay," said the woman. "She can ride with you in the ambulance."

At the hospital, the doctor examined her face and ribs. He sent her to have her head x-rayed. The policewoman reached her arms to take Anne, but Anne turned away. "Can she wait outside the door?" said the technician.

"Behind the screen," Lily said to him. Then she spoke to Anne. "This woman is a nice woman, and she'll hold you for one minute. You'll be safe with her." Lily realized she was saying almost the same things the policewoman had said to her when she was still disoriented. Now she wasn't as disoriented, but her head hurt like hell.

Anne went to the woman, who led her behind the protective wall. The technician pushed the button and came back around.

Afterward, Anne sat next to her in a curtained cubicle, clinging to her.

"Are we going to move again?"

"I don't know," said Lily. "I hope not."

When the emergency room doctor came back, he told her she had a mild concussion and that she should rest in a dark room.

The policewoman had waited outside and asked to take pictures of her.

"No," said Lily.

"We need the evidence."

"You have the doctor's report. I won't have my picture taken. It's religious."

"Religious."

"I believe my soul is sucked out of my body when a picture is taken."

The policewoman looked at her. "Should the doctor know that you're a little delirious?"

"I'm not delirious. I just don't want my picture taken. I'll tell you anything I need to until that sinks into your thick head."

They finally compromised and took pictures of the bruises but not her whole face. Lily knew that if she insisted to the end, the policewoman would get suspicious. She just hoped that the picture Nathan sent to every possible police station was buried in some file where nobody ever looked.

Finally, toward morning, she was able to get back into her apartment. The manager had a new lock put in both the front door and the sliding one. He gave her a stick that she could drop into the slot behind the glass door, making it even more difficult to open. Someone could still get in by breaking the glass, but that was much noisier and took more time than popping the lock.

She called Frances, explaining what happened, and took the day off. Then she called the daycare center. She went back to bed, sleeping until noon, Anne next to her. When she woke, her heart was still beating too fast, and she felt that she couldn't get her breath. She had dreamed that Nathan was the man who had broken into her apartment to rape her. The last time she'd had sex with Nathan was after she had become aware of his controlling nature. Every move he made had seemed contrived, an act, even though he was doing the same things he always did, talking to her, focusing on her, moving slow with his hands. Before long he sensed that she was not into it, and instead of continuing to cultivate her emotionally, he had just taken her fast. She had never agreed to sex again.

"You're sad, Mama," Anne said, laying her hand on Lily's face.

Lily said, "Shall we have lunch at that place with the playground you like?"

"Yes!" shouted Anne.

Lily didn't want to get out of bed, she saw flashes of light and felt lightning pain every time she turned her head, but she got up and they went. While Anne played, she sat with a plastic bag of ice held to the side of her head.

She was anxious about going back to her apartment, but she kept telling herself that the attacker was in the hospital, and even if he was her neighbor and came home, he'd be in no condition to attack her again. Still, she was angry that she couldn't go out on her balcony; that space was defiled for her.

That afternoon, the police had her look at pictures of the man found in her apartment.

"He fits the description of a man who raped two other women across town," the policeman told her. "We don't know for sure, but we're glad we caught him."

The man had a great bruise across his face, the same shape as a bat. Looking at him, Lily realized he was not her neighbor. On their way home, she saw her neighbor entering his place. He looked at her and frowned, but said nothing. Then he came back out. "He hit you?"

Lily nodded.

"Bastard. I heard you knocked him out with a bat."

"Yes."

The man nodded. "Well, I'm sorry you had such a scare." He turned and went inside.

I know from reading that an attacker objectifies the woman, but there is much more hatred involved than with normal objects. Rape is all about violence, anger, and power over another human being. In "Screwed" Janelle Monáe sings,

> Everything is sex
> Except sex, which is power

We live in a rape culture, where a significant percentage of men think that a woman's body is not autonomous but theirs to control. The website of the National Sexual Violence Resource Center, says that 20% of women and 1.4 % of men have been raped. About half of rapists are someone the woman knows, slightly less than that for men. 80% of women who have been raped were first raped before they were 25, 40% before the age of 18. Most men who have been raped were raped before the age of 11. When I first started teaching on the university level, one of the women in my creative writing class wrote an essay about being abused; when we talked, she said that she lived with four other women who didn't know each other before moving in. She said all five of them had been abused. I believe it could be true that almost every girl has the experience of some man saying something to her that invades her privacy and makes her feel demeaned.

In this book I've also considered the other disease in American culture—racism. Our country was founded on racism, repression, and exclusion. In *Playing in the Dark: Whiteness and the Literary Imagination*, Toni Morrison postulates that the US definition of freedom depends on its opposite. We only know freedom in contrast to slavery. Similarly, American culture is sexist: I know who I am in contrast to the feminine Other. Therefore, I am both racist and sexist.

That's a starting point.

TWENTY-NINE

Lily considered leaving Missoula, but she liked her job, and Anne was happy in daycare. She might be in trouble if her assailant was released, but, because the judge had refused to set bail, that would be months away. Besides, the police didn't seem to recognize her. Anne was tired of moving, and she was too.

She decided she would wait a few days and see what developed. She knew it was foolish not to run at the first sign of trouble, but the thought of uprooting made her weary. Also, the wheel said to stay. Still, she was wary, jumpy. If she had lost that fight, what would have happened to Anne? That man might have silenced the screaming child.

Lily decided that she needed to prepare for something else bad happening, so she bought two cheap phones and sat with Anne in the apartment.

"I want you to keep these two phones."

"Where should I keep them? In my backpack?"

"One, yes. The other one we'll put inside your dolly."

The doll had a voice box in back that had stopped working. Lily took out the box, and the phone just fit inside.

Lily showed her how to get it out. They set it on vibration, and Anne practiced answering it.

"This way," said Lily, "if we're ever separated, you can call me, and I'll come and get you."

She showed her how to use #1 for speed dial.

"What do you do if someone tries to take you from daycare and it's not me?"

"I talk to April."

"Or one of the other women. Whoever is in charge."

"Yes."

"We haven't talked much about your daddy."

"He was a bad man," Anne said.

"If he comes, he might have police with him and you might have to go with them. But you can call me with your phone or with the secret phone in your dolly."

"But I can't show anybody the secret phone."

"You can go someplace alone, the bathroom, or a bedroom, and you can call me."

Anne nodded, and Lily hugged her. If Nathan did get control of Anne again, the girl would be frightened of him. Lily wasn't sure that was a good thing she had done to her child.

The women gathered around her and Anne, whom she had brought to work again. They sat in the shade next to the future restaurant, and Bess made Lily tell the whole story. Anne played with sticks that she pretended were a mom and a daughter.

"You're badass," said Bess.

"Are you going to press charges?" asked Frances.

"Yes. The cop said he probably was the perp for two rapes in town."

"Scary to have him break in your apartment," said Andrea. "I would have just run."

"But she had Sam," said Frances. "She couldn't leave her."

"And I didn't have a chance to run."

"You did good," said Frances. "Except you should have also cut off his—" She looked at Anne and stopped talking. "How are you? I mean really."

"You were attacked," said Bess. "I'd be a quivering mass of—whatever."

"No you wouldn't," said Lily. "You'd do better than I did. I was all right until later, after the police left. I was a mess. Then I took Sam out to the playground and we played. I felt better."

"This kind of thing happens too often," said Frances.

"My friend had a boyfriend who wouldn't let her say no," said Bess.

"Did she press charges?" asked Frances.

"No. Nobody believed that it wasn't consensual, so she gave up."

"Hey, maybe you could do training for our farm," said Frances. "Teach everyone how to wield a bat."

"I'd have to also teach them how to get cranked up on adrenaline so they can bash a man's head."

"You have a past," said Bess. "Something has made you strong."

"It was pure desperation. If he had killed me, Sam would have no one. I couldn't let that happen. I was frightened I had killed the bastard, that I'd be accused of his murder."

"You did what had to be done," said Bess.

Lily didn't like summing up her experience in an epigram. She used a deep voice, "A mother protects her young."

Bess and Frances looked at her.

"A woman does what a woman has to do."

Something about it was so silly she laughed. The other two women smiled, but they were twisted, wry smiles, maybe thinking she was a little crazy. That idea made her laugh even harder. Then something shifted, and her laughter turned into weeping. She had held it in so long that she just wept. Anne crawled onto Lily's lap. She held her child and wept.

"It's all right, Mama," said Anne. "It's all right."

The other woman touched her on the shoulder. "Listen to your daughter," Frances said. "You're all right."

A friend read a draft of this novel and suggested that it should cost me more. Specifically she asked what my relationship is to patriarchy, what I think of men like Nathan and some of the others in this book, what I think about myself and my relationship to women. I became a fiction writer to avoid having to answer questions like this one. It's either clear or it's not in the story. But in this novel I've chosen also to essay on issues. My friend wrote, "You have daughters, children who have gone through divorce, who are artists, who have grown up in Utah." She told me that I am embedded in the Patriarchy and I need to make my tone clear if I am to write a book about a woman. I hope it's clear, but I recognize I'm stuck in the perspective of a cisgender, upper-middleclass, white male, and that an essay or a story can't transcend that limitation.

When my wife and I first married, I expected her to leave her scholarship so we could move to a rural Utah town where I could teach junior high English. She sat at home as the wife, until in desperation she started work at the local turkey processing plant, where she used a pair of heavy scissors to cut the gizzards out of newly slaughtered turkeys. Women from the valley and undocumented Mexicans worked together at the factory, members of the same economic plateau. While working there she began having morning sickness from pregnancy and the smell at work became unbearable, so she quit and went back to school. Her life improved. It has taken me decades to figure out that the way we started our lives together was problematic, but she understood this as it was happening.

Alas, I followed a similar pattern of insensitivity to my children's needs. As lord of the house, I thought they should obey me because of my position, not my character, so I often became angry with them and thought them intractable. But I was not their only source of troublesome models and information about the ways adults and children, men and women should relate. As our daughters grew, they were insulted and demeaned by several chastity lessons, the worst being the confusing demonstration of the maple bar dipped in cow shit, an experience I gave to Lily. At first they were just mystified about the meaning of the metaphor, but later the implications became clear—their worth was their virginity—not their intelligence, determination, creativity, independence, or compassion. Even their value as sexual beings was warped by the suggestion that they should feel shame for their bodies, a sense of guilt for the very sexuality that was purported to be their prime worth. They could have been taught by their teacher to respect themselves and their bodies, but instead they were taught fear and revulsion. I'm sure that some religious teachers have intrinsic reasons for valuing purity, as a means of feeling self-worth, for example, but this was not the message my daughters received. I would love to write that we helped them work through this tangle when they came home, but of course they couldn't tell us about the experience until decades later. In addition, we were not open in talking about sexuality. While the version of the chastity lesson that our daughters received was extreme, many girls of faith have received similar lessons. Elizabeth Smart, who was abducted from her home in Salt Lake and repeatedly raped by her abductor, didn't think of escape because she thought that once her chastity was taken, she was worthless.

Binary attitudes about sexuality and gender roles are certainly not confined to patriarchal religions. Gender binaries govern how we think about appearance, leadership style, intellectual capacity, resolve, compassion, nurturing capability, and other social traits that pervade our culture—not to mention inequity in salaries and management opportunity, the hyper-sexualization of women in movies, games, and advertisements, our abusive rape culture, our habit of marginalizing anyone who doesn't clearly fit our prefabricated definitions of masculinity and femininity. Consequently, older Mormons have trouble wrapping their minds around how someone might not fit the binary. I had a friend in college in 1971 who was gay and came out to me, and younger people grow up with people who don't hide their gender. Still, after so many years of living with gay people, we as a culture still brand them as Other and we fear them.

In *Orlando,* Virginia Woolf describes a character that changes from man to woman as he/she passes through centuries of time. Having been both a man and a woman, Orlando can observe differences in attitude that are so pervasive that they are invisible. Orlando found herself adored as a woman, but she also found her actions proscribed. Woolf describes Victorian gender differentiation as a fog clouding Orlando's mind. Even now, women have a narrower range of acceptable public behaviors than men do. Precisely, a woman in an office cannot deal with authority, conflict, collaboration, or innovation in the way a man does, even though she may be doing the job of a man. If she asserts authority, she is butch or a bitch; if she stands up for herself in conflict, she is aggressive or a harpy, but if she doesn't, she's passive, a doormat. She generally has to get used to the idea of men claiming credit for her collaborations and innovations. If she rebukes sexual teasing, she is cold, if she joins in, she is easy, either way disruptive to office harmony. Women must get their appearance right, and then they can be valued for brilliance, industry, or competence.

I do have hope. My two granddaughters are strong and confident, aware of their own power. My daughter posted the following about her daughter, who was five:

> My daughter got a Super Girl doll and squealed, "I love that her head turns left and right! So she can say 'No!' to the other superheroes!"
>
> Then in a stern voice she said, "No Batman! No Superman!"
>
> She kills me. Smash the patriarchy!

THIRTY

Lily watched as Frances shrank in her role as innovator and leader. She still questioned and challenged the others, but did little to shape the outcome. The brewer, engineer, and builder worked together, a synchronous tension that was like a fertile field for new ideas. The cement was poured, and the walls of the brewery rose. Mid-May Lily and Bess transplanted the hops from the greenhouse to the new trellises.

Then later as spring shifted to summer, the hops and barley matured. The best time for Lily was lunch, just before she went to pick up Anne. The women made a weave of conversation, no subject excluded. The brewer and the engineer found more and more excuses to spend time on the farm. The renovation on the church progressed, and the women hired a chef. Her menu was to be combinations of mushrooms, spinach, tomatoes, cheeses, and of course beer—all a woman could want.

Late in the year, they processed the first draft. All the women tasted it all the way through the process, setting benchmarks of when it turned sweet and then bitter, bittersweet.

They formed a circle in the restaurant that would open in a couple of weeks. They drank beer and ate mushrooms on thin toast. Mushrooms that they had grown.

"To Frances," the engineer said, raising her glass.

"To you," said Frances, "and you and you and you and you and you and you and you." She drank. "And to me. We have done it."

Lily mistrusted happy times, or rather mistrusted the blindness that came from happy times, the feeling that it might last forever, that finally life could proceed in a straight line. She is the kind of person who, like me, her inventor, trusts that the bad will happen. She felt the most alive, most in touch with her own being, when things went south.

"What?" said Frances.

"I was just thinking about how drastically my life has changed since I met you." She laid her hand on Frances's arm. "You have given me a great gift."

One of the waitresses came up to talk to Lily. Her name tag said she was Tiffany Cross. "I can't get over the feeling that I know you from somewhere. Are you from Utah? Have you ever been in Bountiful?"

Lily smiled and shook her hand, but her gut tightened like a birth contraction.

"I went to graduate school in Salt Lake," Lily said, "but that was five years ago."

"At the U?" said the woman. "No, I wouldn't have met you there." She shook her head and smiled. "It will come to me sometime. Right now I can't place it. I've seen your face before."

Lily smiled and smiled until she could get out of the room.

She packed the car and then unpacked it, as Anne watched, waiting. She couldn't stand watching that face, saddened by yet another precipitous move.

Lily sat next to her. "We're not going."

Anne put her hand on Lily's face. "I don't want to move. I don't want to leave my friends."

Lily felt foolish. Doom would finally catch up to her, but she still couldn't bear to leave Frances and the farm, not yet at least. Also, the wheel said she still had time. She decided she would stay out of the restaurant, which wasn't where she was supposed to work anyway.

One afternoon, Anne was waiting for her, watching out the window when Lily came to get her from daycare. When she came inside, Anne ran to her.

"Did you have a good day?" Lily asked.

"Yes. I have a new friend. Both Mindy and I like her."

"But you were watching out the window. I thought maybe you were unhappy here."

"I love this daycare," said Anne. "I was just worried because you weren't here yet."

She worried like an adult, and this made Lily sad. She believed Anne was better off with her than Nathan, but he would have hired a good nanny, given her a secure and stable existence, at least until she became independent. Anne was loveable, so the nanny, Brock, and anyone else around her would have loved her, and she would have loved them back.

Lily finally decided it was silly to think that Anne would have been better off with Nathan because he would have owned the child, dominated her soul. The better alternative would be for her to have both Lily and a stable situation—not one where she lived on the street or had to move every few months.

She would not leave. It might be a mistake, but Missoula was their home—at least for now.

Bess tried to get her to go dancing. Lily told her that she didn't want a man. "I have fingers," she said. "What would I want with a man?" Bess rolled her eyes.

"You're going to shrivel up into a narcissistic shell of a woman," she said.

"No," said Lily, "anything but that. My former husband was a narcissist. Last thing I'd want to be. Maybe I'll become a lesbian and marry Frances."

"You'll never talk Frances into that." Bess touched her shoulder. "You need to go out. Going out won't hurt Sam. I'll take you."

Lily nodded, but she was thinking about Sam, the man, not her daughter, and their email exchanges, which had fallen into a pattern:

Sam: I'd like to see you sometime. If you won't tell me where you are, we could meet somewhere.

Lily: It won't work.

Sam: I'm not going to give up.

Bess still had her hand on Lily's shoulder. "You just went into a fugue state," she said. "I'd pay money to know where you went.

"I'll do it," Lily said. "You and me."

She found a neighbor who had teenage daughters and made friends with her. After talking to her in the hallway or a few times over coffee, she trusted the woman enough to ask one of the daughters to babysit for her.

She and Bess went out for dinner. Afterwards they went to a bar on the cowboy side of town. "Saturday night and we're doing what?" shouted Lily over the music.

"Looking at men in tight pants," said Bess.

"Not a safe enterprise," said Lily. "Looking just encourages them."

"Yes, it does, but I dearly love a muscled butt."

"In tight Levi's," shouted Lily.

"The music is too loud to talk," Bess said. "Let's dance."

They got up and started moving around on the floor. Some of the other couples stared at them.

"I forgot this is Montana," said Bess.

"I forget why we chose this side of town to party in," said Lily.

"Heart of enemy territory."

A drunk man tried to move in on them, dancing between them, if gyrating his hips could be called dancing, so they both sat down. He followed them back to their table.

"You don't like being with a real man?"

Lily looked at him. "You're drunk. I'd rather not dance with a drunk man."

"Are you lesbians?"

Bess went to the bar and pointed the man out to the bartender, who signaled the bouncer and pointed to the drunk. The bouncer helped him to the door. He complained all the way, "Bitches!"

Not long after that, a couple of men joined them at their table.

"Can we sit down?" One was tall, and one only a little shorter. Lily couldn't see their faces clearly in the dark room.

"Sure," said Bess.

"You're not regulars here," the taller man said.

"Are you a regular?"

"No," he said smiling. "I'm just saying you look like you're from the other side of the river."

"Right."

"So what are you doing here in Missoula? Going to school?"

Bess glared at him. "Not a good move, saying I look as young as an undergraduate."

"But you are an undergraduate," said Lily.

"Damn you," said Bess. "Don't give away my secrets!" She took a drink. "We're farmers, so we're on the correct side of the river."

The other man stared at her. "You're not joking. You really are farmers."

"No joke. Barley farmers. Beer makers." Lily explained what they were doing. "You? What do you do?"

"Besides picking up beautiful women at a bar? We're trying to start a law firm here. Immigration."

The image of the thin forger in Butte forced itself into Lily's head. "In Missoula?" He was not as quick with his wit or as handsome as Sam, but she felt the tug of attraction.

"Plenty of undocumented workers here who need legal advice. Especially when they get thrown in jail." He slid his chair back. "Do you want to dance?"

"Yes," Lily said.

She heard the other man talking. He and Bess moved away from the booth, dancing not far from her.

They danced a fast song, and Lily felt uncertain, moving with him watching her. Her arms seemed to move in a haphaz-ard, awkward manner.

She leaned forward and shouted in his ear. "I haven't danced in a while."

"You look fine," he said.

Sam would have teased her.

The next song was a slow one. She put her arms around him, and he pulled her close. Her first impulse was to pull away, but she didn't. She followed a much deeper impulse and held him, her chest to his, her hips to his. She felt his erection and didn't pull away, barely stepping, swaying a little. She wanted him. Not even him. She wanted to have someone inside her who wouldn't try to control her, but for now, she just held him, letting the warmth grow from deep in her belly until her whole body felt alive.

She danced another fast one, another, then another delicious slow one. All without talking, just touching and moving to the music.

She felt her phone buzz and saw it was the babysitter. The small voice said into her ear, "I was just wondering when you were coming. It's almost a half hour later than you said."

"Sorry," she said. "The babysitter. I'm late."

"I could come with you," the man said.

She shook her head. "No. No. Not yet."

"Then phone number," he said.

She held her phone up, and he put the number in his phone.

"Thanks for the dances," he said.

She turned away. "Bess," she called, "We've got to go."

After she dropped Bess off and paid the babysitter, Lily sat in Anne's room.

Foolish, she thought. *Dangerous and foolish.*

Still, as she lay in bed, she remembered the feeling of being close to him, of the natural response of their bodies.

"Not yet," she breathed. "Not yet." She wasn't sure her body was listening.

Becoming aroused by the lawyer scared Lily. She realized that she had grown lax, unwary, and hadn't checked up on Nathan for several months. She steeled herself, feeling the old dread that had dominated her life during much of the past two years. She made herself look at Facebook and check the website. The reward was the same, still—$100,000. She looked up her name on the websites of city newspapers. He had renewed the announcement and the put a paid ad in every city she searched: Albuquerque, El Paso, Phoenix, Las Vegas, Los Angeles, Reno, San Francisco, Portland, and Seattle. Then she started checking smaller cities. There was an ad in Billings, Bozeman, Butte, and Missoula. He used the crazy picture of her, hardly recognizable.

Anne was different too. The aged photos that were on the websites didn't look much like her, at least not from Lily's perspective. Anne talked and read and was growing up. Lily didn't look forward to the day she'd have to move again. Anne seemed so happy, and when they were on the move, she wasn't.

Never offend a narcissist, Lily thought. Nathan hadn't lost focus, had in fact increased his efforts to find her. He would never give up. He would be an old man in a wheelchair and he would keep looking for her. She wished she could shoot him with an amnesia gun. Or maybe a complete mind wipe. A lobotomy would be a good start. She thought about using a real gun, but that would only cause her much more trouble than she could deal with. She wondered if her conscience was messed up, because the idea of killing him didn't bother her at all. She just knew she couldn't manage the consequences.

Lily knew he walked the line between narcissism and sociopathy. Environment may have had a part in his condition, but Lily believed, from talking to his mother, that he was born that way.

"His siblings were teachable," she said, "but Nathan never learned to share his toys."

Lily wished she had gotten to know his mother better, but Nathan had not let that happen.

The next week the lawyer invited Lily on a date.

"Ah, youth," said Frances. "I feel it slipping away."

He took her to dinner. Afterward in his car, he asked her if she wanted to go to his apartment for a drink.

"I wish I could. I like going out. I just can't afford a relationship right now."

"I was just asking if you want a drink."

"I know what you're doing, and I just can't."

He reached to brush her cheek, but she blocked his hand and pulled her head back. He took her hand and held it a moment, just long enough to let her know that he was stronger than she was. "Touchy," he said.

"We're done here," she said. "Will you take me home?"

He stared at her for a moment, put his vehicle in gear, and drove to her apartment.

She thought about Sam, her ability to talk with him without awkward pressure to have sex. She wanted sex, dammit, but not just that. She wanted someone to be with, someone who would understand her, so she didn't feel so alone. But she sure as hell didn't like the pressure. She just couldn't afford the whole mess right now.

Anne was asleep, so she paid the babysitter and sent her home.

She sat awake, considering something else that had been taken from her—the ability to be vulnerable with a man.

Images of vulnerability (which anyone obeying the impulse to be hospitable to the Other must have):

- a dog exposing its belly to a human or a wolf exposing its belly to the leader of the pack,
- the leader of a country admitting weakness or culpability for that country's past actions,
- a parent letting a child drive a car for the first time,
- a child driving a car for the first time,
- a man and a woman, after a date, going to one of their apartments,
- a scholar or scientist changing her ideas after evidence doesn't prove what she wanted,
- a child sharing a toy,
- anyone in a community,
- anyone who reflects on their life.

Many people think that being vulnerable is a weakness. Being vulnerable makes me anxious because it's risky, but when I am mindful about it, opening myself to others is rewarding. My father believed that people liked him in the small town where we grew up. He believed his students liked him. He believed this, I think, because he liked them, so it seemed appropriate that it was mutual. Once in a church meeting, he made himself vulnerable by saying this, and someone in the group said, "Not me. I don't like you." My father told it later as a joke that was both self-demeaning and critical of the man who spoke up. Me? Social awkwardness from childhood or adolescence has made me desperate for people to also like me. Unfortunately, this has not made me vulnerable to them in any positive way. That ardent desire sometimes has kept me from going against the grain, contradicting people, becoming vulnerable to their resistance. I have often mistaken my desire to please for being vulnerable.

THIRTY-ONE

Lily and Anne drove up to Glacier Park. They looked at the vistas and at the glaciers, those variegated masses of blue and white. They noticed the signs marking their former levels. A few had shrunk two hundred yards in the past year.

They stopped and watched a herd of elk, huge animals milling.

"Are those cows?" asked Anne.

"Elk. You can tell the difference because they're taller and they have those big antlers.

"They are giants," said Anne. "I like looking at them."

"Majestic," said Lily.

"Yes, majestic. What does majestic mean?"

"That," said Lily. "The trees and the rocks and mountains and the animals."

They sat and drew pictures of the mountains and the elk. They ate at a restaurant and checked into their room in a motel.

Anne asked if they were moving again, or if she could go back to her school and toys.

Lily said, "No, we're not moving. We're going back to the apartment. This is just a trip, a vacation." She wondered if she was saying the truth about not moving. Their lives were structured by movement. "We've moved a lot, haven't we?"

"Yes," said Anne. "We're always moving."

"But we're always together."

"Yes, Mommy, yes."

They went outside and lay on their backs on the deck of their motel, watching the stars. Lily showed her the Big Dipper and the North Star, which was the extent of her knowledge. Then they played at finding patterns in the stars, an elk, a person's face, a snake, a mountain, and a whale.

They drove home the next day, and as she drove, Lily thought that she was caught between two negatives—staying would be dangerous but leaving would also be dangerous, as well as difficult. She hated the prospect of doing it all again, searching for apartment, daycare, job. But she knew it was time to go. The wheel said so.

When she got home, she took out the wheel. It had helped her escape Nathan. She both trusted it and thought she was crazy to trust it. But she knew she'd still do what it said.

The tightrope I walk feels hazardous. I don't think I'm alone among human beings in saying that as I try to immerse myself in my own life, being mindful of my experience, I find myself following rigid, previously-developed patterns of thought and behavior that feel like rigor mortis. Lily has been forced out of her previous life, so she may be less rigid than I am, but desperation has made her adopt a different species of rigidity. As I said before, I hope to at least find balance between certitude, which makes me blind, and lack of certitude, which makes me lost. At least this vision of a chaos of tensions matches what I have discovered about the world: time doesn't work the way common sense tells us it should: neither does mathematics, social hierarchy, fiction, essaying, religion, economics or any other discipline people use to explain the universe and protect their identity. Once, in Austria, my son and I made a quick climb up to a peak near where we were staying. We made it to the top by following a narrow rock ridge, only three or four feet wide in places. As we turned to go down, near dusk, it started to rain, and the rock became slick. Some of the narrowest places also had the farthest drop to either side. My memory of that dangerous, slippery descent feels like my life.

But that doesn't cause me the despair it once did. That trip with my son was sublime in the sense of awe tinged with terror. More awe than terror. That feeling is much better than that of inhabiting safe rooms in palaces built by institutional thinking. Static, controlled, expected.

Right now people are toppling or taking down Confederate statues, because they are monuments of a way of life our country fought to dispel. There was the institution of the South, land-based, slavery-based, agrarian; and there was the institution of the North—money-based, industrial, urban. The North won, but racism didn't disappear. Toppling statues doesn't threaten the fabric of our democracy in the same way that leaving the statues up does. I guess what I'm saying is that I can topple statues in my life—duty based on obedience and fueled by guilt, invulnerable masculinity that makes intimacy either a puzzle or a horror, love of things that others don't have, love of privilege that others don't have, complacency mixed with impotence about reducing carbon-based pollution, inability to talk to my conservative neighbors and relatives and come to compromise about how to move forward. All these monoliths can go.

This sounds like I've come to some answers, the bane of an essayist's creed. They don't feel like answers because how to do these things isn't clear. Also, I know that every moment of certitude, when it seems that I'm balanced on top of the world, is followed by a fall. Which is also true of Lily.

The day before the wheel said she should leave she was even more divided. She didn't want to abandon the work and friendships she'd found. She liked Missoula. She considered telling Frances that she was going to leave, but decided against it. She intended to sacrifice the deposit on her apartment, so that no one would have any warning. She hadn't told Anne, who would certainly complain to her friends. One problem was that the opening night of the restaurant fell on the day she was supposed to leave.

She decided she'd take Anne to the opening, and they'd leave from the farm right after. She could have the afternoon between picking Anne up and the opening to pack everything in the car. After the opening was going well, she could just spin the wheel for direction and distance and go.

But the day of the opening was busier than she'd anticipated. In the morning Lily trimmed weeds, hauled construction scrap to the dump, helped carry boxes of food into the kitchen. By noon her t-shirt was drenched with sweat.

"I'll get Anne from daycare and be right back."

"Thank you," said Frances, who was more distracted than Lily had ever seen her.

After she retrieved Anne from daycare, she considered boxing her stuff and packing it in the car, as she had planned, but she remembered Frances's panicked face and just drove back to the farm.

Through the afternoon she drove a small truck with Anne on the seat next to her. Anne was happy being on the farm, chattering about everything she saw. "What's that, Mommy?" she asked a dozen times. Lily delivered beer from the brewery to the restaurant, took away empty cardboard boxes and smashed them for recycling, mowed the lawn at the house. Toward late afternoon, the jobs ran out. Everyone was still excited, but they seemed less desperate. They would be ready.

Frances even smiled. "Now if only people come."

By evening the parking lot was full, with a line of cars waiting. Lily didn't have as much to do, so she showered in Frances's house, changed her clothes, and grabbed a plate of food that she and Anne ate, sitting on the hillside above the restaurant, watching the people come and go. Frances stood just outside the doorway, greeting the guests, beaming.

At midnight the last guests left, and Frances told everyone to go home. Anne was still excited. "I had so much fun."

Back at home, Lily opened her mouth to say they were moving, but before she could say anything, Anne shouted, "I want stories!" She bounced on her bed.

"Which stories?"

"The one about the mommy princess and the baby princess."

"They wandered the earth. Like warriors."

"I'm Val and I am a warrior." Anne stood in the middle of the bed, her arms raised like victory.

"Once the baby princess was trapped in a city of ogres."

"All the people were ogres, but the mommy princess—" Anne waited.

"The Mommy princess found a magic compass and used it to find the Baby princess. Then they flew away by magic."

"And lived with Auntie."

"You remember Auntie?"

Anne nodded.

"Then they had to run away again because the ogres were after them."

"And then what?"

"One of them found the mommy princess. He was a giant with one eye. The mommy princess stabbed him in the eye with a lance."

"Then the mommy princess and the baby princess lived in a home and they lived there and didn't ever move again."

"Amen," said Lily.

"You're supposed to say, 'The End,' not 'Amen.'" Anne pulled the cover over herself and closed her eyes. Lily decided to let her sleep, just for a little while.

Lily stuffed her clothing into the duffel and carried it down to the car. She put the bike in the trunk. In just a few trips she had everything ready to go. Then she went back up and listened to the faint whisper of Anne's breathing. She thought about Frances and wished she could stay another year, and then another. She didn't want to go through the crying and arguing that she knew would come as soon as she tried to move Anne to the car. She didn't want to leave, didn't want to, so she listened and waited, and then she was asleep on the bed next to her child.

She woke the next morning and saw it was light. At first she was frightened, but then she calmed. She lifted Anne, wrapped the blanket around her, and carried her down to the parking lot. "Where are we going, Mama." Lily buckled Anne in her car seat.

"I'll tell you while we're driving."

"Are we leaving?" Anne sat up, alarmed.

Lily walked around the car. As soon as she reached for the door handle, a group of police officers surrounded her. They all held pistols ready to fire. One had a rifle. She tried to open her door, but a man held it shut. He pointed a pistol at her face and shook his head.

Anne started crying. "Ma, Mama, Ma." A man opened the other door and took Anne out of her car seat. She screamed and twisted, trying to get away from him. Lily forced herself calm. "Please. Let me go to my child. I'm not trying to get away. She's crying, and I can comfort her."

"Hands on the car," shouted the policeman.

Lily did as he said, and he kicked her feet apart.

"I want to see your badges," said Lily. A woman came forward and held her wallet open—FBI.

"Lily Harker," the woman said, "you are under arrest for kidnapping—" She said more, but Lily couldn't hear anything except for Anne's screams, which faded as they put her in another car. She started toward Anne, but a man blocked her way, took her arm and twisted her around. She felt handcuffs close around her wrists. Then he led her to a police car, pushed her head down and shoved her inside. Her hands were still cuffed behind her. As the car started off, she twisted around to look at the other two cars traveling with them, but she couldn't see Anne's head in either of them.

At the freeway, they turned south and soon left Missoula behind. Nobody spoke.

"Where are you taking my child?" she said. No one turned, not even the man sitting next to her. It was as if he couldn't hear her. She fought to stay calm. "Where are you taking my child?" she shouted. "Where are you taking my child?"

"Quiet," said the woman from the front seat.

"Where are we going? I have a right to know."

She said nothing.

Lily tried to slow her breathing. South was Butte, the capitol; maybe they would put her in jail there. She wondered whether they'd take Anne straight to Salt Lake. Nathan wanted the child, but he would also make sure he saw Lily. He would look her in the face through the bars, confirming to himself and her that he had won, so maybe he wouldn't send Anne out of Montana right away.

She wondered how she could manipulate his need to triumph to her own good, and she wondered if she could get her hands out from behind her. She didn't see how escaping would get her closer to Anne. Nothing aggressive would work.

At the jail a policewoman booked her for contempt of court and kidnapping. Lily asked to see Anne. "Yes, I took her from her monster of a father, but I love her and she loves me. She needs me." The woman showed no change of expression. It was like talking to a wall.

She asked for a phone call. First she called Anne's secret cell phone, but that went to a message. "Nobody there," she said as she dialed another number—Frances, who said she'd be there in an hour. She also asked for a lawyer. The officer gave her a number, and she called it. The court would appoint her a lawyer, since she didn't have her own, but it would take a couple of days for a judge to assign one.

They put her in her own cell; it had a sink, a toilet without a seat or lid for the tank, a bed, mattress, and no sheets. They made her put on the jail clothing, a coverall of thick denim. She paced the room, trying to figure what to do. She looked for a vent, but the grate was too small to crawl through. She told herself again that even if she did escape, Nathan would still have Anne. She didn't have her backpack, which had her emergency money, the wheel. She tried lying down, but she couldn't hold still, so she got up and paced again.

Finally, Frances came, and the police let them talk through the bars.

"You need a real lawyer," Frances said, "not one appointed by the court."

"I have $2,000 in my account," said Lily, "but I can't get to it."

"What is your bail?"

"They said I can't post bail, because I'm a threat to Sam if I get out."

"Ridiculous. I'll talk to our lawyer. She isn't a criminal lawyer, but she might know someone. Can you tell me the whole story? Leave nothing out."

"I should have told you before. First, her name is Anne, not Sam." Lily told her everything. Frances listened with close attention.

"Sam, I mean Anne, must be frantic. In a just world you could have appealed."

"Maybe I should have done it then," Lily said, "but I had no credit, no way of hiring a lawyer. The lawyer I had before basically did nothing."

"I'll see what I can do." Frances left, already talking on her cell.

Later that night, the lawyer who worked for the farm and brewery came to talk to her. Frances had told her the details, but she asked Lily a few questions about the original case, date, name of her original lawyer, and details of the custody agreement.

"I just want to talk to Anne," she said. "Explain to her what's going on. I know she's terrified."

"I'll talk to them."

Soon she came back. "She's being taken care of here in town. Her father will be here tonight, and he'll take her back to Salt Lake."

"Can I at least talk to her on the phone?"

She returned again. "It's the opinion of the FBI psychologist that talking to her would only upset her more, because she's going to be returned to her father's custody. You'll have a chance to talk to your former husband in the morning."

"I want someone with me when I talk to him. I want what he says to me recorded."

They gave permission for Frances's lawyer to be with her.

The next morning Lily was weary to her bones because she hadn't been able to sleep at all. She tried to gather her wits and figure a way to get to Anne.

Nathan sat in the chair opposite her, a table between them. His face was somber, but something about his eyes, some sense of triumph, made his expression disjunctive. Lily found herself unable to stop looking at him, but at the same time it was unreal, as if he was a nightmare or a hallucination. Then she looked away, terrified at the idea that Anne was back in his power.

"Are you all right? Despite what you've done, I'll still pay for you to go through psychotherapy."

"Give me Anne back. Or at least let me talk to her."

He sighed, but his eyes showed his real feelings. "I can't do that. I can't trust you even to have visitation. The court will agree." He frowned. "I want you to earn that right. I want you to be stable first."

"Let me talk to her. Let me tell her what's going on."

He wore his compassionate, sad face. "No. That's not good for her. I've told her what's going on."

Lily wanted to say, *You don't even love her!* But she didn't. She knew that's what he wanted her to say.

"Please leave," she told Nathan.

He looked at her sadly and gave the lawyer a pitying look. After the door clanged shut behind him, she turned to the lawyer.

"He's very smooth," said the lawyer. "You're not. You're angry. If I didn't know you, I'd side with him. I can see what you're up against."

Lily was still too angry to talk. She motioned to the guard, who led her back to her cell.

The next day Lily had the chance to talk with Jocelyn, the lawyer, for over an hour. Jocelyn said that there would be a new custody hearing, but that wouldn't be for a month. For now, there was nothing to do to prevent Nathan from taking Anne anywhere. He could take her to Europe, but he'd have to get a passport first.

Lily respected Jocelyn, but she knew she was no match for the lawyers Nathan would hire, and she couldn't hire that good a lawyer for $2,000, even if she could get access to her money. She had zero faith that the system would give her Anne back. She could imagine no way out.

That night she was exhausted and slept. She didn't dream about Anne specifically, but she dreamt that she searched in the dark for something precious that she had lost. But she couldn't remember what it was. Then the lost thing was her, and she looked and looked for herself, and the contradiction filled her with terror.

She woke in the dark, cold and sweating at the same time. She paced in front of the bars, blocked by them, kept inside that room, inside the building, while Anne was alone with Nathan. Because she was trapped, she felt her sanity slipping, claustrophobia growing. Was Anne really in Butte, or in Salt Lake? Nathan had probably found a hotel room in the city and would fly home tomorrow. After that there was no way to know where he'd keep Anne. He wouldn't be careless again. Tonight was the best opportunity, but she couldn't take advantage of it, because of the bars.

She lay awake, evaluating what she knew. Getting a good lawyer was beyond her funds and probably wouldn't help any-way. There was no way to escape. It was risky to use the secret phone to find Anne, who might not be able to describe where she was. There was nothing to do, nothing to do. That night she couldn't sleep, but she dozed most of the next day, too confused and exhausted to think.

Desperate and not consoled by any dogma or hope of heaven, Lily did what she could to get free. She made a noose by ripping strips out of her mattress, tying and twisting them to make a rope. Then she looped it over the top bar and tied it with a firm knot. She pulled against the knot and put the other end around her neck in a slipknot. She tied it short enough that she had to stand on her tiptoes to keep from being choked. Then she undid the noose and waited until she heard the deputy coming with her breakfast. She put the noose around her neck and let her legs go limp. She didn't panic as she went under. As she asphyxiated, her brain depleted of oxygen, she was filled with a beautiful and euphoric feeling, as if she was floating in liquid joy. *Eight*, she thought to herself, *eight, eight, eight*.

THIRTY-TWO

She swam toward consciousness. The code number eight was there in her head, and as she came to herself, she remembered to lie quiet. *Eight*—balanced, calm and quiet, not gasping for breath. No drastic movement. *Eight*. She had an oxygen mask covering her face. She wondered how many people were taking care of her in the ambulance, but she didn't dare open her eyes to see. She limited her breathing, keeping it as shallow as she dared. She held still, still as a rock on the bottom of a pool. She felt the bands around her chest and legs that kept her from rolling off the stretcher. She heard the siren, and soon they came to the hospital. The doors opened, and she kept her body still. She felt herself being wheeled down the hallway. Then into a room. She hoped she had the strength for what she had to do. They took the bands off, and she felt hands under her, lifting her onto the bed. Then she moved, rolling across the bed, feeling the IV tearing out of her arm, shoving a nurse into a policeman. She stumbled once, and then fear and adrenaline took over and she sprinted through the curtain and out the emergency room doors. She heard someone behind her, but she kept running, around the back of the hospital and into a park. As soon as she entered the park, she dove behind a bush and held still, crawling completely under the branches, out of sight.

She waited and then walked back toward the hospital a short distance, then laterally across the back wall of the building and into the side parking lot, far from the emergency room entrance. She looked into the windows of cars until she found one with a jacket laid across the seat. Luckily, the first one she tried was unlocked. She put the jacket on over her coverall. She needed a phone, transportation, maybe a gun. First priority was calling Anne.

Lily walked away from the hospital and knocked on the door of the first house she came to. "Can I use your phone?"

The woman saw her panicked face and asked, "What's wrong?"

"I—I don't have time to explain."

The woman handed her the house phone instead of her cell. Lily punched in the first number and waited until it went to voicemail. Then she tried the second number. Still went to the recording. She'd had Anne record them, so the sound of Anne's voice on the machine, "Sam is not here, but Sam will call you back," ripped her apart.

Distracted, she handed the phone back to the woman.

"Can I help you?"

Lily thought about calling Frances, but the police knew that she had visited Lily and arranged for the lawyer. They would know Lily would try that friend. She didn't want to force Frances into the position of having to lie.

"You could take me to Shopko," she said.

"Shopko? But—"

"My husband works there. I need to talk to him."

The woman agreed.

They drove across town. A police car, lights and siren on, drove the other way. Lily kept her eyes forward, despite a powerful urge to duck down. The woman stopped in front of Shopko and let her out. Lily walked into the store, noticing that she was next to a Home Depot. She grabbed some clothing, a blouse and pants from a rack. Inside the changing room, she quickly ripped off the tags and put on the clothing. She stuffed the jail coverall and the stolen jacket under a rack of dresses. On her way out of the store, she found someone talking on a cell as she shopped. Lily stepped behind the woman, grabbed the phone, and sprinted in the other direction. She grabbed a jacket, put it on, and walked out the front door. She walked into Home Depot, kept going all the way to the back of the store. Sitting on the floor, she called Anne. She stayed there for an hour, calling again and again. She had to keep touching the screen to keep it from locking down.

She hung her head between her knees, the phone dangling from her hand. She didn't know what to do. Finally, when she tried again, maybe two hours later, she heard the ringing stop. She waited for Anne's voice, but it was Nathan.

"I found both phones," he said. "I'm afraid that Anne is playing and can't talk to you. Where are you?"

She hung up and opened the phone, taking out the batteries, so they couldn't use it to find her. She didn't have the wheel, didn't know how to get back into the flow, back to when she could respond immediately to any new challenge, get herself and Anne out of danger. She was next to the lumber section of the store, and she found a stake that had fallen loose from a bundle. She laid it on the floor and spun it. It said south. She walked outside, but just as she started through the parking lot a police car passed. She turned and walked straight back into the building. She threw the stake onto the first shelf she passed.

She stayed in the back of the store as long as she could, sitting on the floor next to the six-inch boards. When the same employee passed her three times, asking each time if he could help, she left the store and ducked back into Shopko. She walked back and forth across the rear of the store, not daring to sit down. At closing time that night, she left. It was dark across the city. Keeping to the shadows under the trees, she wandered along a street that she didn't know the name or number of. She knew she should walk as if she had somewhere to go, or she'd attract attention. She found that she was in the neighborhood of the police station. She turned back and walked the other way. Her mind had nothing in it. Dark, blank. She felt as if she crossed an endless plain at night, starless. Soon she came to a Mormon church. She tried all the windows, but none of them were open, so she lay on the back lawn, under a tree, where no one was likely to see her.

She immediately fell asleep.

The next morning she woke when a group of women drove up. They looked at her as they entered the building. After they were inside, she tried the door and it was still locked.

She went to the back of the lot, where there was a pavilion for picnics. She sat against one wall, out of sight. She tried to rally herself, list what she could count on. She didn't have the wheel. She'd tried spinning something else, but it hadn't worked. Nathan had Anne. No one could help her. Frances might try, but nothing would change the simple fact that Nathan had Anne again. He would never again be careless.

She thought about Sam. Would he drive down, help her to try to find Anne? She had daydreamed of being his lover, but that had been in her head, not his. She thought about praying, about trying anything, and did so. "Dear God, please bring Anne back to me." She had no feeling of response, which every Mormon child was taught was her right. She had no faith anything would change.

She thought about leaving. Trying to forget Anne and build a life. Frances wouldn't risk her business, so she couldn't return to the farm. She might show up on Sam's doorstep, but what if he was living with someone?

She could head south to Mexico, cross the border and learn to speak Spanish. She could return to Canada. She could wander the country, but to what end? What would drive her life with Anne unreachable?

She thought about taking up robbery as a permanent profession. She could figure a way to do it. Or forgery. That might feel good, being a parasite on the flank of the beast that had eaten her guts. She could become a man-killer, finding men who abused or controlled women, murdering them in their beds. That would give her great satisfaction she knew, but in the end, what would it do? She could kill Nathan, but she realized it was just a daydream. She couldn't kill anyone, not even him. She felt too weary to undertake anything that ambitious again. She could become a beggar and survive like any street person, but she'd tried that for brief intervals and didn't want that either, not having a space with walls to hide behind.

Mostly she thought about how weary she was—tired of nothing ever being permanent. Tired of never having a home or friends she could tell anything to. She'd had three friends, Suzanne, whose memory of her was poisoned; Sam, who had probably moved on; and Frances, whom she felt she had betrayed by trying to escape. Now no lawyer could help her.

Around noon, she made a decision. She walked back to the police station, passed through the front doors, and turned herself in.

Isolated in the dark behind my own eyes, I yearn to touch the soul of the earth, to wander through a gate of stars into the depth of the universe. In my meditation I am outside culture and experience—knowing myself as a singular being face-to-face with another singular being. This sensation has little to do with Us and Them, Higher and Lower, or even Wicked and Righteous. There is me and there is another intelligence that I sense. Ours is hardly a relationship between Lord and Underling or Host and Guest. Both of us are dust of the galaxy, particles of light, waves of matter, atoms and energy. A feeling of sight, light and eye. This other, twin to my soul, is ever-present, close as touch, like something at the corner of my eye, always there, but when I turn to look, gone.

They kept her in the Butte jail for a couple of days, then drove her in the back of a car. Once more it had no door handles and a glass plate between her and the driver.

Overkill, she thought. All this to keep a mother from her child. Maybe last week it would have been appropriate, before she had given up, but this week she had no will to act or hope. She could hardly imagine that other self, the one who had driven a shower rod into the throat of a man who threatened her, the one who hit a rapist with a bat, who killed herself to escape a jail cell. That was a dream self, one she couldn't identify as Lily Harker.

They kept her in a cell in Salt Lake while she awaited her trial date. She passed the time imagining Anne, that they were in Maskwacis with Suzanne, or Banff with Sam and Alan or Missoula with Frances and Bess. There was danger, but it seemed far off, something she could manage. All these imaginings were cut short, for different reasons: Suzanne's face always turned sinister, Sam's and Bess's and Frances's faces were also unbearable to see, but it was because she had lost them.

She thought about sitting on the floor of her various living spaces, drawing with Anne, observing the child's bright mind pick up speech faster than Lily thought possible. In her imagination she held Anne on her lap, they had a book open in front of them. Or they drew together. Or they walked in a park, Anne running ahead after a blowing leaf, a bird, another child.

She recreated her child's somber moments. *Are we going to have to move again? Why are you sad, Mommy?*

She started talking to Anne, at first in her mind, but later out loud. At breakfast she asked, "What should we do today? Shall we go to the zoo?" The guard stared at her, then moved away. Because then she could be alone, Lily was glad. She could stay in with Anne or she could go out with her, whatever she wanted.

After her parents' death Lily felt that her mother was close. Whenever some adult said, "I'm sorry for your loss," she wanted to tell them that her mother was not lost. This feeling had nothing to do with religion. She didn't feel inspired by hope or filled with the desire to be so righteous that she would be with her mother in heaven, which was what her bishop, young women's leader, and aunt said she should feel. It just seemed that her mother had not abandoned her. Often Lily spoke to her. The communication was not with words, just a feeling of being with her mother, held by her. Later, in conflict with her aunt, bishop, and school authorities, she gradually lost the sense of her mother's proximity. She thought she had just grown up and could deal with the truth, that her mother was gone forever. Still, she felt nostalgic for that feeling. She had read accounts of Maori and Pacific Islanders who had seen ancestors watching over them, maybe like spectators at a soccer game, cheering them on, or passing essential information. Soon she came to have an anthropological view of what had happened—that the sensation of souls touching was really a product of electro-chemical motions in her body.

She had never had the same sense of connection with her father, even though he died the same day as her mother. Not connecting with him seemed odd when she was fourteen because she had essential connections to them both when they were alive. At first, she thought it was because he was male and not as good at relationships. The years just before he died had been years of tension between him as a person of authority and her as a half-formed entity that rejected control. During that time her father had been on her mind constantly, while her mother just sat there, like water or sleep, something she didn't have to think about. Sitting in the cell, talking to Anne, she sensed something in the corner, standing still, but suffering with her—a being as concrete as the jailer who brought her food or leered at her when she used the toilet.

The FBI agent in charge of her case came to talk to her. She told him everything, speaking into a recorder. He took notes as well. She told him what Nathan had done to her. She noticed that he didn't write as many notes when she talked about that. When he was finished, he stood to leave.

"Can I ask you some questions?"

"I probably can't answer them."

"How did you find out where I was?"

"I can't tell you. Out of concern for the safety of those people."

"Those people?"

"Goodbye."

She didn't think it was Frances, but in this world of greed and desire for dominion, even the woman she trusted could have turned her in. Yet why would Frances try to help with the farm's lawyer? Convoluted. The woman in the Butte shelter who knew her name. Frank or Esther. The siblings of the dead woman whose identity she had stolen. Sam. The truck driver. Her former landlord in Missoula. James. The waitress at the restaurant? It could have been any of them, but it was probably the waitress. Then she thought about her mistrust of Frances, which was ridiculous. She realized she had slipped into a paranoic state where she trusted no one. Still it was what she felt.

She liked it best at night, when she could hold long, whispered conversations with Anne. She talked with her child about memories: when Anne had turned her head toward Lily's voice, even before the nurse laid her in Lily's arms; when as a baby she grinned toothlessly when Lily picked her up and fed her; the primal pull when her milk came as the toothless gums latched onto her nipple; the sound of Anne singing without clear words as she sat in a jumper chair next to where Lily was drawing. Playing with Mikey and Mia; putting on Sam's boots and gloves. "Do you remember when we drove to look at the glaciers, Anne?" But then the woman in the next cell told her to shut the fuck up, so she had silent talks, her lips barely moving. She recognized that talking to someone who wasn't there moved her toward disconnecting from reality. Becoming disconnected from reality was a worthy goal, she felt. Also, she knew Anne well enough to imagine what she would say.

What do you think about your daddy? Lily asked her.

He gives me toys. I have my own room. I have someone who takes care of me. Why won't you come live with us?

I can't. Daddy doesn't want me to see you.

Why?

Because I won't do what he says.

Well then do what he says, said Anne. *If you do that, then you can come and live with us.*

No, I can't come and live with you.

But if you do what he says, then you can come see me.

Lily didn't have an answer to that.

Her days were eating, shitting, pissing, sleeping, and talking to Anne. The court-appointed lawyer visited. He was even less competent than the lawyer she had for the divorce.

"My best advice is to see if you can claim temporary insanity," he said. "Do you want me to proceed in that direction?"

"Insanity?" She shook her head. "Temporary or permanent, what would that get me?"

"A lighter sentence."

"You don't understand," she said. "All I care about is being with Anne."

He put his pen down and stared at her, "Well, your actions have not led toward that eventuality."

"What does Nathan say?"

"Court orders say that, because of your actions, you can have no contact with your daughter."

She stood with her hands down on the table so her face was close to his. He leaned backward, "I instruct you to question that temporary order. If you have to do it, go back to the judge in a new hearing and make it so I can see her. I don't care what conditions they impose. I want to be able to have some parental time. Even a little. Since she was taken from me, I have not been able to talk to her, even on the phone. I have the right to more than that."

"I'll see what I can do."

She couldn't remember when she'd heard a more lukewarm commitment.

"I have money in my backpack. I want access to that money."

"You asked me this already, and I told you that, because we don't know where the money came from, you can't get access to it."

"It's my money. I earned it."

"Working under a false name. The name on your debit card is that of a dead woman. That's identity fraud."

Lily rose out of her chair and leaned across the table, and he backed away. She imagined how he saw her—teeth bared, body tense and ready to jump over the table at him. She knew she wasn't helping herself.

Frances drove down again to visit. She sat across the table from Lily in the interview room. In addition to the locked doors, Lily was shackled, bolted to the table, which was bolted to the floor.

Frances looked around. "I guess Bess was right, you are a badass. What do they think you're going to do?"

Seeing her, the paranoia that Frances had turned her in melted away. "They probably didn't tell you that I escaped once," said Lily. "Strangled myself and ran from the hospital, but I couldn't get to Anne, so I turned myself in."

"We need to get this story in newspapers."

Lily looked up. "I want to know one thing."

Frances nodded.

"Could making me a poster child get me access to Anne?"

Frances pondered. "There are so many people trying to get their fifteen minutes of fame. It just depends. Write something and I'll get it sent out."

"The lawyer I have is crap. He thinks I deserve what I get. I need money, and they won't give me my money."

Frances gave her another long look. "Do you have an idea how much a good lawyer would cost?"

"To go through the whole thing with me? $20,000 or $30,000."

"What good would it do to start with that caliber of lawyer and then not be able to pay her to finish it?"

Lily sighed. "I know it's useless. Unless you could help me."

"I can't give you that much money. In a year I could. Now I'm mortgaged to the hilt."

"I know that," said Lily. "I shouldn't have asked, but I'm desperate."

"I've thought about getting a lawyer that good to take on your case pro bono. I have a list of those in Salt Lake. I'm going through the list. I've got appointments with two of them later today."

Lily felt her sadness welling up. Tears ran down her face. "Thank you," she said finally.

"But that will take time."

Frances touched Lily's hand, which made tears spring to her eyes. Then she was gone.

In the dark she continued her conversation with Anne. *I want to come see you, but I can't. You have to talk to your daddy.*

Daddy? He can't do anything. He wants you to see me, but you broke the law and so you have to be in jail. If you hadn't taken me away, I could see both of you as much as I want.

Yes, said Lily. *That's true. I have never been sure I did the right thing.*

Daddy says you don't want to be with me.

That's not true. That's not true.

Then Anne wouldn't talk to her anymore.

During the last minutes before Anne was born the pain was so intense and the work before her so difficult that everything else around her became less real—the nurse talking in her ear, the pediatrician and the anesthesiologist. They all became less distinct. When the waves of contraction passed through her, she closed her eyes and bore down, feeling the urge to push the baby out, but also feeling the impossibility of forcing something so large down the tight passage from her womb to her vulva. She panicked, knowing that either the baby would die inside her or that she would be split open by the pressure. Again, her belly tightened, such intense pain again, again, and again. Then the pressure released, her baby slid out against her thighs. Everyone was busy and she pushed again, feeling something else slide out, something smaller, a deformed twin? Nobody paid attention to her. Then the nurse laid Anne on her breast, and Lily touched the wonder of her matted black hair, small skull, fingers, she felt the small mouth move against her nipple and she felt the pain of the milk being released.

Sitting on her bed in the cell, knees drawn up to her chest, Lily rocked and moaned, as if she was the one passing through the birth canal.

Lily asked for access to the internet, which they refused. She had wanted to send letters describing her story to every newspaper she could. She hoped that public opinion might make a lawyer interested in her case and that he or she would take it on for publicity. She had written out everything that had happened, and mailed it to Frances, but she couldn't know if any newspapers had published the story yet. She worried, because too many other things demanded Frances' attention.

When she had access to a phone, she dialed Anne's number again, but Nathan's voice came on again, "I told you already. I have taken your phones away from Anne because the court order states you are not to have contact with her." It was a recorded message.

She asked the court-appointed lawyer to help her get her story out, but he told her that would be against the court order. She knew that getting angry and frantic would not help her, but being calm about things didn't help either.

She decided that nothing she did could influence her future.

They had her in a room without even a mattress. She also had clothing that was too thick to tear. It had no belt. None of that mattered, because she didn't hope to escape and join Anne, but it also eliminated suicide as a mode of escaping.

She thought about suicide. It was appealing. Otherwise she faced hours, days, weeks, months, possibly years without Anne. She had no hope that an appeal of the child-custody hearing would change anything. The court would decide she was guilty of kidnapping and contempt of court, and she would receive the maximum sentence. They didn't need to decide whether she was borderline because the previous court had established that. The last silly insult.

Still, her one chance was to present herself well in court.

"How can we prepare?" she asked the lawyer.

"Not much to do," he said. "We just tell them your story. You've written it out, right?"

"Every detail. Who will present it?"

"I will," he said. "I'm an agent of the court. You don't talk unless I call you as a witness."

"My story is our case?"

"What else do you have that would help you?"

"I was hoping that you'd have some ideas about that. I asked you, what is the basis of our case?"

He looked at her for some time. "I don't know that there is a basis to your case. You admit taking the child, in direct contradiction to the order of the divorce court. You took her not only out of state but out of the country. You kept her from her father for more than two years. You tell me what the basis of your case is."

You sanctimonious son of a bitch! she thought. She nearly went over the table after him, but she held herself back.

She talked to Frances's lawyer on the phone.

"As you know, I'm not a criminal lawyer, but I think your best chance is to appeal the original custody finding. You may be able to establish your sanity by taking a psych test from another psychiatrist. I'm not sure how you can establish what you claim about his cleaning out your accounts. You say you got nothing in the division, but that's not what the court document said. It says you got a car and a settlement of cash, which you took in the place of alimony. It will be very difficult to prove that he treated you cruelly if there was no police report. He tried to control you through showering you with money. It will be difficult to make a judge believe that was abuse."

"Yes," she said. "Everything you say makes sense. What about the kidnapping hearing?"

The lawyer was silent. "There's not much of a question that you took her. The judge will focus the case on that question—is it kidnapping or not?"

"What is kidnapping?"

"I don't know the legal definition, but I can look it up for you."

"How about the fact that I didn't think she was safe with him?"

"The previous court made the decision that it was in the child's best interest to have him be the custodial parent. Basically, they already made a clear judgment on that. That's why I suggested that your best bet is to appeal the earlier decision."

"Could you help me with that?"

Silence again.

"That's a major commitment and again, it's not my area. Frances asked me to give you advice. I don't have time or ability to take on a full case, as much as I'd like to help you."

Finally, her court date came. She had insisted on representing herself. She stood and started telling the story of what Nathan had done to her.

Nathan shook his head and smiled, his face the one that made people trust him. His angry, violent face would never appear in court.

"Objection," said Nathan's lawyer, a stout man, balding. His belly stuck out over his belt. "That is not the matter before this court."

"Objection sustained."

"My motives for taking Anne have everything to do with the matter before this court," said Lily.

"Objection sustained," said the judge. "Move on to arguments that pertain to the kidnapping."

"I took my child because her father was a danger to her." Lily said. "His actions toward me show his vindictive nature."

"Objection," said Nathan's lawyer. "She's typifying his behavior without offering evidence."

"Objection sustained. Make sure you offer evidence, not opinion."

Lily took a breath. "I eventually will appeal that decision, but I can't prepare for an appeal when I have no access to the internet or a competent lawyer."

The judge glared at her. "Your last statement that pertained to this case was that you took the child because you were concerned that the father was a danger to the child. Do you have any evidence to support that claim?"

"Just my log," she said.

"Will you read it to the court?"

"Objection."

"What is your objection to her reading this log?" The judge seemed weary.

"Ms. Harker presents this as a log she made at the time. In fact, it was made recently."

"How do you know this?"

"Because the information is wrong. The dates don't match external evidence. In other words, she refers to events, such as the celebration of the 24th of July, but she has the wrong day of the week. Here, she talks about a trip to Moab with her former husband and their child, but again she has the dates wrong. Here is the hotel receipt and here is her log. So the information was made up recently but presented as if it had been written two years ago."

"Is this true?" asked the judge. "Remember that you are under oath."

"Yes," said Lily. "I wrote this last week, but everything I wrote there actually happened. You can look at my sketching journal and see pictures of what happened."

"Did he threaten you or the child physically?"

"He locked the child in a closet."

"Objection. This whole conversation was covered in the custody hearing."

"He threatened us emotionally."

"Objection sustained," the judge said. "I can't see evidence that his statements endangered you or the child."

"It was the way he said it."

Nathan's lawyer stood. "Objection. Tone of voice is not necessarily evidence."

"Objection sustained."

Lily stood quietly in front of the judge. "If you won't let me talk about the previous judgment, I have nothing to say."

Lily felt the slight hope she'd had drain from her. It was no surprise to her when he pronounced her guilty.

THIRTY-THREE

After the verdict, the judge, as he prepared to set her sentence, said, "The defendant doesn't exhibit any sorrow for her act."

Lily considered the proposition: did she feel sorrow? What she felt was emptied out. She had experienced so much sorrow starting when Anne was taken from her that she had exhausted all emotion. She no longer believed that being able to present her story to a judge might make a difference. She was left with only the echoes of loss and terror. Those had returned from the boundaries of her mind, mingling, until she couldn't tell what she felt.

"Ms. Harker," the judge said. "Lily?"

Lily looked up, but she didn't look at the judge. She glanced at Nathan and saw that he was focused on her. His face was impassive, but everything he did was intentional, so she knew that he was trying to either observe something or communicate something.

She didn't want to look at him—something to do with the intuitive sense that it was not smart to look into the eyes of a wild animal, a wolf or badger.

"Ms. Harker!" the judge said again.

But then she did look at him, Nathan, eye to eye. She watched as a slow, slight change came over his face, not quite a smile, not a nod, but some slight change. She knew in her gut that he saw her emptiness and exhaustion. She lifted her head instinctively, not in defiance, but to expose her neck. Also a clear signal.

She rose from her chair and turned toward the judge, ready to receive his judgment. She knew she would receive the maximum sentence of twenty years, but Nathan whispered to his lawyer, who stood and said, "Their child is back with his father, who is not vindictive in nature. He regrets the time lost, but punishing the mother will not bring that time back. He urges the judge to give the lightest sentence possible, to award visitation rights after her release, for two hours every week."

In the short silence after Nathan's lawyer sat down, Lily experienced a kind of vertigo. Words meant their opposite, or not even a clean opposite; they were muddy, slimy as slugs.

The judge gave her five years in prison, with the possibility of parole after a year.

From the jail, she called Anne's cell phone, but the number was no longer in use. She called her appointed lawyer to contact Nathan's lawyer and ask for a telephone conversation with Anne. "Am I your lawyer?" he said. "You fired me."

She got Frances's lawyer to ask for permission to exercise her parental rights, to talk to Anne on the phone. The lawyer hadn't responded by the time she was moved to the prison.

At the Utah State Prison, Lily was put in a cell with a woman who had knifed her husband. She was a big woman. She glared at Lily as if repulsed by her slightness.

"Hello," said Lily. "I'm Lily."

The woman just continued staring at her without saying anything.

By lunchtime the woman still hadn't spoken. She stood once and her impassive face reminded Lily of the woman she had dreamed about, who watched as she passed on the trail. She wasn't the same woman, but the similarity shocked and unnerved Lily. Everything about Cade, which the guard told her was her cellmate's name, seemed indeterminate: her skin was dark and her hair a shock of white. She was also indeterminate as to race, and she might be forty or sixty, Lily couldn't tell. Lily was terrified that Cade would attack her and she would have no way to defend herself.

Lunch was in a room with other women. The male guards prowled the room, daring someone to step out of line.

When one passed her, he leaned down. "You are so hot," he whispered.

The two women sitting across the table from her smirked.

The food was cafeteria food. The room vibrated with suppressed fear and anger.

Back in the cell, the large woman turned to the wall. Lily didn't try to communicate further.

She was given a job in the laundry, stuffing jumpsuits into a row of washing machines and putting underwear into the last one. The guard stood right behind her, and she felt him pressing himself against her butt.

She turned away and picked up more laundry. She longed for her bat, which she could smash against his grinning face.

At the end of the first week, a letter came from Nathan's lawyer, saying that Nathan and Anne were traveling in Europe and would be there until after Christmas. Because it was what she had come to expect, she didn't feel anything at this news. Because Cade, her cellmate, glared when she talked, she communicated with Anne in her mind. One night she found herself unable to visualize Anne's face, or the sound of her voice.

She earned a small amount of money in the laundry, but that was spent on phone calls, trying to contact a lawyer that would take on her case. Frances finally said to her, "I can't do more than I have done. As you said before, what you need would cost $20,000. I'm not in the position to do that." Exasperation was clear in her voice, so Lily stopped calling her. She found her anger grow at Frances, whom she felt had betrayed her. She knew it wasn't rational, but she couldn't get rid of the feeling.

Her story, kidnapping a child because she disagreed with a custody decision, unfortunately was not that rare, so the two Salt Lake newspapers didn't give much space for the story. They got most of the information from Nathan's assistant. As the story died, her hopes for getting a lawyer interested in doing pro bono work also died. Soon the secretaries of the family lawyers in the valley told her to stop calling.

When she wasn't working, eating, or sleeping, she sat in her cell, listening to Cade breathe. She knew the only way out before the end of a year was suicide, but she recognized that she didn't have the will for that. She asked for the wheel, knowing they wouldn't give it to her, and she was right.

CADE IN THE CELL
Automythology (USP)

She knew that once she would have fought ruthlessly and endlessly against what was happening to her, but that person seemed to be a stranger.

If she thought about Nathan and what he'd had the power to do to her, she shook with something like fury. Then that passed, and she felt as if Anne had died. But Anne hadn't died and was somewhere, eating, sleeping, and being watched over by a nanny. Maybe Nathan participated in her teaching, which made Lily's skin crawl.

She hated the idea of Nathan training up Anne—not because he would sexually abuse her but because he would teach her that women were valuable only as they had value to some man. How had it happened that it took her so long to see what he thought of women. And she had become that kind of woman—powerless, submissive, no will. He had mastered her.

One bruised day bled into the next, all the same. The regularity was mind-numbing. The only good thing she had was they let her have a stub of a pencil, a tiny sharpener, a blob of erasing putty, and paper to draw with.

The only change was when the other women fought at lunch, or when a guard touched her. When that happened, she found herself shutting down again, feeling nothing. When she thought about it she realized that everything was diminished. If the wheel was the whole range of emotion she had once experienced, now she felt a fraction of that range.

After about a month Frances came to visit her. Just as had happened before, Lily's feelings of doubt about her friend fled.

"It's hard to call you 'Lily,'" she said. "I'm used to 'Sarah.'"

"I'll answer to either."

"I have a job for you when you get out," she said.

"I'll stay here in Salt Lake," said Lily. "I'll be able to see Anne every week."

"When did you last see her?"

"When we came out to our car the morning after the restaurant opening."

"That bastard hasn't let you talk to her?"

"He says it will damage her to see me in prison."

"You're different," said Frances. "You've given up."

Lily stared at her. "How does it help me for you to say that?"

"Prison has done this. I hate it."

"How is Bess?"

"She got a job on a farm in France. You should write her."

Lily shrugged. She didn't know if she could bear writing to Bess. She'd try to cheer Lily up.

Frances came a few more times, and Lily enjoyed their short talks, but then it was summer and work on the farm was so intense that Frances stopped coming.

Her childhood bishop came to see her. She tried to talk with him, but there was too much distance between them now. He inhabited one universe and she another. He said "I'm sorry" seven times during their short conversation.

One day at lunch Cade came across the table and knocked another woman to the ground. Once she had the smaller woman on the floor, she slugged her in the face, again and again. The guards just watched. Two other women knocked Cade over. One held her while the other hit her in the stomach, face, anywhere that was unprotected. Just as the guards stepped forward to stop the fight, someone threw a chair from across the room, and it hit Lily in the cheek and jaw. Stabbing pain made her dizzy. She felt herself falling, and she awoke in an infirmary bed. It seemed that no time had passed. The med tech told her she had a broken jaw and that the doctor would come the next day to put pins in it. First, they wanted the swelling to go down.

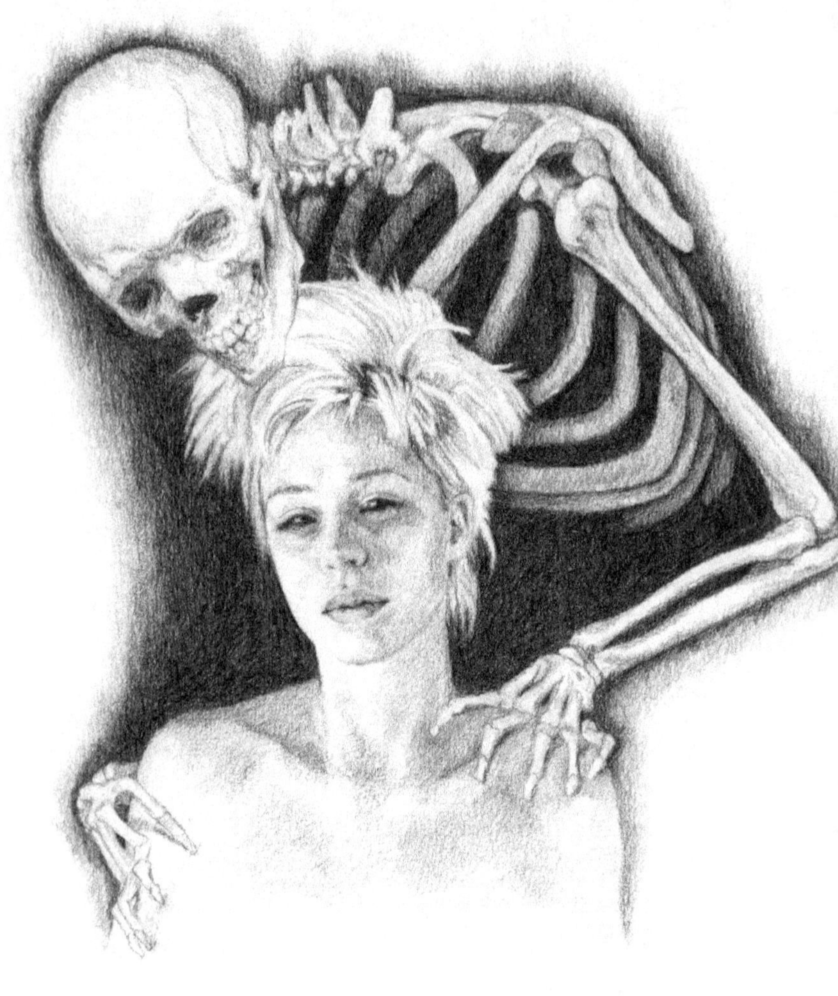

Lily lay in the bed, thinking of the equipment in the room that she could use to kill herself. She could hang herself with the bed sheet, stab herself with the scissors someone had left near the sink. She could find her way to the roof, maybe, and dive off.

Waves of pain and nausea passed over her. They had given her a morphine drip that she could squeeze. It didn't make the pain go away, but it made it so she didn't care about pain. She squeezed it again and again, until it stopped giving her more.

When she woke the next morning, she reconsidered her situation. It would be six months before she'd have a chance at parole. At the end of that time, she might be able to see Anne, unless Nathan changed his mind. Anne would be different. In a year she would have naturally changed physically and emotionally, but with Nathan managing her education, she might have changed in ways Lily didn't want to think about.

Still, seeing Anne was something to hope for. Seeing her child again would be worth the wait. After that, she would have to make more decisions. She would be able to see Anne, in controlled circumstances, every Wednesday. It would be for only two hours at first. If she did nothing wrong, she could work up to four hours each time.

She determined to wait it out. They told her that she would be in the infirmary for six weeks because, in the regular part of the prison, she would be in danger of re-breaking her jaw. She got them to bring her pencil from her cell and she sat in front of the mirror, drawing a self-portrait. She was halfway done, when she looked at it. It seemed nothing like her, so she crumpled it and threw it away.

Eventually, she was released from the infirmary. She asked to be put in a cell by herself, but they returned her to where she had been before, with Cade as her cellmate. She didn't try to talk to Cade and kept as much distance as she could, climbing into her bunk at Cade's feet. The days passed, then weeks, a month, another. She got her job back in the laundry. Soon, even Cade didn't make her afraid. It seemed that she had been in prison forever, that her life on the run with Anne was a dream, and her life with Nathan, before that, a nightmare. Her life with her parents was so distant that it seemed like the dream of a dream.

Worried that she was losing touch with her own life, she decided to draw the people she had met: Jackie, Chris, Mary, Suzanne, Sam, Bess, Frances, and especially Anne. She had dozens of pictures on her camera, but when she asked, they said it was against the rules. She asked again. Still no. Finally, she asked to print them out at the library computer. They let her print a couple dozen. The laundry supervisor arranged for her to get a package of drawing paper with a hundred sheets inside. The sheets were small, eight and a half by eleven, but the paper was good. Then she started drawing in her cell. She sat at the table, with a photo taped to the wall in front of her.

At first she worried that Cade might damage her drawings, so she slept with them under her mattress after putting them between two pieces of cardboard. Once when she laid them out on the table, she found Cade standing next to her. She'd still never heard Cade say anything. Cade reached her hand out, as if she was going to touch a picture of Anne, but she stopped with her fingers a few inches from the drawing. Lily spent several days drawing another and put the first on the wall next to Cade's head.

She drew mostly people she'd met, but she also drew herself as Lilith and Eve. She drew the wheel, the tree she'd slept under next to Brigham Young's grave, a cockroach, strange pictures of the branching internet, her own brain, a skeleton bending over her shoulder. She redid her branching tree from before she married Nathan. She started thinking about the wheel as another Liahona, the ball that had guided Lehi in the Book of Mormon, so she drew a picture of that. Finally, she drew a picture of God's hand flipping a coin to decide her fate, but she drew in the sleeve of a checkered shirt like her father used to wear.

Cade watched all of this, the creation of images from her life. The stolid woman moved her chair close to the table where Lily drew, which unnerved Lily at first but soon seemed normal. Cade started eating lunch at the same table where Lily sat. Whenever a guard or another prisoner got too close, Cade glared at them and they left Lily alone.

She had printed out pictures of Suzanne and Sam, but she found she couldn't draw them, but for opposite reasons. With Suzanne, she couldn't draw the face without making it seem she had a painful secret. She knew she had constructed Suzanne's betrayal on the other woman's frown as they parted. Still, every time she tried, she couldn't get it right, so she finally gave up. Same for Sam, but the feeling was not mistrust, but longing and loss. She knew she still loved him, or had grown to love him. Tracing the lines of his face was unbearable, so she finally tore up the printed picture of him. If she could have drawn them the way she wanted to, the image would have been settled. But their two faces continued in her mind, permanently ambiguous. She wished she could have finished cleanly with them.

One Sunday late in summer, about three years from when she had kidnapped Anne, she attended a church service. She hadn't cared what denomination, but when she went there, she found it was Mormon. Still she stayed. The branch president stood up, announced the singing. His wife led the music and another missionary couple gave the talks. One was about repentance, the possibility of changing one's life through coming back to God. The other was about the eternal nature of life and of the family. Lily left before it was over—it was too painful to think about her and Anne apart for an eternity. She and her child had been divorced because Nathan had more money and power. Even friendship had failed her. The state, the church of her childhood, no system had come to her aid. It may have been, she thought, that the various strands of the social web helped some people, but nobody had helped her. She knew she had become cynical and disillusioned, but that just seemed to be the product of clearer vision. She thought about her own hopefulness earlier in life, and that attitude seemed naïve.

The laundry supervisor, Charise, a woman who had replaced the man because someone had complained about him, asked to see her drawings, so Lily brought them, held between the two pieces of cardboard. She looked through them, careful to only touch the edges. "These are good," she said. "My daughter is an artist."

Lily smiled.

The next day Charise brought a spray can of fixer, and Lily spread her drawings out on the folding table that Charise had covered with newspaper. She sprayed the drawings so the pencil wouldn't smudge.

Charise talked to the librarian and the warden, and they arranged for a show to be held right after the Thanksgiving meal. The librarian arranged for easels and putty so Lily could attach four of her drawings to each one. Lily called the show Automythology Utah State Prison, and numbered the drawings but didn't title them.

Thanksgiving afternoon, most of the prisoners from the women's unit lined up to go into the library. Cade was first. They walked past each drawing. When the first group filed out, Cade stood next to the window. When the guard asked her to leave, she shook her head slightly, and Lily asked the guard to let Cade stay. He ignored Lily and was going to call for help, until the librarian intervened and the guard backed down. Cade stood there and watched the prisoners go past. If one got too close to the drawings, she stepped forward and the prisoner stepped back.

After the show, Lily thought about Cade. She was still frightened of the woman and still kept her distance as much as she could. She knew that Cade could switch from apparent complacency to violence in a second. She thought about the picture of Anne that had somehow appealed to Cade. Maybe it had reminded her of something buried deep. Lily hadn't thought anything could touch the woman, who seemed more like a bear than a person.

As she approached her year in prison, she asked the warden when her parole board would meet. He said they had scheduled her meeting for just after Christmas, January tenth. She opened her mouth to complain that the judge had said her parole would happen in a year; he shook his head slightly. She shut her mouth and thanked him. As Christmas approached, Lily became anxious again. She didn't want to count down the days, so she avoided calendars and tried to let each day blend into the next. During the festive season, various religious groups intensified their focus on the women's section of the prison. One organization gave the inmates candy bars with ribbon wrapped around them. The guards confiscated half and gave the rest to the prisoners. Several times carolers gave performances in the chapel, and the guards demanded that the prisoners go, mostly to preserve a good appearance.

Lily went a couple of times and listened to the old songs that formerly had stirred her emotions: "Silent Night," "Oh, Little Town of Bethlehem," "The First Noel," and a few secular songs like "Jingle Bells." The songs made her weep from nostalgia.

Lily told the parole board that she had changed, that she regretted what she had done, and that she wanted to get a job and an apartment so she could see her daughter every week. They looked at her perfect record and granted her request. She was set to leave prison on February second. She worried that another fight would break out and she'd be killed. She imagined the guards opening fire on the women and the bullets slamming into her body. She knew the guards had no guns and that they were more likely to just let the women fight. She also knew that shooting prisoners was against the rules and seldom happened. Still she hated lunchtime.

She had written Nathan and his lawyer and asked that she be allowed to exercise her parental right and see Anne on February third, the day after her release.

Nathan's lawyer at first said no, so Lily filed a protest with a judge, asking that Nathan be held in contempt of court for not allowing her court-allotted time. They delayed as long as they could and finally permission came for a supervised visit on March fifth. The order said that Lily would need to pay half of the cost of supervision—$200 for two hours. She had no idea where she'd get that much money in just a few days. She only had about $150 from her work.

She would have lodging at a halfway house where she was required to stay for a couple of months. She would also have an ankle monitor while living there, so even if she had wanted to try to run with Anne again, they would find her within hours.

On her release day, Lily was handed her backpack, minus the debit card and cash. She boarded a van for the halfway house.

How to end this book? As soon as Lily was apprehended in Missoula, I asked myself what would happen next. Then I turned the ending over to a random selection method, or nearly random. As I wrote these last chapters, I was in the Mojave Desert with students. They knew I was writing a novel, so I enlisted their help to end it. I didn't have the wheel with me, so I asked them to pick a number between 1 and 15. The number with the highest incidence was 12, which three people chose. I didn't tell them what they were choosing, but beforehand, I had set the following divisions: 1–5 was that Lily would keep Anne, 6–10 that she would lose her and not see her again, 11–15 was a blending of those two—she'd lose her, but be able to see her again.

I could have written those other two options—almost anything is possible in fiction. I could have easily made it so Lily would never see Anne again. This sounds heartless, and as I write this, I feel the sadness of that possibility, but I could have steeled myself. She could commit suicide or Nathan could move to Europe or South America and keep the location from Lily. It could happen. Or the other could happen—fully being with Anne. Lily's old self could return. The officers could return the wheel to her with her belongings as she leaves prison, and she could find Anne and run with her again. Frances or even Sam, if she got in touch with him sooner, might put up the money for a lawyer who could untangle the lies. But what happened is now settled.

What have I learned about and from Lily? Hard question. Lily's flight was a little more than two years, and imagining her decisions was exciting—the ways she might survive through intelligence, creativity, and determination. A seminal book for my childhood was *Kim*; reading how that boy survived through his canny intelligence thrilled me. Despite her certitude about what is best for Anne and her paranoia about her friends, I also admire Lily's love of Anne and her immediate love of these people. I especially love her savage nature when cornered, when she fought back with a bat or a shower curtain rod or her innovative mind. I would have loved to help her and Sam escape to Canada or Europe.

Hardy's *Tess of the d'Urbervilles* ends with Tess's hanging. She had been living with the man who raped her, the one who first claimed her as his property. It turns out that he had known for some time that her husband Angel had returned and was looking for her. He kept this vital information from her. When the lover told her the trick he had played on her, he smiled because he thought he had won again, crushed her spirit again. Earlier she had lifted her neck to him, saying, "Once a victim, always a victim." But this time his smile made her take the knife he was using to cut fruit and cheese and plunge it into his heart. It's satisfying to read, but the satisfaction doesn't last long. Reading the first time, I knew she could never get away. That's the point of a tragedy; viewers or readers are purged through feeling pity and fear, pity for the protagonist, and fear that the same could happen to them. As Victorians read about Tess's treatment by the men in her life, their attitude toward women changed just a bit, certainly not enough. The world is still full of sexism, racism, classism, and other kinds of institutionalized hatred despite all the fiction and non-fiction and all the talking about these problems.

From writing this novel, I've learned again how difficult it is to imagine myself into another person's skin, but I think even imperfect attempts at reflecting on the nature of the Other are worthwhile. Welcoming the guest into the home of one's own mind is difficult not just for writers. Readers of early drafts said they didn't believe that Nathan could take everything from Lily; they didn't believe that she had no friends to step forward and help her avoid becoming homeless. If I had made her brown or black or red, they might have believed the story, but their race and class make it difficult for them to imagine this happening to someone like them. Our own privileged status is generally invisible to us. The news shows that many people in the United States and the world hang on by their nails and live in daily fear that some act by someone in power will unseat their lives. Will reading fiction, autobiography, and the news change the attitudes of middle-class people? People generally only trust writers who already agree with them.

I have also come only to tentative discoveries about myself and how I relate to my family and friends, but finishing this book is not the end of my spiritual journey. Reflection on the nature of Self and Other is not an answer. It's just a method, but it's one we can trust.

THIRTY-FOUR

As she waited for her release, Lily prepared herself for another disappointment. She knew that Nathan would find a way to prevent her from seeing Anne. He could take the child on a trip, he could simply risk contempt of court, although that wasn't his style—to do something illegal in a public manner. He could file a counter proceeding that would take months or even years to untangle. Her only protection was another idiot, court-appointed attorney—an arrogant, incompetent, and self-righteous man, more ruinous to her happiness than any of the seven deadly sins.

She sat on her bed in the halfway house, a nice room, shared with three other women. It felt good to have a small space of her own. When she unloaded her backpack, she found some of the cash, $400, which she had sewn inside one of the padded straps. The discovery brought tears of gratitude to her face. She had enough money to pay for the supervised visit she would have with Anne. She also found the wheel. She held it in her hand, thinking it a strange and awkward device. She tried to figure how it could help her, what decision it could help her make. Randomness no longer gave her any advantage. She put it in her drawer.

She wanted to spin it to see whether or not she would see Anne, but she lacked the courage. If it said "no," she knew she couldn't have borne it.

A woman at the halfway house worked with the community to get ex-prisoners jobs. Lily wanted to get a job in Park City, closer to where Nathan lived, but then she realized he might have moved. Also, the woman said that the job had to be in Salt Lake. Lily was set up with a job at a used bookstore downtown. The owner/manager liked to hire people from the halfway house, they told her.

"Because we're cheap?" she asked.

"That's a cynical attitude," the woman said.

The owner was a portly man with a huge beard, gray and grizzled. He instructed her in the shelving system, which was largely based on his own intuition. She learned the pattern of his brain fairly quickly, and as he watched her shelve books, he nodded and smiled.

"You're going to be fine," he said. "Most people can't grasp my system."

She smiled back. Her habit of random thinking while she was on the run helped her now. Ironic.

When she got back onto her old gmail account, she found emails from Sam that she hadn't been able to answer. They started when she first went to jail, "Where are you? What is going on? Why won't you answer?" They grew more sparse and then stopped while she was in prison. She deliberated about contacting him and finally emailed, "I'm in Salt Lake. I was sent to prison for kidnapping Anne and they've taken her away from me. I was there for a year."

He didn't answer until two days later: "I'm so sorry. You went so long without writing and I was worried. I'm glad you're out."

"I could see you now," she wrote.

"It's not a good time. I'm in a new relationship, and I'm trying to make it work better than Alan's, because I'm competitive. So far it's working. Wish me luck."

"Congratulations, Sam. I wish you the best."

"Thanks."

That is the end of that, she thought. She considered how she felt. After so much loss, the loss of her romantic dream about Sam was insignificant, at least that's what her brain told her. Still she missed—what?—not only him, but the possibility of a future, with him in it, a future that morphed and had unexpected turns.

The day came. She went early to the supervision center. She paid her half of the cost and sat in the empty room trying to calm herself. There was a huge mirror on one side of the room that Lily thought was a two-way mirror, so she could be listened to and watched. She had brought art supplies in a bag, which the supervisor inspected. The inspector looked at the blunt scissors for a moment and then dropped them into the bag, nodding.

The door opened and Anne walked in. She was taller, moving her body precisely, a little like Nathan did. Lily opened her arms, Anne hesitated, then walked forward. Lily wrapped her arms around her child, lifted her on her lap. Anne held her body stiff. Still Lily didn't let go of her. She felt the difference, the larger body, the slight resistance to the hug. Then she held Anne at arms' length and examined her face. A little thinner. Anne looked at the corner of the room not directly back at Lily's face.

"Tell me about your travels," Lily said.

"Daddy and me and Nan lived in another city, Paris."

"What did you do there?"

She thought for a minute.

"I don't know all of what we did. I had lessons in my room. I can speak some French."

"*Comment allez vous?*"

"*Bon,*" she said.

"We went to Disneyland. Daddy, Nan, and I." She became slightly more animated. "Another time I rode ponies that went in a circle."

Lily leaned back and looked at her daughter. Anne gathered herself, a four-year-old, sitting with her knees together, her hands folded in her lap. She wore a dress. A tiny woman.

"Who is Nan?"

"Nan takes care of me."

"Is Nan her name or is she Nanny?"

"Of course that's her name."

Lily swallowed. "What else do you do?"

"Daddy and I talk a lot."

Lily asked, "What does he say?"

Anne shrugged her shoulders. "That I am special. A special girl. He is my Daddy and that I am his special girl."

Lily felt a chill through her body. She still had no concern that Nathan would abuse Anne, but he would make her an experiment in how much he could shape another being.

She found Anne glancing at her, glancing again. A year was forever in a child's life. "Do you remember me?"

Anne looked at her. "Of course I do."

"What do you remember?"

"That you are not well."

"Did your Daddy tell you that?"

She was silent. "He told me that you would lie to me."

Lily wanted to argue, to explain, tell her side of the story. She looked in Anne's face and knew it would be useless and destructive—harmful to Anne.

"You left me," Anne said. "You said you wouldn't leave me, but you did. You said my name was Valerie when it's really Anne."

Lily waited before she spoke. She knew that she couldn't speak against Nathan. Anne wouldn't believe her. Nathan had clearly spoken against her, which was against the custody agreement, but Lily knew there was no way for her to fight for her reputation, not with Anne, not with any judge, at least not without tens of thousands of dollars.

"The police put me in jail. I tried and tried and tried to talk to you, but I couldn't. They wouldn't let me."

Anne put her lips together. The action was not exactly Nathan's, but it was similar. Lily knew it meant that what she was saying violated the child's worldview. She knew the mental action—how can you trust a liar when she says she is not lying? There is no defense against that argument.

"I brought some paper," said Lily. "I have crayons and pencils and markers. Do you want to draw with me?"

Anne was silent. "Why?" she said.

"Don't you draw with Nan?"

"Drawing is for babies."

"So let's be babies." Lily took out the paper and the other things and laid them out on the table. She held a chair for Anne and pulled one up next. She slid a paper toward Anne and put the pencils and crayons and markers close to her. Lily started drawing a picture of the backyard in Canada.

Anne made a mark. "I can't draw like you."

"You don't need to draw like me. Do you remember this place?"

Anne shook her head. "What should I draw?"

"Whatever you want. You can use green or brown or red or yellow. Any color you want."

Anne waited. "I don't know what to choose."

Lily pushed the red and yellow crayons toward her.

Anne made a line, then another, the shape of a dress. Then she drew a head. She picked up a black crayon and drew a head, fast, without care. "See, I can't do it."

"You did fine," said Lily. She did a drawing of the daycare in Banff. "Do you remember this?"

Anne shook her head. She went back to her drawing, frowning and struggling.

Lily drew a picture of Sam's face.

Anne looked at it and smiled. "I remember him, but I don't remember his name."

"Sam."

"Sam. I remember Sam. I chose his name when you made me pick a name that wasn't mine."

"Can I see your drawing?"

Anne reluctantly pushed the picture across the table. It was nearly identical to the first one. "That's nice," said Lily. "You made her hair and face and dress and legs." She thought. "Let's draw without looking."

Anne rolled her eyes.

Lily smiled. "Take your crayon in your hand. Close your eyes. No peeking. We'll do it together."

"I'll draw on the table."

Lily taped paper to the table, three pieces. Then she put another in front of Anne. "Now the table will be clean. Close your eyes. And draw."

Lily moved her hand across her paper, drawing loops and curls and lines. Then she cheated and looked, not at her paper, but at her child. Anne was frowning, trying to draw another triangle for a dress. Lily took her hand and moved it across the page. Then she let go. Anne stopped but then started again, moving hesitantly, in loops.

Then, much too soon, the woman came back into the room. "Time's up."

Lily said, "Can you give me a goodbye hug?"

Anne moved toward her and gave her a tentative hug.

"I'll see you next week."

"When?"

"On Wednesday."

Anne nodded.

Lily said, "I love you."

Anne's mouth pressed into the same flat line.

After Anne was gone, Lily sat, feeling bewildered. The woman came back. "You need to vacate this room. We have someone else coming in."

Lily gathered her things. She walked back to the halfway house. The woman at the entrance nodded and marked a paper. Lily sat on her bed. She drew her knees up and wrapped her arms around them. She felt the ankle bracelet, which sometimes chafed her skin.

She wanted to weep, but she couldn't order her feelings well enough to even do that. She longed for her baby, the Anne who had been.

The next day, shelving books, she felt odd, different. She realized that it was a feeling of pastel joy. The mildest feeling of pleasure. She had work she enjoyed. She could look forward to seeing Anne the next week and the week after and the week after that. She let the pleasure sit in her mind—of seeing Anne's face, of holding her again—until the joy of that hope spread and filled the corners. She remembered a verse from Shakespeare's sonnets, "Love is not love which alters when it alteration finds." She thought she had understood that verse, but she knew she hadn't.

She considered Anne's face, the precise movement of her hands, the hesitant drawing. She thought about Nathan as a sharp presence, like the edge of a nightmare, looming close. She thought about shelving one book, then another, and another.

"This is my life," she thought. "This is my life."

ACKNOWLEDGEMENTS

Thanks to my reading groups—Donna, Bruce, Valerie, Dennis, Mary, Tim, Charlotte, Dian, and Roland; also Madeleine, Katy, Allison, Lauren, and Claire. I appreciate the comments and editorial work of Hadley, Alison, and Brooke. My granddaughter Colette drew the picture of the ouroboros. Of course thanks to Karla who helped me see from her perspective when I was twenty-four and retrograde.

A native of the Utah desert, JOHN BENNION has published a collection of short fiction, *Breeding Leah and other Stories* (Signature Books, 1991), and three novels—*Falling Toward Heaven* (Signature Books, 2000), *An Unarmed Woman* (Signature Books, 2019), and *Ezekiel's Third Wife* (Roundfire Books, 2019). Another novel, *Ruth at the End of the Earth* is forthcoming next year from BCC Press. He has published short stories and essays in *Interdisciplinary Studies in Literature and Environment, Hotel Amerika, Southwest Review, Hobart, Palaver, AWP Chronicle, Utah Historical Quarterly, Journal of Mormon History, Dialogue: A Journal of Mormon Thought, Best of the West II, High Country News, English Journal,* and others. Has retired from teaching creative writing in the English Department at Brigham Young University. For three decades he led outdoor writing programs that use the writing of personal essays to promote student growth. He lives in Provo with his wife, Karla, a writer and psychotherapist.

AMY BENNION is an Assistant Professor at the University of North Florida and has been teaching painting and drawing for the last 12 years—at the University of Utah, Utah Valley University, Westminster College in Salt Lake City, and the Early College Program of the School of the Art Institute of Chicago. Bennion has worked on the Museum Education team of the Art Institute of Chicago and in the Education and Engagement Department at the Utah Museum of Fine Arts. She earned a BFA from Brigham Young University, a Post-Baccalaureate Certificate from the School of the Art Institute of Chicago, and an MFA from the University of Utah. Bennion has shown in galleries across the US and has work in national and international journals.